the bayshore rivals

USA Today Bestselling Author

J. L. BECK
C. HALLMAN

Happy Reading!

JL Beck

© Copyright 2019 J.L. Beck & Cassandra Hallman
Cover Art by: T.E. Black Design
Editing: Kelly Allenby
Proofreading: Stacie McGlaughlin

All rights reserved. This book or parts thereof may not be reproduced in any form, stored in any retrieval system, or transmitted in any form by any means—electronic, mechanical, photocopy, recording, or otherwise—without prior written permission of the publisher, except as provided by United States of America copyright law.

BOOK ONE

when rivals fall

BAYSHORE RIVALS BOOK ONE

USA Today Bestselling Author
J. L. BECK
C. HALLMAN

PROLOGUE

2 Years Prior

"Take the baggie, and put it in Sullivan's pocket," My father orders, not even looking up from the papers sprawled across his desk.

In his pocket? No way in Hell do I want to get that close to that asshole. I'll try and get Shelby to help me with it. I'm not getting within ten feet of him or his brothers.

The Bishop Brothers, Sullivan, Oliver, and Banks are the children of Chloe and George Bishop, our rivals. They're disgustingly handsome, filthy rich, and manipulative liars. Every occurrence I've ever had with them was one that ended with me wanting to stab them in the eye with the nearest object.

I don't know exactly when or how it started, all I know is that the hate between our two families has been growing for the last two decades. Ever since I can remember I've been told about the Bishops and how they were trying to ruin our business, my family's livelihood.

Recently, we had to fire an entire crew right before Christmas. A dozen families out of a job before the holidays and all because of them.

Who does something that cruel? That's not the worst thing they've done either, but it is the icing on the cake. Lately, their antics have been affecting more than just my family. Their wrath rippling down the line and onto our workers. I don't bother to ask what the Bishops have done this time. It doesn't matter. We'll get even. We always do.

Sullivan the youngest of the Bishop Brothers is my age and even though we don't go to the same school, we do occasionally run into each other at events and parties.

Usually, I try to avoid him like the plague. But today I'm going to the same place as him and on purpose. Everyone from every high school across the county will be there no matter the last name.

Tightening my grip on my purse, I ask, "What's in the bag?"

"Don't ask questions you don't want answers to, Harlow. Put the bag in his pocket and I'll make sure the rest gets done," My father answers with a tone that tells me to shut my mouth and do as I'm told.

I bite my bottom lip, wondering if I should push the issue. I don't like the Bishops, in fact, I hate them for what they've done and how they've treated my family for the last couple of years but I'm getting tired of doing my parents bidding. Tired of the constant hate. I decide against making a scene, there's no point. I'll end up having to do it anyway.

"Should I come home right afterward?"

Looking up from the document in front of him he pierces me with a stare from his blue eyes that match my own in depth and color.

A sinister grin finds its way onto his lips. "No. I want you to stick around. Make sure they see who it was that set them up."

"Got it." I nod and grab the baggie from the edge of the desk. The contents of the bag must be light because it feels like there isn't anything inside it.

"Don't forget all they've done to us, sweetie." My father's voice softens. "I wouldn't ask you to do these things if I didn't feel it was justified.

I have to protect you, my businesses, my men and everything those filthy Bishops do is a direct attack against us."

"I know, Dad." My lips pull up into a reassuring smile. Even if I hate what I have to do, being a part of this rivalry, I know there isn't anything I can do to change it. My last name is Lockwood, and it will always be family over honor.

It's my job to protect my family's legacy.

"I'll get the job done," I mumble and turn on my heels exiting his office.

Once in the hall I pause and lean against the wall.

I can do this. I will do this.

I remind myself of how Chloe and George Bishop stare down at me like I'm gum stuck to the bottom of their shoes every time we cross paths. Their three sons are not much better. Annoyingly handsome and full of themselves. Sullivan is the worst. He acts like he is the king of the world and everyone is beneath him, like it's our duty to bow to him.

Tonight, we'll put an end to his reign.

Tonight, he'll find out what happens when you mess with a Lockwood.

1

resent

BAYSHORE UNIVERSITY IS NOT the prestigious college that I thought I would be attending. My whole life I thought I would end up going to one of the best Ivy League schools in the country, like Yale or Harvard, just like every other rich kid from my high school. Instead, I chose to attend this place. A nice but low-key University located on the west coast, hundreds of miles away from my hometown of North Woods. Most kids wouldn't choose to be miles away from their parents, but I wasn't most. I chose this college because it's as far away from my family as I can get.

As soon as I turned eighteen and I got my hands on my trust fund, I was out of my parents' house. There was no way I was going to stay another minute longer. I wanted to disappear, forget about my last name, and what it meant.

After finding out about the things my father had been up to, I didn't want a single thing to do with the family business.

"This is college, and you're acting as though someone has sentenced you to ten years hard labor." Shelby laughs. My nose wrinkles as I look up at the fortress before me. Of course, the place would look more like a medieval castle set in the Scottish Highlands than a university. Ropes of thick green ivy climb the walls like they're trying to escape.

"Maybe not ten years, but at least four, right?" I grin.

"College isn't a dick, Harlow. Stop making it so hard."

"Nice analogy. Where did you pull that one out of?"

"My ass." She grins and slams her hips into mine. I roll my eyes like I'm annoyed with her when in reality I'm grateful she is here. She really had to talk her parents into letting her attend college here. I think the only reason her dad agreed is because he's had a bad year at his law firm and the tuition is cheaper than Stanford, where Shelby was supposed to go originally. She doesn't seem to care though.

Students rush past us in a flurry to get into their dorm rooms, while Shelby and I take our sweet time. We had most of our things shipped to the college, all except our personal belongings so there's no rush for us. We spend most of our time taking in the surroundings. The University itself is beautiful, with huge oak trees, and sprawling areas of lush green grass, that I can picture myself sitting on with a blanket and a good book.

We make it to the crowded dorm and up the stairs to our room without incident. Once inside I exhale all the air from my lungs and sag down onto my small twin size bed. The dorms are small and leave very little room for privacy but that's okay. The place is close to the ocean and has a view that most would dream of.

"Okay, so I was invited to a party by a couple of guys I met over at Starbucks," Shelby says, tossing her blonde hair over her shoulder.

"We've been here less than twenty-four hours and you want to go to a party already?" I knew parties were going to happen, but I'd hoped to avoid them.

"It's a past time set forth by our ancestors, when you arrive at college you must party."

"Sounds like its set forth by Shelby." I roll my eyes.

Shelby juts out her bottom lip into a firm pout, "Oh, come on, Harlow, you only went to a handful of parties when we were in high school and now you don't want to enjoy college. Your parents are out of the picture, you can basically do anything you want."

She has no idea how wrong she is. Yes, I've managed to escape my father's clutches for now, but I'm not going to be able to hide from him and my mother forever.

"If I go will you at least wait a whole month before inviting me to another one?"

Amusement twinkles in Shelby's hazel eyes, "Mmm, two weeks tops."

"Seriously." I cringe.

"It's college, Harlow, and I'm your certified fun helper."

Shaking my head, I say, "You're not a fun helper, you're a get into trouble helper."

She taps at her chin with her finger, "Trouble. Fun. All sounds the same to me. Now, what are you wearing? Better be something sexy. We've got to grab the boys' attention right off the bat. You know college boys, all ADHD squirrel like."

"I'm not catching anything, and especially not any boys' attention."

I'd garnered enough attention from the Bishop Brothers back home. After what I did to Sullivan, I was surprised he could walk past me without wanting to murder me. Let's just say it made social gatherings a little tense.

"Your parents aren't here. You don't have anything to worry about. You're free." Shelby gets up from her bed and puts her arms out like a bird, flapping them until she reaches my bed, slamming herself down onto it, causing me to bounce and a bubble of laughter to escape my throat.

"I'm not worried about them," I lie. I'm worried about them just as much as I'm worried about the Bishops.

Actually, I'm not worried. I'm terrified. For years I've helped my father spread rumors about the Bishops. I've helped ruin their lives and for what? Nothing, it was all for nothing. I didn't know how horrible my father really was. He didn't just want their business, he wanted them gone.

At one point my hate for the Bishops started to diminish, and in its place resentment towards my father bloomed. I didn't want anything to do with my old life, the drama, the hate, the revenge. I wanted to forget that part of my life ever existed.

"Good, because it wouldn't matter if you were. Now, up. Let me see what I have to work with and then what clothing you've brought with you."

"Do we really have to go?" I bat my long eyelashes knowing damn well it won't work. I can't make myself look as innocent and sweet as Shelby does. Plus, I kind of owe it to her to at least go out once. She did, after all, move hundreds of miles away from her family to be a supportive friend.

"Yes." She smiles and I should've known that smile was going to be the death of me.

I PULL on the bottom of the miniskirt that Shelby shoved me into. I'm not exactly skinny, curvy is more like it, and even though I don't have any real self-confidence issues, this thing is so short every single guy here is going to get a flash of my crotch by the end of the night.

If and that's a pretty big *if* I go out with Shelby again, she will not be dressing me.

Brushing a few strands of my silky blonde hair behind my ear I survey the crowded room. The frat house is filled to max occupancy with women and men of all ages. There's dancing, singing, and drinking games. People chilling on the couch in the living room, smoking what I'm pretty sure isn't cigarettes based on the sweet aroma that permeates the air.

"We made it." Shelby huffs, a wide grin on her blood red painted lips. She acts like she just aced a test that she's been studying for all semester. We stand together, side by side, in the middle of the room, watching as people move around it, chatting, and having the time of their lives. The longer we stand there the more attention we bring to ourselves.

I can feel eyes on me, gliding over my bare legs, and my shirt that hangs off of one shoulder. Yeah, I don't like this. Being the center of attention. Feeling out of place and a little timid, I hide behind the curtain of my hair as I turn to Shelby.

"We came, we saw, we had some fun, can we go now?" I whine, tugging on her arm. I haven't been to a party since that night. *That disastrous night.* A shiver runs down my spine at the memory, at the anger, and simmering rage that reflected back at me from all three of the Bishop Brothers.

"We'll make you pay for this, Harlow. One day you won't have your parents' protection, and then what will you do?"

Shrugging I say, "I'm not scared of you. You're weak. Pathetic. Just like your parents."

Oliver entered my bubble of space, forcing me to take a step back or be chest to chest with him, "One day, we'll get even with you. We'll break you. You'll wish you were never born."

"You'll be waiting a long time..." I sneer, feeling the fear slither up my spine and around my throat like a snake.

Wiggling my shoulders, I shake off the unpleasant emotions coming with the memory.

"Nope." Shelby pops the p, and grabs onto my hand, tugging us deeper into the house. The place is huge, similar to the mansion I lived in back home. There are priceless paintings on the walls, crown molding, and chandeliers that cost more than most cars. It reminds me so much of my old life that I have to shake away the creepy feeling slithering up my back. I did my research when selecting a college and I made certain this one wouldn't have any billionaire co-eds.

As far as I know, Shelby and I are the only two people attending this university with parents that make more than a million a year. Which leaves me to wonder whose house it is? Does another student own it? His or her parents? *Why do you even care, Harlow?*

Paranoid. I'm being paranoid. Ever since leaving North Woods I've wondered when my past would come back to haunt me. All the things I said and did. The guilt eats away at me every single day. I let my father lead me blindly into the dark. I let him feed me lie after lie. I thought I was doing the right thing, but I wasn't.

When we enter the kitchen I notice the black marble counters and stainless steel appliances. Off the kitchen is a pair of patio doors that open up to a backyard that butts up to the beach. It's beautiful really, minus all the college coeds that are liquored up.

There's a makeshift bar set up on the huge island and Shelby gets to work mixing us something to drink. *Everything's okay.* I tell myself, blowing out air through my mouth, before inhaling through my nose.

"Here," Shelby says, her pink painted nails coming into view as she shoves a red cup into my hand, the contents sloshing against the sides of the cup. I peer inside of it before bringing it to my nose to sniff.

"What is this? It smells like straight alcohol."

Shelby shrugs, her hazel eyes narrowing, "Just drink it. Live a little, will you? If you promise to have a good time, I'll promise not to push you to go out with me so much. Deal?"

Ugh, as much as I hate to admit it, she's right. I'm eighteen, a college student. I need to live a little, and enjoy the years ahead of me before they're gone and I'm forced to be an actual adult, with a job, and responsibilities.

"Fine. I'll try." I give her a weak smile and take a drink of the pink looking liquid. The burn I was expecting doesn't come and I'm pleasantly surprised by the cherry tang that's left against my lips.

"Good, huh?" Shelby asks, watching me like a hawk.

"Decent. It doesn't taste like I'm drinking lighter fluid."

"Shut up." She giggles, taking a drink from her cup. The hairs on the back of my neck stand on end and I don't understand why. Swinging my gaze around the room I look for anything out of place. *What's wrong with me? I think I'm losing my mind.*

A loud rap song comes blaring through the speakers, vibrating through the masses of bodies and into my skull, causing a dull ache to form there. A book wouldn't give me this kind of headache. Feeling as if I'll need it, I drink the rest of the liquid in my cup and hand it back to Shelby with a mischievous grin.

"Make me another. I'm going to go find a bathroom. If I'm not back in ten minutes send out a search party."

"Don't be so dramatic." She takes the cup and ushers me away. "Go to the bathroom. I'll be here when you get back."

Leaving the kitchen I notice a group of women in skirts shorter than my own enter the house. My heart sinks into my stomach at the sight. *Barbies*. Three girls dolled up like plastic dolls. Fake. Popular. Gorgeous. Every college and high school has them.

They stick out like a weed in a bed of flowers. They giggle, and toss their hair over their shoulders, batting their eyelashes at every man that looks their way, and there are a lot of men looking their way. Turning, I head for the huge staircase before they come any closer, I know their type—they'll either want to befriend me and initiate me into their clan, or they'll make me public enemy number one—I don't want to get on their radar, I want to have an uneventful, low-key college experience. Rushing up the stairs I almost run head first into a couple that is making out against the railing.

I mumble a half-hearted apology and continue in search of a bathroom. I open one door to find an empty bedroom with a large inviting looking bed in the center. How bad is it that I would rather curl up in that bed and read a book than go back downstairs and party with the other students?

When I pull the door shut behind me, a familiar scent coming from inside the room tickles my nose. I can't quite place the unique smell, something like a forest after a rainy day.

I keep walking down the hall and the next door I open is actually a bathroom. I disappear inside, locking the door behind me. It is almost as big as my dorm room. I shake my head at the size and fanciness of it all.

I use to think this is all that mattered, money, pretty things and people who look up to you. That's what my family taught me to think and there was a time when I didn't question anything my parents told me. That time is over. Now I know better.

I'm still thinking about the familiar scent in that bedroom as I wash my hands. Something about it is nagging me but I just can't put my finger on it. Looking in the mirror, I give myself a once over before exiting the bathroom. I really should act more like the other people around here. Have fun and enjoy college life. This is what I wanted. I got away from my family to be normal. All I have to do now is get out of my own head and enjoy this.

I walk back down the hall, forcing myself not to think about the bedroom with its tempting scent. I fight the urge to take another peek inside. Just as I pass it I hear the soft click of a door opening, but before I have the time to truly comprehend that someone is behind me, I'm grabbed by my arm and yanked into the room.

Screaming like someone is about to kill me I stumble into the room, losing my footing as I go. Arms flailing, I prepare myself to land hard on the ground but I'm shocked when a pair of strong arms circle my waist from behind pulling me flush to a firm, warm chest.

Momentarily I'm stunned, like a doe caught in the headlights of a car. My screams cut off, the air stills in my lungs. I can't do anything. I'm frozen in place. *What's happening?*

All I can hear is the swooshing of blood in my ears, my chest heaving up and down with panic. I open my mouth to scream again, but nothing comes out. Suddenly I'm dizzy, the smell of rain fills my nostrils once more and I realize immediately who that scent belongs to.

"Did you miss me? Is that why you're here, in my bedroom? Eager to see what we have in store for you?" Sullivan's dark voice fills the room, and a cold shiver runs through me. I notice then that he's standing a few feet away from me, but his voice affects me as if he is right beside me whispering in my ear. It doesn't matter that I can't fully see him. I don't need to. I know he's looking at me with disgust.

His room? Blinking slowly, I try to digest what he's just said? Confused I'm about to ask him what the hell he is talking about when I realize someone is still holding on to my waist. Their warm hands burning into my skin.

Spinning around I shove at the firm chest in front of me, realizing quickly its Banks, the middle Bishop brother. A sinister grin spreads across his face as he licks his lips. "I think she just missed us, why else would she come here, to our house?"

"Your house?" I finally find my voice again. It's shaky but at least I got the words out.

"Yes, *our* house." A third voice drawls, and my gaze travels across the room and collides with Oliver's chocolate brown eyes. "We bought it recently, figured it would be nicer than living in the dorms."

Dorms? Why would they be living in the dorms?

Nothing makes sense right now. This has to be a dream, no scratch that, this is a freaking nightmare. I shake my head as if I can wake myself up from it. Then I try and take a step towards the door, but Sullivan slaps a hand over the handle halting my movement.

"Not so fast," he growls, his muscled form towering over me. He's bigger than he was the last time I saw him. Taller, scarier, even more disgustingly handsome than I remember. "Let's talk. We want to tell you how this year is going to go."

What does he mean? How this year is going to go? He can't really be saying what I think he is? The Bishop brothers aren't... they can't be... My chest starts to heave, even though no air is filling my lungs. Lord, please tell me they aren't attending college here.

"I don't think she gets it," Banks taunts, devilishly.

"It's not hard to figure out. I mean, we're laying it out pretty clearly. It's a shame really. All that money and her daddy couldn't even get her a proper education." Oliver sneers.

"I'm not stupid." I try and make the words sound strong, but they come out like a soft breeze whispering through the trees.

"Right, you're only a liar," Oliver responds, his words like a slap to the face.

Gritting my teeth, I let the insult sink in. *He's not wrong, I am a liar.* Because of my father I've done a lot of things I'm not proud of. I followed him like a lamb to the slaughter, believing him with blind faith. I knew someday karma would catch up with me. That eventually, I would pay for my wrongdoings, I just never expected it to be so soon.

"Let me put it into words even someone like you can understand," Sullivan leans in so closely, I can feel the heat of his body. I can feel all three of them, their bodies drawn to mine like a magnet.

"Remember when I told you I would make you pay for what you did that night?"

Saliva sticks to the inside of my throat—like honey—making it hard to swallow. Every nightmare I've had over the last year would never have amounted to this. All three of their faces have haunted me in my sleep since that night. I regretted doing it as soon as I did it, but there was no taking it back, there was no changing the course we were headed on. It was like a bad accident, that you couldn't look away from.

As if he can see the worry filling my features his smile widens, perfectly straight white teeth gleam in the moonlight filtering in through the window blinds.

"That little stunt ruined his senior year. Got him suspended from the team. You tarnished our family name, but that was the point, right?" Oliver hisses, his eyes narrowing, his angular jaw—sharp enough to cut glass—clenching.

The Bishops' had money, but nothing could stop the local papers from printing an article about their son doing drugs and getting booted from the team. My father had hit his mark and made them bleed, and worse he'd used me to do it.

"Well, now that our family business is ruined, there is nothing for us to take over, so I guess we all have to go to college after all," Banks explains, and I finally get it. All three of them will be attending Bayshore. *This can't be happening.*

"Please... look...." An apology is sitting on the edge of my tongue, but a hand comes out of nowhere from behind me and presses against my mouth—another at my hip—effectively cutting off the words before I get a chance to say them.

I know who it is that has ahold of me, and I try to wiggle out of

Banks' hold, but he just pulls me closer, until my back is pressed firmly into his muscular chest. Panic, and something else, something warm, and euphoric swirl in my belly.

No. I won't be attracted to them, and their stupid muscles, hard abs, and devilish smiles. They're the enemy, my rivals.

"Shh, Princess. We didn't say you could speak. Keep your mouth shut, otherwise, we'll find a better use for it." Banks' smooth voice tickles my ear as he pulls his hand away from my mouth. His body remains close to mine, too close, but for some reason, I don't move right away. One of his hands remains on my hip and I just stand there for a moment, letting his body heat seep into me, trying to warm the icy cold blood running through my veins.

"I told you... I promised you, that you would pay, and now it's time. It's time to pay your dues." Tears sting my eyes. *Don't cry. Don't cry.* I will not cry in front of them. I won't.

Finding a sliver of strength, I jab my elbow into Banks' ribs. He releases me, even though I know I didn't hit him hard enough to hurt.

"Is that all you've got?" he snickers.

I step toward the door that Sullivan is now blocking with his body.

"Let me go," I grit out through my teeth.

No one moves, or says a single word, it's almost like they're waiting for Sullivan to make a choice and that terrifies me. After a long second, he finally moves out of the way, a smug grin painted on his face. Waving his hand over the door and motioning me to leave, he says, "You may leave tonight, but you can never get away from us. We'll find you wherever you go, and we *will* make you pay for what you did."

2

Running down the stairs as fast as I can, I almost trip, missing the last step. I can't form a single thought besides the one telling me that I need to get out of here. Scanning the crowded room I look for Shelby. She isn't anywhere to be found and I grow increasingly worried with each second that passes.

I can't breathe. I need to go, get as far away from this place as I can. My feet start to move on their own, and I find I'm moving through the crowd of people, pushing some out of the way as I go. Before I know it I've made it to the front door. I suck in a greedy breath of fresh air, my heart racing so fast inside my chest that it feels like I'm having a heart attack.

What the hell just happened?

Reaching into my back pocket I pull out my phone so I can send Shelby a text telling her that I'm outside and ready to go. She appears in the front yard a minute later shaking her head at me.

"What the hell, Harlow? We just got here," when she sees my face her expression sobers. "What's wrong? Did something happen? You look like you've seen a ghost."

"Do you know who owns this house? Who invited you to this party?" As soon as I ask the question her lips curl into a deep frown.

"Well, I didn't at first but I kind of figured it out. I didn't think it was going to be that big of a deal. They just want to be friends. Is that really so bad?" *She doesn't have the first clue what she's talking about.*

"You told them I was going to school here? When? How? And *why*?" I yell, threading my fingers through my long blonde hair. The rational part of me knows it's not her fault. She doesn't know about all of the things that have happened between the Bishops and my family, no one does besides the people involved.

My father made sure of it. He kept our name out of the whole incident not wanting to be tarnished and the Bishops didn't dare accuse me of planting the bag even though they knew it was me. Still, at this moment, I can't help but release my anger on her.

Her hazel—more green than brown in this light—eyes go wide, and she holds a hand to her chest.

"You're supposed to be my friend. How could you do this to me?" Shock and confusion are written all over my best friend's face as I scream the words at her. She has no idea what she's done wrong, and truthfully, I can't blame her.

Right now, I just need to leave. To get away.

Turning around I start to walk away from her, the house, and most importantly away from the Bishops. Everything is ruined now. They've come for their revenge and there isn't a damn thing I can do to stop them. I have no one to protect me now. After all I did for my father, I have no one to blame but myself. I'm the one who needs to suffer the consequences. Tears start to fall and I swipe at them with the back of my hand. I knew coming to this party was a mistake.

"Harlow," Shelby calls after me once, but I continue walking not paying her an ounce of attention. I'll have to apologize later, but right now, I just can't deal with it. Walking down the long driveway I kick at the dirt. Stupid. I was so stupid to think that I could move away, and that my problems would never find me. A slight breeze blows off the ocean and whips my hair in a million different directions, chilling me to the bone. Wrapping my arms around myself I try and forget about all that's lead me here.

All the mistakes I've made, the things I've done. I don't know how long I walk but eventually, I reach the end of the long driveway, just as a car is pulling into it. I don't look up from the ground and hope that the car will continue driving but I'm shocked when it comes to a halt a few feet from me.

To make matters worse the driver's side window rolls down a moment later.

"Hey, you okay? Do you need a ride?" I look up to find a girl around the same age as me peering out the window, a smile on her lips. When she sees my face her smile turns into a frown.

Do I look that bad?

"I don't know," I say more to myself than her. Really, I don't know. I thought coming here would save me, but it seems, it has only trapped me further.

"Come on, let me take you wherever it is that you're walking." I should say no, should just keep walking. I don't know this girl. She could be a serial killer for all I know. But her offer is tempting, and I don't want to overthink it. I'll take my chances of being kidnapped or killed over staying here.

"Sure. I just need a ride to the dorms," I tell her, walking over to the passenger side. She's driving an older jeep, something that, in my old town, no one would be caught driving.

Opening the door I climb in, the small overhead light turning on, casting a yellow glow over both of us. I pull the door shut behind me and grab the seat belt clicking it into place.

"I'm Caroline." She offers, as I get in the car and click the seat belt into place. She gives me another harmless smile that I can only make out because of the giant moon hanging in the sky.

Turning in my seat I take her in. She's young, like me, with short brown hair, she almost reminds me of a brunette tinker bell.

"Harlow," I say, trying to hide the sadness from my voice.

"Well, Harlow, you look like you could really use a drink. Everything okay?"

"Yeah, I'm fine. Just ran into some people from high school. Things didn't end well between me and those people so..." I trail off, staring out of the window.

"Ah, I get it. An old high school flame? Did you see him with another chick?" I almost laugh at her words. I wish it was that simple.

"No nothing like that. It's complicated," I sigh.

"If you want to talk about it I'm a great listener. Hey, which dorms are you in, you never said?"

"South wing, freshmen dorms," I mumble absentmindedly.

"I'm a freshman too. I live in the dorms across the street from you. I don't really know anybody here yet, so seriously if you ever want to hang out, I'm your girl. No pressure though."

"Thank you, I'll keep that in mind," I say when we pull up into the dorms parking lot. "Really, thanks, I appreciate it, and for the ride too."

"No problem. I'll see you around, Harlow," I give her a half-hearted wave and walk towards the entrance of the dorm. My mind is so consumed by my encounter with the Bishop Brothers that I don't realize how weird my encounter with Caroline was. I didn't even ask her why she was so late for the party, or why she was quick to bring me home when she hadn't even stepped foot in the party herself? Does she always pick up random people?

I shove my thoughts about her to the back of my mind and decide to digest them another day. Right now, I have to figure out how I'm going to remain going to school here with those assholes. When I get back to my room, I change into a pair of sleep pants, and an oversized T-shirt. I rid my face of the makeup painted on it, and sag down onto the small twin sized bed.

Tears sting my eyes once again and this time I let them fall. They cascade down my cheeks gently. I'm such a horrible friend. In my fit of panic and rage, I lashed out at the one and only friend I have here. I left her at that party without even thinking. Balling my hands into tiny fists I slam them against the blue comforter. I let those stupid assholes win by leaving, by running away. I want to scream. I've never been the type to run, to hide, but I don't want to fight them. I'm done fighting, done with the lies, with all the drama.

My eyes drift closed and I beg for sleep to come. Instead, images of the brothers filter through my mind. Tall, tan, handsome as hell. It would be so much easier to hate them if they weren't gorgeous and if the things my father had told me were true.

The memory of that night, haunts me, looming over me like a ghost. It's one of the worst and also, one of the best nights of my life all wrapped up in one.

The worst because I ruined the Bishops.

The best because I got my first kiss, even though it was with Sullivan Bishop.

I don't know how I'm going to get close to him. Bethany Kingston's house is packed making it hard to work my way through the crowd, and it doesn't help that I have no idea where he is. Parties aren't my scene and I'm sure I'm drawing attention to myself since I keep stopping and scanning the room, especially since I don't have a drink in my hand. A knot of worry fills my belly. I want to be at home, not out doing my father's dirty work.

The packet feels heavy in my pocket even though it's as light as a feather. All you have to do is put it in his pocket, I tell myself, surveying the room once more for his russet brown hair. The Bishop Brothers stand out amongst the other guys, not just because of their looks but because of the air that surrounds them. They walk with a chip on their shoulders, one that says I'm better than you.

"Come out to play, Princess?" A deep voice says from behind me, vibrating through me, and sending tiny rivulets of heat to my core. I shouldn't be attracted to them, but much like the rest of the female population I am and I hated myself for it.

"Not with you," I sneer, twisting around, coming face to face with Sullivan. Eyes as blue as the sky peer down at me. They're framed by thick lashes that most of the women at my school would die for. I clench my teeth together as I let my gaze roam over his face. High cheekbones, dimples, and full smooth pink lips.

Him, Oliver, and Banks look almost identical, though Oliver has brown eyes that remind me of melted chocolate rather than blue like Banks and Sullivan. They are close in age, Oliver is two years older than us, Banks only a year.

Sullivan's pink lips turn into a pout, "That's a shame. I wonder what it is you do for fun? I never see you at parties like this."

"I don't like the people going to parties like this," I lie. I like most of the people here. I just don't like how people act at parties. I don't like the drinking or the dancing.

"If you don't like the crowd why don't we go out for a walk? Did you see the Kingston's' backyard yet?" I've heard about the backyard. It's supposed to be beautiful. Apparently, Mr. Kingston spends thousands of dollars every few weeks to have the most pristine yard with some of the rarest flowers. But going outside with Sullivan...just the two of us?

"Come on, I won't bite." He winks, giving me a swoon-worthy smile.

"Okay," I say, only partly so I get the chance to plant the baggy. He holds out his elbow and I hook my arm into his as we walk outside together. Stupidly the baggy is in the pocket I can't access with my arm intertwined with his like this.

It's very hard to see him as the bad guy when he is acting so nice to me. I have to remind myself about what his family has done to mine and stop thinking about how lovely it feels to walk so close to him.

As promised, he takes me on a walk, showing me the beautiful garden. We talk about school and the upcoming summer break as we admire the beauty of the unique flowers and warm light coming from the night sky. I hate to admit it to myself, but I'm actually having a good time. Why is he being so nice to me?

Doubt creeps up my spine and settles in the nape of my neck, giving me a subtle headache. I don't think I can do this. Maybe I just go back home and tell my dad I couldn't get to him.

"You okay?" Sullivan suddenly stops.

"Yes, sorry just lost in thought."

"Yeah? Me too."

"What are you thinking about?" I ask curiously. I shouldn't care what he's thinking about I'm not here to ask questions or get closer to him.

"Mostly about kissing you."

My heart freezes inside my chest. Did he just say kissing? Kissing me? I stare at his stupidly handsome face waiting for him to tell me that he was kidding, that it's a joke, but he never does. Instead, he continues talking.

"Would that be okay? If I kiss you, I mean? I know our parents hate each other, and we shouldn't care about each other either, but it's only a kiss." His question hangs in the air for a moment, and I swallow down my nervous anxiety, knowing I'm going to say yes. I don't think I want to kiss him, definitely not, but this is my chance to get close enough to plant the bag.

"Okay.... A kiss... A kiss would be okay, I mean," I whisper right before he brushes a strand of hair from my face. His thumb brushing against my cheek leaving my skin tingling beneath his touch. He leans in, eyes open wide, as if he doesn't want to miss the chance to see my face when our lips touch.

Then our lips touch, pressing together and my eyes close on their own. Tingles of warmth ripple through me. Everything around us fades out as if we are the only two people in the world. All I feel are his soft, full lips against mine. The kiss is gentle, heart-warming, and I lean into him while our lips melt into each other.

I give myself this one second to forget everything, the reason I am here and the reason I should hate him. Butterflies flutter around inside my stomach igniting a deep tremble in my core. A warmth seeps into my bones, melting me like an ice cream cone sitting in the afternoon sun. I want to get lost in that feeling, feel nothing else beside it, but my father's voice rings in my ears right then. I need to remember what his family has done, the pain they've caused.

With a heavy heart and an unsteady hand, I grab the small plastic bag from my pocket and slip it into his before I pull away breaking the kiss.

My first kiss.

The rattling of keys outside the door drags me back to reality. The lock clicks and the door opens a moment later. The light flicks on, blinding me in the process.

"What the hell, Harlow?"

I let my eyes adjust for a moment before getting out of bed and walking over to my friend. "I'm sorry, Shelby," I say as I throw my arms around her and bury my face in her thick blonde hair. "I'm really sorry I yelled at you. You didn't know. I shouldn't have taken it out on you."

"Didn't know what?" she asks, while wrapping her own arms around me. "Tell me what's going on, please."

"Okay." Letting go of her, I grab her hand and lead her to my bed. We sit down together and I wrap the blanket around myself before starting to explain the whole thing. I swore to my parents I would never tell anyone, but they don't control me anymore. So, I tell Shelby about the past, about what happened, and about what I've done.

I tell her about my greatest shame while hoping that she can still look at me the same way after. Hoping that I'm not losing my best friend like I've lost everything else in my life.

3

When I open my eyes on the first day of school, I feel better than I thought I would. It's been two days since my encounter with the Bishops and since I spilled the beans about everything to Shelby. She was shocked about the whole thing, but besides that took it pretty well. She didn't hate me like I thought she would and I'm more thankful than ever to have her as my friend. She promised to never say a word about any of it.

Shelby is already gone by the time I'm dressed and ready to go. She has an early class, while mine doesn't start until ten. I briefly thought about switching schools but decided that I'm not going to run from my problems again, Shelby is here and there is no way her father will let her switch schools again and I don't want to go anywhere else by myself. I'm alone as it is, no need to isolate myself further.

I think the best way to deal with the Bishops is to ignore them as best as I can. I won't play into their games or let them bring me down. I came here to be a normal college student and that's what I'm going to be.

Stuffing all my books and notepads into my backpack, I swing it over my shoulder and head out the door, locking it as I go. I turn around and walk down the hallway with a campus map and my class schedule in hand.

With my eyes trained on the paper, I don't even see the person stepping out in front of me until it's too late and my body is crashing into another. Clutching onto the paper in my hands I look up startled.

I'm about to mumble some apology when I realize it's Banks who is towering in front of me, and judging by the expression on his face, him being here isn't just a coincidence.

"Good morning, Princess," he grins, his blue eyes twinkling with one-sided amusement.

"What do you want, Banks?" I try to push past him, but he blocks my exit and steps in my way, with him being built like a brick wall there isn't much I can do to get by him.

"I was just thinking about how nice it would be for me to pick you up so we can walk to our class together."

"*Our* class?" I repeat his words with disbelief.

"Yup, we made sure at least one of us is always in one of your classes, so we can keep an eye on you," he explains. "We wouldn't want you to have a good time or anything." He leans forward brushing a loose strand of hair from my face. His sweet, intoxicating scent of cinnamon wraps around me making it hard for me to breathe. This close I almost forget he's the enemy. *Almost.* "Remember, we're here to make your life as difficult as possible."

"I got that part, thanks." I swat away his hand and twist around walking in the other direction. I'm not doing this. I can't handle it right now.

The sound of his heavy footsteps following me down the stairs reverberates around the stairwell, but even without the sound, I would know he is there. I can feel his presence. I can feel his body close to mine, just as I can feel each of the Bishop Brothers when they are in the same room as me.

I can't explain it, but it has always been this way. I used to think it was because they were bad and I have a sixth sense about bad people, but I figured out a while ago that the goosebumps covering my skin are not there because they give me the creeps, no it's something much more worrisome than that.

Banks catches up with me and falls into step beside me. My breath hitches at his closeness. Damnit, why does my body have to react this way when one of them is close? Why can't my body get the memo about our mutual hate?

"You are much less annoyed by me being here than I thought you would be. Maybe you even like having me close by," he says, and I can feel my cheeks heating, giving my embarrassment away. "Are you excited to see me? Is that why you didn't pull away when I was standing behind you the other night?"

"Stop," I blurt out and up my pace. Unfortunately, he is much taller than me, his legs longer and even though I'm speed walking now, he is only casually walking next to me, he has no trouble at all keeping up.

Lord, please shove me off the side of a cliff right now.

All I get is two more steps before Banks grabs my arm and pulls me towards him. He twirls us around and pushes my body up against the closest wall. With my back flush against the cold brick, he leans in, so close that his body molds against mine. He dips his head so his mouth is right next to the shell of my ear and I have this strange need, want even, to turn and feel his lips against mine.

Would he kiss me back? This attraction is wrong, but it feels so right.

"Did you like how close I was? How close I am right now?" His breath is hot on my skin and as he talks a shiver runs through my body, from the top of my head all the way down to my toes. This is wrong, so wrong. He is crowding my space, my mind. Making me think and feel things I shouldn't.

Yes. "No," I croak. My lie must not be very convincing, because Banks lets out a soft chuckle at my words. And just like that the moment ends and Banks pulls away, leaving me cold.

"You're still a liar, but that's okay. We'll break you of that nasty little habit."

"Can you just go away?" I try and push down the anger, the shame coursing through me.

"No," he growls. "We won't go away. Not until we are finished with you." He takes a step back, putting a few inches of space between us. "Now, let's go. You might not care about your grades, or classes, but I do, and I don't want to be late on the first day, so get moving or I'll toss you over my shoulder and carry you."

He wouldn't. Would he? My thoughts must be visible on my face.

"Don't tempt me, Harlow. I can, and I will," he whispers so only I can hear him as a group of people walk by. The tone of his voice holds a warning that I shouldn't want to cross but that I feel tempted to.

"Whatever," I sigh, rolling my eyes. If they won't leave me alone, and they feel the need to accompany me to every class, then I'm going to have to come up with a way to make them go away. I'm going to have to come up with a plan.

I'll beat the Bishop Brothers at their own game.

BANKS WASN'T KIDDING when he said they made sure that there would be at least one of them in each of my classes. At first, I didn't think they would be that ballsy, but I underestimated them. Their need for revenge is very real. It also makes it very hard for me to focus.

My first class with Banks wasn't so bad, but the one after that with Oliver was horrible. Girls were talking to him the entire time and he was talking back while trying to include me in the conversation, but not in a good way. Of course, when I tried to get them to shut up the professor yelled at me for disrupting the class. By the time lunch comes around I'm annoyed, hungry, and ready to stab all three of them right in the eyes.

"What are we having for lunch, Princess?" Oliver questions as we leave the economics class.

"*We?*" I ask, coming to a stop in the middle of the sidewalk, taking Oliver by surprise. "We aren't having anything for lunch."

Oliver rolls his chocolate brown eyes, "You can fight this all you want but I'm not going anywhere, and neither are my brothers."

He runs a hand through the thick mop of brown hair on his head. I lick my lips, wondering if it's as soft as it looks. Why am I so attracted to these guys? So what I gave Sullivan my first kiss, who cares, that doesn't mean I should want Banks or Oliver.

"God, I'm fucking hungry." Another voice pierces my thoughts, and I whirl around to find Sullivan walking towards us, his lips like a beacon calling out to me.

Jesus. I need to stop thinking about kissing these assholes.

"Well, you're going to be hungry a little longer because princess here says we aren't eating lunch together."

Rolling my eyes, I say, "Neither of you are eating lunch with me. It's bad enough that I can't even attend class by myself. Girls keep looking at me, staring actually, and I can see them sharpening their claws. Being around you guys adds unwanted attention. All I want to do is go to class and go back to my dorm. Is that too much to ask?"

Sullivan crosses the distance between us in a second, the closeness of his body is almost too much for me, his sweet scent wafting into my nostrils. Having all three brothers around me is like sensory overload and I'm seconds away from tapping out.

"That's the point. What do you think it felt like to have all eyes on me? To have people spreading lies about my parents? To be under scrutiny by an entire town?" His words are clipped, and his tone is dark.

Immediately I'm reminded of the seriousness of this situation. I might be daydreaming about kissing them while being annoyed by their presence, but I can't forget why this is happening, how serious the whole thing is. How much they hate me, and how that's the driving force behind everything they do, to see me suffer. I cannot get distracted by my irrational hormonal reaction to them.

My stomach starts to growl then, reminding me how hungry I am. I could go back to my room and lock myself inside until my next class, maybe they would go away by then. *Doubtful.* But, I have nothing to eat in the dorm.

"Fine," I say defeated. "Let's go get lunch then."

Oliver and Sullivan both smirk triumphantly before escorting me like two wingmen to the campus cafeteria. They make a show of it, opening doors for me like pure gentlemen. I can feel every single pair of eyes on me as we walk. Even the middle-aged lady handing out food is giving me the stink-eye. I want to tell her how much I dislike them following me around but don't. Something tells me she wouldn't care anyway.

When we finally sit down, people at the table next to us start whispering, leaning into each other. I don't know what they're saying but it isn't hard to guess. One of the guys at the table stares at me creepily, and I swear I see him licking his lips as his gaze roams over my chest.

What the fuck?

The girl next to him—who I assume is his girlfriend—gets up to leave, and drags him by his arm out of the cafeteria. If looks could kill, her glare would have struck me dead ten times over.

"Someone might have spread a rumor that you are into some kinky stuff and looking for some more playmates because three guys aren't enough for you," Sullivan snickers before taking a bite of his sandwich. My cheeks heat instantly, and I use my golden hair as a curtain to hide my face from the group of people still sitting at the table nearby.

"You have got to be kidding me," I whisper under my breath. The hunger I felt a minute ago vanishes and is replaced with sickening nausea. I've never even had sex before, and now I'm supposedly into some kinky multiple partner shit?

Shoving away the tray of food I get up to leave.

"Awe, come on, Harlow, it's just a rumor," Oliver teases when I push past him. Grasping on to the strap of my backpack like it could somehow save me, I rush out of the cafeteria, hoping that they'll give me a little space. I need some time to myself, a few seconds to breathe and gather my thoughts.

Darting around the building I lean against the brick wall and press my hands to my hot face. Coming here was supposed to help me forget about my past, about North Woods, about all the things I did for my father, but I should have known better than to be so hopeful. I couldn't just run away from what I've done, away from my problems. It didn't mean I didn't want to try though.

After a few minutes of breathing exercises, I finally succeed in calming down enough to think properly. Running a hand over my face and through my hair, I hope that I look like a normal person and not someone who is on the verge of a mental breakdown.

Straightening up I walk back around the building. Looking at my phone in shock, I realize I've been hiding out behind the building way longer than I thought.

Shit. I'm going to be late for my next class. Still looking down at my phone since there is a text from Shelby that I need to return, I start walking in the direction of the science building when I hear someone calling my name.

I'm grateful that it's not one of the brothers. This voice is feminine.

"Hey, Harlow," the voice is familiar and when I look up from my phone I spot the girl from the other night. *Caroline?* I think that's her name, the tinker bell lookalike.

"Hi, Caroline," I greet, "Sorry, but I'm running late. I have to get to the science building."

"Environmental science 101?"

My brows furrow with confusion, "Ah, yeah. How did you know?"

"I'm heading to the same class," she giggles, her brown head bopping. "I guess we'll be late together then."

For the first time today I smile, because the brothers' are nowhere in sight, and I'm venturing out, making friends. The walk to class is a short one, but Caroline packs our walk full of questions. Like where I'm from, if I'm really dating all three of the Bishop Brothers? Apparently rumors spread faster than I thought in college.

We make it to class five minutes after it starts. The professor gives me a sour look but doesn't say anything. My gaze sweeps around the class to find a seat, more eyes, and whispers.

Great. Only two chairs are free and of course Banks is sitting next to one of those free ones. He gives me a strangely warm smile, waving me over. Jesus, why can't they just go away. I shake my head at him, but then watch Caroline take the other free chair, leaving me with no other option.

"Please take a seat, Miss," The professor scolds, annoyance lacing his words.

With my head bowed in defeat, I slump down next to Banks and open my text book.

"Can I join your harem, Harlow?" Banks asks, and I know he's just being a dick, rubbing the rumor in my face. Using my elbow I hit him in the side, and smile when he lets out a low grunt, letting me know that he didn't see that one coming. Caroline gives me a bewildered expression, and I wonder if she believes me or the rumors being spread?

Banks' jaw tightens, and his eyes narrow as he leans down to whisper in my ear.

"Elbow me again and I'll make a mockery out of you in front of everyone." His warning makes me shiver and I can't help but turn slightly, my gaze colliding with his. The need to ask him what he would do is almost too much. My mind imagining all kinds of things, all of which are wrong in every way.

There's a hurricane of emotions swirling in those blue depths and I want to crack him open, spill all his secrets. Sullivan might have had my first kiss, but something tells me Banks will have my second.

A flurry of whispers fill the room and I realize people are looking at us, smiling, laughing and just like that I've made a mistake. I've fed right into the rumors being spread. The grin that spreads across Banks' smug face tells me that was his point all along and suddenly I'm back to hating him and his brothers all over again.

4

The first week of classes passes without another incident. Other than dirty looks and whispering everywhere I go nothing else has happened and, thank god for that. I have enough to deal with as it is.

I hate to admit it, but classes are harder than I thought. I had always had good grades in high school without even trying too much and I just now realize that it might have had something to do with my dad being a huge donor to school funding.

"How are you holding up?" Shelby asks, while I'm getting ready for a shower. I shrug. Really not sure what the hell I should tell her. Do I tell her about the brothers following me around? About the rumors? I'm sure she has already heard them.

"Everything is okay, I guess, I just imagined college would be different," I admit. "I thought it would be the two of us having fun, spending our days doing whatever we wanted," Shelby is studying art, while I'm majoring in social psychology. I knew we wouldn't have a lot of classes together, but I didn't expect to see her so little.

"I know the guys are getting on your nerves."

"That's the understatement of the year," I scoff. "They just won't let up. I don't know where they get the energy to be so annoying."

"Oh man, that sounds bad." She shakes her head. "I can't believe I used to have a crush on Sullivan."

"You did?" I can't believe I didn't know that.

"Yeah, sixth grade, Miss Holli's class."

I shrug. "Well, don't feel bad, everybody had a crush on him in middle school."

"Yeah, I guess. Hey, listen, I'm sorry we're not spending much time together, and I'm even more sorry for what I'm about to tell you."

"Oh god, what is it? Is something wrong? Is your dad making you move back?" I don't think I can take anything else right now. We might not see each other very much but knowing she is here, with me, it makes me feel better, not so alone.

"No, no, it's not that. It's just…" She seems to skirt around it, and the knot of anxiety in my gut starts to build. "It's just… I got a paid internship at the local art gallery." She finally mutters, head hanging low, as if she's ashamed.

"Oh my god, Shelby! That's great! I'm so proud of you," I screech, lunging towards her and throwing my arms around her neck. "Wait. Why do you sound so sad about it?" She should be excited, jumping up and down, but instead she looks like one of those dogs in the animal shelter.

"Because it means that I'll be gone even more. We will hardly see each other, and I know you need me right now. I'm being a bad friend. I should just decline the offer. I'm only a freshman and I don't really need the money either."

I start to shake my head, blonde strands of hair cling to my face.

"Oh, hell no. You will absolutely not! You will go and rock their world and show them how amazing you are."

No way will I allow her to give something like this up, she deserves to have freedom too. I'll survive, one way or another. She's not going to sacrifice her happiness to be a human shield for me.

"Are you sure? I came here for you, and I don't want to be that friend that skips out."

"Yes, I'm sure. If you don't go, I will make you." I give her my best evil look which only makes me smile. She examines my face like she doesn't believe me, and I narrow my gaze, seriousness overtaking my features.

"Okay! I'll go," she murmurs into my hair as she leans forward. I hold onto her a little longer before pulling away, missing the hug as soon as it ends. "They're asking me to come in today so they can show me around, after classes I'll head over there, and be back later tonight. Maybe we can get a later dinner together or something?"

"Yes, that would be great. And just so you know, I'm so proud of you. You deserve this. Now go and have fun. I have to take a shower anyway. In case you haven't noticed, I stink," I exclaim, fake smelling my armpit as I grab my shower bag.

Shelby pulls back completely, pinching her nose. "That's what that smell is."

"Hey, now!" I complain, giggling.

"Get out of here and get rid of that smell." She teases. Slipping from the room feeling lighthearted and happy I head down the hall to the showers. That's one of the many crappy things about living in dorms, the bathrooms are shared, and so are the showers.

I walk into the bathroom and find two other girls inside glancing at me like they are unhappy to see me. I'm not even in the shower yet and I can hear two girls whispering in the corner. I don't know if they just don't care or if they are making it obvious on purpose but it's annoying as hell. All the rumors, and whispers are soul-sucking. I thought it would die down after a couple of days, but it seems the more I ignore it the louder the whispers get. The fact that one of the brothers is with me at all times just adds to the rumor mill.

Trying my best to ignore them I strip out of my clothes and set them down on the bench in front of the showers.

The sound of a door opening and closing meets my ears right before I slip out of my underwear and get into the shower stall, pulling the curtain closed behind me. Hopefully that was them leaving, as the last thing I want to do is deal with catty bitches after a shower. Fiddling with the water I wait till it turns hot and let the steamy water soothe my stiff neck muscles. As I wash my hair the silence inside the large room becomes too much and I start humming to myself.

Lost in the shower and the song inside my head, I don't hear someone come into the room.

"What song is that, Princess?" A male voice echoes around me. I'm so startled I drop my soap and almost slip and land on my ass in the process. Thankfully I'm able to grab onto the shower curtain and steady myself before I do. With my heart racing out of my chest, and my eyes wide I stand there, shocked, and confused.

Fisting the flimsy plastic in my hand, I pull the curtain to the side just enough to stick my head out and find Banks standing right in front of my shower stall with a smug grin, and a mischievous glint in his eyes. Even though I'm annoyed, I can't help the warm flush that works its way through me at the sight of him. He's wearing a tight fitted T-shirt, and a pair of ripped jeans that hug his toned legs. He looks like he belongs on a magazine cover.

"What the hell are you doing?" I bark.

"Just checking up on you. Making sure you're cleaning all the important spots." His eyes roam over my curtain covered body and even though I know he can't see through the blue plastic, I feel like he can. In the presence of the Bishop Brothers it's like being under a microscope and right now I feel naked and exposed and the worst part is that I'm not embarrassed or appalled by it, not at all.

In fact, I'm curious, excited, and a little turned on.

Bad, Harlow. Bad. I internally scold myself.

"You want me to join?" he asks, a thick brown brow raised. His question making me gulp. *Yes. Yes, I do.* Wait... no... no I don't. When I don't answer him right away, he takes a step towards me.

"N-No... Please leave, you're not supposed to be in here. This is a girls' only bathroom." I state the obvious, trying very hard not to imagine Banks stripping out of his clothes and stepping into the shower with me. Briefly I wonder which of the brothers looks better without their shirts on, who has the bigger...

"Whatever." He shrugs, the blazing fire in his eyes turning to ice in an instant. "Your loss."

"Get out, Banks, or I'm going to report you to the RA."

"Oooo, I'm so scared," he taunts.

We both know it wouldn't matter if I reported him. It's already obvious the Bishops are royalty at Bayshore. I wonder what kind of donation their parents gave the school, god knows new students, freshman at that, wouldn't hold sway like they do.

Pulling the curtain shut all the way, making sure that there isn't even an inch of space at the sides for him to peek in I finish washing my body, keeping my eyes on the shower curtain at all times. Eventually, I hear his heavy footfalls walking away from me, my heart beats a little more, but only when I hear the door open and shut does it steady to a normal rhythm.

I finish showering, shaving my legs, and washing my hair, before stepping out of the shower. I freeze when I look down on the bench where I deposited all of my stuff. Gone. My clothes are gone. My towel is *gone*. That asshole took everything.

I'm standing completely naked and alone in the center of the room, staring at the bench waiting for my stuff to reappear. Moments pass, water droplets still dripping down my body. When I am completely certain that this is reality and I'm not just stuck in a bad dream, I start going through the lockers, hoping, and praying that there is something to cover myself with. At least so I can get to my room.

When I get to the twentieth locker I finally find a towel. It's small, old, and smells horrendous, but it's better than nothing. I don't dry my hair. I just wrap the nasty towel around my body and head back to my room. The scratchy thing is so small it barely covers all my lady parts.

By some kind of freaking miracle no one is in the hallway and I make it to my room without incident. I get to my door and halt for a split second. I don't have my key either, it was in my bag that Banks took, and I don't remember if I locked the door or not. I turn the knob, saying a silent prayer and thanking the universe when the door opens.

Quickly I rush inside, closing my eyes I lean against the door and sigh loudly.

Thank goodness.

"Lose something?" A deep gravelly voice calls. *oh, no, he didn't! He couldn't, right?*

Wide-eyed I spin around clutching the barely there towel to my chest. I'm pretty sure my ass cheeks are showing but it's better than my tits or vagina. I can't believe Banks has the nerve to be here after what he just did. Asshole.

"You." My bottom lip curls with anger when I see him lounging on my bed, a shit eating grin spread across his face.

"Me?" He huffs out a laugh, "What about me? I've been sitting here the whole time waiting for you. It seems you forgot to take your things with you? How is that my fault?" The smile, the fact that he's sitting there looking handsome, and put together while I'm barely hanging on by a thread enrages me.

"Listen, I can deal with you following me around like lost puppies and even the rumors that I know you and your brothers are spreading about me, but this shit, this little stunt goes too far! You need to stay out of my room and out of the showers." I'm so angry, my hands are shaking. *How dare he?* I should have known they would step up their game. That they would do more than just spread rumors and follow me around. This is the last place I have left, my oasis. The only place I can go to get away from them. I can handle a lot of things but this... this invasion of privacy. It's the last straw.

"You crossed the line, Banks!" I yell, feeling my skin heat at the outburst.

"I...I crossed the line?" Banks is suddenly on his feet, and across the room before I can even blink, stopping only inches away from me. The air between us grows thick, making it hard to breath. With his thick finger pointed right at my chest he continues, "You would know all about crossing the line, wouldn't you? About making up lies, and ruining someone's future, their life?" I hadn't ruined Sullivan's life, had I?

"Looks like you're all living a great life, so it couldn't have been that bad..."

"Wasn't that bad, huh?" he mutters to himself in disbelief, "Do you have any idea what you've done to our family? How devastated Sullivan was that he was kicked from the team. People..." He doesn't finish what he says and I'm not sure I want him to. I don't need to hear anything else. I know what I did was wrong, hell, I knew it was wrong before I did it.

When he looks up at me his features are menacing, and I know I should probably be scared right now, but I'm not. Him being this close to me and me being so exposed has my body vibrating with foreign excitement. His heady scent invades my nostrils and all I can think of is him. I forget his anger, forget my guilt, and shame. Everything falls away, leaving just us.

Releasing my hold on the towel I let my arms fall to the sides of my body. Cool air washes over my bare skin, and my nipples harden to tight peaks.

I don't know who is more shocked by what I just did, me or him? I watch his eyes soften and darken at the same time. His pupils dilate as his gaze drops between us, his gaze wanders over my naked form. I watch his chest rise and fall at a faster pace than normal, matching my own erratic breathing.

Shit, I shouldn't have done that.

When his gaze shoots back up and our eyes meet there is a spark there, and that spark ignites an entire fire inside me. Without thinking I take a step forward at the same time as he does. Our lips meet in a furious, almost punishing kiss. There is an urgency to this kiss, and it's completely unlike the one I experienced with Sullivan. Its rage and anger, and I feel like if I don't continue kissing him right now I might combust.

Snaking my arms around his neck I pull him closer. My nipples brush against the soft fabric of his shirt, and I damn near moan at the sensation. His hands easily find my hips and he pulls me closer, so close there isn't a millimeter of space left between us. I can feel my core pulsing, my body melting into his. I know he wants me, the hardened bulge in his jeans telling me so. We continue to kiss, his lips pressing against mine, his hands holding onto me with a possessiveness that excites and terrifies me.

He nips at my bottom lip and I moan feeling the bite deep in my core. I want him, need him. Blood rushes in my ears, and then it ends. Like a cold bucket of water has been tipped over me. Banks pulls away pushing me backwards. I sway unsteadily on my legs. His lips are wet and swollen and all I want to do is run my fingers over them.

"No! You're not going to pull that shit on me," he growls, shaking his head in annoyance. "This might have worked on Sullivan, but you can't use the same trick twice and expect no one to notice."

"He told you?" I respond hoarsely, lust still clogging my throat. My lips swollen and my skin burning where he touched me.

Grinning, he says, "Of course he told us, we're his brothers. Now keep your lips, and your body to yourself, because next time I won't stop. Next time, I'll take and take until there isn't anything left."

Without another look, he pushes me out of the way and exits the room. Bringing a hand to my lips I can still feel his kiss there, the heat of his body burning into mine and I know I'll be thinking about him for a long while to come.

5

Four days pass without Banks showing himself. My little towel stunt must have had some type of impact on him because he no longer follows me around. That doesn't mean I'm allowed to roam around on my own though. Sullivan and Oliver still escort me every place I go. By now, I'm getting used to it. I'm also getting used to the way people gawk at me and the snotty remarks that follow. Turns out college is just like high school, only with more people and less consequences.

"Where are you going?" Oliver asks, falling into step beside me. He's the oldest of the Bishops, and I like to tell myself the smartest. When it comes to cracking them, Oliver will be the hardest nut. "This is not the way to your dorm."

"Great observation skills, Sherlock. I'm going to the library," I snap, hoping it will deter him enough that he will leave me alone. I can't concentrate when one of them is close by and I really need to write this paper. It wouldn't be a problem to do it at my dorm, but the professor is adamant about only using library sources so it's either the library or a failing grade.

"I'll help you study," he snickers, and I already know he is going to do the opposite.

"Look, if you don't let me do this..." I stop, because I don't want to sound weak, or give them any more ammunition, but I also don't really have anything to threaten him with nor do I want to. "I will fail this class if I don't go to the library and then I'll have to leave the school. How will you make my life a living nightmare if I'm not going to school here anymore? Huh?" I mock, the idea of dropping out wouldn't be so bad if I didn't have to face my father.

"We'll just follow you wherever you go," he says nonchalantly, as if he's already thought the scenario through.

"Even back to my parents?"

Oliver's gaze turns dark and he cuts me off mid-step, my body colliding with his, causing me to bounce back off of him. I can feel myself falling backwards when his arm circles my waist and he pulls me into his chest. "Oh, we won't let you get away that easily. We're done here when we say we're done and not a moment sooner. Do you understand?"

This close I can see just how beautiful he truly is, high cheekbones, a strong, sharp jaw, and full lips that draw you in. His hair is a disheveled glossy mass of russet brown that I want to run my fingers through.

Enemy. Bully. Rival. I repeat inside my head, to starve off the indecent thoughts I'm having right now.

"Harlow," Oliver calls out, and I shake myself from the daze I'm in. The dimpled smile on his face tells me I've been caught red-handed.

"You know, I thought Banks was joking when he said you threw yourself at him, but I see it now. That's your thing, isn't it? You use your body to get what you want? How many guys have you slept with to get your way?"

I can't help but laugh at his question as I push him away. I'm a little insulted and for a split second I think about telling him that I'm still a virgin, but that fact seems too personal to share, especially with him.

"Oh no! You got me." I raise my hands into the air like an idiot.

"Harlow, the harlot. I just go around kissing guys and whisking them off into my bed to get them to do what I want. Haven't you heard," I lean into his stoic face, "my vagina is made of gold."

His facial expression combined with the words I'm spewing send me into a fit of laughter that makes my belly hurt. Bending over I hold a hand to my stomach and snort loudly.

"Fucking Christ," he mumbles under his breath, grabbing me by the arm and practically dragging me up the steps to the library.

"I'm guessing you didn't think that was funny?"

We pass a group of people and even with the quick motion I can still feel their eyes on me. Once up the steps I shake off his hold and put some space between us.

"You aren't taking this serious at all, are you?" he asks, his voice threaded with frustration. Little does he know his frustration only makes me feel better. Shrugging, I tuck a couple loose strands of hair behind my ear. My chest is still burning from the laughter and the run up the steps. "This is all a game to you. That's all it's ever been."

"I guess it doesn't really matter what my answer is. You guys will do your worst no matter what I say." I don't wait around to hear his response. Instead I turn and walk inside the library. *My sanctuary.*

Oliver follows behind me like there is an invisible string tethered between us. It doesn't take me long to find a seat, and I pull out the chair making sure I don't scrape it against the wooden floor.

"I'm giving you one hour, that's it. Then I'm putting you over my shoulder and carrying you back to the dorm. I'm not babysitting your ass all night." He growls, throwing himself into one of the wooden chairs. He almost looks too small for it.

"Aww, why not? Got another girl to traumatize?" I whisper getting my notes, pencils, and book out.

"Nope, only you," he says, and somehow his words make their way into my brain and make me feel a way I'm sure he didn't intend. *Only you.*

I start working on the stupid paper, trying to concentrate on my books and not on Oliver sitting next to me. A few times I have to get up and find different books for references, and every time I do, Oliver's there watching me like a hawk, like I'm some criminal that's about to make a run for it or something.

After almost an hour I'm not even close to being done.

Sighing, I set my pencil down. "You know you don't *have* to babysit me, right? I'm not anywhere near being done here and it's painfully obvious you don't want to be here. I don't understand why you have to watch me every second of the day. I'm not a child."

At my words he looks up from his phone, which he's been playing with for the better part of the last hour.

"No, I have a better idea. You gather your stuff up and we'll head back to your dorm. I gave you an hour of my time, if you want more you'll have to earn it." His expression is dead serious, nothing but honesty reflecting in his eyes and that kind of frightens me.

"*Earn it?* What's that supposed to mean? If you think I'm going to sleep with you, then you're mentally ill."

"Pfft, you'd be lucky to ever get graced with such an amazing experience."

I stare at him, my expression blank, "I'm not earning anything. I'm a grown person and if I want to stay here then I will. I'm a human, not an object." I barely get the words out before he is on his feet and reaching across the table. He gathers my papers and pencils stuffing them into my backpack haphazardly.

"Stop," I demand. "I'm not done!" I'm vaguely aware of someone saying *shhhh* but I'm more concerned with Oliver than them right at this moment.

"I don't care. We're leaving." He grits out, and I worry I may have pushed him too far this time. Out of the corner of my eye I spot the librarian getting up from her desk. *Oh shit!* She starts walking toward us, casting a glare our way that says *shut up or get out.*

"I'm serious, I'm not going. I need to finish this paper," I whisper yell as I reach for my backpack.

Oliver's expression turns deadly. "And I'm serious, as well. Walk out or I'll walk you out." I want to slap him so badly, but right then the librarian walks up.

"You two need to leave, right now!" The librarian who looks older than the building scolds, her finger pointing back and forth between us.

"He needs to leave." I hook my thumb in Oliver's direction. "I'm staying. I'm sure you could see I've been working for the last hour. He hasn't."

Before anyone can respond, Oliver zips up my bag, swings it over his shoulder and then squats down, while grabbing onto my hips he tosses me over his shoulder like I'm nothing more than a sack of potatoes. I start to squeal like a pig as soon as I'm in the air.

"Put me down, right now!" I order.

"Out!" The librarian demands. "And don't come back."

"What? I didn't do anything," I yell through the otherwise silent library as Oliver carries me out like a caveman. I'm flustered, irritated, and confused. Balling my hands into fists I start pounding on his back, but it doesn't seem to even phase him. He just continues walking like he's taking a long peaceful stroll through the park.

"Put me down! So help me god, Oliver," I growl.

"Quiet or I'll spank you."

"Excuse me?" I squeak, unsure of how I feel about that.

"You heard me."

"You wouldn't dare. Now put me..." My words are cut off by Oliver's hand as it comes down hard on my ass cheek.

Holy shit, he spanked me. I beat on his back harder, hoping that I'll leave him with bruises, or at least something to remember me by.

"I hate you!" I growl.

"Sure you do," he chuckles into the night air.

We're halfway across campus when I finally give up, exhausted from pounding on his back and getting nowhere, I just slump down on his shoulder. Then I realize that people must have seen the scene in the library followed by Oliver carrying me across campus on his shoulder. This literally couldn't get any worse.

He walks me into my dorm, stopping in my hallway to set me down. I'm still unsteady on my feet, trying to regain my bearings after hanging upside down on the way over here, when I'm suddenly pushed against the wall.

"Do you really hate me, Harlow?" Oliver asks, his fingers moving under my chin to tip it upwards, forcing me to look up and into his eyes. With all the hard plains of his body pressing up against mine it's hard to think or breathe.

My tongue feels like a weight is attached to it. I can't form words, there's something wrong with me, something very wrong.

Oliver grins and then leans down pressing his lips against mine. Our lips crash together like a tidal wave against a cliff. My hands come up landing on his chest and for a brief second I consider pushing him away. I should, my heart is already a mess, my mind in complete disarray. Slowly they're breaking me down, and I'm letting them.

Against my better judgement I cave to my body's need, and instead of pushing him away my fingers clench onto the fabric of his shirt to pull him closer. Again, the kiss is different in comparison to his brothers. Oliver kisses with passion, with a longing that you feel deep down in your soul.

All the anger I felt towards him melts away and is left somewhere in a puddle on the floor. His hands find my hips, pulling me into him. His hardened cock presses against my thigh making my mouth water. My whole body is on fire. His tongue slides across my bottom lip, begging for entry and without hesitation I part my lips, a tiny moan escaping in the process.

The second our tongues touch I'm done for. He tastes like sweet mint and forbidden fruit and I'm reminded of how wrong all of this is, but I can't help wanting him. It's like I'm possessed or something. Like a goddamn dog in heat, I want all three of the brothers.

The blood in my ears roars and I bite at Oliver's lip, the growl that emits from his throat shoots straight to my core, and I clutch onto him harder. This is bad, but it's so much better than all the fighting and hating. I like this, this place where we only exist in the moment, without anyone or anything living in the same world.

Of course, as soon as I start to think that, the moment between us ends.

Oliver pulls away, leaving me breathless, with my swollen lips burning for him.

"Fuck, my brothers were right, you do taste sinful, but oddly sweet too." His eyes reflect hunger and when he swipes at his bottom lip with his thumb I nearly come undone.

He takes a step back to leave, and somehow I find my voice, "Wait, don't leave."

"Stay in your dorm. If I find out you left, I'm spanking that sexy ass until its red." My gaze widens partially because he's so straight forward about the punishment and partially because I kinda want to break the rules just to see if he'll do it.

"But..."

He shakes his head, and lifts a brow in warning, "Be a good girl now." The words come out in a whisper and before I can muster up a response he's gone, walking down the hall. I stare at his back until he's out of sight and then sigh against the door.

What the hell just happened?

"Oh my god, you're totally sleeping with all three of them. Wow, you really are a slut. I better not catch you trying to seduce my boyfriend with one of your kinky fuck fests." Some girl I failed to notice standing in the hall snarls. Horror, shock, and disgust reflect in her features.

Jesus, how long has she been standing there? Scrubbing a hand down my face I ignore her, and only then do I realize that the boys have slowly been making the rumors worse, showing up here, kissing me, leaving my dorm at random times. I thought it was bad having them follow me around but now they're kissing me, touching me, and my body is short circuiting.

"Holy hell," I mumble to myself.

My breathing is still uneven, and my lips feel like they are on fire. Maybe I should heed Oliver's warning, but I really need to get that paper done, I need to get to the library and apologize to the librarian, begging her to let me in. I reach for my backpack—My blood pressure spikes—my backpack, that little shit took my bag with him. I don't even think as I run down the hall, and around the corner to the door.

That asshole with his stupidly good kissing skills distracted me. Shoving the door open I step out into the night, cool air kissing my heated cheeks. I look around the well-manicured lawn looking for anyone that might look like Oliver but find no one.

It's eerily quiet. *Motherfuck!* Descending the steps, I start to head in the direction of the library. I have no way of getting out to their mansion, so I hope he hasn't left campus yet. Along the way I silently scold myself. I'm stupid, so stupid. I let my hormones rule me again. I have got to stop thinking with my vagina. I'm supposed to dislike the Bishop Brothers, not want to ride them like Channing Tatum in the *Magic Mike* movie.

Caught up in my own thoughts I round the corner and collide with another body, a body that's much larger, much beefier than my own. The impact causes me to bounce like a bouncy ball of off the person and land harshly on the concrete sidewalk.

"Ugh." I whine, an ache radiating up my spine. My night goes from bad to worse when I find Sullivan staring down at me. His face lit by the soft glow of the street lamp above us.

"Weren't you told to stay in your dorm?" he accuses, like I'm a child sneaking out and he's my parent.

"The gentleman thing to do would be to apologize and then help me up," I spit coldly, my eyes lingering on him a little longer than they should. *Stop staring.* Stop staring, Harlow. He's got his hands tucked into a pair of worn jeans, and he's wearing a dark Henley that shows off his toned chest, and biceps perfectly.

Boo, why can't they stop looking gorgeous, and while they're at it stop following me around too. These shenanigans are getting old.

"I'm not a gentleman, but I thought you already knew that?" The boyish grin he gives me makes my heart start to race. If these three don't stop fucking with me, I'll be going into cardiac arrest. I feel like every time I escape the frying pan one of them finds me and tosses me back into the fire. It's beyond exhausting.

"Ain't that the truth," I mumble under my breath, I still have the throbbing pain in my spine, but I push through and get up off the sidewalk. I wipe my sweaty hands on the front of my skinny jeans.

"I don't need a babysitter, so you can go and do whatever it is you brothers do when you aren't making my life hell."

"You like us making your life hell."

Narrowing my gaze, I say, "Do not. All I want is to be left alone. I came here to forget about my past, and then you show up here, and ruin everything."

Sullivan shrugs his sculpted shoulders, "I'd say I'm sorry but I'm not. You fucked me over that night, Harlow." He takes a step forward, his huge hand reaching out for me, cupping my cheek gently. I should pull away, run back to my dorm, but I can't. I crave their attention as much as I hate it. I need more, so much more.

"I thought you were different, sweet, and innocent. That night, I was sure I saw a glimpse of a girl that cared, and then like a snake slithering through the grass you showed your true self, sinking your teeth into my skin, injecting me with a nasty venom," he snarls, and even angry he looks beautiful, like a tall wave and I'm the coastline standing in his way.

"I...." My tongue darts out over my bottom lip and his gaze hones in on the movement. The muscles in his throat tightening as he swallows.

"You're a temptress, and I'm weak, so fucking weak for you," he whispers, leaning forward, his hot breath fanning against my lips.

Kiss me. I think to myself, but then decide to take charge pushing up onto my tiptoes I brush my lips against his. A groan resonates from somewhere deep inside of him, and his free hand moves to my hip. My shirt rides up with the movement and I gasp at the feel of his hand on my bare skin. Ahh, it feels heavenly.

"You want me, don't you?" There's a huskiness to his voice and I nod my head, unable to form a single word. There's something in the back of my mind that tells me this is a bad idea, but I push the thought away.

All I want is to feel wanted, loved, cared for, and in some twisted way the Bishop Brothers make me feel all those things, even if they don't realize it.

With a gentle nudge he pushes me against the side of the building and out of the street lamp light. It's harder to see him this way, but not impossible. I can still hear his heavy breathing and feel the hardness of his body brushing against all my softness. Everything is different between us this time, the very first time he kissed me he was gentle, kind, unsure. But this time there's a darkness that clings to him, and I want that darkness to overtake me, to claim me.

He Slides his hand from my hip up my body, until he's cupping my breast through the silky fabric of my bra. My knees shake as molten lava pools in my belly when he flicks his thumb over the hardened nub.

"Sometimes, at night when I can't sleep, I think about what you look like when you come. And I wonder, do you think about just me, or me and my brothers?"

"Oh god," I sigh, my core tightening around nothing but air. I want his fingers there, his tongue, his... it dawns on me then, do I really want him to be my first?

All the thoughts inside my head become fuzzy when he flicks his finger over my nipple again, and leans forward, peppering my throat with hot kisses. Kisses that turn into something more, and soon he's sucking on the tender flesh below my ear. Eliciting quiet mewls of pleasure out of me. Like a tiny kitten I claw at him, pulling him closer.

Lost in my own little bubble of joy, I don't notice someone approaching until a throat is being cleared right beside us.

Oh my god! Without thought I'm shoving at Sullivan's chest. He takes a step back, chest heaving, eyes flickering with fire as he stares down at me with confusion. Without his body shielding mine two girls come into view. They both wear the same look of disgust and I notice then that there's also a guy with them.

"You done with her brother?"

I blink, and for some reason betrayal cuts deep into the tender tissue of my heart hearing Oliver's voice. He's with two girls. He was in a hurry to get away from me to be with them.

"Yeah, you done with that, Sullivan?" One of them snickers. Tears glisten in my eyes. I couldn't stop them from forming even if I wanted to. There's a sick feeling that coats my insides at being caught out here, letting him feel me up like some cheap whore.

Something that looks an awful lot like shame flickers in Sullivan blue depths but before I can read him completely a mask falls into place, overtaking his true emotions. He takes a step back, the street lamp above emitting a soft glow over his features.

"Of course, I'm done. Thanks for the fun, Harlow." The cruelness in his eyes leaves me cold, and I barely keep it together as he gives me one last once over before walking away with his brother and their groupies. Squeezing my eyes shut I tell myself that I won't cry, that I don't care what those girls think of me or how the brothers are using my attraction towards them to make things worse.

After that, I care about nothing, not the paper I need to finish, not the rumors or the betrayal I'm feeling. The boys don't own me, and I don't own them, but it feels like something has changed and I don't know how to deal with all the feelings I'm having.

They're bullies, and I'm the victim of their torment, so why do I feel like falling to my knees for them? Why does seeing them with someone else feel like my heart is being ripped out of my chest?

6

Banks returns to Harlow duty after the embarrassment of the other night. He doesn't mention our kiss, and I hate to admit it but after what happened with Sullivan and Oliver I kind of missed him.

"Why the sad face?" he asks.

I shrug, "Aren't you supposed to be making my life hell? Not asking me why I'm sad? That kind of defeats the entire purpose, doesn't it?"

"Maybe I want to be the one making you sad."

"Don't worry, you and your brothers are the main cause of my misery, so rest assured, you are doing your job. Three golden stars for the assholes that follow me around like they have nothing better to do with their time." It's harder today to hide the disdain I feel for them. Especially since there's a giant hickey on the side of my neck.

I tried everything I could to cover it up, but nothing seems to conceal the purple and red splotch on my pale skin.

"Feisty. Maybe you just need to relax a little, then again from the hickey on your neck maybe you're doing a little too *much* relaxing?" My face deadpans, I'm so close to losing it and punching him, that it's scary.

"Stop following me," I snap and pick up my pace, my shoes

smacking against the concrete. The world wouldn't be turning if he couldn't annoyingly keep up with me, and for a second I think about breaking out into a full on sprint. Then again with Banks' long legs and fitness level, I wouldn't be surprised if he ran circles around me.

He blatantly ignores my attitude and continues talking like I haven't said anything at all.

"Oh, I know the perfect thing. How about a party? You could learn to live a little. All you do is go to your classes, and back to your dorm."

Blinking slowly, I have half a mind to say, *I wonder why,* but I don't because I don't want to engage in any more of a verbal sparring match than I have to.

"That's a hard pass. Thanks for asking," I murmur sarcastically. There is no way in Hell I'm going to a party with him or his brothers. That's practically begging for something bad to happen.

"Suit yourself. But don't whine and cry later on claiming you never get to do anything." Seriously, he sounds like a mixture between my dad and a prison warden.

"I wouldn't give you the pleasure of seeing me cry," I sneer, trying not to notice him, or his toned body. My first mistake was kissing them, my second was enjoying it, because now that I've kissed them, and touched them, my body calls for more, a low warmth simmering deep in my belly every time they're near.

It's annoying, but it also makes me curious.

"Have a totally lame night, Harlow," Banks snorts, as we arrive at my dorm and he shoves his hands into the front pockets of his jeans. *Don't look at him.* Don't let his good looks mess with your head. He's a bully, the enemy, an asshole with a nice face, that's it.

Rolling my eyes I grab my keys and unlock the door.

"Go away, and don't come back." I growl. As soon as I enter the room Shelby jumps up from her bed and runs over to me. I slam the door closed in Banks' face and feel a tiny sliver of power ripple through me.

"Surprise!" She squeals.

"Hey, I thought you'd be gone all night?" I greet and give her a quick hug.

"I know, but then the art show got moved to next week and I wanted to come and surprise my best friend because I miss her, and I'm not the only surprise," her smile widens. "I got us invited to a boat party!" Her eyes light up, and she's beaming like it's the most exciting thing she's ever heard. "A boat party, Harlow! I'm not going to take no for an answer, so don't even waste your time saying it, and if you're worried about the Bishop boys, I'll help you ditch them."

I can't stop the sigh that passes my lips. I don't want to go to a party but I really don't want to disappoint Shelby either. The guys will be there, there's no doubt about it, and if I show up they'll most likely follow me around. On the other hand, I can't keep hiding out in my dorm doing nothing every weekend because of them.

If I stay home, they win. Plus, parties are part of college life, right? I should enjoy this time of my life to the fullest.

Shelby crosses her arms over her chest and gives me the look. What look you ask? The one that shows her annoyance and precedes an hour-long lecture about how I won't always be young, and able to make dumb choices. Her mouth pops open as if she's about to start talking but I cut her off.

"Okay, I'll go," I say and watch her face turn from stern to surprised, and then to excited.

"Holy shit, I was prepared to do some major sweet talking, and a whole lot of persuasion to get you to go, but this thing where you agree so easily is much better. If only you could be this easy all the time."

"If I was that easily convinced then it would be no fun."

"True, and since you didn't take up all my time with talking, we now have more time to pick out dresses," she giggles and runs to the closet. As She starts dragging one dress after the other out of the closet and creating a line up on her bed, I take a seat on the edge of mine.

Crossing my legs, I wait for her to give me my choice for tonight. My phone starts to buzz in my pocket. I dread even looking at it, somehow the guys got my phone number and when they are not busy walking me across campus, they send me text messages or call me. They're the worst.

"I can hear the phone vibrating from over here," Shelby says over her shoulder, "who is it? One of your Romeos?"

"Romeos? Not you too. You know I'm not actually with any of them, right? They are just stalking me to get on my nerves and under my skin."

"Sure, they are."

My brows furrow together in a frown. "What's that supposed to mean?"

She whirls around, a mini skirt in her hands. "Why do you let them stalk you? Did you even try to talk to campus security or the dean's office, or even the police? I mean, they are legit stalking you, but you don't do anything about it, so maybe you don't *want* to be with them, but it's not like you're stopping them either."

Because I deserve it. I think to myself, but the words won't actually leave my mouth, I'm too ashamed to admit how I feel. Instead, I tell her the other reason I haven't said anything yet. "You know how it is, Shelby. They have tons of money, do you really think they haven't thought about this? Haven't made a sizable donation to the school to make sure that they can do no wrong? Plus, the second I say something they'll retaliate by doing something even worse."

"What could be worse than what they've already done? It's not like they would physically harm you. They're a bunch of ankle biting dogs."

"Says the one not being followed by them everywhere she goes."

"Do you want me to say something to them?"

Scrubbing a hand down the front of my face, I mutter, "God, no. Let them do their thing. They only win if I let them. Once they see that I won't react, they'll just give up and move on. I mean, how fun can it be following a girl around all day? Surely they'll get bored of this soon enough?"

She laughs, "No idea. Now put this on, I need to make sure we have enough time for me to do your makeup. If the Bishop Brothers are going to be following you around all night the least I can do is make them want you more than they already do."

"They don't want me. They want to ruin my life. There's a difference."

She tosses a sundress at me, "Don't you remember back in school when they said boys only pick on girls that they like?"

"This isn't elementary school."

"No, you're right, we're adults, so the stakes are higher. They want you, Harlow, and I think you are playing into that."

Before I can think too much about what she is saying, my phone buzzes again in my pocket, too annoyed to let it go on, I finally take it out to see who is calling. I swear to god, if they don't stop tormenting me I'll be forced to do something drastic.

When I see my father's number lighting up the screen I almost gasp out loud. What the hell is he calling me for? Not once has he tried to talk to me since I left. Not once and now he's blowing up my phone?

"Which one of the three musketeers is it this time?" Shelby asks, while applying her foundation with a large makeup brush.

"Neither, it's my dad," I say.

She lifts a curious brow, "Wow, what could he possibly want?"

"Don't know, don't care." If there is one person I would enjoy talking to less than the Bishops, it's my dad. Pushing the decline button, I stare at the screen before powering it off. Whatever it is he has to say, I don't want to hear it.

Despite my better judgment, I let Shelby talk me into a short dress, at least it's not a mini skirt. I know I shouldn't play with fire, but after our conversation earlier the wheels in my head started to turn. Maybe if I made them as uncomfortable as they make me, they would back off a little? Then again, I don't know. Blurring the lines further doesn't seem like a good idea.

I pull at the bottom of the tight material as I sit down in Shelby's car, making sure I'm covered in all the important spots.

I'm not sure if the guys know that I left or that I'm headed to a party. They seem to keep tabs on me pretty well. Sometimes I even wonder if they planted a tracker on me. They're that good at knowing where I am and when.

"I'm so excited. Aren't you excited?" Shelby asks, and I swear she must have drunk two energy drinks and ate a pound of sugar before we left because there is no logical reason for her to be bouncing around in her seat with the smile she's wearing.

"A little, I guess." I shrug. I'm more nervous than anything. Mostly because I haven't been to another party since the night the brothers confronted me. I know it's going to be even worse tonight after all the rumors that have been spread about me.

"We'll have fun. Just don't let them get to you. Just like you said earlier, don't *let* them bother you. In fact, maybe you should find another guy, explore your options." I know she's right, but I can't help it. My track record with parties is horrendous. Every time I go somewhere it ends up being a disaster. The police get called, or I get pulled into dark rooms by brooding brothers.

The list goes on.

We get to the port a few minutes later to find the parking lot leading to the pier is already filling up. We quickly find a spot and get out of the car. The first thing I notice is that most cars on the lot have a Bayshore University permanent parking sticker on the back windshield. I was really hoping that there would be more people from out of town instead of the entire college.

The knot in my stomach grows, the pressure mounting when I see the girl from my building who called me out the other night.

This is a bad start to the night.

Seemingly unaware of my darkening mood, Shelby takes my hand and walks me down to the pier where the yacht is docked. Music is blaring from inside and lights are strung on the outside, illuminating the darkness. The yacht's already packed with people, their chatter meeting my ears.

"Oh my gosh, this is so pretty," Shelby gasps, her excitement infectious. I smile while we are crossing the little metal bridge onto the boat. My best friend's enthusiasm finally catches up with me and some of the tension starts to dissipate.

Stepping onto the shiny deck my wedges hardly make a sound. Shelby drags me across the deck following a string of lights leading to the party.

"What do you want to do first?" She inquires.

"Drink?" It's probably best to get some liquid courage in me before the brothers find out I'm here. Shelby tosses her blonde hair over her shoulder and starts to tug me in the direction of what looks like a bar, the entire thing lined with bottles, and cups.

"I thought you weren't going to come?" My body tenses at the gravelly voice behind me. With my hand still connected to Shelby's I spin around to face Banks. I'm about to spit out a snarky remark but whatever it was I was going to say gets stuck in my throat when I see him standing there. He looks like he's just stepped off a movie set.

My mouth waters, and the muscles in my belly tighten. He looks at me with the same heated gaze that I'm looking at him with, and I swear it's a good thing we're on the water because this entire thing might light on fire with these heated glares.

I drink him in. He's wearing a black button up shirt with the top button undone and tailored gray slacks. With one hand in his pocket, he looks like a fashion model striking a pose, and even worse it takes no effort at all. He's flawless looking without a single imperfection, and while I don't look bad either, I don't look like the other girls here.

"No, no," Shelby raises her finger towards Banks, "she is here with me, not you, so carry on and find someone else to harass."

"We'll see who I feel like harassing later on, for now, you are free to go," he says dismissively as if he has actual control over me. It takes everything inside me not to lash out, and make a scene. There's never been a time in my life where I've been in control. I thought college would be my chance, but it seems I lucked out, once again.

"Get lost, loverboy," she narrows her eyes, and snaps back pulling me towards the party. I don't even look back at him as we walk away, instead I let Shelby drag me through the crowd and straight to the bar. She pours two glasses of champagne and hands me one.

"Just forget about him," she says, as we clink our glasses together.

"Cheers," is all I say before downing the entire glass. I'm not much of a drinker but right now getting a little tipsy doesn't sound so bad. Maybe it'll help me stop thinking about men I have no business thinking about.

"Now we're getting somewhere," she smirks, filling my glass up once again. I don't chug this one but even just sipping on it, it's not going to last five minutes.

Shelby snatches a bottle from the bar, and we find a spot in the corner of the room. I've been on a yacht a time or two with my parents, but it was never like this. With so many people, and copious amounts of alcohol.

Looking into the crowd, I feel like every one of these people are having the time of their lives, all except me. I stop at one of those smiling faces, recognizing it. She sees me a moment after I spot her. Caroline's smile widens even more as she waves at me. I give her a half-hearted wave back, before I return my attention back to my drink.

Like a good friend, Shelby keeps refilling my glass every time it gets empty.

"I wonder how far out we are? We've been on the water for a while," Shelby questions. I just shrug. I don't care how far out we are, or what's going on around me. All I want is to enjoy the night and continue drinking my champagne in peace. The bubbly liquid makes the ache in my chest go away and replaces it with a fuzzy feeling.

"Speaking of water, I gotta go pee. Wanna come?"

"Nah, I'm good. I'd rather keep drinking."

"Okay, don't move, I'll be right back." I nod and watch her walk away, disappearing deeper into the yacht.

"Hey," a male voice calls out, followed by a light touch to my bare shoulder. I turn around a little too fast, losing my balance in the process, and end up landing in the guy's arms, well more like face planting into his chest, but it's the same thing I suppose.

"Oh, I'm so sorry," I apologize holding onto his forearms to steady myself. "I'm such a clutz." I blink up at the blond haired, blue eyed hunk holding onto me.

"It's okay," he laughs, and I notice the twinkle of amusement in his eyes, "I was going to ask you if you wanted to dance, but this is nice too."

The mystery boy smells like expensive cologne, and while he isn't one of the Bishop Brothers, he's handsome, nonetheless.

A nervous giggle escapes me and for a moment I forget why I didn't want to come here. This is fun, the drinking, mingling, and the quietness of the ocean around us.

"Dancing would be nice too," I try to say in a flirty voice, an actual smile pulling at my lips. The words come out slurred and I decide maybe it's time to lay off the champagne for a while.

"Thanks man, I got her from here," a familiar voice cuts in, accompanied by an arm being draped around my shoulders. I look sideways and glance up at Sullivan who is pulling me close to his side, away from the nice guy I'm talking to. His touch seems protective, but even I know better than to assume that's his motive.

He's up to something and it isn't good.

Still, I can't help but notice how delicious looking he is, like a piece of cheesecake just waiting to be devoured. He's wearing something similar to Banks, his shirt a striking red, which seems fitting since I want to make him bleed out right now.

Mystery boy pulls back, eyes wide, while lifting his hands. "Sorry, I didn't know she was here with someone."

"That's because I'm not," I grit out, shoving at Sullivan's side which causes him to drop his arm. His lips turn up into a cruel smile, and to anyone else it would look as if he's on the verge of laughing but not to me. No, I can see the evil monster lurking underneath, waiting to come out and play.

He wants to hurt me, and even though I deserve it, it pains me that I can't just have one night to myself.

"It's not your fault, man, she likes to make me jealous by sleeping around. No hard feelings. I'll keep an eye on her for the rest of the night, make sure she doesn't suck some random guy off in the bathroom, *again*." Sullivan says dramatically. My mouth pops open, shock overtaking me.

What. The. Fuck?

The other guy's eyes grow wider, if at all possible, his cheeks turning crimson red, before he mutters a sorry and walks away. Once the poor guy is out of sight I turn towards Sullivan with my fists clenched, anger burning in my veins.

"Who the hell do you think you are?" I yell, shoving at his chest with both hands.

I expect him to say something, do something, anything, but instead he tips his head back and starts to laugh, and not just a normal laugh either. This is a belly shaking, laugh your face off laugh. If he wanted to embarrass me, to make me feel like dirt then he's succeeded, again.

"You're a piece of shit, Sullivan, and I wish that I never kissed you that night. I'm sorry for what happened, okay? I'm sorry, but this? This is too much. I don't care that I hurt you, nothing warrants this. Nothing." I growl and shove at him again. My little outburst is gathering attention, and I can already hear the whispers swirling around. Twisting around on my wedges, I start to walk away, but I make it less than a step before Sullivan's meaty paw lands on my shoulder halting me.

"We're done, when I say…" All logical thinking goes out the window, all I feel is rage, red hot rage and before I realize what I'm doing, my hand is moving through the air. Even over the music I can hear the loud slap of skin on skin as my palm makes contact with his cheek. Pain lances across my hand, but I don't care if I hurt him.

His words hurt me more than he could ever know. The blow causes him to take a step back, and out of the corner of my eye I see his gaze widen, his eyebrows lifting up to his hairline with shock. Like a fish gasping for air his mouth pops open. Lifting a hand to his cheek he touches the red mark left behind as if he can't believe that I actually slapped him.

There's a tightening in my chest, and it feels like my heart is breaking. Those blue eyes of his—that I've seen filled with compassion, and maybe even kindness in the past—fill with anger.

"Leave me alone. I'm done playing your games," I say feeling defeated, and this time when I turn to walk away, he lets me. My eyes are burning with unshed tears as I make my way through the crowded dance floor pushing anyone who doesn't move fast enough out of the way. I'm not sure my night can get any worse, and then it does.

Right before I walk out, I spot Oliver and Banks lounging on a leather sofa near the door. Each of them have a girl cuddled up beside them. I know it shouldn't bother me so much seeing them with other girls, hell, it shouldn't bother me at all, not after what just happened. But I can't help the sting of jealousy that lashes through me. It's like someone poured acid in my chest and I'm being painfully burned from the inside out.

They both look up as I approach. My chest heaves and I feel like I can't get enough air into my lungs. Oliver meets my eyes first, his smug smile turning into a frown but I don't know why. Before I can study his expression further, the long-legged blonde slides onto his lap and covers her lips with his.

Lips that I kissed only days ago. Lips that I can still feel on mine.

I clench my hands into tight fists and glance over at Banks, his eyebrows are drawn together almost as if he's concerned. It doesn't make sense, none of them really care. I've dug my own hole, and pushing them, letting them kiss me, touch me has just buried myself deeper. Unable to stand there and look at them a second longer I start walking out the door.

"That's right. Run along little girl," the bimbo on Banks' arm calls after me. I don't give her a second glance. She's not worth it. Not worth the anger. The pain. She deserves Banks. I just push out the door and into the cool September night. The tipsiness I felt moments ago completely vanished. The reality of it all hitting me is more sobering than a bucket full of ice water raining down on me.

Wrapping my arms around myself, I try and keep myself together in more ways than one. I don't want to be here right now, on this stupid boat. Feeling the panic inside me rise up I start walking around the deck, looking out into the vast darkness of the ocean. We are so far out I can't even see a single light past the water.

The wind is chilly and barely having anything on doesn't help to keep me warm one bit, but I would rather freeze to death out here than go back in there again. Hopefully Shelby will notice that I'm missing and come out and find me soon.

Walking back to the far end of the yacht where I'm hidden by the darkness, I let go of the pain that's painting my insides. Tears start to fall down my cheeks, even though I told the bastards to stay inside. Placing my hands on the cold metal railing I let my head fall forward.

How did my life become so sad?

The question has been running through my mind for a while now. How did it come to this? Was is all my fault? My father's? Or maybe it was nobody's fault and we all just need to live with the cards we were dealt? Somehow, I don't think that.

One tear after the other cascades down my face, and into the dark blue ocean beneath me. All I want is for someone to hug me. To take me into their arms and tell me I'm going to be alright, that everything is going to be okay.

A brisk wind blows through my hair and I bite my lip to stifle the sob threatening to rip from my throat. I'm torn from my hug daydream by a hard shove from behind.

Everything unfolds so fast that I don't have even a second to react. One moment I'm standing by the railing, the next I'm being shoved over the edge, flying through the cold air.

A gut-wrenching scream rips from my chest, rushing past my lips a moment before my body hits the unforgiving sea.

Pain ripples through me on impact, petrifying my bones as a terrorizing darkness swallows me whole. Panic grabs onto every cell in my body, robbing my brain of any thought but one. *Survival.*

It takes everything inside me to push aside the feeling of a thousand needles prickling across my skin that the ice-cold water leaves me with. My lungs burn, begging, pleading for air. Squeezing my eyes shut I overcome the stiffness in my limbs and start kicking my legs with everything I have left to give.

I push and push, giving it my all, but if I've learned anything, it's that sometimes giving someone or something your all isn't enough.

7

My chest constricts the muscles so tight that I can barely breathe. I try and swallow but my throat, and lungs hurt so badly that it feels like an elephant is sat on my chest.

Somehow, I manage to get air into my lungs, though it feels like I'm breathing through a straw. Darkness still has a hold on me, its claws sinking deep into my subconscious refusing to let go, and let me open my eyes.

While I can't open my eyes, my ears still work. There are voices surrounding me, most of which I don't know. There is a gasp and a flurry of whispers that float around me like clouds wisping through the air.

Two voices stick out, reaching deep inside of me, making my shallow heartbeat, turn into a hard gallop.

"She's breathing," Oliver exclaims. I can hear him panting, attempting to catch his breath and I wonder what happened. There's a hand cradling face and somehow, I know it's his. I want to nuzzle into his touch, sink into his warmth, but I can't. I can't move at all. It feels like I'm floating just barely clinging to this world.

"Harlow, can you hear me?" Sullivan's voice caresses my ear. There's a pleading to his voice, telling me he's concerned, and I try my best to answer him, or at least, open my eyes, but I'm unable to do either. My lips part, my mouth opening, but words never come. All I get are my teeth chattering together.

Only now, with the touch of Oliver's hand do I realize how cold I am. More than cold, freezing.

"We need to get her dry and warm," Banks says, right next to me, two strong hands rubbing up and down my arm.

A second pair of strong arms slide underneath me and lift me into the air. My body curls in on itself as if out of instinct and my head falls against a firm shoulder.

"Everything's going to be okay. I've got you," Sullivan whispers into the shell of my ear while cradling me to his chest.

Strangely, that's all I need to hear to know it's going to be okay. He said he's got me, and for the first time, I believe him because I know, deep down, he won't let anything happen to me. In his arms I'm shielded, secure, and protected, at least for now. I let sleep pull me under once more. Even in the darkness I feel safe knowing he is holding me.

Awareness comes back to me slowly and the coldness that was threatening to eat at my limbs has vanished. My body still aches all over, but the freezing cold water has been replaced with something warm, something that smells delicious, and something that makes me melt into a puddle of mush. I try and stretch, but my muscles are stiff and tingling like I've been laying on them wrong. A pained moan escapes my lips as I try and move.

"Shit," I hear Sullivan's voice right by my ear. It's strained, and thick with restraint. "She's grinding her ass over my dick."

"I don't think she's doing it on purpose," Banks snickers.

"Tell that to my dick, asshole."

"Just think about something else," Oliver chimes in. "Or we can trade places, if this is too *hard* for you."

"Funny. I'm good right here. I'll deal with the blue balls later. You already did your part by jumping in to save her. When are we getting back to land and where the hell did Shelby go?" Sullivan growls.

Save me? Oliver saved me?

"Calm down. I sent her to get Harlow something warm to drink and to try and find her some dry clothes."

My eyes still feel impossibly heavy like there are boulders weighing them down, and now that the coldness has dissipated, I feel every single ache but intensified by twenty.

What happened to me?

"Why would she do that to herself? Have we really been that horrible to her? Is death easier than us?"

For a moment I'm confused. What are they talking about? I didn't hurt myself. I would never do that. Much like the waves cresting against a beach, pushing and pulling the sand my memories start to resurface in my mind.

Slapping Sullivan.

Walking out.

Crying.

Someone shoving me off the boat and into the water.

Oh my god. I almost died.

"I don't know, Sullivan, maybe we've been miscalculating this whole thing. She looked really bad when she was running out of there," Banks tells him.

"If you ask me, we've been kinder to her than her family's ever been to us." Sullivan says, this time. "But I don't know, maybe you're right. Maybe we've taken things too far."

"Stop. We don't know anything yet, not until she wakes up." Oliver says, in a low voice, a voice that says his word is final.

Digging deep I find the strength to pry my eyes open. It takes what seems like hours to do but can't be more than a minute. I blink a few times, my surroundings come into view. We're still on the boat that much I can tell from the slight bobbing motion, but we're in what looks like one of the cabins below deck.

The room is small and with all three brothers inside it, it seems even smaller. Banks is sitting on a chair to the left of me, and Oliver is sitting on the edge of the bed. A throat clears and I lift my head just the slightest, finding that I'm lying on a bed with Sullivan spooning me, both his arms wrapped tightly around me. Wiggling a tiny bit I feel soft fabric against my bare skin.

Naked? I'm naked.

As if he can read the horror on my face Banks says, "We had to undress you. We didn't touch, and we didn't look expect for when we had to, I promise." The wink he gives me is one that I'm sure is to ease the tension, but it doesn't.

"Yeah, you were freezing, your lips blue, and your skin ashen." Oliver says, and my gaze swings to him. I can see the pain in his deep brown eyes, but I don't understand it. I don't know why they care if I live or die? They certainly didn't care earlier with those chicks on their arms. My eyes fall closed for a moment as I try and gather my thoughts. I can't think about any of that right now. I almost died, someone pushed me off the boat.

"I... I didn't jump." I croak, my throat feeling raw, my voice sounding like someone else's and not my own.

"We're just glad you're okay." Banks whispers, his voice thick like honey. Weakly I turn my head and glance at him, the blue of his eyes blaze with anger, and sadness, the two emotions swirling together, bleeding into each other.

"Someone pushed me... I don't know..." My voice cracks again, and pain fills my chest. Who would push me? Who hates me enough to want me dead?

Before all of this, I would have thought they did? But then why would they save me? It makes zero sense.

"Shhh, we can talk about this later." Sullivan soothes. I want to tell him I'll talk about it now but I'm too exhausted to care, or to fight back. I let the warmth of his body heat encompass me. It wraps around me like a blanket holding all my broken pieces together. Slowly I breathe him in, he smells like rain, and citrus, it soothes the ache forming in my chest.

Closing my eyes again, it doesn't take long for sleep to drag me back down. It's a lighter, more carefree sleep this time. As if I'm just taking a little afternoon nap instead of recovering from almost drowning.

The next time I come to, I am being carried off the boat. I can't even move my arms because my whole body is swaddled in a blanket. Blinking my eyes open, I squint up and find that Banks is the one carrying me this time. I stare up at him for a long moment, taking in his features. I know it's stupid and that I have other, much bigger things to worry about but I kind of want to kiss him. Just to see if all of this is real, if I really did almost die, if they really did save me.

"Where do you think you're taking her?" Shelby squeaks. She sounds out of breath, like she's been running or something.

"We need to get her to the hospital," Banks snarls, his tone razor sharp.

His response pulls me from my dreamlike state and I start to panic.

"No," I croak. "No hospital." His pace slows when he hears my voice, concern etched into his handsome features.

"Please, I just want to go home and go to sleep," I plead. The last thing I need is to go to the hospital because then my father will be called, and I'd much rather die than deal with him right now.

Eventually Banks stops walking all together his gaze flicking around. When I follow his gaze I find Sullivan, Oliver, and Shelby all standing around us.

"I told you she wouldn't want to go. She hates hospitals," Shelby says, all matter of factly, her arms crossed over her chest.

"Are you sure?" Sullivan asks, looking at me, his eyebrows pinched together as he examines my face, like it's hiding all my secrets.

"I promise. I'm fine. I feel better already. Nothing a little soup, and sleep can't fix."

The guys exchange a look, what this look is, I don't know. I can't even really explain it. It's like they're agreeing on something without even speaking.

All three of them nod their heads and then Sullivan speaks, "Fine, but you're coming with us."

"What?" Shelby practically screams.

"She's coming with us, at least until she's feeling better," Sullivan announces, which only seems to peeve Shelby off further.

"Wait, you're telling me that you're going to take her back to your house? You guys? The same people who hate her?"

"We don't hate her." Banks interjects.

"Pfft, could've fooled me, it was probably one of you that pushed her off the boat."

The statement is a bold one, and whatever response Shelby was trying to get out of them she earns because Oliver takes a menacing step towards her, his finger pointed at her.

"Oh yeah, because I'm going to shove her off the fucking boat, and risk my life jumping into the same waters to save her, for what? Fun?" Oliver's face twists, morphing into something I've never seen before.

Shelby snarls, "I don't know, maybe? It seems like all of this is a game to you guys. Who's to say you don't want her dead? Or maybe you just want to play the hero?"

A cruel bubble of laughter pushes past Oliver's lips, "If we wanted her dead, she'd be dead already."

Okay, so I felt that one right in the heart.

"Enough you two." Sullivan barks, "It's already been decided. She's coming with us." He turns toward Shelby who is rolling her eyes.

"You don't own her. Nothing has been decided at all. I'll take care of her." She argues, and I swear I see her stomp her foot in anger.

"Shelby, it's okay. I'll just go with them."

"Fine," she finally huffs. "But they better not hurt you," she gives all of them a stern look, one that says don't fuck with me or my friend.

"You okay?" Banks leans down, whispering into my ear.

Am I okay? Someone tried to kill me. I don't know. I don't have the strength to fight with anyone right now. All I know is I don't want to go to the hospital and if that means I have to go with them, then I will.

"Can we just go?" His grip on me tightens and I can feel the tension in his muscles. He gives me a lopsided grin that would normally leave me feeling all fuzzy inside.

"Of course, Princess." He says and starts to walk again.

"Dude, where are you going?" Oliver's voice filters into my ears.

"To the house. If you guys want to stay and argue you can, but I'm taking our girl home. She needs a warm bath, rest, and something to eat."

"If anything happens to her, I'm coming for all three of you!" Shelby yells, somewhere off in the distance, but all I can focus on is Banks' words.

"I'm taking our girl home."

Our girl.

∽

WHEN WE ARRIVE at the mansion I'm alert enough to walk by myself, but Banks being overbearing insists on carrying me.

"You're not even wearing shoes," he points out and I look down at me feet, my toes wiggling freely. I guess he's right, still I don't want to be a damsel in distress. I may have almost died, but my legs still work.

Oliver walks ahead and unlocks the door for us. Walking inside, Sullivan switches on lights as we go. It's strange to be alone with all three of them, almost intimate, like we're in our own secret little world where we don't have to hate each other.

"Alright, I'm going to go and get out of these wet clothes and into the shower. I'll be out in a little bit," Oliver says, before disappearing up the stairs. As soon as he's out of sight I feel it, this strange tug at my heart. Like being away from him is losing a piece of my soul.

Something clicks in my brain then. He saved my life. He jumped into the ocean in the middle of the night and somehow found me, pulling me out.

Thinking it once doesn't quite hit home, so I let it run through my head again.

He saved my life.

Oliver saved my life. My mind is still reeling from this revelation as

Banks and Sullivan take me upstairs and into the bathroom attached to one of the guest bedrooms.

I watch Sullivan turn on the water and pour some bath soap into it, while Banks sits down on the edge of the tub, still cradling me to his chest, wrapped up in a blanket like a newborn baby. I watch the water fall into the huge corner tub, the bubbles building little cloud like mountains as it fills up. When it's about half way full, Banks starts to peel the blanket back.

"What are you doing?" I gasp, grabbing onto the blanket like it's my protective barrier. I kinda guess it is since it's the only thing shielding me from their eyes.

"You gonna take a bath with the blanket around you?" Banks asks, his thick brow raised curiously.

Shaking my head, I feel my cheeks start to heat. "No. I can take a bath on my own though."

Banks exchanges a disbelieving look with Sullivan before shaking his head. "I don't think you should be alone right now."

Clenching my jaw, I say, "I told you. I didn't try to kill myself. Someone pushed me. I'm not making this up. I swear. Someone pushed me right over the edge. One minute I was standing there and the next I was in the water."

"Did you see who it was?" Sullivan asks, his gaze colliding with Banks'. It's almost like they're communicating in some strange brother way, and whatever they're thinking or saying they don't want me to know.

Even stranger is Sullivan's reaction, it's like he believes me.

"No. I was holding onto the railing looking out onto the water and someone just shoved me from behind. I didn't hear or see anyone coming."

Remembering it makes me shiver. Who would want to hurt me? No one other than the Bishops, but the brothers didn't do it, they saved me.

"Either way, you almost died tonight, you shouldn't be alone right now. Let me help you into the tub and then we'll just sit down on the floor to keep you company."

Biting my bottom lip, I contemplate it. I guess they've already seen me naked, Sullivan was holding me under the blanket, and I let him feel me up the other night, so there is really no reason to be shy now.

"Okay, but don't look...I mean, at me... again," I say suddenly feeling self-conscious. I'm not anything spectacular to look at, nothing like the girls they were with tonight. My hips flare out, and my thighs are a little thick, my boobs are pretty stellar or at least I've been told. I'm short, with hair the color of sunshine but I'm nothing special and yet, Banks and Sullivan are staring at me like I am.

Banks helps me stand up and frees me from the blanket. My cheeks feel like they are on fire as soon as the fabric is pulled away. As promised neither of them look directly at me as I step into the bath on shaky legs. Never in my life did I think I would be in this situation. The Bishop Brothers are supposed to be my enemies and yet here they are caring for me.

Banks places his hands on my arms to steady me until I'm submerged in the tub. The hot water soothes my sore muscles immediately and I sink down into the bubbly water with a soft moan.

"Your back is bruised a little bit. I can put some arnica cream on it when you get out if you want me to?" Sullivan asks, as he and Banks take a seat on the floor next to the tub. I'm not sure what arnica cream is, but anything that he wants to rub on me right now sounds good. My entire body is one big aching mess.

The water fills up until it's almost at the edge before Sullivan gets up and shuts it off. For a few minutes I just soak in the water and let the tension seep from my body.

"Do you want to call the police? If someone tried to kill you..." Sullivan suddenly breaks the silence.

"No," I cut him off. "I don't want to call the police. One, I don't have anything to tell them. I didn't see anything, plus I was drinking...*underage* drinking. I'm already the center of attention at school, there's no need to make things worse for myself. Maybe whoever pushed me didn't want to kill me. Maybe it was just a joke that went too far? I don't know but I don't want to do anything that might add to my problems."

"You really believe that?" *No*, but I want to believe that that's all it was, because the alternative is too scary to consider.

"I don't know what to believe, but I do know that I want this to be over. I want to be a normal college student and forget this whole thing ever happened. I'm probably the laughing stock of the campus now." I frown staring down into the bubbly water. "Well, more than I was already."

"Look…" I glance up at Sullivan. Those blue orbs of his bleed into mine, making my heart skip a beat or five. I can almost see the apology forming on the tip of his tongue. I shake my head slightly, hoping he understands. I don't want an apology. I should be the one apologizing. All of this is my fault.

"You should stay here for a few days," Banks interrupts. "If someone really did push you, maybe it's not safe for you at the dorms anymore." Logically speaking he's not wrong, if it wasn't just some sick joke then that means someone's out to get me, but who?

"You don't really want me here, we all know it." I avert my gaze so they can't see the sadness flickering in my eyes. I'm ashamed over how weak I am for these men, how much I want them, when I know I shouldn't.

"If we didn't want you here we would tell you to leave, you should know that. I want you to stay, and although I can't speak for my brothers, I'm sure they feel the same."

"Feel the same about what?" Oliver says, walking into the bathroom, droplets of water clinging onto his hair. He looks clean and happy.

"Harlow staying here for now," Sullivan explains. "Banks thinks she shouldn't go back to the dorms if someone tried to kill her and I agree. It would make watching over her easier."

"Yeah, I agree too," Oliver says, without thinking about it. "It's settled, she stays." He decides clapping his hands together.

"Mhm, *she* is right here, and *she* should get a say in where *she* goes, right?" I say into the room, knowing damn well that they're all going to disagree with me.

"No." All three of them say at almost the same time. Each of their faces hold the same expression, a mix between *fight me*, and annoyance.

"Whatever." I roll my eyes and sink down a little deeper until I'm chin deep in the water. If they want to play hotel for the next few days, then so be it. It's not like they don't have the space here for an extra person and I'm not going to lie, this is much nicer than the dorm shower stalls. I allow myself to soak a little longer while all three of them stand and hover over me broodingly, like someone could possibly get to me in their guest bathroom. It's kind of cute how protective they're being. Almost enough to make me forget their bullying ways.

When it's time to get out of the bath it's just as awkward as it was getting in. The guys kind of avert their gazes but insist on helping me out. Sullivan wraps me up in a large fluffy towel and before I can take a single step he bends to pick me up. I don't even say anything knowing he's not going to put me down. What's the point in wasting my energy?

They want to treat me like fine china then I'll let them.

We walk back through the guest bedroom, but instead of putting me down on the bed like I expect him to, he keeps walking until we're in another room, a room that has to be his because it smells just like him. The room is vaguely familiar and I realize it's the same bedroom they cornered me in the night of the party. Except now the lights are on and I can see the contents of the room. Dark sheets, grey walls, a wrought iron bed, close to the floor. The room screams masculinity.

Reaching the bed Sullivan sits me down on the edge of it, and I sink deep into the memory foam mattress. It feels like heaven. I consider rolling over in the towel and letting the mattress swallow me whole when he walks over to his dresser and pulls out a shirt and pair of shorts. My eyes feel heavy and my muscles ache. It's starting to feel more like I fell down a flight of stairs and less like I was shoved off the side of a boat.

"You'll stay here tonight," he says, returning to the bed and placing the clothes beside me.

"I know, we discussed this already," I say mid-yawn. Our eyes meet and there is a warmness within his gaze that I've never seen there before.

"No, I mean *here*. You'll stay here, in my bed tonight. Tomorrow you'll stay with Banks and then Oliver. We'll switch off and on."

"Wait, what?" I tighten my hold on the towel, needing something to hold me to this reality because what he just said makes zero sense to me.

"Your dreams are coming true, Princess, you'll get to sleep with each of the Bishop Brothers," Banks teases from the doorway and I give him a disgruntled look.

Pfft, this is not my dream. Totally not my dream. I don't know what he's talking about.

"No. There has to be like three extra rooms in this house. I'll just take one of those. I don't need to be babysat while I'm sleeping."

Sullivan shakes his head, his features hardening as he leans forward and into my face. I should shrink back, get up, run for the door, leave this house but I can't, not only that, but I don't really want to.

His big hand reaches out and cups my cheek and I bite my lip needing something to focus on so I don't nuzzle my face into his hand like an unwanted dog needing pets.

"Don't fight us, please, because you won't win. There are three of us and one of you. One way or another we'll get what we want. So let us do this for you. Let us take care of you. It's the least we can do."

The compassion in his voice tugs at my heartstrings. I must be having a mental break down because I'm on the verge of tears.

"Don't lie to me, we're enemies, rivals, you don't want me here," I whimper, my emotions breaking through the surface.

Sullivan smiles, really smiles and when he speaks, I swear my entire body breaks out into a shiver, "Rivals or not, I've always wanted you here." He pulls back, his hand dropping from my cheek, the moment ending all too soon. "Now, let's get you to bed. We can figure stuff out tomorrow."

Nodding my head I try to understand the feelings coursing through me. They should hate me, and they do, but there's something else there. The feeling is like a snake bite, the wound festering, the venom spreading through my veins. I look up from the floor and find all three of them staring at me. I've never felt so confused and complete all at once.

This makes zero sense but I'm too exhausted to try and figure it out right now. Maybe I'm so tired that I'm making this all up in my head. I should just go to sleep and reevaluate this whole day tomorrow.

And that's exactly what I do. I quickly slip into the clothes Sullivan laid out for me with the guys turning around like the gentlemen they are. I cuddle up on the king size bed, Sullivan stripping down to his boxers and crawling into bed next to me.

I gulp down the nervous anxiety of having him so close to me while being damn near naked. Banks and Oliver say their goodnights and leave the room. Exhaustion starts to tug at me and I'm only vaguely aware of the door closing and Sullivan leaning over to whisper in my ear.

"Sleep tight, Harlow," his voice carrying me off into a dark slumber.

8

When I wake up it's not yet light outside, the sky through the shades casts a dark shadow inside the room. Slowly I turn, lifting my head to find Sullivan still asleep. He looks so at peace. A Greek statue, with hard edges, and well-defined muscles that makes my mouth water.

I'm mostly laying on top of him my leg draped over his, my arm wrapped around his middle, those perfectly shaped abs pressing against my skin, with my head resting on his firm chest. I don't remember falling asleep like this, but I'm not complaining about waking up in this position.

My cheek is hot where my skin is pressed up against his and when I try to move, I realize his arms are caging me in, holding me tightly to his side. I know I shouldn't, but I feel secure, and protected in his arms. I'm content, so content that I almost forget that I nearly died last night. The unpleasant thought sends a shiver down my spine and I nestle even deeper, like I'm trying to embed myself into his skin.

"Are you cold?" Sullivan's sleepy voice vibrates through me. It's husky, and strokes something deep in my belly. My feelings for him—hell for all three of them—are spiraling out of control.

"I'm fine," I whisper, my own voice raspy and my throat sore from swallowing all that ocean water yesterday.

"How is your back? Are you hurting anywhere?" He questions, his voice strong.

"Just sore, but I'll be fine. I'm stronger than I look," I tell him as he starts to gently rub his hands up and down my back. I bite my lip to stop myself from making any loud mewling noises.

"Let me see it. I forgot to put some cream on it last night. I can do that now," he offers, nudging me off of him. I scoot away and lay down on my stomach beside him. This is bad, but oh so good. He peels the blanket away and gently pulls the shirt I'm wearing up.

The cold air of the room kisses my bare skin and I hiss out through my teeth at the sensation.

"Don't move, I'm getting the cream." He orders and gets up from the bed. God, he's so bossy, it's almost infuriating. I don't watch him, instead I bury my heated cheeks into the mattress. His scent swirls around me, it's inside me, in my pores, swirling around my head. I'm supposed to hate him, but hate is the last thing I'm feeling right now.

He reappears a moment later with a tube in his hand. Sitting down next to me, he squeezes some onto his fingers and starts to lightly massage my back. His touch is gentle, and sensual at the same time. It sends small jolts of pleasure up my spine and then back down again, and into my core.

"Oh god, that feels good." I groan into the mattress without thought.

"I told you I could make you feel better," he whispers, his hot breath caressing my ear. I can almost see the smug look on his face, the glint of mischief in his eyes. It doesn't take long for me to turn into a pile of mush beneath his strong hands. His fingers trail across my skin, the cream he used penetrating deep into my muscles. He pulls away and I'm not sure what overcomes me, but I feel the need to apologize, to tell him that I'm sorry for ruining everything for him last year. I never should've listened to my father, believed his lies, not when he was far worse than the Bishops.

Pushing up off the mattress I settle onto my knees, the shirt falling back into place. When my gaze finds Sullivan's, I see the heat in his eyes. Instinctively my eyes drop down to his boxers, a sizeable tent having formed there.

Shit, he's huge, and hard as stone. I lift my gaze back to his face before I say something to embarrass myself.

"I... I just want to say sorry, for that night, for ruining..."

"Shhh," Sullivan reaches out, pulling me into his arms. My lips press into a firm line at his touch. The organ in my chest starts to pound and my chest rises and falls in an unsteady rhythm. With his hands on my hips he moves us back towards the headboard. I gasp as his stiff cock presses against my center. He must be able to feel the affect he has on me.

"I don't want to talk about the past, in fact I don't want to talk at all." Fingers ghost over my hips and I wiggle against him, enjoying his hardness against me. His grip tightens and he groans, and I swear to god it has to be the sexiest sound I've ever heard in my entire life.

Lifting my hands I place them on his shoulders and lean in, my lips finding his full firm ones. The kiss is saturated with lust, with a primal need for something more and like two souls trying to find their place in each other we collide with a heat that could rival the sun. Sullivan's tongue slips past his bottom lip, and presses against mine begging for entry into my mouth. Without hesitation I part my lips and our tongues meet, stroking each other tenderly.

My hands move all on their own gliding over his strong shoulders, and down his firm chest, over his eight pack abs, and to his tapered waist, before moving back up again, until my fingers find purchase in the longer strands of his hair, in this light it's almost a rusty color that suits him.

Breathlessly, he pulls away, the blue of his eyes the color of a thunderstorm before it rains, his pupils dilated, "Fuck, Harlow, I want to kiss you everywhere, taste every inch of you."

His confession should frighten me being how inexperienced I am, but it doesn't it excites me, because I would love nothing more than to have his lips on my skin, his tongue stroking me in ways I could never imagine.

"Do you want that?" He questions, leaning in to press a kiss over my throbbing pulse. Pressing down on his cock I swivel my hips, the pleasure that zings through me is indescribable.

"Yes." I reply hoarsely feeling only a little timid when he pulls away and grabs the hem of the T-shirt I'm wearing, pulling it up and over my head. The shirt falls to the mattress beside us, and suddenly I'm sitting in his lap, my breasts exposed, and my cheeks feeling fifty shades of red. Instinctively, I lift my hands to cover my breasts but Sullivan isn't having it, he shakes his head, and grabs onto my wrists, bringing my hands back to his shoulders.

"You're beautiful, and you shouldn't hide that beauty."

He just called me beautiful. I soak in the words and sink my teeth into my bottom lip when he leans forward and sucks one of the stiff nipples into his mouth. His eyes drift closed, and he moans around the tip, the sound pulsing through me.

My pussy clenches around nothing but air, and I wish so badly that he would alleviate the ache forming there. Pulling away he releases my nipple with a loud pop and moves to give equal attention to the other one.

"You smell like sweet vanilla. You're intoxicating, and taste like freshly picked strawberries. Fuck, I could kiss you all day, and suck on these pretty pink nipples for hours." Goodness, his words aren't helping matters.

I can feel something building deep inside me, it mounts higher and higher as he sucks my nipple, swirling his tongue across the hardened peak while kneading my other breast, his thumb and forefinger rolling the hardened nub gently.

"I'm... that feels good, even better than the massage."

Pulling away he palms both breasts, his eyes flashing with barely restrained need and in this moment, I want him to snap. I want him to take me, give me the pleasure that I know he can. The pleasure that he'll give, if I ask.

"I need you…"

"Grind your pussy against my cock. I want to see what you look like when you fall apart." He croaks, and like a kid being told they can have dessert before dinner I press my pussy against his cock—our thin layer of clothes doing nothing to hide our arousal—taking whatever he will give me.

At first contact I gasp, my pussy throbbing, and heat spreading through my core. Maintaining pressure, I swivel my hips and smile when a deep moan passes his's lips.

"So pretty, so fucking pretty," he murmurs, looking up into my eyes, his fingers plucking my nipples with a steady rhythm. I let my body's reaction to him overtake me, and start humping him, finding the perfect angle that brings me just enough pressure to set me off.

My movements become wild, my hips moving faster and faster, as the pleasure rises higher, and holy hell, I wish there was less fabric between us right now.

"Come for me, Harlow, show me how much you want my cock and maybe next time I'll give it to you." The deepness of his voice, and the erotic words set me off, heat pools inside me and then like a firework I explode. My entire being quaking, my pulse pounding in my ears as my pussy clenches over and over again around nothing.

"Fuck…" Sullivan grits out, his fingers digging into my skin.

Sagging forward I fall onto Sullivan, my ear pressing against his chest, the sound of his own ragged heartbeat filling me with warmth.

"It's been a long time since I came in my fucking boxers, but you, Harlow, hold a power over me that is both frightening and exciting. But believe me, next time I come, it will be inside of you."

My eyes widen and I gulp, wondering when the next time will be. My stomach is in knots, but the rest of my body is relaxed, a puddle of mush. I pull away, my mouth popping open with a question on my tongue, when the bedroom door opens and Banks walks in. I can't imagine what he's thinking as he takes us in, his face is a mask of unshown emotion and before either one of us can say anything he exits the room, closing the door behind him.

I turn back to face Sullivan bashfully and he brushes a few strands of hair from my face. I'm a fucking mess. I just humped one of the guys I'd been taught to hate for the first eighteen years of my life. The same guys who've spent countless hours bullying me and making my life miserable. So why does this feel so right, yet so wrong? Having Banks walk in on us, is leaving me with a whirlwind of emotions that I don't know how to deal with.

"We can't help it, all three of us want you. The question is, do you want all of us?"

And if that isn't the million-dollar question, I don't know what is.

Breakfast isn't as awkward as I expected it to be and Banks doesn't mention what he saw in Sullivan's room. Still, this feels anything but normal. Part of me is still wondering if this is real at all. How can we go from hating each other to enjoying breakfast after cuddling all night? Then something dawns on me. Did we ever really hate each other? Or were we just conditioned? Did we just hate the versions of each other our parents made us see?

Looking back on it I can't really say I ever felt like I hated them myself, as in, they never did anything to hurt me directly. Everything I ever heard about the Bishops came from my father and now that I know my father lied to me I can't help but wonder if he lied about other things too. My mother never spoke of them, but when she did it was with the same disdain my father had.

Thinking about my parents always leaves a bitter taste in my mouth. I take a sip of coffee and try to wash down the unwanted memories. Instead of dwelling on the past I look over at the three men sitting at the table with me. I've never seen them so relaxed and carefree.

"I'll be gone most of the day, but I'm sure Banks and Oliver can keep you busy," Sullivan says, in between bites of his bagel.

"Where are you going?" I ask out of curiosity, only after the words leave my mouth do I realize how nosy I'm being. I internally curse at how ridiculous the whole thing sounds, Jesus, Harlow, he gave you an orgasm, not a wedding ring.

"Just have to deal with some stuff," he looks over at me briefly, obviously not willing to share. I take the hint and don't ask him to elaborate. It's none of my business really.

He leaves right after finishing breakfast and I try to help Oliver and Banks clean up the kitchen, but Banks instructs me to stay seated which leaves me feeling weird and out of place.

"I should probably just go back to the dorms," I announce, feeling as if I might be intruding or something. "You really don't have to do this. You don't have to take care of me, watch over me. I don't need…"

"We already talked about this. You are staying here until we figure out who pushed you off the boat." Oliver's voice holds a finality to it, like what he says goes, and I know once again I've been shot down. I frown and cast my eyes to the floor, crossing my arms over my chest. I'm still wearing Sullivan's shirt. No bra, of course, and his shorts, with, you guessed it, no panties.

Even with the clothing I have on I feel naked, and out of place.

"Why don't we watch a movie or something?" Banks suggests, clearly trying to lighten the mood. "We can spend the rest of the day on the couch, maybe order some takeout, lay around and be lazy."

"Actually, that does sound really nice," I smile. "But, I need to at least call Shelby and let her know I'm okay. I know her, and by now she's probably worried herself into a frenzy. She'll be waiting around all day for me to call or come home."

Banks claps his hands together, the sound echoing around the room loudly, "It's decided then, lazy couch day it is. Here, you call Shelby," he says, sliding his phone across the table towards me.

"I'm hopping in the shower."

"And I'm going to pick a movie. Return to the living room in ten minutes," Oliver demands, his gaze burning right through me. I can't place the emotion I see there, but I can't look away. It's like he has be in a trance. He slips from the kitchen a moment later and I feel like I can finally breathe.

What the hell was that? Whatever it was it was intense. With the phone in hand I dial one of the few numbers I know by heart.

Shelby answers on the second ring with a dramatic gasp, "Hello?"

"Hi, it's me. Just calling to say I'm alive."

"God, Harlow, I've been worried sick about you. I don't think you staying there is safe. I feel like a shitty friend to have let this happen. I should have called the police instead. God, please tell me they haven't hurt you. I swear I'll murder them. I know how to hide a body."

"What? No! Stop, Shelby. I'm fine." I assure her, but I can tell from the heavy breathing she's doing through the phone that she's on the verge of a meltdown.

"You almost died, Harlow. Do you have any idea what it felt like to see them pull you from the water like that? You do know you weren't breathing when they pulled you out, right?" For a moment I don't say anything. That explains the pain in my chest, I guess. Someone must have done CPR on me. I lick my lips, preparing myself to say something, to reassure her that I'm okay, but the words won't come. I didn't know that, and honestly, I'm not sure I wanted to know that. I don't want to be reminded of how close I was to never waking up, to never seeing Shelby, or the guys, again. Swallowing down the fear, and sadness bubbling up inside me I force myself to speak.

"It was a freak accident. Probably just a joke that went wrong. I promise, I'm fine," I say weakly, wishing I was strong enough to believe the words I'm saying. She sighs deeply into the phone and I know she doesn't believe me. She's known me long enough to know I'm not okay, but she also knows I'm not ready to talk about it.

"Fine, but call me if you need me and oh, I almost forgot. This chick came by our room this morning, asking if you were okay. Carole I think was her name."

"Caroline?"

"Yeah that's it, she said she was worried about you last night and wanted to check up on you."

"That's sweet," I say, wondering how she knew what room I lived in.

"I'm going to the gallery for a few hours, but I'll have my phone on me, and I mean it. Anything, Harlow, even if you just want to talk."

"I swear, I will call if anything happens," I assure her. "Thank you for being an awesome friend, I love you."

"Yeah, yeah. I love you too, bestie. Talk later." I press the red end key on the phone and stand there for a moment, regaining my composure. I wasn't breathing? I literally could've died, I was so close to death, but Oliver saved me.

He saved me.

9

If someone would have asked me two days ago how I was going to spend my Saturday, this would have been by far the furthest scenario from my mind. Banks, Oliver, and I are stretched out on the oversized sectional, each eating out of a box of Chinese takeout, while watching all the *Die Hard* movies.

We are already at the end of the second one and Sullivan still hasn't returned. I wonder where the hell he is, but I don't want to seem nosy, so I keep my mouth shut and enjoy this day without worrying.

"How is your back?" Banks asks, when the movie ends.

"It's better, that stuff Sullivan put on there really helped."

"Is that what you two were doing this morning?" he teases. "Maybe I can put some *cream* on you too."

Oh God. I don't know if it's the reminder of what I did with Sullivan, or the suggestive tone in Banks' voice, or maybe the way Oliver's smoldering eyes are burning into me right now, but something has my core tightening and moisture building between my legs.

"You're cute when you're blushing," Oliver says as he sits up and leans over to me. "Let's see your back." He tugs on my shirt urging me to lift it up.

I scoot to the edge of the couch and lift my shirt up on my back. I don't plan on showing more skin than that, but when Oliver starts running his fingers slowly up my spine, I have this overwhelming need to take my shirt off all the way. I turn my head and look back over my shoulder just as Banks reaches out for me as well. His fingertips grazing over my ribs.

With both of them touching me at the same time my senses go into overdrive. Before I know what I'm doing, I pull my shirt off all the way and drop it onto the floor by my feet.

"Fuck yeah," Oliver exclaims. Grabbing me by the hips, he spins me around and pulls me onto his lap. I straddle him in nothing but a pair of thin shorts, the fabric already soaked at my crotch.

I can't hold back a moan when I feel his very hard cock pressing up against my clit. With his hands sprawled out on my thighs he grinds me over his length, but I really lose it when he takes one of my nipples into his mouth and swirls his tongue around the tight bud.

My head falls back as pure lust overcomes me. Suddenly I don't care about how wrong this is, all I can think about is their hands on me, their mouths, their tongues, their...*oh my god*. I can't believe this is happening. Am I going to lose my virginity during a threesome?

Oliver sucks on my puckered nipple and I lose my train of thought again.

"Don't be so greedy, brother," Banks growls from beside us and Oliver releases my nipple with a pop.

Banks smiles and cups one of my breasts before leaning down to take the other one into his mouth while I'm still straddling Oliver. The wrongness of it all is so exhilarating. I had Sullivan this morning and now I'm with his brothers.

I busy my hands threading my fingers through tufts of soft brown hair while Banks swirls his tongue around my hardened nipple. The sensations they both stir inside me are maddening.

Suddenly he stops and pulls away gently. I whimper at the loss of contact, my head too dizzy with lust as I try to figure out if I've done something wrong.

"Lay across our legs," he orders, tugging at my shoulder. With shameful eagerness I oblige, readjusting my legs so I can lay across both their laps. My upper body is on Banks, while my ass is nestled against Oliver's hardened cock.

"You want us to make you feel good?" Oliver inquires, his voice heady, while running his hand up and down my inner thighs. My heart starts to beat rapidly desire pooling deep in my gut.

"Yes," I say breathlessly, my tongue darting out over my bottom lip to wet it.

"I want to touch you," Oliver purrs.

"You are touching me," I tease, even though I know exactly what he means.

Grinning he uses his hand to nudge my legs apart.

"I want to touch you here," he murmurs and lets his thumb ghost over my shorts covered pussy. Taking the hint, I spread my legs further for him. He takes the invitation and trails his fingers over the fabric before he dips his thumb into the waistband of my shorts and starts to pull them down.

I lift my hips to give him better access and then watch as he pulls the fabric down my legs slowly, ever so slowly, leaving me completely bare. My eyes dart between both of them as they look down at me like I'm an all you can eat buffet and they are two starving men who haven't eaten in weeks.

Banks cups my cheek and tilts my face towards him. Leaning down, he presses his lips to mine, this kiss consumes me, ripping the air from my lungs. I'm so overwhelmed by that kiss that it's hard for me to keep track of where Oliver's hands are.

Pleasure builds further when Banks' free hand finds my breast and he starts kneading the flesh. At the same time Oliver's hand moves between my thighs to cup my mound, his thumb finding my clit with ease.

"You want us to make you come?" Banks asks, his voice unnaturally deep as he pulls away just enough to speak.

With his thumb firmly on my clit Oliver moves a finger to my already drenched entrance. This is insane, we should stop, but I don't want to, I don't know if I could stop right now. The world could burn to the ground around me and I wouldn't care. All that matters is the scorching fire flickering in my belly.

"Yes, please," the words come out on a gasp because right as I'm speaking them, Oliver slides one of his thick digits into my slickness.

"Fuck, Banks, she's tight as hell." Oliver's voice is strained, the muscles in his neck tight. He looks like he's ready to explode.

"Mmm, so tight and ready for us," Banks murmurs against my lips, before deepening the kiss. Seconds later my nipple is being rolled between two fingers, my chest heaving. My body shudders with pleasure at the explorative hands of these two men.

I whimper the moisture between my legs growing, dripping now. I'm so wet, so ready, it's almost embarrassing. As if he can sense my discomfort and need for more, Oliver starts to move, his finger pumping in and out of me with shallow thrusts.

"Fuck, you're so beautiful, Harlow, your pussy's taking my brother's finger with so much ease. I can picture you with my cock stuffed inside."

Dear lord, my cheeks heat at the admission. Could I handle being taken by two of the Bishops? Even more so, would I want to be? I already know the answer to that question and as wrong as it might be, yes. I would want to be taken by them, together.

Banks is filthy, his words egging me on, pushing me closer and closer. My legs fall apart completely, my hips rising slightly with each shallow thrust, while Banks continues to pluck at my nipples, alternating between the two while whispering filthy thoughts in my ears.

"You're so greedy, so willing and ready for us," Oliver growls, adding a second finger. He pauses briefly, before moving again, giving me time to adjust to him. It's almost like he knows that I've never done this before.

I feel full, so full, and the pressure in my womb builds as Oliver does this strange thing where he crosses his fingers inside me, rubbing at the tender tissue at the top of my channel.

"Shit," I gasp, into Banks' mouth and arch my back, pushing my breasts further into his hands. I'm full on panting now, my body moving on its own, my hands reach around, trying to find something to do.

One ends up in Banks' hair, my fingers digging into his brown locks. My other hand grabs a fist full of Oliver's shirt, pulling him towards me, as I teeter on the edge of insanity between the two of them.

"That's right. Come for us. Come all over his fingers, gush that pretty pussy all over his hand," Banks whispers against my heated skin, coaxing the orgasm right out of me. My thighs quake and my muscles tighten, the pleasure blinding me as it zings through my being from head to toe. I feel my channel spasming around Oliver's fingers, gripping onto him, and refusing to let go. My teeth sink into my bottom lip to stop the scream of pleasure from escaping, but some spills out anyway, ripping from my throat and from somewhere deep inside me.

"Ahhhh...." The noise vibrates off the walls. I squeeze my eyes shut and enjoy the last wave of the orgasm as it ripples through me like little aftershocks. Slowly I float back down to earth like a leaf falling from a tree.

Seconds tick by and I squeeze my lids tighter wanting the moment to last forever, but as the euphoric pulses of pleasure leave me, I'm left wondering what happens next?

I've not only kissed all three of them. I've done sexual things with all of them too.

Where does that leave me? Sandwiched right in the middle? Blinking my eyes open the first person I see is Oliver. He withdraws his hand from between my thighs, and brings the two fingers, now dripping with my arousal to his lips.

He slips them into his mouth, his eyes drifting closed as he sucks. He takes his time, like he's sucking on a lollipop. He's tasting me, tasting my arousal, my come and I'll be damned if it isn't as hot as hell to watch.

"You taste divine. I can't wait to have those thighs of yours wrapped around my face, with my tongue in your pussy."

Using my arm to shield my face—which is most likely cherry red—I hide from him.

"Don't be ashamed, that was amazing." Oliver assures me, his eyes darkened with arousal.

"Fuck yeah, it was. That's going in my spank bank for next time," Banks chuckles, while gently smoothing his thumb across my forehead. My breathing returns to a semi normal pace. My heart on the other hand is still galloping out of my chest and I don't think it will return to a slower rhythm any time soon. Not with Banks and Oliver looking down at me like they're about to devour me all over again.

I can feel both of their cocks straining against my bare skin, and for a second I'm scared of what's to come next. I want to satisfy them both like they've just done for me, but can I?

Can I take both of them, at the same time?

Banks must see the worry flashing in my eyes because he starts to shake his head.

"You don't have to do anything," he assures me, while running his fingers through my hair. The feeling is, there is no way to describe it. It's like a massage but for your scalp.

"I want to, it's just..." The sound of a door opening and closing echoes through the house, followed by heavy footfalls heading towards us. *Sullivan.*

I know I've done nothing wrong, Sullivan and I aren't an item, but I still scramble off both their laps with my shirt in hand, grabbing my shorts off the floor. I tug the shirt on over my head, and it just clears my tits when Sullivan comes strolling into the living room. Stopping in the doorway, he takes in the scene with his eyebrows raised, like he is trying to solve a puzzle.

"What the hell is going on here?"

"Oh, with us?" Banks grins, leaning back against the couch with his hands behind his head. My eyes dart between Sullivan, Oliver, and Banks. Sullivan's got a dark look in his eyes, while Banks is grinning like a fool.

"Well? Someone better tell me what the hell you guys are doing?"

Sullivan pauses, his gaze raking over me once, and then a second time, except this time his gaze lingers on my bare legs. I feel like I'm being inspected.

I try and look anywhere but at Sullivan or the other two but my gaze keeps catching on two hardened cocks straining against the fabric of shorts. Fuck, that looks like it hurts.

"Why are her shorts off?" Sullivan asks, and Banks bursts out laughing. The tone of Sullivan's voice is deep, protective, alpha-like and I wonder why? Is he trying to stake claim to me? It sounds that way.

"Oh, we were just putting some cream on her back, like you did this morning, remember?" Oliver teases, a thick brow lifted, and though his response is directed at Sullivan his eyes are boring into mine. I swear if my cheeks weren't already on fire, they would be now.

Sullivan's eyebrows draw together, and then his lips twitch before pulling into a smile, "I see you've made your choice then," he says, reminding me of the question he asked me earlier that morning.

Did I want all three brothers? *Hell yes.*

Could I handle them? I don't know.

Is this a horrible idea that will blow up in my face, *yes*. This is wrong and not just because they are supposed to be my enemies, because our families have hated each other for years. No, it's wrong because I'm falling for three men who bullied me, who I thought for sure hated me, but clearly didn't hate me enough.

And if things end badly, which I'm sure they will, I'm the one that will get her heart broken, not them.

Turning on the balls of my feet I walk out of the room. I need some space, to be somewhere where I'm not surrounded by them and their intoxicating scents. Somewhere I can breathe without having a Bishop stuck up my ass. I don't know what's happening anymore, all I know is that we aren't enemies anymore.

"Hey, wait, where are you going?" Sullivan asks, the sound of his feet pounding against the floor behind me tells me he's following me. *Great.*

"Can you give me something to wear? Like some sweatpants or something?" I ask, stopping in the middle of the hallway.

Sullivan reaches out for me, his hand is heavy on my shoulder as he turns me around to face him, and I let him because I'm weak. Weak for him, weak for all three of them.

"Yeah, sure, whatever you need." He responds. Keeping my eyes firmly on his chest I say, "Thanks," and go to turn around, but the hand on my shoulder tightens and my stomach starts to flutter for some stupid reason.

He leans in to me, and I lift my head, unable to resist the closeness of his body. My nostrils flare as I breathe him in. All I can smell is rain, the smell of a thunderstorm, "Are you okay?" That voice of his is soft, wrapping around me like a cashmere sweater.

Suddenly my throat, lips, it all feels dry. "Yeah." I say, the tone of my voice softer than I expected it to be, "It's just all a little much and everything is happening so fast. I mean, one day you hate me and the next you want me to..."

"Whoa, slow it down. I've always wanted you," he admits, for the second time. Peering up into his eyes I see nothing but honesty reflected back at me.

"Well, I didn't know that," I say, chewing on my bottom lip.

"Well, you do now. Come on, let's get you dressed," Sullivan says, taking my hand and leading me to his bedroom. I take a seat on the edge of the bed and watch him dig in the drawers of his dresser. He hands me a pair of sweatpants and socks which I put on right away.

Once I'm dressed I feel a little better, less exposed and more put together, but not safe. These men have the power to strip me bare with a single look.

"Tonight you'll be sleeping with Banks," he reminds me, and I swear I can sense a change in his demeanor. He runs a hand through his hair as if it's a nervous tick.

"Okay, if that's what you want." I murmur, coming to stand fully.

Even though I wouldn't consider myself short the brothers still tower over me like giants.

"You aren't ready for what I want yet, but you will be, soon, so very soon." The seductiveness dripping from his words nearly has me ripping my clothes off again. Stupid hormones, stupid feelings. I have to stop thinking with my vagina.

There's this low chiming sound that resonates through the house. Sullivan's eyebrows furrow together in confusion. Did someone just ring the doorbell? At ten o'clock at night?

"Who the..." He grumbles, but doesn't finish his question, he just turns around and heads for what I assume is the front door.

He makes it about two steps into the hall before all hell breaks loose.

10

They say there is always a calm before the storm, but there was nothing calm about what was about to occur. Three distinct voices pierced the air all at once. All three of which I knew, but one that I haven't heard in months. Not since the day I left home.

No. It can't be.

Each of the voices are coated with venom as they carry through the house vibrating the walls angrily. Sullivan gets a running start but I'm not far behind him as we both bound down the hall and then the stairs towards Oliver and Banks. Panic creeps up my throat, and the closer that we get to the foyer the clearer the voices become.

Oliver, Banks, and my dad. They're arguing, words being thrown like punches through the air. "You have fucking balls coming here, after what you and your daughter did to my brother, my family." My hearts racing out of my chest, the worst thoughts possible taking place in the forefront of mind.

"Where is she?" *His* voice is like acid raining down on me.

No. No. No.

What the hell is he doing here?

My feet don't even touch the bottom step and my mother is on me, wrapping her slender arms around me, hugging me with all her might, and it seems as if she cares, as if she's worried.

"We're here now, you're safe," she says into my hair with a relieved sigh her arms tightening around me, squeezing the life out of me.

I'm so baffled by the whole situation that I almost forget to push my mother away, almost. I push her away with a gentle nudge, and she looks at me with a stunned expression like I'm supposed to welcome her with open arms. I couldn't care less about her feelings though. I look past her to meet Oliver's gaze. There is a fury stirring in his brown depths, eyes that just a short time ago had passion, lust, and need for me in them. But that's long gone now, I can tell before I even open my mouth to ask what's going on.

"Get the fuck out of my house and take your lying daughter with you!" Oliver demands, his entire body vibrating as he takes a step forward to stand toe to toe with my father.

Lying daughter? What the hell is going on?

Confused, I look between my father, my mother, Oliver, and Banks. My head feels like it's on a swivel.

"What..." is all I get out before Banks starts yelling at me.

"I can't believe we fell for your lies again. You're one hell of an actress, I'll give you that," his words drip with hate. The way his eyes rake over me with pure disgust leaves me feeling like a piece of garbage floating in the wind.

The knife of betrayal slices through my skin cutting me so deep I'm sure I'll never survive the injury. I haven't lied about anything, haven't done anything wrong.

Shaking my head, I swing my gaze to Sullivan, maybe he'll talk to me, try and figure this out, but I should know better. His confusion turns to hatred before my eyes. He won't let me explain. He is making up his own story in his mind, and in that story, I'm the bad guy.

I look at his face and take in his contorted features I know it's over. His expression will haunt me for a long time, maybe even forever.

Disappointment, despair and hate...so much hate, cloud his vision. No longer is he the man that gave me my first kiss, my first orgasm.

Instead he's the vile nightmare my parents always made his family out to be.

"I..." I start but am cut off.

"Shut up! Shut the fuck up and get out! You Lockwoods are nothing but garbage, liars, and thieves." The words hurt, and my cheeks sting as if he's slapped me. I'm so stunned that I can't move. All I can do is stare back at him wondering if I will ever see the Sullivan I love again.

"I didn't..." Oliver takes a menacing step towards me and I take one backwards out of instinct, my body telling me to run. The look he's giving me right now frightens me to the core. But not just because of the disgust in it, but because of the hate and the unforgiving rage. He wants to hurt me, make me feel the betrayal he's feeling right now.

"Touch my daughter again and I will have the police on your asses faster than you can call your pathetic parents," my father sneers.

Someone grabs onto my hand and starts pulling me towards the door. My legs move, but only because it's walk or be dragged and as badly as I don't want to leave, I don't want to be dragged out of the house like some fool either. It's obvious I've already done enough wrong, there is no point in standing here, begging for forgiveness. Tears sting my eyes, my heart thunders in my chest, and my stomach clenches with anxiety over the unknown.

What is going on?

I almost trip on the way out the door but right myself at the last minute. I blink rapidly like that might wake me up from this nightmare. I can't help but flinch when the door behind us is slammed shut, the noise vibrating through me. I'm dumbfounded, completely at a loss as to what is going on. Why are my parents here? What did my father say to Oliver and Banks that made their opinion of me change so drastically?

My mom drags me across the driveway to their car, rocks dig into the bottoms of my sock covered feet, digging deep enough to cut through, but I don't feel the pain, if there is any. Nothing could hold a candle to the pain residing inside my chest. My father opens the back passenger door and my mom ushers me into the back seat. I'm broken, confused, a shell of myself.

They get into the front seats and we speed off down the driveway, gravel kicking up under the tires.

"The Bishops, Harlow? What were you thinking? Did you sleep with one of them? Oh god, please don't tell me you let one of them touch you." My mother whines, pure disgust in her tone. She hurls about ten more questions at me before I manage to find my voice, my thoughts swirling and panic rising.

"What the hell just happened?"

"We saved you from the biggest mistake of your life," my father barks. "That's what happened." His blue eyes clash with mine in the rearview mirror.

"What did you tell them?" I'm shaking now, fire filling my veins. I should've known. I didn't hear the whole conversation but in that one-minute Sullivan and I were upstairs my parents had found a way to make the brothers hate me all over again.

"That we know they had something to do with you almost dying last night and that we have plenty of people who were on that boat willing to testify to it."

Oh, my fucking, god. "You let them think I set them up... again. Didn't you?"

Instead of answering my question, my dad asks his own. "What if they had something to do with it?"

No, they didn't, they couldn't. It wasn't the brothers.

"There is no way they did! None of the Bishops pushed me in. Oliver was the one who saved me. How do you even know about the boat?"

"It doesn't matter how we know. Did you really think we would let our only daughter go off on her own without watching over her?" My mother asks, and I suppose I shouldn't be surprised. I should've known better, known that someone would be watching me, reporting back to them with every little detail.

"Yes, you should have! I thought I made myself clear the night I left, that I don't want to see you again? If I wanted something to do with you I would have answered when you called me. I would've visited you over the summer." I can count on one hand the number of times I've yelled at either one of my parents, but tonight it feels like déjà vu. I yelled the night I left and I'm yelling now, with good reason. How fucking dare they show up here, spouting lies, and interfering with my life?

"Don't be so dramatic, you don't have to stick up for them anymore. I've spent my entire life fighting against that family and I refuse to let my daughter be corrupted by such evil bastards." My eyes bulge out of my head at my father's words.

"Evil? You are the evil ones," I grit through my clenched teeth. "Drop me off at the dorm and leave me the fuck alone!"

"Harlow, language," my father warns as if he holds some kind of hold over me still. This might have been the first time I ever cussed at my parents, but I couldn't care less. I'm so angry with them. I didn't think I could hate them any more than I do, but once again they've proven me wrong. They've ruined everything by showing up here, everything.

"I hate you," I mutter, crossing my arms over my chest. It feels like my heart is breaking. I might sound like a hormonal teenage girl who is having a bad day, but I actually mean it. I hate my parents. I hate them for how they've raised me. I hate them for deceiving me, for not letting me be who I want to be and for destroying everything I love.

They took my image of people and distorted it. They twisted me, molded me into the person they wanted me to be. My entire world is crumbling, and I can't manage to pick up the pieces fast enough. I feel like I'm speeding down a hill in a car without breaks. What am I going to do besides crash?

"Swear to me, Shelby, swear it wasn't you," I beg, looking deep into her eyes.

"I swear, Harlow. It wasn't me! I haven't seen or talked to your parents since before graduation. I promise, I didn't tell them anything." I watch her face closely and find nothing but sincerity. My shoulders sag in defeat. *It wasn't, Shelby.* I've known her long enough to pick out a lie and she isn't lying, but if it wasn't her, then who was it?

Holding my head in my hands I say, "I'm sorry. I shouldn't have accused you. It's just my parents can be very manipulative. They could have you doing their dirty work without you even knowing it."

"I know, and don't feel bad you've been through a lot lately." She places her hand on my shoulder, and I lift my head. She gives me a weak smile. "So give me the deets did you send your parents packing?"

"I told them to leave me the hell alone or I would go to the police." I didn't want it to come to this. Even after everything, I hate that I actually threatened my parents, but I didn't see any other way of protecting myself.

I'd already moved hundreds of miles away, told them I never wanted to see them again and still they followed me, tried to control me, manipulate me. What else was I supposed to do to get away from them?

"Police?" Shelby asks, baffled.

"Remember when I told you how I overheard my parents talking about setting up the Bishops?"

"Yeah, of course."

"Well, I didn't tell you the whole story…"

It was already late and a school night, that's why I was sneaking down to the kitchen to get a snack. I was surprised when I heard voices coming from the living room because my parents usually went to bed early, but I didn't think too much of it until I heard a third voice that I didn't recognize.

"As always, it has been a pleasure doing business with you," *a man spoke, his voice deep and there was a captivating darkness about his tone that had me stopping mid step.*

"Likewise, Mr. Rossi," *my father replied.*

"I think we've been associates long enough for you to start calling me Xander," *the man said.*

"Very well, Xander," *my mom purred. Followed by a girlish giggle.*

"Thank you again for helping us with the Bishop situation." My mom said their name as if it left a bad taste in her mouth.

"No problem at all, framing people is my second favorite work."

"Oh, what's your favorite?"

I can already tell the answer isn't one I want to hear.

"Killing people," the man confessed, without an ounce of sarcasm in his voice.

Nervous laughter bubbled from both of my parents' throats while bile rose in mine. I clasped my hand over my mouth and ran back up the stairs. I barely made it to my bathroom before vomiting out the contents of my stomach.

Once I was able to get up from the bathroom floor I went back into my room and opened the laptop. Xander Rossi was his name, I typed it in the search bar and hit enter. Immediately I had one article after the next pop up. Most of them were from the local news channel and newspapers.

Xander Rossi was the head of the local mob.

My parents had been doing business with the fucking mafia.

Shelby stares at me silently, and then her lips part, "The mob?" she finally asks, her tone filled with disbelief.

"Yes, *the* mob," I confirm. "That's when everything started going downhill. I confronted them the next day, I started digging, asking questions. Once I opened my eyes, I couldn't look away. All the lies, all the things I believed that they told me. I destroyed someone's life because of them, because of their lies."

I'm not looking for pity. I've taken responsibility for my actions, my parents on the other hand, have not.

"Wow, that's...wow," she says, her eyes wide.

"Yeah, so I'm done with them. I don't know what they were trying to do by showing up here and acting like nothing happened, but I shut them down."

"Good. You don't need that kind of negativity in your life," she says, and she is right, I don't need them in my life, nor do I need the Bishops. They were so quick to turn against me and didn't even let me explain. Which hurt like hell. They were too busy hating me to listen to my side of the story. I thought we had moved passed our differences, let the past go, but instead it feels like they were just waiting for a reason to turn on me.

They want to be enemies again. *Fine.* I don't need them, nor do I want them. They were pains anyway, or at least that's what I tell myself as I get ready for classes.

11

I spend the next two days torn between wanting to reach out to the guys and trying my best to avoid them. Apparently, they're doing the latter, because neither Sullivan nor Banks showed up to the classes that we share.

Like the moping teenager I am, I walk to the local coffee shop in the afternoon, getting a hot cocoa and the biggest chocolate fudge brownie they have.

"For here or to go?" The girl with bright pink and purple hair from behind the counter asks.

"To go, please."

"Hey, Harlow," a familiar voice calls. I turn to find Caroline standing a few feet away. "Looks like you had the same idea as me," she smiles. "I'll have the second biggest brownie," she tells the barista.

"Hey, Caroline," I take in her warm smile. Shelby's been busy at the gallery and suddenly sitting down with a friend seems more appealing than sitting outside on a bench in the quad by myself.

"Want to sit and stuff our faces with sweet goodness together?" I ask.

"Sounds amazing,"

We pay, get our orders, and sit down in the corner of the coffee shop, near a bookshelf that's brimming with books.

"How have you been?" Caroline asks, as I shove a piece of brownie into my mouth. It tastes like Heaven and chocolate had a baby.

I shrug, "Okay."

"You really scared us all on the boat, the other night. When Oliver pulled you out of the water your lips were blue. I was worried you weren't going to make it."

"It really wasn't that big of a deal," I lie. It was a huge deal, someone had wanted to hurt me, who, I didn't know, but I also didn't want to worry Caroline with that admission either. I hope she doesn't ask me if I jumped.

I don't want people thinking I'm suicidal either, though I'm sure if I put my ear close enough to the ground within the gossip circles I'm sure I'll hear a rumor being spread about me.

She jumped, no one pushed her. She's crazy.

"Mhm, then why do you look like you're having the worst week of your life?"

"Well, I just have some personal stuff going on, and you know not to be weird, or anything, but every time I feel like I need a friend or someone to lift me up you appear like a fairy godmother."

A soft giggle escapes her pink lips. "That's me, the fairy godmother of friendship." Soft chatter surrounds us as we nibble on our brownies together. I wash mine down with even more sugary goodness, hoping that the sugar high will give me enough strength to get through the rest of my day. As badly as I don't want to admit it, the brothers have ruined me.

I've grown dependent on them. Where having them around, and following me, annoyed me at first, I kind of grew accustomed to it and now that they aren't I just feel alone, discarded like trash. I'm sure that's the point though, to make me feel like shit.

"Are you sure you're okay?" Caroline asks again, placing a gentle hand on my shoulder, concern flickering in her eyes.

I look up from my brownie, "Would it be weird if I said I was in love with three guys?"

Caroline blinks, a neutral look on her heart shaped face, "It's 2019, who cares if you love three guys? Love is love, right?"

"Right, but..." I swallow my throat suddenly feeling dry. "What if they're three guys that you shouldn't want to be with? Like they're bad for you, but you can't help yourself?"

"Ooo, kinda like these brownies?" She says, wiggling her eyebrows, and popping another piece of gooey goodness into her mouth.

"Yes, kinda like these brownies."

"You indulge, I guess. I don't know, do what you think is right?"

I want to tell her I have no idea what is right or wrong, but I don't. I won't bore her with the details of my dramatic weekend. I don't want to send her running for the hills.

We finish our brownies, sneaking in a little small talk here and there. By the time we're finished my belly is full, and I'm back to smiling again.

"If you're still struggling with English, I can help you. We could meet up in the library or something one of these nights. Go over notes?"

"You would do that for me?" I ask, as we walk out of the coffee shop and towards the quad where I will most likely end up seeing at least one of the Bishop Brothers. It's strange, because now that they're not following me around like lost puppies I find myself watching for them. I want to see them. Hell, I crave them, my belly tightens, heat blooming deep down inside me when I think of them.

"Of course, you've got a lot going on and what kind of friend would I be if I didn't offer to help you?"

"Honestly, a typical one. In case you haven't noticed I don't have many friends here." I mumble, wrapping my hand around the strap of my backpack. In the back pocket of my jeans my phone starts to vibrate. Laughter meets my ears, but I'm too busy unlocking my phone and looking through it to look up and see what has people laughing.

"Harlow..." I can hear the worry in Caroline's voice without even looking at her face to confirm it.

My phone continues to vibrate, and vibrate, and vibrate and I'm starting to get flustered with all the incoming text messages. Lifting my head my gaze catches on the east campus building where I notice a banner blowing in the wind. Bright pink lettering painted across the white canvas. *What the hell is that?*

Harlow Needs More Dick- Send Pics If you're DTF!

Below is my cell number, which explains all the incoming texts. The letters are so bright you couldn't miss them if you tried.

Joy. Another stunt from the Bishops. I should've known things would go from bad to worse.

"Like, oh my god, its Harlow the whore in the flesh," a girl sneers from a few feet away. I look up and see it's one of the groupies from the other night. The one that was crawling all over Oliver, or maybe it was Banks I don't remember, and I don't really care. Her name's Tiffany, that's all I know.

I tell myself to look away, to push my feelings down, swallow my pride, and turn the other cheek but I can't help myself. Like bile rising up my throat, the anger, and red-hot rage burns through me, and I find myself crossing the distance that separates us without thought.

"Did you do this?" I growl, pointing to the banner behind her.

She shrugs, purses her lips, and juts her hip out looking at me like I'm a peasant and she is the queen. To think that I used to be treated like a queen. If only she knew where I came from, the power I used to have, the power I no longer care to have.

"Maybe. Maybe not? Why's it matter? Last I heard if you can handle three you can handle them all." Laughter bubbles out of her, and the girl standing beside her. She looks familiar too, but my bone isn't with her, it's with her friend.

She thinks she's perfect with her platinum blonde hair, and painted on face, but she's just like the rest, a snotty bitch. My hands curl into fists, my nails digging into my palm.

"What are you going to do if I did?" She narrows her gaze and taunts me with a shit eating grin on her lips. I've endured enough bullshit. I came here to escape, to get away from the pain, the drama, but it seems it just followed me and I'm done, so done.

I react without thought pouncing on her like a cat. I pull back my fist and slug her in the face. Pain radiates up my arm while a scream that sounds like I'm murdering her pours from her lips. We scuffle across the grass, her fingers digging into my hair, pulling at the strands, causing a burning pain to flare across my scalp.

Bitch. I do the same, and when she starts to shriek like a pig, her arms flailing and her hands landing anywhere they can, I smile, feeling completely satisfied with myself.

"Harlow!" Caroline is grabbing onto my shoulders, and pulling me back, but not before I land another punch on the bitch's nose. Chest heaving, and heart racing I take a step back and look at the girl lying on the grass, droplets of blood dribbling down from one of her nostrils.

"You're trash. Nothing but a trashy whore," Tiffany snarls, shoving up off the grass. I smooth a hand over my hair and down the front of my jeans. By now a crowd has gathered around us, and I fully expect to be called into the dean's office for this little stunt. Whatever the punishment, it'll be worth it.

"I know what she did was wrong, but you can't just go around beating people up," Caroline scolds while shaking her head, sending strands of her dark hair across her panicked face. Shit, I know she's right but, god that felt good. Caroline starts pulling me away from the crowd and I follow her gladly, ready to get away from the gawking audience.

"Well, look who it is," a familiar voice hisses and it has me stopping mid step. "Can't get enough attention, can you?"

I turn and find Sullivan, Oliver, and Banks staring at me. Sullivan looks unimpressed with my little stunt. Banks has a stupid grin on his face that I would like to wipe off with my fist. And Oliver casts nothing but a cold glare my way. I know I should just walk away, I have already made the target on my back bigger by fighting Tiffany like this.

Unfortunately, my anger gets the better of me and before I can get a grip on it, words are pouring out of my mouth.

"I hope you're happy," I spit at them. "I'm guessing you had something to do with this?" I point at the banner.

"It's not our fault that you're such a slut," Banks says, and I see red. Like a bull I charge him, pushing his chest so hard he stumbles back a few steps.

"You are just making this worse for yourself," Oliver sneers.

"All you had to do was let me explain!"

"We are done listening to your lies, Harlow. You made your bed, now it's time to lay in it," Sullivan growls, his voice sinister.

For a moment I just stand there looking at them, trying to see the men who kissed me just a few days ago, the guys who held me and made me feel safe. I search for that compassion deep in their eyes, but all I see now are guys who hate me and want to hurt me.

"Harlow, we should probably..." Caroline places a hand on my shoulder.

"Yes, we should," I whisper. We walk away from the crowd with me trying to ignore the nasty looks and condescending murmurs following me.

"It's going to be okay, Harlow," Caroline says, "We'll figure this out."

"I wish that was true." Oh god, I hope she is right. Is everything going to be okay? Can I figure this out? Or is this going to be my life from now on?

Caroline walks me to my dorm. She asks me repeatedly if I'm okay and I give her the same answer, *"yeah, I'm fine."* She wanted to come up and watch a movie, probably thinking she would be able to take my mind off this whole thing, but I know there is no hope, so I send her home.

My room is empty when I walk through the door. Shelby is gone again and when the realization I am alone hits me, I break. I crumble to the floor like a rag doll, covering my face with my hands as I let it all out.

All I wanted was to escape but it seems I've traded one prison for another, the only difference is this time my heart is paying the price.

THE NEXT DAY goes just as badly, maybe even worse. I can't go anywhere without people looking at me like I'm a piece of shit. Sneers, laughter, and shitty remarks follow me wherever I go. Ignoring my surroundings is getting harder and harder to do.

I try to keep my head down and in one of my books, but my mind keeps wandering to the Bishops. I can't get over the way they looked at me. I'm so angry at them, for refusing to let me talk, for further embarrassing me in front of everyone, but I'm hurt at the same time. My heart a bleeding mess because for some reason I thought maybe they cared, that maybe they *loved* me.

Stupid, so stupid.

This all could've been avoided if they would've they just let me explain.

As I'm walking to my next class across the west side of campus, I notice two guys walking in my direction. Even though my gaze is on the ground I can still see two dimpled grins forming on their lips and I just know they are going to make a comment about me when they pass. Everyone else has, so I don't expect them to be any different.

Grabbing on to the strap of my backpack, I mentally prepare myself for the verbal assault that's to come, but as they pass neither says so much as one word. And it's then that I learn there are far worse things that can be done then spouting nonsense.

Instead one of them does something worse, he grabs my ass. The jerk grabs my ass, his meaty fingers sinking firmly into the fabric of my jeans. Then he squeezes, hard.

Yelping, I whirl around, my fists clenched, and nostrils flaring, "What the hell is wrong with you?" I grit out through my teeth.

"What? Not kinky enough for you? You need something better?" He grabs onto his junk and shakes it a little bit before releasing a chuckle into the air.

He moves away, following his friend who is a couple steps ahead, also smiling and laughing. *Assholes.* They're both lucky they walked away. I would've kicked their asses if I had to.

It's not until I make it to the classroom that I realize I'm shaking. I'm not sure if it's from anger alone or if I'm a little shook up from that guy grabbing me. My emotions are so out of control it's hard to pinpoint their origin.

Sinking down into the chair, I start to unpack my books and notepad. This is the class I normally have with Banks, but I don't expect him to show up. That's why I'm shocked when I look up and see him walking into the room.

Like magnets drawn to each other, his eyes find mine immediately. For the shortest moment I think he is happy to see me, a smile ghosting his lips, then as if he remembers where we are, his face turns to stone. With a mask carefully placed over his features, he walks in and takes a seat two rows in front of me. My heart starts to beat wildly, my throat tightening, and my chest aching.

Seeing him is torture, especially right now when all I want to do is run up to him and bury my face in his chest and inhale his sweet scent. I feel weak for needing him and it feels so wrong that I still want him like I do.

Taking a deep breath, I try to shake the unwanted thought away. Just when I get my heart rate back under control, and my chest stops heaving, someone else walks in. *Tiffany.* Shit, I forgot she was in this class too. Guess I should think about who I share classes with before I decide to throw down with them.

She lifts up her nose and struts through the room like it's her own personal runway, and I hope someone would put a foot out so I can watch her tumble to the ground. Naturally she takes the seat beside Banks, who of course puts his arm across the back of the chair. Exhaling I grit my teeth together.

I tell myself it doesn't matter, she doesn't, he doesn't, but that would be so much easier if I could actually believe what I'm telling myself. Peering at me over her shoulder, she gives me a smug smile, like she won something, and I can't help but appreciate the way her smile is a bit uneven. She might have been able to cover up the blue and black skin with makeup, but she can't cover up that her cheek is still swollen from where I punched her. I had expected to get into some kind of trouble, but it never happened.

I don't know if that's because of the Bishops or if Tiffany's just worried that I'll kick her ass again if she says something.

"Stop staring," she scoffs.

"Stop looking so hideous," I respond, crossing my arms over my chest. She already thinks I'm a bitch and I'd rather be seen as that than a push over. I've laid down, took the hate, let the Bishops bully me, but I'm done.

I don't want their hate anymore. I want something else.

"Awe, is Harlow jealous?" Banks chimes in, twisting around in his seat. My entire body lights up, ripples of electricity dance across my skin at the deep baritone of his voice. The coldness in his blue eyes reminds me of the ocean the night that I fell off the boat, cold, and unforgiving. Lifeless and impossibly deep.

"Not jealous," I lie, because let's be honest, I am jealous. "Mostly angry, but also, I feel sorry for you, that you had to stoop so low and hook up with someone like this," I lift my chin to Tiffany. "It's sad that you're trying to replace me, as if she ever could, but whatever, she can have my sloppy seconds."

Those cold depths of his flicker with fire, and his chiseled jaw turns to stone, he looks like he wants to snap me in two and knowing that makes me sit up a little straighter in my chair. It makes me a little happier, knowing that I still have some type of hold on him, even if it's not the kind I'm really after.

"Watch it, Harlow, my brothers and I can bring you great pleasure, but we can also bring you great pain."

He doesn't give me a chance to respond, the professor walks in a second later, and Banks turns around in his chair to face the front of the class. But I don't miss the warning in his voice. He wants to scare me, but the only thing that scares me is losing my chance with them.

12

The alarm on my phone goes off, the annoying ringing letting me know my laundry is dry. Putting my kindle down, I grab my spoon and chuck it into the sink and put the ice cream tub back into the freezer. Most people my age are out partying on a Friday night, but me, I would much rather be reading, and chilling out in the dorm. It would be nice if Shelby was here, but they have some really important artist coming to town, so she's stuck working at the art studio all weekend. It's whatever though, as long as she is happy, then I'll be happy for her.

I leave my dorm and head downstairs, my slipper covered feet making hardly any noise against the steps as I head outside to the side building. It houses the student laundry. If my mom ever found out I was doing my own laundry she would be appalled. I didn't wash my first load until a few weeks ago, and even though it was kind of a nightmare at first, for both Shelby and me. I'm proud to say that I've kept the accidental dye jobs and bleach spots to a minimum.

Its past ten and most students are out partying, which leaves the dorm area quiet and empty. I make my way around the building in the darkness of the night. Only two street lights illuminate the sidewalk as I hurry around the building. I'm probably imagining it, but I have this weird feeling that someone is watching me. Like a sixth sense, the hairs on the back of my neck stand up as a shiver runs over me.

The feeling doesn't ease up, even when I finally walk into the communal laundry room that holds about ten washers and ten dryers. The space is completely empty, silent. It almost seems deserted.

Scurrying across the room I grab my basket off the top of the dryer and set it on the floor.

I open the dryer and start grabbing my clothes, stuffing them into the basket without folding them, because who the hell has time to fold. It isn't until I grab the second handful that I notice something black on one of my white T-shirts.

Plucking the T-shirt from the basket I lift the fabric and stare at the front of the shirt in horror. Written there in large black block letters is the word *SLUT*. What the fuck? Shaking my head in disbelief, that someone would even be that immature I pull out another handful of clothes. I pray that's the end of the cruelty, but I should know better. One of my favorite sweaters has been destroyed. I cringe when I see the word **WHORE** written into the pink fabric, streaks of black ink bleed into the shirt and I know I'll have to toss it out. I know it's just a shirt, but it's mine, it belonged to me.

One by one I check every piece of clothing. Every single one has something written on it, something horrible, and offensive, and something that doesn't represent me as a person at all. But the person who wrote these hateful words wouldn't know that, because they believe only what they want to.

Angry with the world I stuff all the clothes into the basket and slam the dryer door shut. The sound so loud it echoes through the vacant space. My hands are shaking as I grab the basket and place it against my hip to carry it. I will myself not to cry, but the tears well in my eyes anyway. College wasn't supposed to be this bad, high school totally, but college? People were supposed to act like adults, be mature, make good choices, and stick up for others. I guess I never expected the brothers to follow me. That threw a wrench into my perfect future.

They wanted revenge, well, they had gotten it and the next time I see them I was going to tell them that. I'm going to let them see how broken I am. I deserved the pain, the hate, the anger the first time around, but this? No. Enough is enough. My parents showing up wasn't my fault, someone set me up, just like with the boat, and if they would've listened maybe things would be different.

With my laundry basket of destroyed clothes in hand, I speed walk back to my dorm. My vision is blurry with unshed tears that I try to blink away. There's a tingling on the back of my neck, it's the same feeling I got earlier.

Someone is watching me. What if it's the same person who shoved me off the boat? Panic claws at me and I take the corner a smidge too fast, catching the edge of the basket on the wall. The impact sends the basket to the ground knocking it out of my hands. Clothes spill out on the sidewalk and into a big pile of textiles.

Fuck my life.

I'm tempted to just leave them and run back to my room but decide not to give someone the satisfaction of seeing them sprawled out across the concrete. The last thing I need is my panties strung up like lights across campus. Angrily I bend down to grab the last shirt off the concrete, my fingers brush against the fabric when I get this strange feeling in my gut, like something bad is about to happen. I have this sudden urge to scream, and so I do.

A blood curdling scream rips from my throat just as a large figure appears next to me. I scramble backwards, landing on my ass, pain flaring across both cheeks as the figure crouches down next to me. His large hand reaches for me and if I hadn't recognized the face attached to that hand, I would have probably suffered from a heart attack.

"Calm down," Oliver's deep voice pricks my ears, his eyes scanning my face. Can he see the tears, the sadness in my eyes? "What's wrong with you? You look like someone kicked your dog and pissed in your cheerios."

"What's wrong with *me*? What's wrong with *you*? Actually, what's wrong with all of you? Have you been watching me, again? I can feel eyes on me."

"Stop, no one has been watching you." He says it like I'm crazy for thinking it, and hell, maybe I am, maybe it's all in my head.

Picking up the basket and its content, I get back up onto my feet. Oliver reaches for something on the ground and to my embarrassment it turns out to be a pair of my panties. Sadness overrules my anger and humiliation. I'm sad because having Oliver this close after everything is hard. So hard. I hate not being able to fall into his embrace and feel protected. Instead, he's standing there holding my panties that have the word CUNT written on them.

I try my very best not to cry, but my best is not good enough today, my only hope is that the light from the building is not efficient enough to show my tears. Snatching the piece of cotton from his hands I start walking away from him, but to my utter surprise he grabs my wrist and pulls me back towards him.

"What's wrong?" he asks again, his voice softer and I can't help but burst into laughter. It's not a 'ha ha that's funny laugh', it's a humorless, sad laugh with a sob in between.

"Did you seriously just ask me that?" I'm surprised by the question, but I'm even more surprised when he takes his hands and cups my cheeks, he drags his thumb over the delicate skin under my eyes and wipes the last few escaping tears away.

And like a river with overflowing banks the words flow freely past my lips.

"You want to know what's wrong? I want you, I want all three of you, even after everything, I want you, and trust me, I know I shouldn't, I know it's wrong and it will never, ever work, and I know you're back to hating me. But, at least I admit how I feel." A moment of silence settles between us as he lets the words sink in while continuing to stroke my cheeks with such softness it takes everything in me not to sink into his touch.

I can see the turmoil in his chocolate gaze, "You're right, it won't work and it's all kinds of wrong..." I wait for the unspoken but, but it never comes. I don't miss the pain and want in his eyes though. I'm too familiar with both not to notice it. "We all want something that we can never have, and you, Harlow, are the one thing my brothers and I can never have."

I swear my heart breaks a little more inside my chest when he leans forward and presses a soft kiss to my temple. His lips burn into my skin and my whole body starts to tremble.

When he starts to pull away, I say, "I didn't call them, my parents. I don't know who did, but I didn't, and I didn't tell them that it was you or your brothers that pushed me off that boat. Someone set me up."

Oliver nods, taking a step back, while exhaling a breath. He looks so conflicted when he says, "It doesn't change anything. We were born rivals and we'll remain rivals. Your family's damaged mine and I can't betray my parents by loving the enemy."

Love? I watch his Adam's apple bob up and down as he swallows. He turns to walk away, and I anchor my feet into the ground to stop myself from going after him.

"You love me?" I croak, unable to stop the question coming out.

Oliver blinks, his long lashes fanning against his cheek, "Don't waste your love on somebody who doesn't value it," he says before giving me his toned back and walking away. He's speaking in riddles, does he mean I don't value his love? Or they don't value mine?

My head is a cluster fuck, my emotions sprawled out across the concrete like my clothes were a short while ago. Someone is out to hurt me, to destroy me and I can't tell if it's the three men I'm falling for or someone else.

I turn and take one step before I come to a sudden halt yet again. Standing a few feet away from me with her arms crossed over her chest is Shelby.

"What the hell are you doing, Harlow? Haven't they done enough?" She scolds me.

"It's complicated, I..." I start but can't come up with any further explanation. "You don't understand."

"You're perfectly right, I don't understand. I don't understand how you can be so naive and keep letting them play you like this. Haven't they proven over and over again that they are out to get you? They don't love you, they don't even like you. You let them do this to you, you *let them* break you and then I'm the one you go to in order to pick up the pieces."

Her words slice into me like a dull knife. They hurt incredibly bad, especially because on some level I know she is right. I let them close, I let them touch me and kiss me, because I wanted them to, no matter the consequences. They wanted to hurt me, and I let them, but the way Oliver just looked at me, the words he spoke. He said love, he said he loved me and deep in my heart I feel that he wasn't lying. He loves me and I love him.

"I'm sorry you feel that way, Shelby. But I can't help the way I feel, and I think deep down they feel the same about me."

"Then you are stupid. They don't care about you and I'm done watching this train wreck. I can't stand seeing you like this, with *them*," she spits, and I don't miss the hateful tone in her voice.

She turns on her heels and before I can say another word, I watch my best friend walk away. The only person who has stuck with me throughout the years is walking away from me, and there is nothing I can do to stop it.

With my head hung in shame and my heart a bleeding mess I walk back up to my dorm, of course there is a group of girls snickering in the hallway. All three of them give me the stink eye as I pass, but I don't care. I don't know if it's them that massacred my clothes, or Tiffany maybe? Maybe it's even the brothers, I don't know.

All I know is they can cut me with their eyes, and kill me with their hatefulness but I will still rise the next day, like the sun hanging high in the sky I won't let them stop me from shining.

13

The next morning, I wake up with swollen eyes and a crust sticking to my eyelashes from crying all night. Rubbing the gunk out of my eyes I sit up in bed, for a moment I think my vision is fudged up but then I see that the twin size bed across the room from me is vacant.

I'm alone, Shelby's bed still made, letting me know she never came home last night. Did I lose my best friend? I grab my phone from the nightstand and check to see if she called, or even texted? When I see that she did neither, my heart sinks a little deeper into my stomach.

What is happening to me, to my life? Moving here was supposed to help things, but it seems like it only isolated me, made me weaker, sadder, which is hard to believe since I was sure nothing could destroy me like my father's lies had.

Wrapping my arms around myself I cuddle deeper into Sullivan's sweatshirt, which I'm still shamelessly wearing almost every night. It has long lost the smell of his laundry detergent, but in a weird way it makes me feel closer to him. I should probably burn the damn thing after all he's put me through, but I can't.

It's like a bandage for my heart, a security blanket, because even though I know he's not here and probably never will be again having an article of his clothing makes it seem like he is.

With a heavy heart, I peel the sweatshirt off my body and pull on the last clean pair of jeans I have. I pair it with an old sweater from the bottom drawer of my dresser, while making a mental note to go shopping later and replace everything that was destroyed yesterday.

Going through the motions of my morning routine, I wash my face, brush my teeth, and comb my hair. I don't bother putting on any makeup, since I'm not trying to impress anyone. My eyes catch on the reflection of the person in the mirror. I don't recognize her, the bags under her eyes, and the sadness in her dark gaze. My life wasn't perfect before I came here, but it wasn't this crazy, not this sad. Pulling up my mop of blonde hair into a messy bun, I take one last look in the mirror.

I can do this.

Who cares that someone's after me, or that half the school looks at me like I'm a sasquatch and the other half like they want to hurt me? Or that the three guys I had to fall for are the biggest bullies of them all.

I put my books and notepads into my bag and grab a granola bar to eat on the way to Social Psychology. It's the one class I share with Sullivan and I've been dreading going all week. Of the three brothers, Sullivan has avoided me the most.

Dragging my feet to the class, I make it there just in time. Sullivan is already sitting in his seat, his eyes trained on the professor, as if he can't wait for him to start the class. His arms are folded across his chest, the fabric of his shirt straining, making his arms look even more muscular. Internally I curse myself for even noticing, for thinking about how strong his arms felt when they were wrapped around me, making me feel safe, secure.

There is seriously something wrong with me.

I should not be lusting after one of the men that have made my life hell, after the enemy, the bully. But like a bad habit I just can't kick my addiction to the Bishops. The entire walk to my table I watch him out of the corner of my eye. Sullivan's eyes never move away from the board. He doesn't even glance up at me as I pass him, but I know he can tell

I'm there. I don't need him to look at me to know my presence affects him.

I know he can sense when I'm near just like I can do with him and his brothers. I can tell by the way his jaw flexes and his back oh so slightly straightens out, as if he is on edge. If he was a dog, his ears would be perked up right now, listening, and watching for danger.

When I reach my seat, I slump down into it, trying my best to pretend like I'm not affected by him being here. Placing my books, and notebook down on the desk I busy myself, making it look like I'm doing something. The professor starts his lecture, but no matter how much I try and pay attention, I can't.

Like a nervous tick, I spend the entire class chewing on the end of my pencil. I've written some notes down, but to be honest I didn't listen to half of what was said, my mind occupied with the brown haired, blue eyed asshole sitting five seats away from me, the asshole who hasn't even looked my way once. I expected him to be upset about my parents showing up, about the things that they told his brothers, but I never expected him to turn his back on me. I guess if anything I'm disappointed in him, in the fact that out of all three brothers he didn't even hear me out.

Lost in thought, I didn't even realize the professor had dismissed the class until people started getting up to leave. Sullivan is out of his seat and out the door before I even blink, the only proof that he was actually here is his rain water scent wafting through the air. Standing I shake my head in disbelief, how mature. Gathering up my book and notebook I shove them into my backpack and zip the thing before putting it on. Even with all the tension and awkwardness between us I feel a twinge of loss at his absence. I wish I didn't feel this pull towards him, like my heart is breaking when he fails to acknowledge that I exist.

Everything about us is wrong. Wanting to be with them, it's forbidden, like poisoned fruit that's dangling right in front of me. But, they're always slipping through my fingers. I escape the confines of the room and walk out the double doors and onto the sidewalk.

With my backpack slung across my shoulder and my English Literature book under my arm, I start walking towards my next class. I hurry, not wanting to be late for another class. Putting one foot in front of the other, focusing on my steps I don't notice the person approaching me until it's too late.

My lungs deflate and a scream claws up my throat as my backpack is ripped from my shoulder, tugging me backwards with it. My book slips from beneath my arm and tumbles to the concrete.

"What the hell?" I yell, whirling around to face my assailant. When I do, I realize that there are *two* people instead of one, and not just people but men. Fear trickles down my spine. I don't recognize either one of the two guys, but one thing appears in my mind in bright neon, I don't want to know them.

"Why haven't you answered any of our text messages?" One of the guys sneers at me, his eyes menacing in the afternoon sun. It takes me a moment to grasp onto what he's said. First, I think he might just be mistaking me for someone else but then he continues speaking and it's clear that he is talking about the banner with my cell phone number painted on it. "What the fuck? I sent you some nice dick pics, cock, and balls, and I expected you to send me something back."

"Don't you know it's rude not to return the favor? I suppose we can let it slide, but only if you let us see what you've got going on under that sweater," the second guy chimes in, licking his lips like I'm a medium rare steak waiting to be devoured.

"Get lost, douchebags" I spit as I bend down to retrieve my book. *Assholes.* This is just another reason, another thing that proves why I should forget about the brothers. If it wasn't for them, I wouldn't be dealing with this right now.

With the book in my hands I straighten. Mentally I've already made a plan to escape, to get away before this can escalate further, but as I turn to walk away from them, one of the fuckers grabs me, his meaty paw landing on my skin like a hot branding iron.

"Whoa, where the hell do you think you're going? We aren't done here, sugar. I showed you mine and now you're going to show me yours," he leers, his gaze roaming over my chest and even though I'm not showing cleavage, or any real skin, I feel exposed.

"I don't think so," I snap, trying to wretch my arm free from his grasp, but that only encourages him more, and he digs his fingers deeper into my flesh. To make matters worse, the second guy gets a hold of my other arm and before I can stop them, I'm being pulled towards the back of the building.

"Let go of me!" Panic is coating my words. I might as well have not said them at all because they ignore me as if I hadn't said anything..

Panic settles deep in my gut and I'm seconds away from starting to scream at the top of my lungs when a third figure appears beside us. Oh god, and I thought this couldn't get any worse, now there are three of them.

I'll never escape, never be able to fight them off. Inky black dread clouds my mind, and I feel the tears forming in my eyes.

"Usually when a woman says no, she means no." Sullivan growls, the sound of his voice soothing the panic threatening to take over my body. I'm so relieved that I could sink to my knees on the ground to thank him.

"Come on, man, don't be a dick, you can't keep her all to yourself, obviously she likes getting banged by more than one guy, hence you and your brothers using her," he retorts. His chuckles sounding strange.

Sullivan doesn't answer, at least not with words. With superhuman speed he catapults his fist into chuckling asshole's face, shutting both of them up in an instant. The guy staggers back from the hit, releasing my arm as he does.

His friend follows suit and flings my arm away like it's on fire.

"Fucking asshole," the guy moans, holding his hand to his jaw. Blood dribbles down his chin from a cut on his lip.

Momentarily I'm stunned, like a deer in the middle of the road, two headlights shining on it. The other guy balls his hands into tight fists, and it looks like all three of them might start fighting but then Sullivan takes a threatening step forward, his chest puffed out, his face set in a furious scowl, those massive paws of his clenched into tight fists. He looks like a Viking on the warpath, ready to destroy and kill everything, and anything in his way.

Even though there are two of them and one of him, they cower to him, taking a few steps backwards before turning around to walk away, well, more like run.

I rub at my arms where the skin feels bruised from them gripping it so tightly. Sullivan glares in the direction of the two assholes, before he turns his attention back to me. With a clenched jaw and murder in his blue eyes it looks like he wants to chase them down, to teach them a lesson. Only then do I let what almost happened, what would have happened if he wasn't there sink in. Fear floods my veins, turning the hot blood to icy slush. My whole body starts to shake, my heart threatening to beat out of my chest. A sheen of sweat forms against my brow.

"Has this happened before?" He demands, his hand gripping at the corded muscles of his neck. Tension seeps off of him, and slams into me. I'm terrified, but beneath that fear is something else, anger, sadness, pain, and it pushes through to the surface like a submarine breaking ocean water.

"You mean guys propositioning me? Grabbing me and asking to see me naked? Well yes, actually, see that kind of stuff happens when everybody thinks I'm into it. Wasn't that your plan all along?"

He sighs and looks away, as if he can't look into my eyes any longer. As if he feels ashamed. I cross my arms over my chest, mentally giving myself a hug. Silence stretches on between us, being this close to him is fucking with my head. I want to kiss him and smack him. Tell him that I did nothing wrong, and make him beg for forgiveness, but before I can do any of those things his sultry voice breaks the silence.

"Oliver isn't coming to English class, so come on, I'll take you there."

Without even looking at me, he starts walking towards the main building. I know he expects me to follow him, but I can't make my feet move. Standing there like I grew roots I watch him walk away. He stops after a few feet when he realizes I'm not following him. I want him to keep walking, but I also want to beg him to turn around, to take me into his arms. I'm conflicted, confused, *broken*.

"Don't be stupid, let's go, I'm not going to do anything to you. I'm just making sure that you make it to the class," he says over his shoulder.

Shaking my head, I say, "I think I've had enough for today. I can't do this right now. I'm going back to the dorms," I tell him, but still my legs won't move forward, it feels like I'm stuck in mud. Not stuck, drowning. All I want to do is go back to my room, lock myself inside, crawl into my bed, and pull my blanket over my head and forget. Forget the brothers, what just happened, the rivalry and all the family drama that comes with it. I want to bury it all, dig a hole and toss it inside.

"Fine, I'll take you there instead." He spins around and starts to walk back towards me, but still I don't move, unless you count my knees knocking together. When he realizes that I don't plan to move he sighs, as if I'm inconveniencing him.

I don't want to need him, them, but I can't help it. I'm weak, weak for the one thing I shouldn't want, the enemy.

Surprising me further with his actions, he steps closer and snakes an arm around me. Holding me close to his side, he gently starts to guide me back to the dorms. My steps are still unsure but with him by my side, steadying me, my legs seem to do just fine. The walk to the dorms isn't a long one, but today it feels like it's taking forever. Which I don't mind, not when it gives me more time with Sullivan.

Sullivan doesn't say anything, and neither do I. Instead I inhale his intoxicating scent that's wrapping around me like a blanket, sheltering me from the cold. Having him this close after everything that happened, his hands on me, his body close enough for me to feel the heat rippling off of it, it feels like heaven, like a healing balm against a wound. My vision blurs, and big fat tears start to fall from my eyes streaking down my cheeks. Crying is weak, but I'm exhausted, tired of barely holding it together.

We reach the dorms, and Sullivan starts to pull away, but I can't let him, for some strange reason I can't. Turning I wrap, both arms around his middle and press my face into his chest. He feels like him, and as stupid as that is to think I know he's the only thing that makes sense right now.

"Harlow," he whispers, pressing against my shoulders gently. I should have known he would still react with anger, with venomous rage. He peels me off his chest, holding me at arm's length. *He doesn't want you idiot, stop throwing yourself at him.* Let him go.

"I'm... I'm sorry..." I stutter, keeping my eyes on his chest, my head hung in shame so that he can't see how heartbroken I am, how lost I am without him and his brothers.

His hand comes into view, and then he's placing it beneath my chin forcing me to look up at him. With a heavy heart I let our gazes collide. God, he is handsome, like a Greek god, and GQ magazine model had a baby together. That jaw of his is clenched tight, and I itch to trace the sharp contours of his face. The tension in his face seems to ease away, and his gaze softens as he takes in my tear streaked cheeks.

"Do you want to stay here, or do you want to come with me?"

"Come with you?" I question, confused.

"Yes, with me, to the house?" His thumb brushes across my bottom lip. The touch caresses something deep inside me, something primal, and something that's waiting to bloom and break free. I can't explain it, but I feel it.

"You still want me?" How the words manage to slip past my lips I don't know.

Sullivan's blue eyes flicker with heat, "Want isn't exactly the word I would use. We need you, just like you need us. The way you're acting is how Oliver, Banks, and I have been acting since your parents showed up."

"But they hate me," I croak, my throat aching.

Sullivan shakes his head, "Come with me, at least for tonight."

I should say no, walk into my dorm, and go lay down in my bed alone, forever alone, but I can't. Physically, emotionally I can't, and I don't want to. I need them, just as they need me.

"Will you tell them it wasn't me, that I didn't call my parents? Will you help me make them understand?" I ask.

Something swirls in his eyes, and I can't pinpoint the emotion.

"You believe me, right?" The air deflates from my lungs as I wait for his response. I watch his Adam's apple as he swallows.

"Yes, Harlow. I believe you, now let's go. I'll talk to my brothers, get them back on team Harlow." Brushing his arm away I wrap myself around his middle again, holding onto him tightly, just to make sure this is real and not some sick dream.

"You're okay now, everything is okay." Sullivan whispers, a hand smoothing down my back. I squeeze my eyes shut and relish in his words.

It isn't okay, not yet, but it will be soon.

14

I fall asleep on the way to the Bishop residence, my side snuggled into the door of Sullivan's jeep. My eyes blink open as the car comes to a stop. It takes me a moment to realize we've arrived at the house. I'm beyond exhausted, my life is officially falling apart, and all I want to do is crawl under a rock and hide from the entire world. I stare at the monster of a house in front of me through the windshield. I'm worried. Afraid of how Oliver and Banks are going to react when they see me walk through that front door.

"Afraid?" Sullivan asks, as if he could read my mind. I twist around in my seat to face him. He's not smiling, in fact, he looks as cold as a statue. Impassive and cut off from the world. I think on his question. *Am I afraid?* Hell yes. Afraid of losing the last shreds of my heart, afraid of the unknown, afraid of where we will go from here. Is there any hope for us?

"A little," I confess, feeling like all my emotions are on display.

"It will be okay," he murmurs soothingly before getting out of the car. I open my own door and slip out. The short walk to the front door goes by in a flash. Sullivan twists the knob and walks in with me following closely behind.

I follow him step for step as he walks into the living room, almost as if he is my human shield, protecting me from the wrath of his brothers.

"Hey, what..." Oliver stops mid-sentence when he sees me hiding behind Sullivan. "What the hell is she doing here?"

Banks is sitting beside him, glaring at me, but not saying anything and I have the urge to turn around and run back out the front door.

"Just listen for a minute," Sullivan starts, while Oliver and Banks are already shaking their heads, anger wafting off of them. "She's going to stay here tonight," he announces despite his brothers' obvious disgust.

"Fuck that. There is no way we are letting her stay here," Banks speaks for the first time, his voice as hard as his facial features. "I'm done. I'm done with this whole thing." He declares.

My heart sinks even further. They're going to kick me out. I knew they would, but it still hurts to accept it. I let my head hang low, tucking my chin against my chest, and turn around to leave, but Sullivan stops me, his warm hand gripping my elbow.

"Go upstairs to my room, I'll be right there," he tells me, lifting his chin towards the staircase.

"Are you sure?" I ask, looking up at him, not daring to glance over at his brothers. Their icy gazes are shattering my still beating heart.

"Positive," he assures me. "Go, I'll be right there." He gives me a reassuring smile and call it weakness or a need for attention but against my better judgement I do as he says. I let my feet carry me up the grand staircase.

"This has to stop, Sullivan, we agreed this wasn't going to happen, that you weren't going to..." Oliver's voice drops dangerously low and I block it out, finishing my walk up the stairs. I drag my feet across the carpeted hallway, until I reach Sullivan's room.

Twisting the door knob, I open it and walk inside. I close the door behind me, taking in the space and smell. This strange feeling comes over me, I can't explain what it is, but it feels like peace, like safety, like nothing can get to me when I'm in this room. Slipping off my shoes, I let my body pull me towards the bed. Sinking down onto the mattress I almost moan, the tension seeping right out of me. I press my face into

Sullivan's pillows and inhale, his heady scent swirling in my veins. A warmth blankets my body, and for the first time in forever I don't feel alone. I don't feel afraid.

My eyes drift closed, as I slowly breathe in and out, the air passing my lips with ease. I stay like this for a long time, until eventually the exhaustion, fear, and pain of pretending everything is okay overtakes me and I drift off to a blissful sleep, with Sullivan's calming scent surrounding me.

OPENING MY EYES, I yawn, my gaze sweeping around the room, grey walls, black sheets, it takes me a moment before I realize where I am. The sound of running water coming from the attached bathroom pricks at my ears. I rub my eyes with the back of my hands and look at the door. It's cracked open, steam escaping from the room.

Sitting up on the bed, I run a hand down my chest flattening my now wrinkled sweater. The water shuts off and I hear the shower door open and close. Only then do I realize that Sullivan must be behind that door, and obviously very much naked. My cheeks heat stupidly and my lower belly tingles at the thought.

The door opens, and Sullivan enters the room wearing nothing but a white towel wrapped around his waist. My mouth goes dry and I think my heart actually skips a beat. I don't know where to look first, at his chiseled abs, or his shoulders, or his face, or the delicious V of muscle that leads down to a land that I shouldn't be thinking about. No man should look as good as he does, it's just not fair.

"Hey, you're up. Sorry if I woke you," he says nonchalantly, completely uncaring to the fact that he is not wearing any clothing. Droplets of water cling to his hair, and he shakes it a little bit sending water in every direction.

My chest starts to rise and fall, my nipples hardening against my bra.

"I-I mean, n-no... you didn't... I was..." I stutter, my tongue feeling heavy. I'm flustered even though I'm the one dressed and clearly have nothing to be embarrassed about.

Sullivan starts heading towards the bed, with each of his steps my pulse picks up, thrumming loudly in my ears. I nibble on my bottom lip, trying my best to ignore his presence but it's a lot harder than one would think. I shouldn't be thinking about him like this, naked, wet, our bodies gliding together. By the time he's standing in front of the bed, and only a few feet away from me, my pulse is all but racing.

"You're looking at me like you're scared I might eat you." The grin he gives me could set panties on fire.

"I-I just woke up," I say, mostly because I can't think of anything else to say.

"I noticed," that signature smirk of his widening, as if he knows the power he holds over me. "Do you want to take a shower too?"

"With you?" I ask like an idiot. He smells like soap, and water, and bad choices, really, really bad choices.

"Well, I just took a shower, but I could help you out of your clothes? And with other things, of course." His thick brows wiggle playfully.

Oh my God. He wants to help me out of my clothes. He's basically naked, besides the towel and he wants to get me naked. That would mean we would both be naked. *Together.* I might be inexperienced, but I'm not stupid. I know what happens when people get naked together, and they don't do much talking.

I swallow, but there's no saliva left in my throat, my mouth feels dry like I swallowed a cup of sand. "Okay," I answer meekly, my cheeks burning.

Sullivan blinks, his gaze widening, the playful grin slips off his lips, "You're serious? You want this?"

I lick my lips. Do I want this? Him, and his brothers? Obviously, I want them, but do I want to have sex? Do I want my first time to be with the same boy who took my first kiss, my first orgasm? I shouldn't want it to be him, not after everything, but it feels like I'm whole when we're together and I want to be whole, so badly.

"Yes... I want this... you, I mean... I want you." I stutter out, and grip onto the hem of my shirt, trying to build up the courage to pull the thing off and toss it onto the floor.

With a grin, he moves closer, his movements sleek, smooth, like a cat striding through the night. My body is burning up, it feels like I have a fever. I start to lift my shirt up and pause.

"What about Oliver and Banks?" I ask, needing to clear the air before we take another step. I want them as equally as I want Sullivan, but they don't want me right now, and I need this, the connection to be back in place. I need all of them.

"You want them too, don't you? You want all three of us." There's no judgement in his eyes, no anger. He's simply speaking the truth.

Releasing my lip from between my teeth I say, "Yes, I do."

"And you can have them, all of us, but not tonight. Tonight you're all mine." His voice is low, seductive. Reaching for me, he brushes some lingering strands of hair from my face, the simple touch sending my already stimulated nerve endings into overdrive.

I consider telling him that I'm a virgin but decide against it. What if he changes his mind because of it? I don't want to ruin the moment. I'm given little time to dwell on the thought before Sullivan pounces on me. The towel around his waist slips to the floor, and I gasp, just as he takes my cheeks into his hands. He kisses me, gently, but with an underlying hunger that has me eager for more. He kisses me until I'm breathless, until my chest is heaving, and my hands are shaking, until my lips are swollen. Until there is nothing but the two of us.

He only stops kissing me long enough to help me out of my clothes. Dipping his fingers into the waistband of my jeans, he drags them down my legs along with my panties, leaving me bare to him. Slinging them over his shoulder, they land on the floor somewhere behind him. My bra is next to go. He reaches around me and with skillful fingers he is somehow able to undo the clasp. My breasts fall forward without the support of my bra.

With a devilish grin that I feel deep down to my toes he flings the contraption over his shoulder just like he did the rest of my clothing.

Then there's silence as he takes a moment and just looks at me and I do the same in return.

His pupils are dilated, his eyes seem black instead of their normal stormy blue. His chest rises and falls rapidly, and his jaw is set in a hard line. He looks ruggedly handsome. My eyes wander lower, past his well-defined stomach and down the trail of russet brown hair leading me straight to his very erect penis. I gulp, I've seen dicks before, but nothing could prepare me for one *that* size entering me.

"Scared?" Sullivan asks smugly, stroking the thing leisurely, like he has all the time in the world.

"No." I shake my head, lying while trying to hide the nervousness from my voice. "I've just never…"

"Been with a guy as big as me?"

Arrogant asshole.

"Yeah, you could say that."

"I'll go easy on you, Princess." His wink makes me smile shyly, I can't help it. I have no idea what the hell I'm doing here. "But first…" He leans over me, his body hovering above mine as he lowers his head to my breast. His hot, wet tongue drags over my swollen nipple before he closes his mouth around the tight peak and starts to suck.

Sweet baby Jesus.

I moan into the room, my hands roaming over Sullivan's toned back and shoulders, pulling him even closer. Unable to lie still, my body moves like a snake underneath his touch, wiggling restlessly, my back arching off the bed. My body begs for more, it needs more.

He cups my other breast with his warm hand, kneading it, then he starts rolling my nipple between his thumb and index finger just as Banks had done. The sensations spiraling through me are explosive.

"Lie back," he orders gruffly, and I follow his command without thought or hesitation, coming to rest against his soft sheets. "So fucking pretty," he murmurs, nudging my legs apart. I can feel his eyes on my flesh. "I'm going to taste you, so be a good girl and stay nice and still. I need you soaked with need before my cock comes anywhere near your pretty pussy."

I swallow around the lump of fear forming in my throat and nod my head, my hands fisting into the sheets as he situates himself on his belly, spreading my legs wider to accommodate his huge form between my thighs.

He lowers his head, bringing his mouth to my center. I can feel his hot breath on my already slick folds, and I shiver at the onslaught of sensations rippling through me. I'm barely grasping onto reality, hanging on by a thread and then I feel his tongue dragging across my most sensitive parts. It's a brief touch, a caress, the feeling so foreign, so intense, I can barely handle it. No one has ever done this to me, no one's ever touched me this way and all I can think is that I want more, need more. Like an addict I'm desperate, willing to sell my soul for my next hit.

My hands leave the sheets and find their way into his thick silky-smooth hair. Threading my fingers through the strands, I rake my nails over his scalp. He releases a throaty moan, the sound vibrating through my core, coaxing a moan past my own lips.

"Ahhhh..."

"You taste exactly like I knew you would. Like strawberries and cream," his skillful tongue swipes over the sensitive bundle of nerves and my hips lift, a jolt of pleasure rippling up my spine.

"Sullivan," I whine, wanting more of him, feeling this deep, primal need trying to escape out of me.

"Patience." He tsks, with a light chuckle before getting back to work on tasting me. Using his fingers to spread my folds and suck on my swollen clit. The need builds, starting from behind my eyes and through every inch of my body, out of reflex I squeeze my thighs together, but Sullivan doesn't care, he continues to lick and suck as I grow slicker and slicker, my arousal damn near pouring out of me.

When I'm positive things cannot possibly get any better, he slips a finger into my channel, while still keeping pressure against my clit. He pumps in and out of me a few times, before adding a second finger and stretching me deliciously. Thrashing against the pillows, I bite onto my fist to stop myself from screaming out loud as he fingers me, while sucking on my clit with unforgiving need.

A blinding light flashes before my eyes, and my hips rise and fall as an indescribable pleasure lays claim to my soul. Sullivan's thrusts slow, as I slide down the mountain of pleasure.

"Oh my god," I whimper when the last ripples of pleasure have run through my body. Sullivan chuckles against the sensitive flesh of my thigh, his breath tickling me.

I don't even want to know how good sex will feel if it feels this amazing and all he did was use his fingers and tongue.

Before I can catch my breath, he starts kissing that same patch of skin and continues moving upwards, peppering open mouth kisses over my thighs, belly, ribs, and all the way back up to my breasts.

By the time he gets to my collarbone I can feel his enormous erection pressing up against my leg, his smooth skin caressing mine as he moves his body between my thighs. I'm panting now, salivating.

He reaches over to the nightstand and opens the drawer, digging around inside it. The break of passion gives me a moment of clarity. What the hell is he doing? A second later he pulls his hand out of the drawer, a small foil package in his hand.

Condom. *Oh shit, I almost forgot.* Looking down at me with raw need he rips the silver square open with his teeth. Taking the condom out, he reaches between us with one hand. Part of me wants to take a peek and watch him put it on, but I don't think I can actually tear my eyes away from his. It's like we are tethered to each other, an invisible hold binding us.

With his hand still between us, I feel him guiding himself to my center, and I spread my legs even further for him. The smooth head bumps against my still sensitive clit and my thighs automatically squeeze together at the sensation.

"Relax," he whispers into my ear as he starts to rub the head of his cock up and down, through my folds, spreading my juices over his cock before he brings himself back to my entrance.

Holding himself up with one arm his lower body against mine, his hips press into mine like a missing puzzle piece, the head of his cock pressing against my entrance. With a gentleness I didn't know he could possess he enters me slowly, stretching my walls, making me take all of his thickness.

He lowers his head, nestling his face into the crook of my neck, and I am glad he does, because I don't know if I could hide the tiny surge of panic and discomfort I'm experiencing right now. Needing to touch him, I grip onto his biceps, my nails sinking into the flesh leaving small half-moon indents behind.

I feel full, so full, and I know he's only inside a few inches. I gasp as a small sting and a slight burn ripples through my core as his cock breaks through the resistance, taking my virginity. I've given him all my firsts, and my heart. Sullivan must not even notice it, because he just keeps pushing inside of me until there is nowhere else to go, the head of his cock bumping against the back of my channel.

His lower body is now completely pressed to mine, leaving no space between us. With minimal effort he hitches my leg up, and swivels his hips, pressing deeper inside me. My chest heaves up and down, my heart fluttering so hard I'm sure even he can hear it.

"Fuck, this is a tight fit." Sullivan blows out a heated breath, sweat beading his brow, and I wonder if he's ever done *it* like this.

Seated deep inside me, he lifts his head his eyes moving from where were connected to look up at me. I can tell by the tension in his muscles that he's restraining himself. His lips part, and his gaze darkens.

"Do you want me to fuck you hard and fast or slow and gentle?" The edge to his voice, and crudeness of his words scares me a little, but I remind myself that this is Sullivan.

My Sullivan.

"Slow, please," I answer with a strong voice. With a clenched jaw he pulls all the way out of me, the air rips from my lungs with the sensation, and before I can fill them again, he's entering me, slowly, so slowly.

"Do you wish it was all three of us doing this with you right now?

That we got to take turns with you? Making you come over and over again."

"Yes," I answer breathlessly. "I would like that," I admit shamelessly. Sullivan smiles, his eyes lighting up, as he continues his slow leisurely strokes. Pulling out and pushing back in. In and out. In and out. Eventually the dull ache gives way to red hot pleasure that spreads out through my abdomen like lava erupting down the side of a volcano.

"I always knew it would be this good." Sullivan grunts, and he looks so beautiful right now, his eyes closed, his body straining above mine. I want to remember this moment for the rest of my life, the one singular moment in history when a Lockwood and a Bishop became one. Because that's what this is history and we're going to rewrite it.

"I've got to speed it up, Princess," Sullivan pants, his hot minty breath fanning against my throbbing pulse. "This slow pace is killing me."

"Okay," I give him a little nod and turn, pressing a kiss to his mouth. I drag my tongue across his bottom lip, silently asking for entry.

He opens for me all the way and our tongues meet for a sensual dance while he starts thrusting inside of me, his hips piston upward, going deeper, harder, and faster. His cock rubs against something deep inside me, and I feel the pressure building in my womb. He breaks our kiss and stares down at me, a wealth of knowledge and secrets in his gaze.

"I want you to tell me when you're close," Sullivan orders, and I nod unable to form a cohesive word.

He changes positions then, pulling away and pressing back onto his knees. He grabs onto my hips pulling me into him and in this position he seems even deeper, like he's a part of me.

My lips part into the shape of an O. And each time he bottoms out inside me a sliver of pleasure ripples through me. With a feral grin Sullivan places his thumb against my overly sensitive bundle of nerves and with all the sensations overtaking me it doesn't take long for me to reach my peak.

"I'm-I'm...coming," I gasp, barely getting the words out before my thighs start to quiver and my toes curl. My back arches off the bed, and Sullivan starts to curse as he holds me in place my pussy squeezing his cock with an evil vengeance.

"Fuck me," his pace grows faster, his grip on my hips harder, his head tipping back as euphoric pleasure overtakes his body. And then I feel his cock pulsing inside me as he lets out a deep animalistic growl before slamming into me one last time.

He collapses on top of me with a huff, his sweat covered body, blanketing mine with warmth and safety. I relish in this moment, having him so close, where no hate, no parents, no drama can reach us. I know the moment can't last forever, but I can hold onto it, keep it close to my heart. He rolls off me a second later, falling to the mattress beside me.

He reaches down and pulls the condom off with a wince, before throwing it into the trash bin next to the bed. I look down at my thighs, hoping that I didn't bleed onto the sheets.

Not wanting him to stop touching me, I roll over with him, planting my head on his chest and draping my arm over his torso. I close my eyes and suck in a deep breath. With my ear right above his heart, I can hear the steady rhythm clearly, like my own personal lullaby.

As if the sound was just made for me, calming and soothing me, I'm lulled to a deep slumber and for the first time in a long time I'm falling asleep knowing that everything is going to be okay now.

Everything will be fine, as long as I have Sullivan.

15

"This feels nice," I whisper into Sullivan's skin the next morning. Taking a deep breath, relishing in his scent, I run my fingers over his stomach, tracing each muscle as I go. I've been up for ten minutes, which I spent every second of cuddling and touching Sullivan.

He only woke up about five minutes ago and I'm not sure if it's because of all my touching and teasing or if he is just having morning wood but his cock is hard as steel. A sizable tent forming between his legs. My head would like to repeat what we did yesterday, but the dull ache between my legs says otherwise. So instead of instigating sex, I simply keep running my fingers over his skin.

"Yes, it does feel nice. I wish it was real," he says almost absent-mindedly.

I smile at his words. "Of course this is real, why would you think anything else?" I ask, without looking up.

"I know this isn't real for you. I know you don't actually want me." My hand on his stomach stills. Confused I raise my head so I can see his face. I take in his somber expression wondering why he is suddenly in this mood.

Still smiling, I ask, "If this isn't real for me and I didn't like you then why would I have given you all my firsts?"

"All your firsts?"

"Yes," I admit. "I gave you my first kiss, you gave me my first orgasm, and last night I gave you my virginity."

"Stop, Harlow," he growls, suddenly pushing me off of him. My mouth pops open and I'm completely dumbfounded by his sudden mood change. "I know…I know this is all a game to you. Do you really think I would believe you? Believe that I was your first kiss? That you were a virgin?" He tips his head, back and chuckles, "I might be stupid, but I know a liar when I see one, and you, Harlow Lockwood, have and always will be one."

I'm so stunned by this whole situation, that I'm literally speechless. He shakes his head and pushes off the bed. Stomping to his dresser, he pulls out the drawer with such force it almost comes out all the way. He grabs a pair of shorts from within and puts them on, damn near ripping them in the process.

"Sullivan, I'm not lying, last nig…" I say, once I find my voice again. Why does it feel like we're falling apart?

"You deserve an Oscar, you know?" He cuts me off, whirling around with a coldness in his gaze. "Your acting skills are on point. Maybe you'll start your acting career with the video I took of us fucking last night."

The air stills in my lungs, the only sound I hear is the thump, thump of my heart. It feels like it's being ripped in two and at any given second I expect it to stop working. His confession destroys me and shatters my world.

"You… you… filmed us having sex?" I stutter, my hands shaking, tears forming in my eyes instantly.

A smile spreads across his face and even though it seems forced, it wounds me deeply. Disgust and hurt spread through my body and I can't stop it. I scurry off the bed and gather my clothes from the floor, putting each piece on as I go. I can't do this anymore. I can't keep being their punching bag, reliving a past that I'm so helplessly trying to break free from.

With everything but my jeans on I glance over at Sullivan who just stands there watching me with an unreadable expression.

"You're right, I *am* a great actress. So committed to my role, I grew back my hymen for you, to make this more believable," I spit out, shoving my legs into my pants, I point to my thighs which still have streaks of blood on them. Sullivan follows my gaze, his mouth pops open when he sees the small smudges of blood. "Don't believe me asshole, check the condom, or maybe think back to the way you fucked me, of how nervous I was," I pull my pants up the rest of the way and button them.

Sullivan looks like he's about to say something, but I'm done. I'm not waiting around to hear what it is he has to say. Some lame-ass apology that means nothing. Because I mean nothing to him. To them. I'm so done. Done with the lies. Done with the games. Done with him and his brothers, his family, all of it. Just done!

"Have a nice life," I murmur on the way out of his bedroom door. Tears escape my eyes as I run through the house.

"Wait," I hear Sullivan call from upstairs just before I slam the front door behind me.

How could I have been so stupid? I gave myself to him. I loved him, I loved all three of them and all they did was play games. I'm nothing more than a pawn to him and his brothers.

I run down the sidewalk, my shoes pounding on the pavement, and the tears running down my face uncontrollably. Pushing my legs as far as I can, I only slow when I become lightheaded. Needing to catch my breath after running through the neighborhood for I don't know how long. My chest aches, my lungs burn, and a killer headache has formed right behind my eyes.

I stop and look around, taking in my surroundings, and I realize that I have no idea where I am. Reaching into my back pocket I pull out my phone and find the contact info for the only person I can think of right now.

Caroline answers after the third ring. "Harlow, what's up?" Her voice is cheery, as usual. Completely oblivious to my despair.

"Caroline," I sigh with relief, "can you come and pick me up?"

"Of course, are you okay?" She loses her cheery tone, concern replacing it.

"Yes, no, god, I don't know. I'm at…" I look around me, trying to find a street sign. "McKinley Road," I say when I finally find one.

"I'll be there in ten minutes."

Ending the call, I sit down on the curb and let my head fall into my hands. I vow to myself never to be dumb enough to fall for their tricks or antics again. By the time Caroline's car pulls up, there must be a puddle of tears in front of me, because I haven't stopped crying since I got off the phone with her. She jumps out of the car and runs around to where I'm sitting.

"Oh my god, what happened?" She kneels down next to me, her arms circle around me. "Please, tell me. What's wrong?"

"It was all a lie… Sullivan and his brothers played me," I say in between sobs. "I loved them and…"

"Oh, Harlow, I'm so fucking sorry. Come on, girl, let's get you home."

"No, I don't want to go home. I need to talk to Shelby. Can you take me to the gallery downtown?"

I need to apologize to my friend, she warned me about the Bishops, and I didn't listen. She's been the only constant in my life, the only one who always stood by me. She is the only one I can trust, and I've been neglecting her. I need her, now more than ever.

"Of course, come on," she ushers me into the passenger seat, and even buckles me up when I don't move to do so myself.

"Are you going to tell me what happened?" Caroline asks half way through town.

"I…I don't even know. Everything was fine one minute and then it wasn't." Which is the truth. One minute it was pure bliss and the next, utter horror.

She doesn't ask me any more questions and I'm more than grateful for the silence. I don't think I could answer anymore of her questions anyway.

"Thank you, Caroline," I gaze over at her once we've stopped in front of the art gallery. "I mean it, thank you. You've been a great friend."

"Any time, Harlow. Call me if you need anything." We hug before I exit the car. My face is still red, and my eyes are still swollen from crying but I'm past being self-conscious.

Taking a deep breath, I push the gallery's doors open, a bell rings above my head and I walk into the clean space. Modern looking sculptures are sitting on hip high pedestals in the center of the space and pictures of all sizes are decorating every wall in the room.

A petite woman walks into the showroom greeting me with a wide smile. She is wearing a skin tight pencil skirt, a matching crop top, and four-inch high heels that look like they could break some ankles.

"Hi, can I help you?"

"Yeah, I'm looking for Shelby. I'm sorry to show up here, I know she is working but this is kind of an emergency."

"Who?" The woman looks genuinely confused, her eyebrows drawing together.

"Shelby," I say louder, she must have not heard me clearly.

"Doesn't ring a bell. Is she one of our artists?"

"Oh...ah, maybe... maybe, I'm at the wrong gallery, I'm sorry," I say embarrassed, before turning on my heels.

"This is the only gallery in town, miss."

I freeze with my hand hovering inches away from the doorknob. My mind goes blank and then this feeling of utter dread creeps its way up my spine and settles into the base of my skull.

Nothing makes sense, everything I thought I knew is wrong. My life built with building blocks of lies and deceit and like a Jenga tower someone pulled the one piece that has it all crashing down.

I feel like I'm trapped in this moment, my mind frozen in time. My thoughts hovering somewhere in between disbelief and unbelievable despair.

"Are you okay, miss?"

No... no, I'm not okay and I don't know if I ever will be.

I walk back outside and down the sidewalk. I know there are people walking down the side of the road like me, cars driving on the road, I know they are there, but I don't see them clearly. Everything around me is a blur. My mind overwhelmed with everything that has happened today.

My body's numb, my emotions in disarray. I feel like I'm not even here, like I'm only a shadow of myself, a ghost who isn't part of the world at all.

Putting one foot in front of the other, at least I think that's what I'm doing. I look up, the scenery changing around me, the ground beneath me suddenly seems different. Sounds piercing through the fog surrounding my brain. Someone is screaming, but I can't make out what is being said. Then something catches my eye. I look up to see two bright lights heading straight for me. But I'm not fast enough, there is no time...

∼

DARKNESS.

Nothing but darkness.

I'm not sure where I am. But wherever it is all I know is darkness. This place has no end, no beginning, no up, down, right or wrong.

There is no love or hate, no pain, but also no happiness.

I try to remember how I got here, or where I'm from but my mind is nothing but a wasteland.

All I am and all I know is darkness.

Until one day, when there was more.

BEEP.

. . .

Beep.

Beep.

A steady rhythm calling me from somewhere unknown. The sound seems close and a million miles away all at once. For a long time, that's all there is.

"It's been ten days," a woman's voice suddenly breaks through.

"Mrs. Lockwood, these things take time. Harlow suffered a major brain injury. It will take time for her to recover. I can assure you that she is in the very best hands here at the clinic."

"She better be, considering what we are paying you," another man's voices meets my ears. It's deep, scary even and I make a mental note not to mess with that man.

After that, I hear the opening and closing of a door, followed by chairs moving around.

"You heard the man, love, let's go home, there is nothing we can do for her right now."

Suddenly, I have the overwhelming urge to open my eyes, I want them to see that I'm here, that I'm awake. I don't want to be left alone in the darkness again. Willing my eyes to open, it takes every ounce of strength I have. I feel like my eyelids have turned into lead and my strength has diminished to one percent.

Still, by some miracle my eyes slowly blink open. The bright yellow light coming from the ceiling overhead blinding me momentarily, but I keep squinting and blinking until I can make out the room and its contents.

"Oh my God! She's waking up!" The woman's high pitch voice hurts my ears a little but her hands covering mine are soft and warm and make up for the pain. "Oh, Harlow, you're okay. Everything is going to be fine now, I promise."

I blink, confused, then I look down at her hand and pull mine out of her grasp.

I look up into her big tear-filled blue eyes, horror, and shock reflect back at me and I ask the only question that I can, "Who are you?"

BOOK TWO

BAYSHORE RIVALS BOOK TWO

USA Today Bestselling Author
J.L. BECK
C. HALLMAN

PROLOGUE

Sullivan

I spend all night letting yesterday's events run through my mind. Fuck, how could I have been so stupid? The moment I saw the red smudges on the insides of her thighs, my heart fell into my stomach, and I knew she wasn't lying. I still don't understand how I didn't see it before. How could I have been so blind? What we had was real and I used her. I broke her.

I could see it in her beautiful blue eyes, the moment her heart cracked and shattered into a million pieces. The light inside them dimmed and all because of me. Fuck, my gut hurts just thinking about it. I wish I could forget, but I won't.

We could have been happy, but it doesn't matter now, it's too late. Nothing I say will undo what's already been done. The only thing left to do now is figure out why our parents would have told us these lies about Harlow.

After hiding out in my room for most of the day, I walk downstairs to get something to eat, hoping Oliver and Banks are gone. I don't know if I can handle more of their hate right now. We agreed on not going through with our plan and I did it anyway. They believed her and I didn't. They were right and I was wrong, so terribly wrong. I let everyone down, because I believed lies, so many fucking lies.

When I walk into the kitchen, I almost turn around. They are both there, sitting at the kitchen table, talking about getting a new car.

They stop talking when I enter. I'm immediately met with hardened glares. I open the fridge to grab some sandwich meat and a pack of cheese. Turning around, I find both Oliver and Banks looking down at their phones, apparently, they're ignoring me now. I have half a mind to start telling them I'm sorry again, but I don't, it won't do me any good anyway.

Instead, I continue putting my sandwich together as quickly as I can to escape the suffocating tension in the room. I need to get back to my room so I can wallow in my own misery. With my sandwich made I start to put everything back into the fridge, the buzzing of my cell in my pocket interrupting me.

I fish it out, hoping the entire time that maybe, just maybe, it's Harlow. My clammy hands nearly have me dropping it as I swipe the screen to unlock it, disappointment striking me through the heart like an arrow.

Tension coils in my gut. It's just Marc, one of the guys from school.

I'm about to shove the device back in my pocket without looking at the message when Oliver turns to me, his face a mask of horror, "Oh, my God, did you get Marc's message?" The tone of Oliver's voice tells me instantly that whatever Marc sent him is serious, so I do the only thing I can. I open the message.

Inside the message is a link, which I click on, which leads me to a newspaper article from the Bayshore newspaper. First, I'm confused, but then I start to read the headline and my heart sinks into my stomach.

Bayshore student left in critical condition after hit and run.

I don't know why, or how, but I know without a doubt the student they're talking about is Harlow. Call it a gut feeling or whatever you will, but I know. Still I continue reading, my eyes unable to move fast enough.

A young woman, who reportedly is attending Bayshore University, was struck by a car downtown, near the art gallery, witnesses say. The car then fled the scene and the woman was rushed to the hospital. The incident is still under investigation...

Unable to read another word, I turn off my phone and place it down on the marble counter, before sagging against it.

I did this... this is all my fault.

"It's her, I know it's her," I say, more to myself than to my brothers. When I look up, Oliver is staring at me, there's a feral look in his eyes, one that I've never seen directed at me before and I'd be lying if I said I didn't hate myself in that moment.

"If she dies, then you might as well be dead too." The anger and hurt in his voice chills me to the bone.

"You know I didn't intend for any of this to happen."

Oliver shakes his head, before getting up, the sound of his chair scraping across the floor. Banks doesn't even look at me, obviously, disgusted beyond belief. Oliver walks over stopping on the other side of the island. His hands are clenched into tight fists at his sides and I wouldn't be surprised if he tried to slug me right now.

It's not like I don't deserve it.

"It doesn't matter if you intended for it to happen, it did, and the consequences are resting on your shoulders now. I just want you to know that if she dies, it will be partially your fault. If you would have believed her, she would be with us right now... safe. She didn't deserve what you did to her." His voice trembles, his gaze hardening, and I nod acknowledging his words, because like always, he's right.

He was right when he said we shouldn't do it. He was right when he said Harlow was more important than any family rivalry.

I should've listened to him. I should've followed my heart, but I didn't, and now the one person who shouldn't have paid the price, has. But I'm a Bishop, and above all, a man, so I'll do what I need to do to make things right.

Harlow Lockwood will be ours again, and this family rivalry ends now.

16

HARLOW

ONE MONTH LATER

Staring down at the pale blue comforter, I try and piece the jigsaw puzzle called my life back together again, but every time I start to think about it, about anything, nothing pops up. It's been three days since I was released from the hospital. I've been living in this huge house that is supposed to be my home... but it just doesn't feel like it.

There are no memories; happy or sad, there is nothing—a dark, endless sea of blank space. It's so strange to think that one day you are whole, your life full and vibrant, and the next you're merely a shell of what you used to be. A soft knock sounds against my bedroom door, and I look up, knowing it's the woman that calls herself my mother.

"I know this is a lot for you to take in and all, but your father wanted me to let you know that Matt, your fiancé will be stopping by tomorrow. Your appearance while he is here is very much appreciated."

I will my mouth to work, for words to come out, but they just won't. Every day since I got home, either my mother or my father have been with me, trying to make me remember a life they say I enjoyed. Though deep down in my gut, none of it feels right; this huge house, the expensive dresses, and maids to do whatever I want. It doesn't seem like something I would've liked, let alone enjoyed.

In fact, this place feels like a prison, but I don't understand why. I'm sure any girl my age would enjoy having the world at her fingertips, which clearly, I had, and still do, so why does it feel like none of those things mattered to me.

"Harlow!" my mother barks, and I blink from the blank space in my mind.

"Yes. I'll be here." I tell her softly, unsure of how I should respond, how I would've responded before. Am I being myself? I don't know. It occurs to me then, where else would I be? I have nowhere to go, no friends, besides Shelby, who came to visit a few times, but was of no help. A fiancé that I don't remember, and haven't met, because he's not been in the country until now.

My mother's icy gaze softens, "You've been in your room almost all day, maybe you could come downstairs and have dinner with us? I had Margaret make your favorite; baked spaghetti." *Baked spaghetti?* Hmm, it wouldn't hurt to see if eating this so-called favorite meal of mine jarred a memory.

"Sure, I would like that," I tell her, as I climb off the four-poster bed, and pad across the floor. She smiles at me, but the smile doesn't reach her eyes and looks forced, awkward even, as if it's not something she often does.

Silently we walk down the hall, and then down the grand staircase before entering the dining room. There's a chandelier that hangs above the table, giving the room an elegant feel. My father is already sitting at the table and gives us a tense smile when we enter.

"It's very nice of you to join us for dinner, Harlow. Have any of your memories returned?" he asks, almost in a robotic way. I pull out the chair next to him, and sag down into the seat, though I would much rather have taken a seat at the far end of the table.

Margaret, as well as another maid, brings out dinner, placing plates down in front of us like it's a restaurant, and we're not capable of making our own plates.

"So, what did I do for fun? Did I go anywhere? Hangout with anyone?" I blurt out, causing both of my parents to look up at me like I just asked them to solve a math problem. "The doctor said I'm supposed to do things I did before to jog my memory, but I don't exactly know what that was, and I've been kind of bored. So, what did I do?"

Dad places his silverware back down on the table, glancing over at my mother before turning back to me, "Ah well... you liked to go shopping, and hang out with Shelby. You and Matt used to go out on dates, but once he went to France to run the French branch of his father's company, you talked on the phone a lot."

I stare at him, dumbfounded, "That... that sounds great. Anything else? Bike riding? Hiking? Did I like to do homework, or did I hate it? Was Shelby my only friend or were there others?" His face seems to grow tenser with each question, a vein in his forehead bulging under the pressure.

Why is this so hard for them to talk about?

"That's really it, you spent most of your time with Shelby or Matt after you graduated high school. Like we already told you, you wanted to take a year off before thinking about college," he finally answers, seeming angry, but how would I know, maybe this is his normal behavior.

"Okay, maybe I can go shopping tomorrow morning before Matt comes over?" I ask because honestly, I'm not sure if I have to or not. I'm an adult, yes, but feel more like a child right now. A lost child.

"Sure, why not. I can come with you..."

"You don't have to," I cut my mother off before she can finish. "I can go by myself. I don't want to burden you guys any more than I already have."

"I don't know if that's such a good idea." Dad's voice cuts through the air, and I glance over at him, shocked.

What does that mean?

That I can't leave on my own? As if he can hear my thoughts, he clears his throat, and says, "What I meant was, you don't know this area yet, you need to get familiar with everything again before going out into the city by yourself. It's not safe."

Right, that makes sense.

"I'll be happy to come with you, dear," Mom chimes in. "We are long overdue for a mother-daughter shopping trip."

"Perfect, let's go together then," I say, forcing a smile because I'm not sure how to genuinely smile yet.

THE NEXT MORNING is spent going from one high-end boutique to the next. My mother has already bought a fortune worth of clothes while I only hold one measly bag with some pajamas. I picked them out at the last place to keep her happy. This is clearly her element since it seems she's thoroughly enjoying herself; smiling, laughing, and trying on clothes like she's a doll. I, on the other hand, am bored out of my mind and have been annoyed since store number two. I can't imagine ever enjoying this. Tossing money around like it's nothing.

I'd have more fun watching paint dry.

"Okay, last stop is Macy's, and then we'll go have lunch at the little Italian place across the street," Mom says, utterly oblivious to my lack of enjoyment. I cringe at the thought of enduring another three hours of shopping this afternoon.

We climb into the car that's pulled up in front of the boutique, and the driver takes us to the large department store, which is a couple blocks away, dropping us off at the main entrance, like we are too good to walk across the parking lot or something. All I can think is, this isn't me, no way. It doesn't feel right. It doesn't seem like me. I might not know who I am, or have any memories of who I once was, but in my gut, I know this person isn't me.

Once inside, Mom heads straight for the shoes, dragging me behind her. With my hands hanging down at my sides, I watch her try on about twenty different pairs before we head to the dresses section of the store.

As if she finally notices that I'm with her, her gaze sweeps over my empty hands, "You haven't bought anything yet, you need to buy something here. Something nice to wear this afternoon when Matt comes by. How about this?" she suggests, handing me a strapless summer dress with cherries on it.

"Maybe," I tell her while inspecting the dress. It's not terrible, maybe a little shorter than I like, but still wearable.

"Well, go on, go to the dressing rooms and see if it fits," she orders, her eyes not even meeting mine but roaming over the racks. "Oh, look at this one over here..." she trails off and walks away, acting like a child distracted by a shiny new toy.

Standing there, I stare at her for a long moment, with the dress in my hands, before deciding to try it on. Getting a stall without any hassle, I place the dress down on the hanger and start to pull off my shirt. The fabric barely passes over my head when the door suddenly bursts open. A scream lodges itself in my throat, and before it can pass my lips, the man who has invaded the small space uses his hand to cover my mouth. Peering up into his blue eyes, I feel this strange wave of deja vu overtake me.

"Shh, Harlow, don't scream, please. I've been trying to get to you for weeks. You have to hear me out," the strange, but very attractive man pleads. Shaking my head, I feel anything but fear for the person in front of me, which makes zero sense, it's almost like... I know him.

"Please, Harlow, just one minute and then I'll be gone, I promise I'm not here to hurt you." My brow furrows in confusion. He sounds sincere and honestly kind of desperate, and I don't know what to do. If I should scream and push him away or let him explain himself.

"I'm going to pull my hand away, please don't scream." Those eyes, those big piercing blue eyes hold mine, and something compels me to nod my head. Letting the stranger know that I won't scream, even though I know I should.

Slowly, he pulls his hand away, and I suck in a ragged breath of fresh oxygen, letting it filter into my lungs. With it comes his intoxicating scent; raindrops, and sandalwood, like the forest after a storm. A kaleidoscope of butterflies seems to take flight in my stomach right at that moment. Whoever this man is, I knew him, and so did my body.

"Harlow, you don't belong here, I know that probably doesn't make sense, but you have to believe me, your parents are lying to you. You weren't happy here. It's all a lie. Do you understand me?"

I stare up at him, listening to every word that passes his lips, trying to make sense of each one. Who is this guy, and why is he saying all of these things to me? How does he know my parents? How does he know that I wasn't happy here? I have so many questions, but there are no answers, at least not within sight.

"My brothers and I believe that you're in danger here. I want to help you, will you please let me help you?"

"I... I don't know who you are..." I stutter.

The man smiles coyly, "Sullivan Bishop, and we have a past. Some I wish you could remember and some I hope you never do."

Puzzled, I ask, "What does that mean?"

Sighing, he says, "Nothing, right now. I didn't come here for my own wants. I came here because I'm worried about you. You almost died, Harlow." His voice cracks at the end, showing the raw emotion he's feeling.

"I'm not in danger," I answer without hesitation. "I was in a car accident."

"You don't understand," Sullivan growls, pressing a clenched fist to his lips. "What do you remember? Anything?"

I shake my head, growing more and more confused. The air becomes heated between us, and all I can feel, and smell in the confined space is him. It's annoying and comforting all at once.

"Harlow, sweetie, how does the dress fit? Let me see it." My mother's voice filters through the closed door. Before I can open my mouth, Sullivan presses a finger to my lips.

Panic fills every crevice on Sullivan's face, and he grabs me gently by the shoulders, leaning into me, his hot breath caressing my ear, "She can't know I'm here," he whispers so only I can hear him. I nod, letting him know I understand. He releases his hold on me and takes a small step back. He's trusting me and deep down I know I cannot let him down.

"It didn't fit. I'm about to come out," I call through the closed door. Only then do I realize that I had taken my shirt off and have been standing here with nothing but my bra and jeans on the entire time. Heat creeps up my chest and into my cheeks and Sullivan crouches down picking up the shirt which I dropped when he stormed in here. He hands it to me, and I take it from him mouthing a thank you, before slipping back into it.

He didn't even look at my chest, just my eyes and face.

"Awe, I really wanted to see you in it. Doesn't matter, you've got plenty of dresses at home. We need to go if we're going to be home when Matt and his father get there."

"Coming, just a second..." I answer. Sullivan's gaze turns murderous, but he doesn't say anything else. I want to ask him what she said that angers him so much, but I don't. I watch as he presses himself all the way to the wall so I can open the door without him being seen. I grab the dress, which never left the hanger and step out of the dressing room like nothing ever happened.

"You okay?" Mom asks, looking up from her cell phone, her eyes roaming over my face, "You look a little flustered."

"Uhh," I clear my throat, "I'm fine, just ready to go home is all."

She stares at me as if she's trying to determine if I'm telling the truth or not, and I start to sweat, my gut tightening, twisting and turning.

"Okay, let's have lunch, then we can go home and freshen up."

"Great." I plaster a smile on my face, and we head out of the store, but with each step I take, I can't help but wonder, who is Sullivan Bishop, and why does he think I'm in danger, especially in the presence of my own family?

I try to forget about him and the whole conversation in the dressing room, but I can't. By the time we get home, my head is about to explode from trying to figure out what he was talking about.

"I'm going to go hang up these new dresses," my mother says, heading up the stairs.

"Mom?" I call after her, making her stop to look back at me, smiling. "Who is Sullivan Bishop?"

As if I've brought up a terrible memory, her face falls, and her eyebrows pull together. "Where did you hear that name?"

Oh shit, I didn't think about that.

"I-I... remembered it," I lie.

"Just the name?" Mom questions nervously.

"Yeah, do I know that person? Who is he?"

"Oh gosh, Harlow. Sullivan is a terrible person, he terrorized you all through high school. Bullied you and turned all your friends against you. Shelby, bless her heart, was the only one who stuck by you." Well, that explains why I have no other friends, I guess.

"His parents are no better. They've been trying to ruin our business for years. Those are not the kind of memories I wanted you to remember, honey. Sullivan Bishop is someone you want to stay away from, as far away as possible. He is a master manipulator, and for whatever sick reason he's always hated you and has tried everything in his power to hurt you."

Hated me? I don't know why those words hurt so much, but there is a distinct ache in my chest. Why would he hate me? Why would anyone hate me?

"Harlow, if he ever comes near you, I want you to tell us, okay?" she says, but it almost sounds like a warning.

"Do you hear me, Harlow?"

Blinking from the trance, I say, "Yes, of course." Though it's a lie. Sullivan Bishop already approached me, and for some strange reason, I get the feeling that there is more than just hate between us.

17

After looking through my closet for what seemed to be the better part of the afternoon, I've managed to find a yellow sundress, and I've paired it with a some wedged sandals, that look like they've never been worn. Once dressed, I look at myself in the mirror. I feel as if I'm wearing a mask, hiding behind these clothes, and make-up.

This isn't you, Harlow, whoever you are.

The dinging of the doorbell, though faint, meets my ears. Matt and his father must be here. I apply a small amount of lip balm before I turn and walk out of my room. I wonder what Matt is like. Have we known each other since we were kids? My father never really explained to me how our relationship had come about, and it seems that whenever I ask questions, I get nothing in return, no answers, just more confusion.

If I didn't know any better I would think that my parents were hiding something, but that's the thing, everything seems as if it's a secret, hidden beneath a veil, that's what it feels like when you can't even remember what your favorite color is, or your favorite food.

Exhaling as I descend the stairs, each step I take toward the dining room, making me more, and more nervous about this dinner. I know this *Matt*, whom I'm supposed to marry, even less than I know my own parents, and I hardly know them at all.

This couldn't be more uncomfortable. Ever since I woke up in the hospital, I feel like I'm in a constant state of being uncomfortable. Not knowing things I should, always feeling behind and left out of every conversation.

All I have to go on are the things my parents tell me, and it's clear they're only telling me what they want me to know. Which leads me to wonder...what if that guy, Sullivan, from earlier was right? What if I don't belong here, what if I was never happy here? And if I wasn't happy here, where was I happy? Was I happy at all? I need more answers.

The questions swirling in my head start to cause a throbbing behind my eyes that has me dizzy by the time I reach the bottom of the stairs.

"Harlow," my mother calls for me as she enters the foyer, a shocked look in her eyes as if she's surprised to see that I actually came down on my own, or I dressed up. It could be either one, I suppose.

"You... you look beautiful, it's been a while since I've seen you in a dress." Her eyes brim with joy, an infectious smile cresting her lips.

"Thank you." I smile back at her, it slips a little when she grabs my hand and pulls me toward the dining room.

"Matt's father, Richard, is a close friend of the family. You and Matt basically grew up together. He is only two years older than you. We used to spend the summers together in the Hamptons." I can hear the sadness overtaking her voice as she speaks. "Anyway, Matt will be the perfect gentleman, and he knows that you're still working through your memories, so he promised to give you space and lots of patience."

I almost snort, he promised to give me space and patience? She talks as if he's my owner, as if what he says goes? We're not married, and in my eyes, we aren't even engaged until I remember the engagement. I cannot be with a man that I don't even know or remember. He needs to wait until I do, or he has to make me fall in love with him again.

Three deep voices filter through the walls, they're chatting over a football game or some type of sport, I don't really care. It ceases as soon as we enter the room. Like a trained dog, Matt gets up and walks over to me, and for the first time, I look up into a pair of deep brown eyes that belong to the man I'm supposed to be madly in love with. So, why don't I feel anything? I felt a connection to Sullivan, and we're supposed to hate each other.

"Hi, Harlow. I'm sorry I wasn't here to see you in the hospital, and when you returned home," he smiles, and though he has a sweet smile with perfectly straight white teeth peeking out past his pink parted lips, nothing about him seems friendly, or kind. Yes, he's handsome with an angular jaw, and perfectly sculpted cheeks, and he's tall with hair you could run your fingers through, but nothing about him appeals to me.

It feels like I'm looking at the off-brand version of what I would really like.

"Hi, Matt. I'm sorry I don't remember you, or our engagement," I give him a half-hearted smile because honestly, I am sorry. I want to remember probably as much as everyone in this room wants me to.

"It's okay, we can always make new memories. Our relationship was mainly long distance. We had agreed to get married when I returned home, but I suppose that's not happening now." He leans down and presses a kiss to my cheek, startling me.

For a moment, I forgot that we weren't alone in the room, until he moves away, pulling out my seat for me. I take the spot directly beside my mother, and let Matt scoot my chair in.

Dinner passes at a snail's pace, and while the food is delicious, my appetite is non-existent. When Richard and my father move to his office to discuss business, I plan to part ways and go upstairs to drown myself in a book. Whoever I was before this, at least had excellent taste in books.

Pushing from the table, I move to get up when my mother places a hand against my arm, her eyes bleeding into mine.

"Why don't you and Matt take a little walk around the mansion?"

"Uhh…" I flounder, my eyes darting to Matt who seems to perk up at the suggestion. "Sure, though I have no idea where anything is… I'll probably just get us lost."

"I've been here enough times for both of us," Matt says, moving toward me. My mother smiles obviously pleased with herself. So much for escaping this dress and shoes for my PJs, bed, and a good book. Looks like I'm taking a walk around the house that I don't remember with a man that I don't know. Sounds like the start of a serial killer movie.

Matt takes my clammy hand into his and guides us out of the dining room, tugging me toward a pair of French doors off the kitchen, which lead outside. Nibbling on my bottom lip, I wonder apprehensively if I should allow him to hold my hand or if I should pull away. I certainly don't feel like holding his hand.

Before I realize it, we've reached the garden, a massive water fountain is in the center, and for a moment, I'm mesmerized, caught in a trance over the profound beauty before me.

Matt releases my hand, the loss of contact startling me.

"I was hoping by showing up here tonight I would get laid."

Holy shit, this guy didn't just say that? I must have misheard him, right? My mouth pops open, and I cross my arms over my chest, flames of angry fire flickering in my belly. I want to slap him, kick him in the balls, and shout at him, but I don't.

"Okay, I take it that's a no," he says, chuckling and for the first time, I see him smile, really smile. He sighs and sinks down onto one of the marble benches that overlooks the garden. I watch as he taps on the bench beside him, obviously signaling for me to come sit with him, but the last thing I want to do is sit next to him now.

Actually, I can think of a couple hundred other things I would rather do.

Frustrated about my lack of movement, he growls, "Jesus, Harlow, it was a joke. I know your memories are gone, but I didn't think your sense of humor was too."

"Didn't sound like a joke," I sneer.

He rolls his eyes and pulls out a pack of cigarettes from his pocket, "Whatever, your sense of humor obviously sucks, by the way."

"Maybe you just aren't good at telling jokes," I tilt my head to the side, watching as he lights up the end of his cigarette, a bright cherry appearing at the end. Sucking in a deep breath of nicotine, he holds the air inside his lungs for a moment before releasing it, a pillar of smoke snaking out of his nose and into the chilly night air.

"Did you miss me?" he asks, his eyes piercing mine before I break the connection and look away.

"No, I wasn't lying when I said I didn't remember you."

"I can help you remember me..." his voice trails off, "I mean if you want me to." I know I should be shoving my foot up this guy's ass by now, but my curiosity outweighs my need to hurt him.

"Did we ever... you know?" My cheeks start to flame as the question rolls off my tongue.

"Fuck?" Matt hisses into the air, "No, you never let me inside those cotton panties of yours." He takes another drag of his cigarette, exhaling the smoke, before rubbing the end against the bottom of his shoe. His insult doesn't go unnoticed. It's clear to me that I was a good girl before all of this happened, or at least somewhat of one if I held onto my v-card.

"Why the hell are we engaged then?"

Matt smiles again, and I swear the brown in his eyes grows darker, "'Cause it makes sense. It will be good for both of our families and good for business. So, let's just get it over with. You did agree to marry me at one point, that's the truth, and I think we still should, we don't have to be in love for this to work. We don't have to hate each other either. This could be a mutual benefit for both of us, so let's just be adults here and do what's best for everybody."

I'm left speechless by his admission. That's a lot to take in, and I need a minute to actually grasp onto everything he just said. Even though his confession hurt, in a way, it was also honest, and after feeling like my parents have been hiding stuff from me, I do appreciate that honesty. Still, hearing that I agreed to marry for reasons other than love makes my chest ache.

Was I really that kind of person?

"How would it benefit us to get married?" I ask after gathering my thoughts.

Matt shrugs, "Mostly because our fathers do a lot of business together, and they are planning on merging their companies after our marriage. It would show the board members that this would still be a *family business,* which your father has always claimed it to be. Also, my father wants me to take over the company in a few years, and I might have a bit of a wild side. Hookers and partying all night. It's kind of a turn off for some of the investors, getting married and *settling down,* would ease their minds."

"So, what you're saying is, we're getting married for show, to boost our families images?"

"It doesn't have to be that way. I mean, I do like you… you're really pretty," he says, his eyes briefly scanning my body.

"Ah… thanks." I guess he said that to compliment me, but it feels more like an insult. Are my looks all he likes about me? Is that what he bases my character on?

"We could have a good life together, and I would take care of you. I mean, I'm an asshole, but I protect what's mine."

"I don't know. I don't remember you, or anyone for that matter. I don't know what's real and what's not."

Matt nods as if he understands, "I see that this is something you need to think about. If you could do me a small favor and not tell your parents that I told you the truth about us, I would appreciate it. They asked me to tell you we were in love and all that shit. Just a precaution in case we do get married. I don't want to piss off the in-laws right off the bat."

"I won't tell them, and thanks for being honest with me. I really appreciate it."

"No problem, here is my number. Call me if you want to talk more." He hands me a business card. I take it and hold on to it tightly like it's a lifeline. I feel like I might need his honesty in the future.

Turning around to leave, something dawns on me, I have one more question burning in the back of my mind, and I want only an honest answer.

"Can I ask you something else and you be honest with me?"

Matt stares at me, his face blank, "Ask away, sweetheart."

"Do you know Sullivan Bishop?"

At the mention of the name, Matt's face scrunches up like he just caught a whiff of something nasty. He leans forward on the bench, staring up at me, "I know the Bishops alright, and so do you, well, did. Your family and the Bishops' have been enemies since forever, for as long as I can remember. It's funny you ask that actually because you and Sullivan have history."

My eyes widen, and I wonder for a moment if that's why I felt so connected to him. As if Matt can see the wheels inside my head spinning, he continues, "Not that kind of history. I think you would much rather kill each other than screw. You two have hated each other since you were kids, and senior year you planted drugs in his pocket at a party. Got him arrested and kicked out of school. They did an article in the paper about it, plastered the Bishop family name everywhere. Sullivan lost his scholarship to play ball, but their family lost much more than that. They've since disappeared from town."

"I... I destroyed someone's life?" I blink, not even sure I believe what he's saying. Why would I do something like that? What caused me to hate this family so much?

"You act so surprised?" Matt's brow furrows with confusion, "I know you don't remember stuff, but I'm sure you can still tell who you are inside, right? Plus, it's not like they didn't deserve it. Your father has reasons for doing the things that he does."

There's a gnawing in my gut, something that tells me if I look deep inside myself, I won't like the person I find, the person I was before the accident. I don't want to be her...I don't want to do whatever my father had me doing.

"I don't care what his reasonings are, that's not me. That can't be. I don't want to hurt people, deserving or not." Matt scrubs a hand down his face and lets out a frustrated sigh.

"The damage is already done, Princess. Sullivan Bishop has been out for revenge for a long time, so don't be surprised if he comes for you next."

"What does that mean?" I ask because I don't understand. I don't understand anything, and the frustration over it grows inside me the roots sinking deeper and deeper. It's like everyone is speaking in tongues, a language I used to know but no longer understand.

Matt gets up from the bench and walks toward me, he stops a foot away, leaving just enough space between our bodies, so I don't feel suffocated by his presence. Still, his body towers over mine, and I don't like it. I don't like the fragileness I feel. There's a sweetness to his scent, and it tickles my nostrils. His fingers lift my chin up, forcing me to look into his eyes as he speaks.

"It means if he or his brothers fuck with you, there will be consequences. Your father just got you back, and I doubt he's going to let anything happen to you again."

When he releases me, I feel compelled to ask him what he means about my father getting me back? Is he referring to the accident? Or is he referring to something else? Matt doesn't give me a chance to digest my thoughts fully before he takes hold of my hand, tugging me back the way we came.

"It's time for the Princess to go to bed."

"I'm an adult you know, not six-years-old, and I'm not a princess, stop calling me that," I growl under my breath as he leads me back into the house.

He stops once we reach the grand staircase, a tight-lipped smile on his lips, "You might be an adult, but you're fragile, like the most beautiful piece of sea glass, and right now you need your rest. You are still recovering, and if you don't take care of yourself, you will never fully recover and come to remember the life you lived."

I guess I can't argue with him there. I've been exhausted, my headaches have been more constant than normal. It's like my memories are trying to come back, pushing against the barrier my brain has put up. I want to remember, no, I *need* to remember. I need all the missing puzzle pieces so I can figure out what the hell is going on.

"I want to kiss you, Harlow," he murmurs, and before I can object, he's leaning in, cupping me gently by the back of the head, his fingers threading through my hair. His lips descend brushing against mine in the faintest way, but it's still enough to send an electrical shock through my body that sparks something inside my brain.

A memory, a thought... the barrier separating the two spaces, my past, and my present, cracks a little and I push through the crack grabbing onto the thought with two hands, letting it drag me into the darkness.

"Okay.... A kiss... A kiss would be okay, I mean," I whisper right before he brushes a strand of hair from my face. His thumb brushing against my cheek leaving my skin tingling beneath his touch. He leans in, eyes open wide, as if he doesn't want to miss the chance to see my face when our lips touch.

Then our lips touch, pressing together and my eyes close on their own. Tingles of warmth ripple through me. Everything around us fades out as if we are the only two people in the world. All I feel are his soft, full lips against mine. The kiss is gentle, heart-warming, and I lean into him while our lips melt into each other.

I give myself this one second to forget everything, the reason I am here and the reason I should hate him. Butterflies flutter around inside my stomach igniting a deep tremble in my core. A warmth seeps into my bones, melting me like an ice cream cone sitting in the afternoon sun.

I want to get lost in that feeling, feel nothing else beside it, but my father's voice rings in my ears right then. I need to remember what his family has done, the pain they've caused.

With a heavy heart and an unsteady hand, I grab the small plastic bag from my pocket and slip it into his before I pull away breaking the kiss.

Try as I might to hold onto that memory it slips between my fingers like tiny bits of sand, the kiss with Matt ends as well and I'm left wondering what the hell just happened.

"I'll see you later, and like I said...call me if you need anything." Matt trails his thumb over my cheek, and I turn on my wedges, damn near falling on my face, as I do.

Thankfully, I catch myself against the railing and start up the stairs, all but racing toward my bedroom. By the time I reach my room, I'm panting, my chest rising and falling in such a manner, I wonder if I'm going to have an anxiety attack.

Slipping inside the room I close the door behind me and turn the lock into place. Then I slide down the door, my ass hitting the floor with a hard thud. That was definitely a memory from my past, and it was obviously with Sullivan, and it proved my biggest fear. I had hated him, but not enough to not give in to the temptation of kissing him, and if that's not the scariest part of all of this, I don't know what is.

If Sullivan was supposed to be an enemy, if we were fated to hate each other, if I hurt his family, and him, then why the hell were we kissing each other? And why did he find me and say he wants to help me? None of this makes sense, and as badly as I want answers, I know I won't get any unless I dig deeper, unless I find them out for myself. Pushing up off the floor, I get ready for bed, putting my PJs on, and washing my face.

By the time my head hits the pillow, I'm partially asleep. My mind drifting to someone I shouldn't have anything to do with.

18

*L*ike every morning, for the last few weeks, I wake confused. It takes me a while to grab onto my bearings and make sense of anything first thing in the morning. I'm always looking around the room for something familiar...something that makes me remember this place, but it never happens.

Each day I wake up here, I feel like a visitor, a guest staying in a five-star hotel. Still in my jammies, I wander around my room, having the sudden urge to find something, anything that looks or at least feels familiar.

Walking over to my bookshelf, I let my fingers trail over the spines of the books, there are countless books, some of which I've read and loved, but nothing seems recognizable. Pulling the nearest book out, I search between every page, looking for something, anything, but nothing comes up. I do it with each of the books, but the outcome is the same.

Frustrated, I move to my desk and start to go through all the drawers, old notebooks, and pencil cases, but again, nothing worthy of investigation. I scour through the rest of the room meticulously, before I move on to my closet, touching every piece of clothing, every pair of shoes and accessories inside the large space. *Nothing.* Always nothing.

Tears prick my eyes, the frustration inside me boiling over. All I want is a thought, a memory, good or bad, it doesn't matter. I just need something to keep me going. God, please give me something to show me that I'm not going crazy.

With my head hanging low, I exit the walk-in closet, but as I cross the threshold, I spot something out of the corner of my eye. A backpack. It's thrown carelessly in the corner beside the door. It's hidden in plain sight, and I wonder why I've never noticed it before.

Bending down, I pick up the old worn backpack. It looks nothing like the clothing and purses that adorn the hangers in my closet. It looks like... *me.* Urgently, I move to my bed and unzip it, pouring the contents out on my comforter.

Books, papers, folders, and loose pens fall haphazardly onto my bed. This must be my high school backpack. At first glance, nothing out of the ordinary sticks out to me, and I start to feel depressed again, but when I start to put all the contents back inside, something slips out of one of the books and lands on the floor at my feet.

My gaze darts to the rectangular laminated Student ID card. I know it's mine because there is a picture of me on it, and my name is printed across the top right corner, below the words: *Bayshore University.*

Picking it up, I inspect it further. Written next to my picture is my name, my birthday, and my Student ID number. I realize then that this isn't my high school backpack. It's my college one, but if I wasn't in college, then why do I have a student ID for one? Turning, I sit down on the edge of the mattress.

Flipping the card over there is an address, phone number, and website link.

My eyes dart to the sleek cellular device sitting on my nightstand. Since coming home, I've looked at it a handful of times. There's nothing on it. I've looked through it, it contains a few numbers, but that's it. It's practically brand new, and I'm doubtful it has ever been used.

Grabbing it, I decide to make a phone call to the University just to make sure that I was attending college there. My fingers shake as I dial the number, my heart beating wildly in my chest. If I was really going to school there, then why am I at home right now? Why didn't my parents tell me?

Pushing the thoughts away for a moment, I press the green call key, and the sound of the phone ringing fills my ears.

"Bayshore University Admissions, how can I help you?" A woman greets joyfully.

"Hi, yes, I was wondering if you had a student by the name of Harlow Lockwood in attendance there?"

"Hi, and who am I speaking with?"

"Harlow Lockwood."

"Umm," she pauses, obviously confused.

"It's a long story, but I can confirm my date of birth and possible student ID number if that helps any?" The click of fingers on a keyboard fills the speaker of my phone.

"That would be great. Whenever you're ready."

I recite the information on the card back to her, and within seconds, she confirms what I had suspected.

"Okay, Harlow, I can confirm that you were a student here. It looks like you're still enrolled but on a leave of absence. Was there anything else that you wanted to know?"

Leave of absence?

"No, thank you." I hang up the phone catching the beginning of her wishing me a good day, knowing damn well that won't be happening.

My hunch was spot on, my parents have been lying to me, and have definitely been hiding stuff. The question is, why? Whatever their reasoning, it had better be good because no longer will I stand by and be made a fool of.

With my ID card in hand, I storm out of the room and down the hall heading toward my father's study. I need some answers, and I need them now. As I get closer to the door, I notice it's cracked open, Dad's voice filtering from within. He's either on the phone or talking directly to someone. Since I'm barefoot I'm able to creep closer without making a sound, at the door, I peer through the slit into the room.

From what I can see he's alone, no one else is in the office with him. Thankfully he's turned toward the window, his back to me.

"I told you that I would meet you tonight at the hotel…"

The person on the other line must say something because a moment later he answers with, "Yes, wait there, naked on the bed, like always, and please next time don't call my office. Anyone could answer. I have to get back to work, I'll see you later, baby."

Blinking, I try to absorb what I just heard. My father is… is he having an affair? It sure sounds that way. I know I should be angry, maybe even sad, but it's almost like I have no emotion toward it. It's like… I don't care. Which is strange, because I should definitely care.

Impatiently, I wait another minute before entering the room. I don't want him to know that I heard the conversation. Shoving it to the back of my mind, I concentrate on the anger boiling in my veins over him lying to me about college. If he lied about this, then what else has he lied about?

Certain that enough time has passed, I march into the room without knocking. My father's head snaps up from the papers he is working on at my appearance.

"Harlow?" Shock fills his features. Why is he so surprised to see me? I don't dwell on the thought for long since there are other pressing matters.

"Why did you lie to me about college?" I bellow, getting straight to the point. Walking up to his desk, I toss the ID card at him. It slides across the polished wood, coming to a stop right in front of him. As if he had this all planned out, his lips part, and he looks up at me, shame flickering in his eyes.

"Harlow, you don't understand. I'm trying to protect you."

"Protect me? From what? Getting an education?"

"From being hurt. You were not safe there. Someone tried to kill you, twice!" he growls, "You're a Lockwood, and as your father, it is my job to protect you."

"Protect me from the truth? If there was really someone trying to kill me, then why wouldn't you tell me? Why would you hide that information from me?"

"What do you want me to say, Harlow?" He tosses his hands into the air, frustration seeping into the space between us. "There was no way you would have healed if we had put you under more stress. I brought you home and kept things from you because I wanted to help you heal faster, and I wasn't going to have you miles away from your family, only for someone to succeed in killing you."

My heart sinks into my stomach, "I feel trapped here. If I was away at college, then that's where I should be right now. That's why I don't remember anything..." My voice trails off, "I don't remember anything because I wasn't here. This place isn't my home anymore. The doctor said I should be where I was before the accident, but I'm not."

Something that resembles anger ignites in his gaze, "That's a lie, and you know it. This is your home, and it will always be your home. You've lived here your entire life, why would you say such a thing?"

Truthfully, I don't know, all I know is that if this place were home, if it was where I belonged, then surely, I would remember the simplest of things. As it is, I can't even walk around the house without getting lost.

"I want to go back to college, and even if you don't want me to, I'm still going."

"And who do you think is going to pay for that, young lady?" he spits, and I have the sudden urge to stomp my foot. Him treating me like a child, makes me want to act like one.

"You will," I snap back at him. "Because if you don't, I'll tell Mom about your affair." Dad looks at me like I've just slapped him. A short silence settles between us, and I can see the uncertainty in his eyes, he's trying to figure out what to say next.

"How did you find out about that?" he finally says, his voice oddly calm.

"I just heard you on the phone before I came in." I don't see the point in lying to him, I've got leverage now, and I'm going to use it.

"It's not what you think..." He starts, but I interject.

"I don't care who you're with, or what you're doing. All I want is to go back to Bayshore. I don't belong here."

"You do, but I wasn't lying about being worried about you. Someone is trying to hurt you, and I can't protect you from here. So, if you must go, then I'll be sending two of my men with you."

"Two men?" I'm bewildered, and I'm sure my face shows it. "What? Like as bodyguards?"

"Yes, exactly like that. You must think I'm stupid if you think I'm sending you there unprotected."

Annoyed and thoroughly done with the conversation, I roll my eyes, "Fine, send who you want, as long as they stay out of my way." I spin around and head for the door when he calls after me, making me stop midstep.

"Harlow, like any family, we have had some disagreements in the past. We are not perfect, but you must believe me when I say, I truly care about you and I don't want anything to happen to you." The sincerity in his voice is unmistakable, but still, I can't fully forgive him for lying to me. If he's lied once, he's most likely lied before.

I stare at him, feeling an ocean of space between us. "You don't lie to the people you care about," I say, and walk out of his office without looking back. When I close the door behind me, I smile, because for the first time since I came here, I feel like I might just have a grasp on my life.

19

With my worn-out backpack slung over my shoulder, I walk across campus for the first time. Well, the first time that I can remember. I'm not sure if it's me or the two bulky guys following me that has everybody looking my way curiously. Either way, I feel a little like a walking sideshow with everybody gawking at me like this.

I try to ignore all eyes on me as I walk into the classroom. Thankfully, my two goons, Ernie and Bert, as I like to call them, wait outside the door. I take a seat all the way in the back and get out my textbook. It's in the middle of the semester, and I have no chance of passing this or any other class, but that's not why I'm here.

Flipping through my textbook, I'm waiting for the professor to start class when someone clears their throat in front of me getting my attention. I look up from my book, and for a second, I think I'm looking into Sullivan Bishop's eyes… but I blink and realize it's not him.

It's just someone who looks a lot like him, same russet brown hair, the same shade of blue eyes, and even something about his soft smile is familiar.

The similarities between the two are startling.

"Harlow," my name falls from his lips as if he's said it a million times before. "We were really worried about you," he continues, taking the seat beside me.

"Do I know you?"

He nods, his smile widening, "I'm Banks," he introduces himself, extending his hand out to me.

"I'm Harlow, but I guess you already know that." I lift my arm, reaching out to shake his hand. The moment we touch it feels like a lightning bolt shoots through my body and straight to my brain...

"Shh, Princess. We didn't say you could speak. Keep your mouth shut, otherwise, we'll find a better use for it..." Clear as day, Banks' voice rings in my ears. Another snippet of a memory starts invading my mind. *My back pressed into his chest as he whispers the threat into the shell of my ear.* Panic rises up inside of me like a volcano, and I push the memory away. I don't want to remember this.

Pulling my hand away, as if his touch burns my skin. In the same motion, I get up. The chair falling over behind me, the sound of it making every head in the class turn in my direction.

"What's wrong?" Banks asks, his face etched with concern, while I gather all my stuff and shove it in my backpack.

"I... I've got to go, wrong class..." I mumble. Grabbing my bag, I scurry out of the class, my heart pounding like a jackhammer against my chest.

Escaping the room, I run past the two guys standing guard at the door without looking back.

"Hey, where are you going? Did something happen?" One of the guards calls after me.

"I just want to go back to the dorm." I don't bother explaining myself any further. It's none of their business anyway. I know they'll follow behind me, but I don't really care. I drown out everything around me and speed walk across campus and back to my dorm.

When I burst into the room, I'm disappointed to find Shelby

standing beside her bed, a pile of laundry before her. I had hoped to be alone.

She's mid-fold, her eyes widening when she sees me.

"Hey, you're back early?" she greets, and when I don't respond right away, and instead walk over to my bed, she asks, "You okay?"

"Yeah, just couldn't take another second of class," I mumble tossing my backpack onto the floor before throwing myself down on the twin-size mattress.

"And why was that?" she questions.

I'm about to start telling her about Banks and about the snippet of memory I recalled, but I get this churning in my gut that tells me not to. Something in the back of my mind tells me to keep this to myself until I know the whole story, so instead, I decide to lie.

Groaning, I say, "I just didn't get anything the professor was saying. It's useless, I'm not remembering anything." The lie glides off my tongue easily, one would think I lie all the time, and maybe I did, before.

"I don't know why you go anyway. I mean, I know why, but you can do other stuff around here to jog your memory. College isn't all about classes."

"Then what's it about? What else can I do to help?"

"I told you already," she rolls her eyes, "We went to parties before. We should go to parties now, it might help you remember something, and if it doesn't, maybe it'll help to meet people, to get out and about."

I remember her telling me these things, but honestly, I don't want to go to parties, and it's hard to believe that I enjoyed going to them before. But Shelby has no reason to lie to me, so it has to be somewhat true. Gazing up at her face, I can see the excitement growing in her eyes as if she knows that I'm about to give in and agree to go with her.

A second later, I say the words, "Okay, I'll go with you."

And she breaks out into a giggle, slamming down onto the mattress beside me.

"Yes! This is going to be so much fun. I swear, Harlow, you loved dressing up and going out. Gah, I can't wait to help you choose your clothes." She wraps her arms around me and hugs me tight to her chest, "I missed you, Harlow, I really did, and I'm so glad that you're okay."

IT TAKES a little finagling to get out of the dorm without my *bodyguards* finding out. Thankfully the university told them that they can't stay inside the dorms, so after a short while they leave to head to their rental, and that's when Shelby and I make our break.

When we arrive at the frat house, the place is packed, even the front yard is brimming with people. Inside is even worse, and by the time we make it to the kitchen, I'm ready to turn around and go back outside. Shelby keeps a tight hold on my hand like she knows I'll bail at any given second. As I look around the room, trying to take in the sights and see if anything about this place or the people here jolt an emotion or even a memory, I feel eyes on me.

Across the room, someone is staring at me. I know it. I can feel the heat of their gaze creeping up my back. Turning my head in their direction, and my gaze collides with chocolate brown orbs.

In the endless sea of people, it shouldn't be all that surprising to make eye contact with someone, but this isn't just *someone*, this person's eyes are like melted chocolate, and brimming with concern. They captivate me, grab onto me, and refuse to let go. Breaking eye contact, I let my gaze roam over the stranger's body, realizing he looks just like Sullivan and Banks.

Leaning into Shelby, I ask, "Who is that?"

"What?" Her eyes follow my line of sight.

"That guy standing in the far corner of the room with his arms crossed over his chest, who is he?" I ask again.

Shelby's face sours, "Oliver Bishop. We don't associate with *them*, Harlow. They're trash." *Them*. That makes me think of what Matt said, "*Sullivan and his brothers,*" I suppose that explains why they all look alike. Sullivan, Banks, and Oliver must be the *brothers*. Brothers I'm supposed to stay away from.

"Everyone keeps warning me away from them," I bite my bottom lip, the memory from earlier entering my mind once more. Banks said *we* in that memory... were his brothers with him that night? Did they all threaten me? Even though I tried to forget it earlier, now I wish I had held onto it, maybe I would remember the whole thing then.

Still biting my lip, I feel compelled to look back over at the elusive Oliver, but as I do, I realize he's no longer standing there. My heart skips like a stone skipping across the water.

Where did he go? Is the first question that pops into my head, and the second is, why do I care? A pop song filters through the speakers, and Shelby squeals with excitement, her eyes glittering in the bright lights.

"Oh my god, I love this song," she shouts, either ignoring my question or having not heard it at all. As she bops her head to the song, belting out the lyrics, she tugs me along, until we reach the island that is scattered with cups and liquor bottles. There's a beer keg centered in what would be the breakfast nook area with about five frat guys around it. They're all laughing at something that one of the guys said, distracting me momentarily.

That is until I feel a heat creep up my back, it feels like the sun is beating down on me, and I release Shelby's hand and whirl around, to find Oliver mere feet away, a smile ghosting against his lips.

Up close, he looks even more handsome, like an older version of Banks and Sullivan. Each of the brothers reminds me of those Roman soldiers from the 15th century, all muscled, and beautiful, only missing their togas, and a sword, and shield.

Their faces angelic-looking, with sharp jaws, and high cheekbones. Their teeth perfectly straight, and white, and their hair styled to perfection as if they just walked off the cover of a romance novel. No one should be able to look as good as the three of them do, and yet, they do.

"Nope, I don't think so," Shelby interjects, but Oliver rolls his eyes, ignoring her, and closing the distance between us in one single step.

"She can talk to who she wants to, you aren't her keeper." Oliver's words are directed at Shelby, but he doesn't look away from me as he says them.

"You're trouble, Oliver, and Harlow doesn't need trouble," Shelby growls "go away."

"I.... I know you..." I blink slowly, speaking more to myself than him. Inhaling slowly, the zingy scent of citrus, and rain fills my nostrils calming me almost instantly.

"Yes, you know me," he smirks. His smile makes me want to smile, and I don't really understand why. "Why are you here? You hate parties."

"Don't be ridiculous, Oliver, and don't tell Harlow what she likes and doesn't like," Shelby snaps at him like a momma bear protecting her young. "Come on, Harlow, let's go outside," she grabs my arm and starts pulling me toward the back door before I can even protest. A dark look crosses Oliver's face, but he doesn't make an effort to stop her. Not even a second later, I'm walking into the cool night air, a shiver rippling down my spine.

"Ugh, those Bishop boys are so annoying." Shelby rolls her eyes. "Stay here, and I'll go inside and make you a drink, and seriously, stay away from them, they're nothing but trouble, plus you're supposed to hate them."

"Supposed to hate them?" I ask, but Shelby doesn't answer me, and instead, walks back the way we just came. I stand there for a minute or two by myself, and when she returns with two red cups in her hands, I smile.

"Here, drink this, let loose, and let's enjoy the night." I take the cup from her hand and take a big sip, letting the fruity liquid soothe my nerves.

"Mhh, that's really good," I admit.

"Of course it is, it's your favorite," Shelby winks, and I take another drink, gulping half the liquid down without thought.

We talk for a bit, laugh, and dance, and before I know it, my cup is empty, and I'm feeling a whole lot better. As if the alcohol gave my mind a break from trying to remember something and make sense of everything, I feel a bit calmer, more at ease, and suddenly, I want another drink.

"What is this? I want some more," I tell Shelby.

"I'll get you some, stay here, girlfriend," she laughs, clearly a little tipsy herself. I watch her walk back into the house before looking around the back yard. There are a ton of people outside, most of them playing drinking games. A few couples are dancing on the grass, the atmosphere out here seems more chilled than inside.

Scanning the crowd, I hope to spot Oliver again, but no matter how much I look, I don't see him anywhere, it's almost like he disappeared.

"Harlow?" An unfamiliar voice calls startling me, and I twist around faster than necessary, coming face to face with some guy that I don't know. He's holding a red cup in his hand, which he extends out to me, "Shelby asked me to give this to you. She said she'll be right back."

"Oh, okay..." I take the cup from his hand and watch him turn and walk the other way. *Weird*. Not dwelling on it, I take a sip from my new drink and look around for Shelby.

Where the hell is she?

I take a few steps toward the door that leads back into the house when someone steps in front of me, cutting me off and causing me to stop or run head-on into them.

"Hey, Sexy, glad to see you back on your feet again," the guy that cut me off says. He looks vaguely familiar, but I can't tell why. I think he was sitting at the table inside earlier. Maybe I even knew him from before, either way, I already don't like him. Not only because of how he called me *Sexy*. No, there is something else about him that I don't like. Something that leaves me feeling sick.

"Thanks," is all I say as I push past him, trying to get inside.

His hand snakes out at the last minute, and he wraps his fingers around one of my wrists tugging me back toward him. "Not so fast, I wasn't done talking yet," he slurs.

Now that he's close, I can smell the alcohol on him, it pours from his mouth, causing my nose to wrinkle with distaste. He smells like a damn distillery. "My friends and I want you to come back to our place. There are three of us, three fat cocks, just the way you like it," he snickers, peering over his shoulder, at what I would assume are his friends.

His statement leaves me feeling sick, my stomach churning, bile rising up my throat.

He talks as if that's something I like or something I did before.

No way would I have had a threesome, right?

"Let me go," I growl into his face, wrenching my arm from his grasp. I take a few unsteady steps backward. "Don't fucking touch me again, asshole."

He holds his hands in the air as if he's surrendering, but something tells me that if we weren't at a party with a bunch of people watching us, this situation would have ended a lot differently. Turning, I walk away from him, and into the crowd, suddenly feeling safer there. I take another gulp of my drink, hoping the cold liquid will cool my heated blood. That guy's an asshole, a douchebag.

For a moment, I close my eyes and forget about the world around me. I almost laugh out loud. I'm trying to forget when all I've been doing for the last few weeks is trying to remember. Sucking a deep breath of air into my lungs, my eyes flutter open again. I feel different. There is a weird feeling in my stomach that seems to be spreading throughout my limbs at a rapid pace. Taking a few steps, I notice how my legs are wobbly and unsteady, like a newborn fawn.

Did I drink that much alcohol?

People run into me, as I make my way back inside or am I running into them? My perception is off. I can feel my mind becoming more clouded by the second. With each step I take forward, I become more confused, more unsure, less coherent.

What the hell?

I look up to see if I'm still going in the right direction, but I can't make out the door anymore, all I see are people dancing, talking, and drinking. The world is carrying on around me while I'm slowly slipping away, and there is nothing I can do about it.

"Changed your mind, sexy?" The creep's voice from earlier filters into my ears while clammy fingers circle my wrist, pulling me away from the dancefloor. I want to scream, but nothing comes out. I want to fight him, but my limbs won't move. Panic floods my veins, and all I can think of is how stupid I was to come here.

20

Somewhere in my panic-stricken state, and confused mind, meaty fingers are replaced with soft hands. The smell of sweat and alcohol is replaced with the clean scent of citrus and rain. The terror I feel inside, replaced with an eternal calmness.

Without knowing how or even why, I know that I am safe.

"Don't ever touch her again..." A familiar voice growls the sound vibrating through me as my ear presses against a warm, firm chest.

"We were just having some fun, Oliver. Don't get so butthurt."

"You are lucky there are people here, if it was just you and me, your jaw would be broken right now," Oliver threatens the creep. "Maybe some fingers too..."

He doesn't say anything else, just wraps his arm around me and starts leading me somewhere. My legs barely work, and I know he is half carrying me. At one point he just picks me up as my movements become more sluggish.

The music and the noise of the party fade away until it is almost completely silent around us. The only thing remaining is the steady rhythm of Oliver's beating heart.

I'm not sure how I got there, but the next time I open my eyes, I'm in the backseat of a car. My body feels heavy and useless, my limbs weak like they have boulders tied to the ends of them. When I try and sit up to look around, I realize I'm not alone. Oliver is with me, and I'm lying across his lap, his arm cradling my head.

"Hey there," he whispers, his fingers brushing over my face, making my skin tingle and something deep in my mind sparks with life.

"You want us to make you feel good?" I can hear Oliver's voice in my ear, but I'm not sure if this is real or a memory.

He runs his hand up and down my inner thighs. My heart starts to beat rapidly desire pooling deep in my gut.

"Yes," I say breathlessly, my tongue darting out over my bottom lip to wet it.

"I want to touch you," Oliver purrs.

"You are touching me," I tease, even though I know exactly what he means.

Grinning he uses his hand to nudge my legs apart.

"I want to touch you here," he murmurs and lets his thumb ghost over my shorts covered pussy. Taking the hint, I spread my legs further for him. He takes the invitation and trails his fingers over the fabric before he dips his thumb into the waistband of my shorts and starts to pull them down...

"Are you okay, Harlow?" Oliver asks, dragging me back to reality. "You're breathing funny... please, tell me you are okay."

"I'm okay," I say, my voice comes out weird and broken, but at least I got the words out. Trying to keep my eyes open, I want to look at his face, but my vision is blurry, and I can't make out all of his features. So I close my eyes and try to remember him instead, but when I do, it's not Oliver I see... it's Banks.

"You want us to make you come?" Banks asks, his voice unnaturally deep as he pulls away just enough to speak.

I'm so confused... is Banks here? No... I think I'm dreaming or remembering something. Unable to hold onto reality, I let my mind pull me under, drawing me in, deeper and deeper.

"Yes, please," the words come out on a gasp because right as I'm speaking them, Oliver slides one of his thick digits into my slickness.

"Fuck, Banks, she's tight as hell." Oliver's voice is strained, the muscles in his neck tight. He looks like he's ready to explode.

Slowly the puzzle pieces fall into place, painting a larger picture in my head. I was with both of them, Oliver and Banks. I was lying across their laps, while they were touching me... and I liked it. I wanted it, even asked for it.

I try to open my eyes once more, I want to ask Oliver what happened between us, but my eyelids are just too heavy, my head too muddled. I feel his hand cup my cheek, his thumb running over my skin gently, and I take comfort in that. His touch is tender, kind, and before I know it, I'm drifting off to sleep.

The next time I open my eyes, the fog circling my head has lifted a bit. My mind is clearer, my thoughts sharper. I'm still in the back seat of a car and Oliver is still holding me in his lap, although his eyes are closed now, his head tilted back resting on the backrest.

For a long while, I just lay there staring at his sleeping face. It is completely dark outside, but there is a streetlamp not far from us that shines enough light in the car to let me see how peaceful he looks. So angelic, I don't want to wake him, but I also want to talk to him. *Need* to talk to him.

"Oliver," I whisper calling out to him. Stirring lightly, his eyes blink open and like two magnets drawn together, our gazes collide.

"Hey, you. Feeling better?" His sleepy voice is gruff, but the hand cradling my head is warm and gentle.

"Yeah... I don't know what happened, I think I drank too much," I admit. Only then do I remember the creep who got handsy with me earlier. "Thanks for helping me with that guy earlier."

"There is no need to thank me." Oliver's voice drops, and I involuntarily shiver at the deepness of it. "We're friends, and that's what friends do, they protect each other."

I don't understand why if everyone is telling me to stay away from them, why he would protect me, or even say we're friends. Am I dreaming still?

"Are we friends?" I ask, sitting up, and slowly turning to face him. "Everyone keeps telling me to stay away from you and your brothers because you are trying to hurt me."

"We're friends." He answers, his voice clipped. "And hurting you is the last thing any of us want to do." The sincerity of his voice causes a slow heat to unravel through my lower belly.

"Were... were we ever *more* than friends?" I stutter over the words, asking the question. Do I really want to know the answer? All these memories, and thoughts, the things that guy said to me earlier about wanting three... cocks. It was almost as if he was implying that I was sleeping with all three of them.

"It's complicated... just know that we care about you and we are trying to watch out for you. No one is going to hurt you, not ever again."

"And by *we* you mean you, Banks, and Sullivan?"

"Yes, we all care about you." His eyes dart away, and he looks out the window into the darkness of the night. There's a long pause before he speaks again, and it's almost like he's gathering his own thoughts. "I should take you back to your dorm, now that you're feeling better."

I'm about to object, but he's already out the door, leaving me alone in the backseat. He climbs into the front and starts the car, the engine roaring to life, and filling the quiet space.

The entire ride back to the dorms he's quiet, and so am I, unsure of what to say or do. I should ask more questions, investigate him and his brothers further, but as soon as I open my mouth to start speaking, we pull up in front of the dorms. The two goons my father sent with me walk up to the car as soon as Oliver puts it into park, almost as if they expected us to be here.

One of them opens the door for me, a somber look on his face. "Miss Harlow, you should have stayed in your dorm. That was very dangerous, and because of your reckless behavior, we have to report this back to your father."

"Oh no, anything but that..." I say, sarcastically, letting out an exaggerated gasp and rolling my eyes. "You do realize that I'm an adult, right? That I'm in college, and that I'm not actually required to listen to you or him?"

"Your father just wants you to be safe." So he keeps saying, almost like he's trying to convince everybody around me that his intentions are pure, but not everyone knows the things I do, or the gut feelings I'm experiencing.

"Goodnight, Harlow," Oliver calls from the front seat before I get out of the car, obviously having heard the entire exchange.

"Goodnight," I respond and shut the door behind me. As soon as I do, he speeds off. I guess he couldn't wait to get out of here. Shrugging, I walk back into the dorm, ignoring the two lugs that follow behind me until I make it to the door. Escaping inside, I walk up the stairs, stopping once I reach my dorm room door.

I realize then that I never did find Shelby, and the thought of her alone at that party is unsettling. Maybe I can go back and get her? No, I'm too exhausted for that. I'm seconds away from having a breakdown when the door to my room opens, and Shelby appears before me, her thin arms wrapping around me, pulling me into her chest. I'm briefly aware of her tugging me inside the room and closing the door behind us.

"Oh my gosh! I was worried sick, Harlow. I went looking for you, and someone said they saw you leave with Oliver. What happened? Did he hurt you?" The panic in her face has my knees buckling. All this time I was worried about her, while she was here looking for me.

"He didn't hurt me," I mumble as she helps me to my bed. There's a throbbing directly behind my eyes that makes it feel like I've been beaten over my head half a dozen times with a brick. "He saved me," I add.

"Saved you?" Shelby says, completely baffled.

"Yeah, some guy was getting handsy with me, and he told him to go away. He helped me out to his car and then I fell asleep for a little while. When I woke up, I felt better."

Shelby looks, well, like she's about to be sick, "Oliver didn't protect you, Harlow, he set you up. The entire time I was inside, it was because he refused to let me come out to you. I went in to make you a drink, and he blocked the exit when I tried to come back outside. Then he put something in the drink I made you and gave it to some guy, told him to bring it to you saying it was from me, but I would never do that to you." Shame fills her eyes. "He drugged you, Harlow! He wasn't trying to save you, he was trying to use you, hurt you, and this isn't the first time this kind of thing has happened. I think it's time I tell you the whole truth."

"What whole truth? What the hell are you talking about?"

Shelby sits down on the mattress beside me, "I wanted to tell you, but your parents thought it would be too stressful, so I've tried not to say anything, but you have to know about the Bishops for your own sake, and apparently, your safety now too."

My stomach drops, and I stare at her, waiting for her to start speaking.

"Before the accident, the Bishops followed you here, to Bayshore. They wanted revenge, and I'm pretty sure, though, I don't have proof, I'm positive, that it was one of them that hit you with the car. It wouldn't surprise me, at all. They tried to kill you once before, by pushing you off a boat we were partying on. You almost drowned!"

"Why? Why would they do that? Why do the police not know about these things?"

Shelby scoffs, "They're not stupid, they covered their tracks, but if you are looking for proof that they've tried to hurt you, I can give you a lot of that and then some."

"Proof? What proof?" My chest hurts simply thinking about Oliver trying to hurt me. He was so nice earlier...so kind, and tender-hearted, and I felt safe with him. Can I really be that bad of a judge of character?

Shelby grabs onto my hand, a frown overtaking her lips, "They didn't just try to hurt you physically. They bullied you the entire time you were here. You can ask almost any student at the university. Most of them know about it or have seen it first-hand. They spread rumors about you, saying you slept with a bunch of guys, and even worse they told people you liked threesomes, kinky sex, and that you were pathetically lovesick over them because they rejected you."

Shelby shakes her head and pulls her phone out, searching for something on Facebook. "As if that wasn't enough, they even made a banner and hung it up on campus with your number on it." She hands me the phone. There are some photos pulled up from a profile of some girl named Tiffany. The first one is of her sitting on Oliver's lap nibbling on his neck. Jealousy floods my system, and I don't know what to make of that. I hold no claim over him, and apparently, I never did, so why the hell do I feel this way?

Scrolling down the pictures, it only gets worse. More of her and Oliver, others of her with Banks. Then Banks with another girl. Sullivan is in some as well. All of them make me feel the same way. Jealous and betrayed, neither one of those feelings is justified or explainable.

Then I find one picture that hits home. Tiffany, two other girls, and the Bishop brothers are standing in front of a banner, posing with it and laughing. It reads **Harlow Needs More Dick- Send Pics If you're DTF!** A number, which I assume used to be mine is written with it.

"It was terrible. Your phone wouldn't stop ringing, you had to get a new number. Guys would harass you walking across campus. I don't know why they were so cruel to you."

I don't understand. I can feel my heart struggling to beat. It feels like I've been gutted, and I'm struggling to hold myself together.

"I'm sorry, Harlow. I tried to stop it, but it was pretty much the whole school against us two. Then the accident happened, and I was so worried about you." Her eyes shimmer with unshed tears.

"Thank you for being a great friend, Shelby, you've always stuck by my side... through everything, even when I didn't remember who you were," I force a smile because honestly, I feel like crying right now. I'm not sure why, but I do. It's like the very thought of them doing those things taints the perfect images I have of them inside my mind.

"Well, what are friends for if not to protect those that they care about. You would have done the same for me. Now let's try and get some sleep before the sun comes up."

I nod in agreement, while Shelby gets up and starts to put on her PJs. I don't even bother. All I do is slip out of my shoes and skinny jeans before curling up in my bed. When the lights are out, and the room is blanketed in silence, I wait for sleep to come, but it never does, and instead, I find myself staring up at the ceiling wondering why if the Bishop brothers were so mean to me, if they bullied me, why do I feel so connected to them? Why does it physically hurt to think about them being with someone else?

21

It's been two days since the party, but the ache in my chest from what Shelby shared with me hasn't stopped throbbing. It feels like a bruise that's continually being prodded at, never getting the chance to heal. Luckily, I haven't seen any of the Bishop brothers, and I'm more than okay with that. I'm not really sure how to approach them now that I know the truth. Hell, I don't even really understand all of this.

My emotions are a rollercoaster ride, up and down with each curve, then a loop as the final blow. I want to hate all three of them, but deep down in the pit of my stomach, there is this flicker of doubt that I could ever hate them. If I could just get my stupid memory back, maybe I could finally make sense of everything.

Walking into class, I'm reminded of Shelby's words, *"They followed you here to get revenge."* Those words alone, coupled with the ones Matt told me, *"I think you would much rather kill each other than screw."*

Then there are the pictures on the phone... the things they did.

Everything points to what everyone has been telling me... we have been nothing but enemies, *rivals*.

Pushing the thoughts away, I find a seat at one of the empty tables at the back of the chemistry class. There are small lab stations already set up in the center of each table, and the look of it makes me nervous. I have no idea what I'm supposed to be doing here, hopefully, whoever decides to sit beside me knows what to do.

A petite looking girl with short brown hair appears out of thin air, sliding into the seat beside me. She smiles blissfully, and as I stare at her, maybe a little too long, I can't help but think she looks like an adult version of Tinkerbell.

"Hi, Harlow. I'm Caroline."

She must know me.

"Hi," I try and make myself smile back, but there's no point. There's too much going on inside my head, and honestly, I'm not happy enough right now to muster up even the tiniest of smiles, and faking it just isn't cutting it anymore.

"I'm guessing we knew each other, and that's how you know my name?" I try not to sound annoyed, because truly I'm not, but this memory loss thing is starting to weigh on me, among other things.

"Yes, we are friends, or at least I hope we still are," she raises an eyebrow as if she's awaiting a response.

"Maybe... I guess we have to start all over again. My brains a little like scrambled eggs right now."

"I'm up for that," she smiles and extends her hand out to me. "Hi, I'm Caroline, it's nice to meet you."

Taking hold of her hand, I give it a gentle squeeze. "It's nice to meet you, Caroline."

"I'm so glad that you're okay, minus the memory issues and all." She smiles again, and I wonder how she does that, appears to be happy all the time.

"Hi, Harlow," another girl says, as she saunters up to our table. Looking up at her, I realize she's the Tiffany chick from the pictures that Shelby showed me the other night. My mood sours even further then.

I don't need this reminder of how I was treated and how the Bishops played me. Without greeting her, I pull out my textbook, and open it up, pretending to find some imaginary page I'm looking for. Anything is more interesting at this point than reliving the hell of something I can't remember.

"What's the matter? Too good to say *hi* now?" Tiffany huffs, leaning against the table, the bracelets on her wrist clanking loudly against the wood. "Seems like you remember me just fine. So I'm guessing the whole losing your memory thing is just a scam to get attention? Do you think that's how you'll get the Bishops to notice you?"

"Don't talk to her," Caroline snaps back.

"Well, look at you, growing a backbone, and shit." The muscles in my jaw tighten, my teeth grinding together so harshly I can hear the sound of them clashing together in my ears.

"She doesn't want to talk to you," Caroline wrinkles her nose, "and honestly, you don't even deserve to be in her presence. You're nothing but a big bully."

Tiffany narrows her eyes and leans even further across the table, and I have half a mind to shove her arms back and watch her fall face-first against the wooden surface.

"That's rich, as if the Bishop brothers had nothing to do with it? Who do you think told me to do it? You think the banner was my idea? Think again."

"I'm sure you had to be talked into it," Caroline glares, her eyes burning like molten lava. "That you didn't enjoy even one second of it."

Scoffing Tiffany fires right back, "As if she wasn't enjoying all the attention, too bad it wasn't enough to hold the Bishops' interest. At the end of the day, they come to my bed."

"Tiffany, please find a seat." The professor shouts from the front of the classroom, his voice ringing through the space, drawing excess attention to the three of us.

"You're lucky, both of you," Tiffany practically spits the words, before turning on her heeled feet to find an empty seat. As soon as she's gone, I all but melt into my chair.

Well, that was enjoyable, not.

The professor tells us to open our books to page seventy-five and starts talking about something from last week's class. I try and focus on the board and on the notes, but every time I look toward the board, I see Tiffany's stupid blonde head.

Caroline leans over and whispers, "I'm sorry you had to see that, and that we talked as if you weren't here. She just makes me so angry. Always playing the victim." Fire still flickers in her eyes, and I know her intentions are pure. She's just trying to be a friend.

The rest of the class goes by in a flash, that is, once I forget about the blonde skank sitting a few feet away. With the memory of her fading, I actually start to enjoy myself. That is right up until it's time for the hands-on experiment to take place.

Nervously, I look over at Caroline, "Do you know anything about this chemistry stuff?"

"You're looking at a straight-A student," she winks, and I watch her turn on the burner before reorganizing all the beakers and test tubes. "You just sit there and look pretty, and let me do all the tough stuff," she giggles and cracks her knuckles.

She starts mixing some of the liquids together and sets them over the flame, while I watch half curious, half wary of what may happen next. When the liquid starts boiling, she turns the knob for the burner down, but the flame gets bigger instead of smaller. Distress signals start to go off in my brain like bright red traffic signs.

"Mhh, that's weird," her forehead creases and her words must be loud enough for the professor to hear because I see him approach out of the corner of my eye, "I think this burner might be broke."

Professor Keller walks over to our table and takes a closer look, when he touches the knob, the flame shoots up as if he had turned it up all the way. The flame is so large that I can feel the heat of it on my face. Out of instinct, Caroline and I both push away from the table, while Prof. Keller tries to turn off the burner. As soon as he touches the switch, the whole thing blows up in his face. A scream catches in my throat as the entire classroom breaks out into chaos.

Everything happens so fast my brain can barely keep up. Prof. Keller's face is badly burned, and even though I want to help him, I don't know how. I'm in too much shock to know anything right now. Caroline grabs my arm and pulls me away further, as some guy helps the professor sit down on a chair nearby. Others around us are running out of the class, and two people are on the phone with emergency services.

A couple other teachers burst into the room telling us to walk outside. Caroline never leaves my side as we make it out of the building. Where a group of people have gathered. A lot of the girls are crying, and even the guys look like they are about to breakdown.

When I look over to Caroline, I realize that she has her phone out and is texting someone. I briefly wonder if I should text someone, do I need to let Shelby know that I'm okay? My thought is interrupted when the ambulance and police sirens approach at rapid speed.

"Let's get out of the way," Caroline tells me and starts tugging me away. I follow her mindlessly to the side of the building.

"Don't you think they would want to talk to us? Maybe we should go back," I point out when we are already at the corner. Caroline stops and faces me, an unreadable expression on her face.

"Harlow, listen, you have to believe me when I say that I am your friend. It might have not started that way, and I'm sorry about that, but I am your friend now, and I'm doing this to help you."

"Doing what to help me?" I barely get the words out before someone grabs me from behind. A hand slaps over my mouth, muffling my scream. A pair of muscular arms circle my waist and pull me to a firm chest as I'm dragged backward.

My eyes seek out Caroline, and I see her face before I'm turned away. It is blank as if she is trying to ignore my struggling, as if she doesn't want to acknowledge my fear. In the midst of my raging anger, my fighting instinct kicks in, and I start kicking my legs out and flailing my arms around me, but it's no use, I'm basically immobilized. Tears dwell in my eyes, and fall down my cheeks.

When I realize my assailant is pulling me toward an old truck, I dig my heels into the ground, but he just picks me up and carries me to it.

The driver's door opens, and a second guy comes out. As soon as he comes into view, my heart stops. *Banks.*

Banks opens the back door so whoever is behind me can push me in. I'm guessing it's either Sullivan or Oliver who has an iron grip on me. My chest tightens, and more tears escape my eyes, making my vision blurry.

"Don't cry, we won't hurt you," Oliver's smooth voice tickles my ear, confirming my assumption. I expected him to push me into the back, but instead, he keeps a hold of me as he slides into the backseat himself. Banks shuts the door behind us and climbs into the front seat. As soon as he does, we speed off.

The world seems to spin around me. I'm sitting on Oliver's lap, his hand still covering my mouth and his other arm is like an iron bar across my chest.

Only then do I realize how much danger I'm in. I'm being kidnapped. They're taking me to god knows where, with the intent of doing who knows what.

Every bad scenario runs through my head. Dread and terror spread through me, making my whole-body shiver in fear.

"Shh, it's okay," Oliver tries to soothe, his voice low and comforting. I can't help but wonder if this is a sick game to him. He can't actually expect me to believe him. Of course, he doesn't know that I know now. "I'm gonna take my hand away. I'd prefer if you didn't scream."

I'd prefer? What an ass.

Slowly he removes his hand from my mouth, and I suck in a greedy breath. I don't scream, mostly because there really is no point. We are in a truck driving down the road.

Who is going to hear me?

Digging deep, I find the strength to speak, to fight back. "Where are you taking me? What are you going to do?"

"I've already told you, we're friends and we are trying to help you."

"We're not friends," I growl, trying to fight against his muscled arms. "And you've hurt me. I know you have. Shelby told me everything. There's no point in trying to hide it."

"And what's that?" he asks, slightly amused.

"I know you drugged me the other day at that party."

"I don't know why she would say that, but I can assure you, I did no such thing. What would be my motive for doing that?"

"I don't know, why don't you tell me? She told me you wouldn't let her go back outside and told some random guy to bring me a spiked drink."

"First of all, why would I drug you, and then sit in a car with you for three hours until you sobered up, just to drive you home? Second, if I would have really done that then why didn't Shelby call the police?"

His words have the fight in me stopping dead in its tracks.

Why would he, and why didn't she call the cops?

It doesn't make sense to me. Shelby's supposed to be my friend. She's supposed to help me, not hurt me. Why would she do such a thing? Banks takes a sharp turn making us slide across the leather seat. The movement interrupts my thoughts.

Air swooshes from my lungs when I nearly make impact with the window. I would have hit my head against it if it wasn't for Oliver's strong arms wrapped around me.

It's then that I realize I'm still sitting on his lap. Pushing off of him, I scurry off his lap, and take the seat next to him, and attempt to gather my thoughts.

I'm confused, beyond confused.

"I don't know... but I do know what I saw. She showed me pictures of you and Tiffany. I know you terrorized me at school, that you hung up a banner with my number and spread rumors about me."

Oliver's face falls at the mention of those things, and I know that they're true.

"I'm not gonna lie to you, Harlow. All those things are true, but that was before..." His voice trails off, and it sounds like he's ashamed.

His words hurt more than I anticipated. I already knew the truth, but part of me was hoping that it wasn't true, that maybe he would deny it, or had an explanation for his actions, but he doesn't. Disappointment and jealousy settle deep in my gut.

"Why would I believe anything you say now? You just admitted to bullying me. You made my life hell, and now suddenly you want to *help* me?" I scoff, they can't actually expect me to buy this bullshit story.

Oliver looks scorned, but not defeated. "You aren't innocent, either. Yeah, I've done things and so have my brothers, but you did something just as bad. We wanted to ruin your life because you ruined our lives when you planted drugs on Sullivan."

Banks takes that moment to say something for the first time, "What you did two years ago affected our entire family. Our father's business went bankrupt, we had to move, completely start over again. So yeah, we wanted revenge. But we would never physically hurt you... *never.*" For some stupid reason, I look to the front seat, my eyes meeting Banks' in the rearview mirror.

"Everything you just said only proves further that you should hate me and that I shouldn't trust you."

Oliver sighs loudly and scrubs his hands down his face in frustration, "You're just gonna have to trust us, I guess."

"We're almost there," Banks says, and I wonder where the hell *there* is. Looking out the window, it's clear that we've left the city, given all the trees. Banks turns off the highway and on to a smaller road. After a few more miles, he turns down a dirt road, and my panic starts to mount.

"Where are we going?" I ask, doing my best to keep my voice steady.

"We bought a cabin up here to get away from school when we want to. We're gonna stay there for a few days until we can figure out who is trying to hurt you."

"No one is trying to hurt me, and if they are, I'm better off back at the dorms with dumb and dumber than I'll ever be here with any of you." At the end of the day, the Bishops and I will always be rivals, and nothing they tell me will ever change that.

"Sure, you can think that all you want, but you aren't getting out of our sights until we decide it's safe to do so," Banks hisses.

Crossing my arms over my chest, I stare out the window, watching as we drive deeper and deeper into the wilderness.

"You can tell me whatever you want, I'll never believe anything you say." The words come out stronger than I anticipated, even though it feels like I'm a piece of crumbling rock on a cliff's edge.

Oliver speaks this time, "That's fine. Maybe you won't believe us, but you can't deny the truth when it's right in front of you, now can you?"

"I'll believe it when I see it, and kidnapping me is not looking too good for you." I don't dare look at him, because deep down, I know he's right. Deep down, there's no way I can look away from the truth. Now the real question is... what is the whole truth?

22

We pull up to a cabin out in the middle of nowhere. We're probably miles away from any other house, and even though I don't know which way to run, I won't just let them take me inside that cabin.

Banks cuts the engine, and I push open my door at the same time. Before they even realize what I'm doing, I'm sprinting away from the car, leaving the cabin and them behind me.

"Harlow, stop!" Oliver calls after me, but I don't listen or turn around. Pushing my legs to go as fast as I can, I run like the wind. Trees whooshing by me as my feet pound over the soft forest floor. I don't hear anyone following me, and I'm confused that they're not.

Then, out of nowhere, a body slams into me, arms circling my waist as I'm tackled to the dirt-covered floor. I'm about to hit the ground face first, but mid-flight my assailant twists us around, so he lands hard on the ground, with me on top of him.

Still, the impact is harsh enough to knock the air out of my chest. Closing my eyes, I gasp for air, while my heart beats unnaturally fast in my chest.

Someone grunts heavily behind me, but his grip on me stays the same. "Shit... that hurt. Are you okay?" Sullivan groans into my ear.

"Let me go, and I'll be better," I snap back. Instead of letting me go, he rolls over so we can get up together. Keeping one hand tightly wrapped around my arm, he walks me back to the cabin I just ran away from.

Oliver and Banks are standing at the door, both of them have their arms crossed over their chest, giving me a disapproving look. Oliver actually shakes his head at me when I walk past him, and I have this urge to kick his leg.

"Don't look at me like you're my dad, and I just missed my curfew. You kidnapped me, did you really think I'd just let you and not try to get away?"

"You're a pain in the ass," Banks mutters under his breath somewhere behind me.

I ignore his comment.

Crossing the threshold, I step into the small cabin, which is basically one large room. My eyes dart around, there's a kitchenette, a living space with a flat-screen, a recliner, a sectional, and angled off in the corner is a king-sized bed. There's only one other door besides the front door, and I'm guessing that leads to a bathroom.

No. Hell no.

"I'm not staying here," I yell. "Take me back to campus, right now," I demand, but when I turn around, coming face to face with all three guys.

I find they're each giving me a different looking level of sternness.

"No," Oliver takes a step forward, forcing me to take a step back. "Stop fighting us."

"Never," I curl my lip. Taking another step backward, I nearly trip over my own feet. Sullivan comes to my rescue, once again, his hand gripping onto my bicep gently. The heat of his touch sears my skin, and instead of wanting to pull away, I want to lean into his touch, let him wrap both his arms around me.

"Well, this is going well," Banks sighs, shutting the door and turning the lock. The noise of it draws my attention. Shit, I'm stuck inside this cabin with all three of them, with no way out. Fear slithers through my veins, but there's something else there, something residing just beneath the surface. It's warm and makes my stomach do summersaults. I don't understand it, and nor do I want to. These men are my enemies, nothing more.

With his hand still wrapped around my upper arm, Sullivan turns to his brothers. "Did you explain to her why she is here?"

Oliver tosses his hands into the air, his handsome face riddled with frustration. "We told her she was in danger, of what we didn't explain. It doesn't matter right now, because she's not going to believe a damn thing that we tell her. Shelby's got her so brainwashed it isn't even funny. Nothing we say is going to sink in."

"Okay, let's just sit down and take a breather," Sullivan suggests, leading me to the sectional. We sit down, and Banks and Oliver follow suit. Oliver sits next to me, leaving me wedged between him, and Sullivan, while Banks sits down on the recliner.

A long, tense moment of silence fills the room, and all I can think about is what they are going to do next. *How long can they keep me here? How long before someone notices I'm missing?* They haven't actually hurt me, and they've already had plenty of opportunities to do so, so maybe they are telling the truth, at the very least about that.

"Hypothetically speaking... say I do believe you... that you do want to help me and keep me safe from some unknown threat. Why? You already admitted to hating me at one point. Why not anymore? What changed that?"

"Well," Banks snickers and I swear he gets even more handsome when he smiles. "*You.* You kind of changed that all on your own. We weren't lying when we said we were out for revenge. I guess we never accounted for that hate to turn into something else, something that started to look a lot less like hate. We each spent a lot of time with you, and I guess you grew on us, in more than one way." A mischievous grin appears on his lips, and it tells me that he is talking about something besides friendship.

"Oliver said we were *just* friends."

"I don't think *friends* do what we did," Banks chuckles.

My eyes dart between all three of them. They can't really be saying what I think they're saying, can they?

"I...." My cheeks heat and a boulder the size of Texas starts to form in my throat. That guy from the party, he said I was into threesomes. Assuming what they're saying is true, then he was right?

"Did I... Did I sleep with all three of you?" I cringe as I ask the question, though there's a tiny spark, a tiny flame of curiosity that flickers inside of me. Ashamed, I bury my face in my hands. This is wrong, so wrong.

"You didn't sleep with all three of us. Only Sullivan." Oliver speaks through his teeth, his tone, filled with venom, signifying his distaste over the subject. Dropping my hands from my face, I turn to face Sullivan.

Shame and guilt mix inside his ocean blue eyes and I know immediately that there is more to this story than what they're telling me.

"Tell me. What happened?"

"I don't think now is the right time to talk about this," Sullivan interjects before anyone can say anything.

"Why's that?" Oliver hisses like a snake, and Sullivan's gaze turns to steel, his jaw clenching so tight you could cut glass on the edge of it.

"You know why," he grits out.

"Yeah 'cause it would paint you in a shit light, and god forbid that happens," Oliver snarls, and I notice that he's vibrating with rage, his entire body tense. "I'm going outside before I do something stupid."

Oliver tries to get up, but I grab his arm pulling him back. "Don't go." I'm not sure what compels me to say it and with the feeling behind it, but as soon as the words are out, Oliver relaxes next to me. "Please tell me what happened... all of it. The good and the bad. I want to remember it, but I can't, so I need you to tell me."

"We followed you to Bayshore, we wanted to mess with you, try to sabotage your school year, maybe even get you expelled," Oliver starts explaining. "We followed you around, spread rumors..." His voice trails off, shame filling his eyes at the memory.

"Then we got close, really close," Banks continues. "We actually got to know you, and we were working on forgiving you, but then you betrayed us again... or so we thought."

"You denied setting us up *again*," Sullivan says as if he's lost in thought, "at the end, Banks and Oliver believed you, but I didn't... I was so caught up in my own anger, so caught up in feeling like we had given you the knife to stab us all over again, that I secretly filmed us having sex."

My eyes go wide at his confession, my heart all but lurching from my chest.

Filmed us having sex?

My mouth pops open, and I don't know if I'm angry, shocked, or ashamed.

"Why? Why would you do that?"

Sullivan blinks, his eyes finding mine. "I was angry, I thought you'd made me fall for you as part of a plot against us. I had no idea you were so innocent. I was going to publish the video for all to see, show you as the dirty slut I thought you were, but I didn't. I swear to you that I didn't, nobody ever saw it. I knew the second that I saw the blood on your thighs, it was me who had wronged you. Both of our parents wanted to ensure we remained enemies, and I had gobbled that bullshit right up. They had me eating right out of their hands." Shaking his head, he looks away, as if he couldn't take looking at me any longer.

"Do you still have it? The tape..."

Sullivan turns, his eyes snapping up to mine. "Why?"

"Do you or do you not?" I ask again. The air grows thick as all eyes move to Sullivan.

His face pales just a bit, and then he says, "I swear no one's seen it but me."

"But you still have it?" I push.

"Yes," he finally admits. "Yes, I still have it."

"Jesus dude, you didn't delete it?" Oliver barks, and I swear he's just looking for a reason to clobber his brother. Then again, I'm kinda interested in seeing it.

"I can't believe you, you really are a dickhead," Banks chimes in, just as disappointed in his brother as Oliver is. "I should kick you in the nuts right now."

"I want to see it. I want to see the tape." I don't even think about the repercussions or how it's going to make me feel afterward. All I want is to see it, because maybe, just maybe, reliving my past will make me remember it fully. Sullivan pulls out his phone and thumbs through it, pausing as soon as he finds the video.

Slowly, he hands it to me, shame and guilt, among a slew of other emotions paint his features. Ignoring how that makes me feel, I take the phone, and without any hesitation, I hit play.

The video starts, Sullivan and I are in a bedroom, already lying on the bed, naked. His body is covering most of mine, but I still feel weird with Oliver beside me, who can clearly see the screen.

"Do you want me to fuck you hard and fast or slow and gentle?" Sullivan's voice comes through the speaker and my breath hitches. He sounds different, his tone laced with lust, his voice deeper, reaching into the tiny crevices of my soul.

"Slow, please," my voice comes out strong, and I watch intently as he starts moving, his hips thrusting forward with determination. The muscles of his back ripple and he looks like a man on a mission, a mission of pleasure. As I watch, heat creeps up my neck and cheeks, while tingles of warmth spread throughout my core.

"Do you wish it was all three of us doing this with you right now? That we got to take turns with you? Making you come over and over again." Holy shit. I almost drop the phone. Why would he ask me that? Swallowing loudly, I glance up at Oliver and Banks, who are both staring holes straight through me.

"Yes," I answer, sounding breathless. *"I would like that..."*

Hearing my answer, I drop the phone. It slips out of my trembling hands and falls to the hardwood floor landing with a loud clunk.

Moaning sounds fill the room before Sullivan can snatch the phone from the ground and turn off the recording.

My cheeks are on fire, and my head feels like it's about to burst into flames. I basically just watched myself in a porn video while three guys were watching me.

Though embarrassing, it was needed, because it showed me that they weren't lying. I had sex with Sullivan, not all three of them, but I wanted to sleep with all of them, that much was obvious which all but tells me they all mean something to me.

"So..." Banks clears his throat. "Did that help jog your memory?"

Someone, please kill me now. Or at least let me disappear for a little bit.

"You don't have to feel ashamed, Harlow," Oliver says. "All three of us knew what we were getting into. We had talked about it at great lengths when things started to change between us. We want you just as badly as you want us."

"Wanted, you mean?" I correct him, though, we all know that I'm lying. Even if I don't remember them fully, in some ways my body does, it's drawn to each of them in its own way, each of them taking something different from me, and giving me a little piece of themselves back.

"Stop denying it. We know you want us, and you know that we want you. Enough damage has already been done, enough time has been wasted, and I don't want to play games anymore." Banks states, matter of factly.

"It's not that easy for me. My body remembers you, but my brain doesn't. I'm afraid, okay? How can I trust anyone or anything, when I can't even trust my own brain?"

"You can trust us," Sullivan assures, his hand reaching for mine.

"Brain injuries take a while to heal, and sometimes the memories never come back, but that doesn't mean we're just going to walk away or let something happen to you." Sullivan's fingers interlock with mine, and for the first time today, I feel safe.

"Why don't we get something to eat and talk about what happened today?" Oliver suggests, and everybody nods their heads in agreement.

They must have had this planned because both the fridge and pantry are stocked with food. Sullivan heats up some ready to eat grocery store meals, and we all sit at the small dining table. The guys shovel food into their mouths at an alarming rate, while I take small bites, trying to decide if I'm hungry or not.

Looking between the three of them, I start to talk. "It was just Caroline and me at the table. So, if someone rigged the burner, it happened before we came into class. The only other person who came to our table was... *Tiffany*." I really tried to say her name in a normal voice, but the dislike for her clearly reflects in my tone. "She told me you guys had a thing..."

Banks chuckles, "Of course she did. You don't have any reason to be jealous of her though. We used her to make you jealous, nothing more than that."

"Did you sleep with her?" I don't know what compels me to ask, but I have to know.

"No, none of us slept with her or any of her friends," Sullivan cuts in. Through all of this, I know I should be more apprehensive, should be concerned about what's happening, but I'm not. The brothers are the only people who have been honest with me. They're the only people that have made an effort to tell me about my past, *our* past.

"Well, I guess that makes me feel a little better," I say the words out loud, though, I didn't mean to.

"We missed you, so much, and we did kick Sullivan's ass for you. After what he did, he's lucky we didn't disown him," Oliver states, before laughing and the sound slices through me. It's so deep, and warm, and I just want to tell him to keep talking, and laughing, but that would be weird, right? Dropping my gaze down to my food, I shove the pieces around with my fork.

It hits me all at once why I'm here then, all the pieces stacking up inside my head, leading me to this very moment. My father had said I was in danger, and now the brothers were saying I was in danger. But who was I in danger from?

"Who would want to hurt me?"

"Honestly, we don't know. First, it was the..." Banks' words cut off when a soft knocking sounds against the door. All three brothers exchange a look as if they're talking with nothing more than their eyes. Oliver pushes away from the table and goes to the door, letting in whoever is on the other side. Immediately, I start to feel nervous, dropping my fork onto my plate.

"How is everything? Is she okay?"

Caroline? I shove from my chair, nearly sending the thing to the floor. She's stood in the doorway, her face scrunched together, guilt flickering in her eyes.

"Harlow, I'm sorry," she says, as soon as she crosses the threshold. Deep down, I know I should be angry with her for leading me here, but I'm not. I can't be. It seems the Bishop brothers and Caroline are the only people telling me the truth, or really anything right now.

"Don't be. It's okay." I assure her with a soft smile. She nods as if accepting my word, and Oliver closes the door, sealing us all inside.

"What's the lowdown, Cuz?" Banks implores.

Cuz? I stare, thinking maybe I've misheard him. Sullivan catches my bewildered facial expression and interrupts before Caroline can start talking.

"Caroline is our cousin," he announces, and I stare at him blankly. I have half a mind to say *no way, really*, but I feel like sarcasm really isn't needed at this point.

"You didn't tell her yet?" Caroline whispers, elbowing Oliver in the side.

"When would you have liked me to tell her? Trying to keep her in this cabin has been enough work." Oliver quips before giving me a dashing smile, the effects of said smile send a ripple of heat all the way down to my toes.

Caroline shrugs, "I guess, it doesn't matter though. It's a good thing you got her out of there. I don't know what the hell is going on. There was no evidence of anything, no foul play, they're claiming it was the burner that malfunctioned, but we all know that would just be too much of a coincidence."

The way she says it, with so much conviction, it scares me a little.

"We'll figure it out. Don't worry, Harlow," Sullivan says.

"Want something to eat, Cuz?" Banks offers and Caroline nods furiously.

"I'm starving... let me get some of this," Caroline points at the meatloaf. I realize that there are only four chairs, and all of them are taken, so I get up to sit on the couch.

"I'm done eating, you can have my chair," I say, but when I try to walk past Banks, he reaches out and grabs me by the hip, pulling me into his lap.

"Don't be ridiculous. You can sit with me," he grins, as my ass makes contact with his leg. I should pull away, but sitting on his lap feels normal, and it feels even better to have his heavy arm wrapped around my middle, holding me tightly to him.

Jesus. There has to be something wrong with me.

Caroline eats and talks a little more before saying her goodbyes. When she leaves, I'm left feeling anxious and unsure.

One cabin. Three brothers, and me.

23

The guys talk amongst themselves for a while, and then we all move into the living room and watch a little tv. The room seems so small with all four of us in it, and I swear the temperature rises too. Sandwiched between Banks and Sullivan on the couch, my eyes start to grow heavy with exhaustion.

"Ready to go to bed?" Oliver asks, obviously seeing my drooping eyes. I glance over to the lone bed in the room. "To sleep, nothing more," he clarifies, seeing my apprehension.

"Are we all going to sleep in one bed?"

"Nah, we'll make Sullivan sleep on the couch. It's a king-size bed, it will fit three of us, so, you, me, and Oliver can sleep in it together. Unless you're not okay with that?"

"No... it's fine." My eyes dart back over to the bed. It's huge, and it wouldn't be fair to make two of them sleep on the floor while I had that huge bed all to myself. "You're right, it's big enough for the three of us."

Banks smiles, and I get this stupid urge to trace his lips with mine. I wonder what he tastes like. If he's as intoxicating to my taste buds as he is to my other senses?

Sullivan gives me an oversized shirt and shorts to wear to bed, and I get changed in the bathroom. I have the weirdest feeling in my gut as I do so. It's a mixture of excitement and wrongfulness. *I'm about to sleep in a bed with two guys, with a third one in the same room.* All guys that I admitted wanting to sleep with. I'm not sure what that says about me, if anything.

Shaking the feeling off, I step out of the bathroom and find they have already gotten comfortable. Sullivan is sprawled out on the couch with his hands behind his head, his shirt's missing, and his perfectly sculpted body is on display. Wetting my lips with my tongue, I try and look away, but it's so damn hard. The dips and planes of his chest beckon me onward.

Finding some internal strength, I pull my gaze away and mumble a goodnight beneath my breath. Oliver and Banks are both in bed, laying on either side shirtless just like their brother, and having left me a lot of space in the center.

Sweet baby Jesus. My ovaries are going insane, and the heat I felt once before pulses low in my abdomen. From the foot of the bed, I crawl into my designated spot and slither under the covers. Oliver rolls then, one of his thick muscled arms wrapping around me, drawing me into his chest.

"If this bothers you, tell me, but I want you close. Just to hold you, nothing more," Oliver whispers into the shell of my ear, and I shiver at the hot breath skating across my cool skin. I can feel the hardness of his body molding against mine like two pieces of clay coming together.

Tucked tightly into his side, I inhale the clean scent of soap and rainwater. It calms me and makes me feel warm and cozy. Banks shifts against the mattress before rolling over to face me. Like his brothers, he looks like a Greek god, carved from stone, his body perfectly sculpted, his jaw tight, and his hair tousled. Our eyes collide then, and in the depths of his gaze, I see a hurricane of emotions swirling.

With a gentle hand, he reaches out and brushes away a few stray strands of hair from my face.

"I never thought we would see you again." Banks' admission surprises the hell out of me. He comes off as the jokester of the group, but right now he looks anything but to be joking. In fact, he looks serious, so serious it's almost scary.

"Well, I'm here now." The words barely make it past my lips. It feels like I'm caught between fire and ice, my body being pulled in two different directions.

"Yes. Yes, you are." He smiles, his thumb drifting over my bottom lip. His eyes follow the motion, the color of them darkening, lust, and need swirling around, and around.

Kiss me. I scream internally, though, I'm not sure why. The pull I have toward these guys is magnetic, and even if my brain can't remember why they matter, my body and my heart do.

"Goodnight, Harlow," he whispers a second later, pulling his hand away, pouring an ice-cold bucket of water all over my desire at the loss of contact. His eyes drift closed, and he rests his hand against the mattress in the small space between us.

"Sweet dreams, Harlow." Oliver nuzzles into my hair, and I feel his words in my bones. The room grows quiet, and it seems to take me forever to close my own eyes. After a while, the heat in my veins dulls, and exhaustion wins out, pulling me deep into the darkness. With all three brothers in the room, nothing can touch me, hurt me, and I let that sink deep into my mind as I lull off sleep.

I'm standing on the deck of a boat. My hands are on the railing as a brisk wind blows through my hair. It's cold, so cold, and I bite my lip to stifle the sob threatening to rip from my throat. My emotions are out of control, short-circuiting. Out of nowhere, a hard shove from behind me causes me to lose my grip, the cold metal disappearing out from underneath my fingers. In seconds I'm flying through the cold night air, my body waiting for the pain to come.

A gut-wrenching scream rips from my chest, rushing past my lips a moment before my body hits the unforgiving sea. Pain ripples through me on impact, petrifying my bones as a terrorizing darkness swallows me whole. Sinking like a rock to the bottom of the sea. Panic grabs onto every cell in my body, robbing my brain of any thought but one. Survival.

It takes everything inside me to push aside the feeling of a thousand needles prickling across my skin that the ice-cold water leaves me with. My lungs burn, begging, pleading for air, but I have none to give them. Squeezing my eyes shut, I overcome the stiffness in my limbs and start kicking my legs with everything I have left. I will not die without a fight.

I swim through the darkness and toward the surface, giving it my all, but it's not enough. The current is too strong, the water too dark. I'm too weak.

The sea is swallowing me whole...and all that is left is death.

It's finally come for me...it's finally time.

Air fills my lungs, and my eyes pop open as I feel around me to gather my bearings. *Where am I? What's happening?* For a moment I'm suspended in time, unsure of everything around me. Sweat dribbles down the side of my face, and the sound of my heartbeat swooshes in my ears. Something moves beside me, and I look over, slowly coming back to my senses.

"It was just a nightmare, everything is okay, you're okay," Oliver soothes. My throat tightens, words refusing to come out at that moment. I wasn't okay though. I was dying, drowning, alone in the darkness. The sea swallowing me whole.

Tremors of fear ripple through me as I remember the dream as if it actually happened to me, and then I realize... it did. I almost drowned. Someone did push me off a boat. Someone wants me dead, and I don't know why. The fear inside me spikes and I find myself rolling over, and burying my face into Oliver's bare chest. Inhaling his masculine scent, I try and push the worries away.

"Shh, I'll never let anything happen to you again," Oliver murmurs, his lips ghosting against my forehead. My entire body is shaking now, but I believe him. The hand slung over me rubs soothingly up and down my back, the motion alone pulls me from the foggy fear surrounding me. With every stroke of his hand, I feel less afraid, and more turned on. A fire sparking deep inside my gut.

Tipping my head back, I peer up at Oliver, his face is creased with sleep, but his eyes are magnificent, deep and dark, like melted chocolate.

"Are you okay?" Banks' muffled voice sounds from behind me. The sheets rustle and then I feel him closer, his hard body brushing against mine. Oliver moves his hand and Banks moves even closer until he's sandwiched me between him and Oliver.

"I almost died. In my dream, I was dying, and no one saved me, and the water was rushing in," I whimper, unable to hold it together a second longer. Oliver caresses my face with his hand, his thumb brushing against my lip, while his eyes bore into mine.

"I jumped into the water that night to save you. There was no way I was going to let you drown. You weren't alone, Harlow, and you never will be again."

He saved me? He jumped into the water and saved me? Before I can fully grasp the significance of the statement, his lips are on mine. I'm vaguely aware of Banks' fingers sinking possessively into my hip, pulling my rear into his hardness. With Oliver's lips on mine, Banks brushes away the hair at my neck and peppers my skin with kisses. Instantly my body melts, my insides turning to molten lava.

Oliver cradles my face in his hands, and continues his assault on my lips, kissing me like a man starved of food. He sips from my lips like I'm a sweet nectar, his tongue slipping into my mouth and caressing my own. The tiniest of whimpers slips past my mouth as the hold Banks has on me grows harder, his fingers digging into the tender flesh. Oliver swallows up my whimper but not before Banks can hear it. Again, he squeezes the flesh, kneading it in his hand, his fingers playing with the waistband of my shorts.

Oh, hell, I want his fingers in me, *no,* I need them in me. I need the ache forming between my thighs elevated before I combust.

Breaking the kiss, I suck in a precious breath of oxygen before I whisper, "I want to do with you what I did with Sullivan." I speak to both of them, and, though, I can't see Banks' face at that moment, the deep growl that emits from his mouth and against my skin tells me he approves.

"You don't have to. That's not what this is about. Yes, we want you, but it's deeper than that. It's so much more than sex, Harlow."

I can't comprehend his words right now, not with Banks' lips on my skin, and Oliver beside me, his lips swollen and his eyes wild with need.

He's saying one thing, but his body is reacting in another way, the large bulge pressing against my thigh giving him away. He wants this so badly, just like I do, and I need to prove it to him.

"I know it's not about sex, but I want you, both of you. It feels like I'm burning up inside. I don't understand the need, or why, all I know is that I have this connection with each of you, and I want to strengthen it. It pains me to be so close and not have the same things with you two that I do with Sullivan. I want that connection to grow."

"Sex or no sex, we're connected. That won't ever change," Banks whispers against my skin, his voice deep and smoky.

"Please," I plead one last time, and as if the word alone holds power, Oliver's resolve snaps. Pulling away, he shucks his shorts. Banks does the same, and then together, they help me out of my own clothing. Rolling me over onto my back, Oliver slowly peels my shirt off while his brother does the same with my shorts. It doesn't take them long, and before I know it, I'm completely bare, not only in a physical sense but in an emotional one as well. It feels like I'm giving each of them a piece of my jagged heart.

Banks leans forward, pressing his lips to mine, his kiss is hotter, deeper, wilder than Oliver's and he brands me with his lips, leaving me burning. I can feel Oliver moving against the sheets, and then I feel his fingers, gently skimming over my tummy, moving lower and lower. My legs part all on their own, and I tremble with anticipation.

"Your body is a temple, Harlow, and it deserves to be worshipped," Oliver whispers, his tone gravely and zinging straight to the epi-center of my core. I want to respond, but I can't. My lips are molded to Banks' and the possessiveness of his kiss tells me he won't let me go, no matter what.

"I'm going to taste you, lick, and suck, nibble, and devour every inch of your pink pussy."

Oh god, yes, please, yes. My fingers fist the sheets, and my heart gallops in my chest when I feel the first lick of Oliver's tongue.

Banks breaks the kiss, and a low mewl escapes my lips. "So fucking pretty, and perfect. You were made for us, your body, your heart, and your soul," he hisses, his hands finding both my breasts. He kneads the flesh, rolling my puckered nipples between two fingers. With wide eyes, I stare up into his crystal blue orbs, becoming entranced by them. I arch into his touch while at the same time lifting my hips, needing more, so much more.

"Greedy. Such a greedy girl," Oliver chuckles against my folds, and as if he has a direct line to my mind, he starts to devour me, nuzzling his nose against my clit, he tongues my entrance. In and out, in and out, his tongue swirling around in a circle.

"I can see how wet you are, how much you want us. Come all over my brother's tongue so we can claim you..." Banks commands huskily, and I swear his voice alone has some type of spell on me. The heat in my belly spreads outward, and as Oliver licks me faster, alternating between licks and sucks, I find myself being pulled closer and closer to the cliff's edge.

Two fingers enter me without warning, spreading me. I expect there to be some pain, but there's none, in fact, there's nothing but pleasure. It sparks, igniting my orgasm like a rocket that's heading toward the moon. One more pluck of my nipple, and two more dips inside my tightness and I'm soaring through the air, my entire body burning, like a shooting star, I burn up across the night sky.

A gasp catches in my throat as I tumble through nothingness, my eyes fall closed, and my nails sink into flesh that I didn't even know I was holding onto. Oliver growls deeply between my thighs as he licks my orgasm clean. I blink my eyes open and find Banks staring at me, the look in his eyes is possessive and tells me that tonight means everything to him. Oliver pulls away, and I'm left reeling, a thousand different emotions prickling the surface.

"Roll to your side," he says, gently nudging me to roll over. I do as he asks, resuming the same position we were laying in before. Oliver is in front of me, and Banks is behind me. The only difference now... we are all naked.

I can feel Banks' hard length pressing up against my ass cheeks as he kisses my bare shoulder, before grazing my ear with his teeth,

"Tonight, we're going to make slow love to you. Show you how much we really care about you, and how we truly are one. You belong with us, and you never have to be alone again."

Swallowing, I push any, and all, thoughts away. Whatever happens tomorrow, I will deal with then, my emotions, my thoughts. All of it can wait. Falling into the feeling of nothing, but the two of them, I moan as Banks once again starts to kiss me, his lips sucking at the tender flesh beneath my ear.

Oliver lifts my leg and drapes it over his, opening my center up to him. He pulls me into his body, his cock brushing against my sensitive clit as he lines himself up with my entrance. A soft gasp fills the air as he slips inside, stretching me slowly, so slowly, I think I might die.

Banks groans into my ear as if he was the one to slip inside me. His hands roam over every inch of flesh, my chest, neck, and hips, while his brother inches himself inside of me, deeper, and deeper until I feel nothing but him. Air rushes from my lungs, and my body once again feels like it's burning up.

Once seated fully, he gives me a moment to adjust to his size. I feel so full, but also content, like this is exactly what I needed. For the first time, I don't worry about my memories returning. I don't feel broken or lost. All the confusion in my mind is gone and replaced with the feelings Oliver and Banks are giving me. There is no need to worry because, in this room, I have everything I'll ever want or need.

Oliver pulls out of me almost all the way, only to thrust back inside. His movement causes my back to press more firmly into Banks. Every nerve ending in my body starts to tingle, needing more, and as if Banks understands that need, he begins to touch me again, running his fingers all over my back, shoulders, arms and coming to rest against my ass. I wonder if he wants to claim that part of me too.

"I know you're thinking about it. About letting me take your virgin ass, and I will, just not tonight..." *Oh lord.* The growl he emits could wake the dead, and when his teeth sink into my shoulder, a spasm of pleasure radiates out of my core, causing me to clench around Oliver's length. Oliver holds onto me tightly, his fingers digging into my skin while he stares at me with so much need and conviction, I could cry. His body is wound tight, his muscles trembling with every thrust, telling me just how much he wants this, how much he needs it.

"I've dreamed about this night, about having you for the first time, about coming inside of you." His eyes are wild and full of life. It's risky, I know that but I'm on the pill, and I know they would never put me in danger like that.

"Yes," I pant, feeling the distinct build of pleasure filling my veins. The idea of him coming inside me only turns me on more. Banks plucks at my hard nipples, and grinds his cock against my ass, making Oliver hit something deeper inside of me. I can't help myself, there's no holding back the pleasure that comes rippling through me.

"I'm going to come inside you..." Oliver groans and I nod, as pleasure overtakes me.

My entire body trembles and my chest rises and falls like I'm running a triathlon. Like a rubber band pulled too tight, I snap, euphoric pleasure floods every cell of my body, and my channel grips onto Oliver's shaft with a vengeance, refusing to let go.

He continues to thrust through my orgasm, his teeth gritted, and his grip tight, until he finds his own release only a moment later, his cock swelling before his sticky hot seed fills me.

Oliver stays inside me for another moment, his cock softening. We are both panting, unable to catch our breaths, but he doesn't care about that, and neither do I. His lips find mine again. He kisses me with nothing but raw passion, and I moan into his mouth.

I can't get enough of him... *them*.

Our lips are still touching when he pulls out of me. As soon as he does, Banks' grip on my hip tightens, and he pulls me into his groin. His cock slides between my folds from behind with ease, coated with his brother's release and my own.

"Fuck, Harlow... I don't know if I can do slow," Banks admits, his hot breath fanning against my shoulder. "I want you so bad, and I've wanted you for so long that I haven't had sex since that first night we kissed. I was done for after that night, completely mesmerized by you."

"Take me however you want," the words come out on an exhale.

Slow, fast, it doesn't matter to me. All I want is him inside of me.

"Lord, help me, you make it so hard to be a gentleman when you say things like that." Without warning, he slips inside of me, bottoming out with ease, the head of his cock meeting the end of my cervix. Again, I'm full, so full, but like my body should, it adjusts to Banks' length the same as it did to Oliver's.

Pleasure overtakes me as Banks fucks me, literally fucks me, his thrusts as harsh as his kisses, and as hard as his love is.

Oliver lowers his head, taking my nipple into his mouth and between his teeth. Gently he bites down, and a lightning bolt of pleasure zips through me, causing my toes to curl. A loud moan fills the room, *my* moan.

For a split second, I think I should be quiet, but I can't come up with a good reason why. We are out in the middle of nowhere, who is going to hear me? *Sullivan?* I've already had sex with him, and he knows I want his brothers as much as I want him. If he wakes up, I'm certain he won't care, that is if he's not already awake.

"Shit, you're so tight, and perfect. You've ruined me for anyone, you're it, Harlow." Banks grunts every word, and it sounds like he's barely holding on. His grip tightens, his force bruising, and I want to fall deep into his touch. I want to let him swallow me whole.

"I can hear how wet you are, the sound of all our juices coming together. It's hot as fuck, the hottest thing I've ever seen or heard." Oliver declares, his lips pressing hot kisses over my chest. Oh, god. It's happening again. I don't know how but it is… the pleasure is building, and this time it almost hurts. It feels like it's being ripped out of me.

"Come with me…I need to come…" Banks is unhinged, wild, a beast that is staking his claim on my heart.

"Yes… yes…" I moan, panting so hard, I might pass out. Pleasure blooms inside me like a flower opening up for the first time. Oliver sucks on my breast so hard that there's an edge of pain to the pleasure. Using his other hand, he kneads the sensitive flesh, walking the line between pleasure and pain.

Banks' fingers dig into the skin around my hips as he holds onto me with all his strength as if he is scared I'll disappear. He thrusts inside of me over and over again, and it feels like he goes deeper every time. It feels like he's branding himself inside of me, making sure I will never forget what it's like to have him there.

"I'm coming," I just barely manage to get out before I explode, going off like a bomb. The orgasm is so powerful, I see stars before my eyes, every muscle in my body convulses in their holds. Every cell in my being is on fire, and for a moment, I don't know where I am, all I know is unyielding pleasure.

Banks grunts and stills inside me after one last powerful thrust. My swollen lips part, and a gasp releases from inside my chest when I feel the warmth of his release flood my channel. With his face buried in my hair, we both come down like floating feathers, from our high.

Oliver's head is nestled against my chest as the room grows quiet. Moans and pants slowly turn into even breathing. Banks is still inside me, and he doesn't make a move to pull out. We all just lie there, our bodies intertwined.

"Are you okay?" Oliver asks, peppering soft kisses against my skin.

"More than okay. I feel whole... like we belong together."

"That's what I've been telling you, haven't I?"

"Yes, and I'm sorry it took me until now to realize it."

"That's okay, I'll forgive you." I can almost see the smile on Banks' face at my back, which causes me to smile. My eyes feel heavy, and I feel so content I could sleep just like this, and maybe I will. Banks slips out of me, and they both wrap me up in their arms, creating a cocoon. My breathing starts to even out when I hear someone moving, only then do I remember why I should have been quiet.

Sullivan.

"You guys seriously fucking suck," he mutters under his breath. Banks and Oliver chuckle next to me, the whole bed vibrating with their laughter, but I feel bad. A second later, I hear Sullivan get up off the couch and the sound of the bathroom door closing. I briefly consider getting up to go and find him, to give him something too, but decide against it. Sullivan had me first, and he'll have me again, soon.

I discover then, as I'm part-way between sleep and wakefulness that it doesn't matter if my brain can't remember them, because my heart and my body, they'll never forget.

24

The next morning, I expect things to be a little awkward, but I'm pleasantly surprised when they're not. In fact, it's quite the opposite. Everything just feels right, like it's meant to be. I'm deliciously sore and end up spending a good thirty minutes in the shower letting the hot water beat against my back before I get out and get dressed.

When I return to the living area, Oliver is standing in front of the stove making breakfast, while Banks disappears into the bathroom. Sullivan is sitting on the couch, surfing the channels, so I decide to join him. I sit next to him, leaving a few inches between us, but he shakes his head and grabs my arm, pulling me into his side.

"I think I deserve some cuddling, at least," Sullivan grins, and I can feel my cheeks heat thinking about last night.

Cringing, I mumble, "Sorry you were kind of left out..."

"Don't be," he interrupts. "One, I deserved it. Two, I didn't share with them the first time I had you. Three, this is all about you... and you sounded like you had a good time, a great time, and to me, that's all that matters."

"You kids want pancakes?" Oliver questions from the stove.

"Yeah, I'm starving," Sullivan answers. Just then, my stomach growls so loud that I know he can hear it, and with a chuckle, he adds, "Harlow is too."

A few minutes later, Banks comes out of the bathroom, freshly showered and dressed for the day, and we all sit down at the table to eat together.

"So, what are we going to do now?" I ask as I spear a piece of pancake with my fork. "Are we just going to hide out here or can we go back to classes today?"

"We need to figure out who is trying to hurt you first," Oliver mumbles while shoving a piece of pancake past his lips.

"We are not going to figure that out here, though, are we? Plus, what if the burner was an actual accident? Freak accidents happen all the time," I reply, grabbing my glass of milk.

"And you being pushed off the boat? And hit by a car? And drugged at a party? All of that coincidence? Each of them a freak *accident?*" Sullivan points out, and I can't argue with that. One of those I could consider being an accident, but all of them, yeah, no. Which means I need to come to terms with the fact that someone is trying to kill me.

"We've already caught Shelby in one lie, maybe she had something to do with it?" Banks suggests.

"I don't know..." I think back on all the time I've spent with her in the last few weeks. There's never been anything off about her. She seems like a great friend, my parents seem to love her, and there were pictures of us in my room, pictures in which I looked very happy.

"Why would my best friend want me dead?"

"I'm not sure," Banks answers. "I really don't know why anybody would want you dead."

"You hated me at one point, so what's to say that other people don't?" At the mention of our past, Banks' face tightens, the muscle in his jaw jumping.

"I don't think our hate was ever fully deserved, not for you, anyways. I think your dad is mostly to blame... actually all of our parents. Before your accident, we always went off what our parents told us about your family, but after we hired our own private investigator, we found out that even though your father seemed to be the main instigator, our father wasn't as squeaky clean as he made himself out to be."

"Do you know why our parents have had this feud for so long?" From what I can gather so far, our families rivalry started years ago over some business. They blamed each other for trying to destroy the other's business, sabotaging property deals, and taking away high-profile customers. It sounded horrible for everyone involved.

"Here is the thing..." Oliver places another pancake on Banks' plate. "We always thought this was about business, that's what our dad told us. When we had the private investigator look into your father, he dug some stuff up about his past... about both of our fathers' pasts." He gets a plate for himself and takes a seat, and I'm sitting there waiting with bated breath for him to finish his statement.

"What did he find?" I ask, trying not to sound overly eager.

Sullivan answers my question as Oliver starts to devour his pancakes. "Apparently our dads have known each other for much longer than they like to talk about. In fact, they grew up together and believe it or not, they even used to be friends."

"Friends?" The way I heard my mom talking about the Bishops makes it hard to believe that there was ever anything besides hate between those two, but it makes sense. To hate someone, they have to have wronged you in a way that cuts deeper than the surface.

Tucking my hands under my chin, I ask, "What happened? What made them become enemies?"

"That, we don't know." Oliver answers this time, "But we're going to find out. We're done being our parents' puppets, and we're done letting your parents control you."

Control me? Had my father asked me to plant those drugs on Sullivan? Was he using me, or did I make the choice to do it on my own? Looking at the big picture now, yes, but before I don't know. I know my father is having an affair with someone, but does that mean he lied to me about everything else... or wants me dead? I can't possibly think my own father would want me dead, but I don't know what's true and what's a lie anymore. Even the few memories that have returned to me are blurred... like they've been run through a blender.

"I'm sorry about all the stuff that happened between our families. I don't know if I apologized before, but..." My voice trails off as I get lost inside my own head.

"No apologizing. We've all done things we regret doing, things that were done for someone else. We aren't those people anymore." Sullivan soothes, and I want to lean into him, let him hold me in his arms but instead, I extend my hand out to him. He takes it, rubbing his thumb over the top of it, slowly soothing the ache in my chest.

"I wish I could remember everything. If I could then maybe I would be able to help more."

Banks shakes his head, "It would be nice for you to remember, but you remembering wouldn't change anything, I don't think. You didn't see who pushed you off the boat, and I doubt you would be able to recall who hit you with the car."

"Yeah, I guess you're right. I just feel so useless," I mumble.

"It's okay, the memories will come back eventually, or maybe they won't. Either way, we will make new ones to replace the ones you lost," Oliver says, his sculpted lips turning up into a dazzling smile.

"So, what now?" I ask.

"The same private investigator we hired back then is looking into the incident at school. Let's wait it out here for two days, and if he can't find anything, we'll go from there. No matter what, our biggest priority is making sure that you're protected."

WHEN I WAKE up the next day, everyone else is already up, so I take my time crawling out of bed. The smell of freshly brewed coffee and bacon permeates the air, and my stomach, of course, has to growl to let me know that it approves.

"Look who's finally awake?" Oliver teases, as he busy's himself in the kitchen. My eyes catch on Banks who is sitting at the dining room table, his eyes glued to his cell phone. Sullivan isn't anywhere in sight, so I assume he's in the bathroom or maybe even outside.

As if he knew that I was thinking about him, the bathroom door opens, and Sullivan appears. I try to avert my gaze, but what's the point? Instead, I let myself drink him in, my eyes roaming over his freshly showered, and sculpted body. *Damn.* I nearly swallow my tongue, the same tongue I would like to use to lick the remaining droplets of water off his skin. Jesus, I need to stop thinking with my vagina. But it's so damn hard when besides the thin towel hanging low on his hips, he is entirely naked.

Must look away. When my cheeks start to burn, I avert my gaze to his face.

His hair is wet, making the russet brown color look almost black, which draws out the ocean blue of his eyes, making them appear brighter. Knowing damn well I'm checking him out he gives me a cheeky grin.

"See something you like?" He wiggles his thick brows, and I swear my face turns fifty shades of red. I shouldn't be shy about this, about them, but for some reason, I still am. I mean, I've slept with each of them, so I have no reason to turn all red-faced over simply checking them out, but I can't stop myself.

Banks looks up from his phone, "Sullivan, stop trying to seduce Harlow, and put some damn clothes on. No one wants to see your pecker, including her."

"Are you sure? It looks like Harlow wants to see my pecker, maybe even touch it."

Lord, please save me.

"What do you think, Miss. Lockwood? Would you like to touch it?" Sullivan chuckles.

Shaking my head in embarrassment, I move to get up and go into the bathroom when a memory pops into my head.

"Harlow, this is not up for negotiation. You're a Lockwood, and you're to protect this family, its name and business. If that means doing some things to people that deserve it, then so be it."

That's the thing. I don't care if they're guilty or innocent anymore. I'm tired of being a Lockwood, tired of doing my father's bidding.

"I'm done. I'm not going to be your puppet anymore. Find someone else," I speak through my teeth, shoving out of the chair to leave his office. I want to be my own person, and I cannot do that while being stuck underneath my father's thumb.

"It's not like the Bishops are innocent, Harlow. They brought this on themselves."

Anger simmers in my veins, nearly reaching boiling point, "Sullivan didn't bring this on himself. You made me plant those drugs! You made me ruin his life. I never should've listened to you. If this is what being a Lockwood means, then I don't want to be part of this family anymore!"

A look of shock overtakes his features, "You don't mean that."

Curling my lip, I let every ounce of rage I'm feeling coat my words, "I do. I'm done. I want out. If you don't let me go, then I'll find another way. One way or another, this charade is over." I don't bother to look at him as I walk out of his office. I've made my choice because in my eyes while the Bishops aren't innocent, neither is my father.

I blink the memory away. My father did make me do it. It wasn't my own choice, and that thought soothes me more than I thought it would. I didn't realize how much not knowing was weighing on me. I thought I was a terrible person. Maybe I wasn't so bad after all.

"Hey, are you okay?" Sullivan's voice is coated with concern, his teasing tone gone. "I was just joking… I'll put some clothes on."

"No, it's not that."

"What's wrong?" Oliver drops what he is doing in the kitchen and walks over to the bed. He cups my cheek and examines my face as if he's going to find some underlying ailment. "You look pale."

"I just remembered something… a fight with my father. It must have been before I came here. I told him I was done. I didn't want to be a Lockwood anymore." The room goes silent around me, all three brothers staring at me. A sick feeling settling in my insides. "You don't think it's… He's my father, he wouldn't want me dead?" I ask, looking up into Oliver's concerned eyes.

"I don't know. Nothing and no one is off the table at this point." I nod in agreement. I guess he is right, even though my gut tells me otherwise... it couldn't have been my own father. This is a slippery slope we're walking, and if his hate runs as deep for the Bishops as I feel it does, then it very well could have been him.

"I also remembered something else, that my father was the one who made me plant the drugs on you, Sullivan."

"We figured that already," Sullivan says, as if doing what I did, didn't ruin every aspect of his life. From the way Matt made it sound, he had it all, and then I came along ripping all of it right out from underneath his feet.

"Well, you might have. I kind of thought I was a bitch before my accident, and I even thought that it might have been my idea to destroy your life. So it's nice to know that at least it wasn't my idea. I wasn't the one who wanted to do this to you. I was merely a pawn, fed lies and told to do things in honor of the Lockwood name."

"Whatever we did in the past, is in the past now. Don't blame yourself for anything. I forgave you a long time ago, and I'm just glad you forgave me in return," he says, taking my hand, and just like that, I feel much better. Yes, we both made mistakes, but everybody does, some just bigger than others.

∼

ON DAY three of our cabin getaway, I start to get antsy. We all decided that we would wait until the end of the day to see if the private investigator could find something. If he came up empty, then we would be going back to Bayshore tonight. The hours drag on, and Banks continues to check his phone to see if anything turns up.

"I'm going for a run," Oliver announces, getting up and walking over to his duffel bag. He rifles through it and pulls out a pair of worn Nikes. He puts them on and starts for the door, pausing briefly with his hand on the knob. "I shouldn't be gone long, so if I'm not back in an hour, call out a search party." He grins and slips out the door, closing it softly behind him, leaving Banks, Sullivan, and I alone together.

I look between them, and they're both looking at me with a heat in their eyes that I know fairly well now. It has been three days since I had sex with Oliver and Banks, and since that day, it has been harder and harder to push away my wants and needs for all three of them. I want them all together, but I'm not sure I could handle that just yet.

"I'm going to take a shower." *A cold one.*

"Okay, you want me to join?" Sullivan wiggles his eyebrows back and forth, the grin he's giving me goes straight to my core. I bite my bottom lip to stifle my moan. If I said yes then that would leave Banks all alone out here, and I couldn't do that to him.

Standing, I roll my bottom lip between my teeth and stare down at him batting my eyelashes seductively, "What if I did? Would you come?"

"Oh... I would more than come. I'd come, and then you would too." He winks, but I don't miss the way his gaze darkens at my words.

"If you're bringing him into the shower then I'm coming too," Banks informs us, also giving me a panty-melting smile, which is fine since I'm not wearing any. I only had one pair, and after washing them once, I decided just to wear my shorts.

Sullivan and Banks exchange a look, their smiles widening as if they had come up with some secret plan that I knew nothing about. Standing up, they stalk toward me while I walk backward. I'm not afraid of them, if anything, it's quite the opposite. I'm excited, my blood humming, my entire body electrified waiting for one of them to make a move, to put their hands on me.

"Since the other night, I've wondered what you would look like with my cock in your mouth." Banks licks his lips, and I can't pull my eyes away from the motion of his pink tongue as it sweeps across his bottom lip. All I can think about is that tongue, against my skin, flicking against my clit until I explode.

"And all I could think about was how jealous I was that my brothers got to have a taste of you, but I didn't," Sullivan smirks, his hand moving to the front of his loose-fitting gym shorts. "My cock's been hard for days replaying that night in my head over and over again. The way you fell apart as they brought you to orgasm again and again. Your gasps and pants. The sweet sounds you made will forever be embedded in my mind."

I nearly gasp when the back of my knees make contact with the bed, and thankfully so, because they're wobbling so badly, I'm sure I'll fall over any second. I watch as Sullivan prowls toward me from the front, while Banks comes at me from the side. *Such a predator.*

They both reach the bed at the same time, Sullivan reaching for my shirt, relieving me of the fabric without a word.

In seconds, I'm naked, and I'm not even sure how it happened so fast. All I know is that the cool air feels nice against my heated skin. I fall back upon the soft comforter, as the two guys look down at me with feral gazes; like I'm a lone doe wandering the woods and they're two wolves who haven't had a meal in weeks.

"It's your turn," I say cheekily, looking over their still clothed bodies. Banks moves first, pulling off his shirt with ease, and tossing it to the floor beside him. Then he pulls down his shorts, his massive erection springing free.

Holy shit, that was inside me?

I didn't have a chance to look at it before, with it being dark and all, so now I'm staring at it like it's a gold bar that someone's placed in front of me. It's thick and veiny, the mushroom-shaped head looking soft, and I wonder what it would feel like against my lips.

My core clenches at the mere thought. I want him desperately. I'm so enamored by it; I barely notice Sullivan stripping out of his clothes. Banks curls his fingers around the thick shaft, giving it one hard stroke. My nipples pebble, hardening instantly, and I can feel a gush of moisture between my folds. This is so erotic. Me, them, naked. Me watching him with his hand wrapped around his cock. It's the icing on a three-tier triple chocolate cake, and I'm the one holding the fork.

"You want this?" Banks questions, his voice low, and thick. Touching something deep inside me. Nodding my head eagerly, I bite into my bottom lip when he asks me the next question, "Where do you want it?"

Answering him without a breath of hesitation, I say, "In my mouth."

Banks grins, and my attention is dragged away from him when my eyes catch on Sullivan, who is also standing before me, naked as the day he was born. His body is magnificent, and my mouth pops open as my eyes move over each perfectly sculpted muscle. Shoulders that are built and look as if they're made to hold the world, washboard abs, that make me want to lick between each divot.

I want to kiss and touch him. My entire body is aching for these two men. Leaning forward, Sullivan grasps my chin with two fingers and pulls me toward him. His lips land against mine, the kiss is fire and teeth and all-consuming passion. The sheets rustle beside me, and I feel Banks moving closer to me.

His fingers ghost against my shoulder as he brushes the silky blonde strands away. "One day, I will fuck you so hard you'll feel me in every cell of your body for the rest of your life."

What a bold statement. I want to tell him, but all that comes out is a throaty moan that's muffled by Sullivan's lips as he nips at my bottom lip, his teeth raking over the tender flesh. Banks peppers the side of my throat and shoulder with hot kisses, sucking on the skin harshly before lapping away the pain with his tongue.

"Get on all fours for me, baby," Sullivan murmurs, his chest rising and falling rapidly. It takes me a moment to start moving, my head still in the clouds, but once I reach the hands and knees position, I'm back. Panting loudly, I realize that my arousal is dripping embarrassingly down my thighs.

"Fuck, you're so wet. It's such a fucking turn on knowing that we do this to you." Sullivan trails a hand down my spine, and I peer up at Banks who is looking down at me, his eyes hooded and dark. He looks like the big bad wolf, and I desperately want to be eaten.

He moves closer to me, using one hand to bring his cock to my lips, and the other to tip my chin upward. The velvety smooth head of his cock brushes against my lips, right as Sullivan enters me with two fingers. *Good lord.* My mouth pops open, a breathless moan filling the air as a warmth ripples through my veins. I flick my tongue out, over the slit and under the head of Banks' cock, a tangy saltiness exploding against my tongue.

Banks' eyes seem to grow wider, as I do this again and again until he's groaning and I'm riding Sullivan's hand, rocking back and forth against his fingers.

"Suck his cock, Harlow. Take his cock into that virgin mouth and let him come inside of it," Sullivan encourages, and I can't help it. I do as he orders, sucking just the head into my mouth. Banks let's go of his cock and tips his head back, a groan that sounds more like a growl ripping from his muscled chest.

Swirling my tongue around the head, I try and focus on pleasuring Banks, but Sullivan is making it damn near impossible to. His fingers working some type of voodoo magic on my pussy. In seconds, I'm more than just panting. I'm humping his fingers, chasing a release I know only he can give me.

I'm so close, so damn close, a scream catches in my throat, and my chest tightens, my legs start to tremble and then just when I'm about to detonate, he removes his fingers. I whimper around Banks' cock.

"Shhh, he'll give you your release…" Banks soothes, his thumb grazing my cheek. Inch by inch, he slowly enters my mouth while Sullivan brings his cock to my entrance, coating his thickness with my arousal. His hands find my hips, holding me their possessively as he pulls me closer to his groin.

By the time Sullivan enters me, Banks has his entire cock in my mouth, his hips thrusting gently. The tip of his length hits the back of my throat, and I gag, but that doesn't stop Banks or even Sullivan.

In fact, it's like the sound encourages them because Banks continues to thrust into my mouth, smiling, his eyes twinkling with their own darkness as he hits the back of my throat, while Sullivan starts to move faster, and faster his hips pistoning, his balls smacking against my ass.

The room filling with nothing more than our moans, and the slap of his skin against mine. I'm burning up, sweat forms against my brow, and I moan around Banks' length as Sullivan's grip on my hips tightens. Fingers digging into my skin, I know there will be bruises, and I want there to be. I want to remember this, feel it for as long as I can afterward.

"Fuck, you're so tight, so warm..." He plows into me, and it's like I'm balancing perfectly between the two, with every thrust, I suck Banks harder pushing all three of us closer and closer to the imaginary finish line.

"I'm close..." Banks hisses through his teeth, his face tightening. "I'm going to come in your mouth. If you don't want me to, you need to stop now." In reply, I suck harder, and he laces his fingers into my hair, encouraging me to go faster. Drool dribbles down my chin, as I let him use my mouth like his brother is using my pussy.

"You're perfect, so fucking perfect, Harlow," Sullivan chants, as he leans forward and presses a hot kiss to my shoulder. Banks' cock seems to grow in size, and with a grunt, he starts to come, his fingers holding my head in place as his sticky come fills my mouth. I swallow as much of it down as I can, but a little escapes my mouth when Banks pulls his cock free, the tip gliding over my bottom lip.

With my chin pinched between two fingers, he forces me to look up at him, "It's your turn, baby. Come all over my brother's cock."

"Yes..." I pant, feeling nothing but Sullivan as he enters me, over and over again, fucking me like a ravaged beast.

"I'm close, so close..." He growls.

"Me too..." I inhale a sharp breath, every single muscle in my body tightening. I'm burning hotter than the sun, my entire body bursting into a ball of flames once I finally reach my orgasm. Sullivan falls apart right along with me, my walls clenching him so tight it almost hurts.

"Holy fuck, Jesus," I've never heard Sullivan sound so breathless, as he does in that moment. Banks releases my chin, and I slump forward feeling Sullivan's sticky come coating the inside of my womb.

"That was..." I gulp into the comforter.

"Amazing," Banks quips.

"Intense," Sullivan adds.

"All of the above," I say after a moment, my breathing, and heartbeat slowly moving back to a normal rate.

"I think Oliver is really going to regret going on that run," Banks chuckles, which causes me to start laughing as well. Sullivan slowly pulls out of me and presses a soft kiss, to my ass cheek. Right then, the front door to the cabin opens and in walks a sweaty Oliver.

"What did I miss?" he asks, his eyes taking in the scene before him.

Banks crawls off the bed, and pulls his shorts back on, "Just the sexiest fucking thing ever, but I'll be sure to tell you all about it later."

Oliver rolls his eyes, but I don't miss the primal look he's giving me. Eventually, I'll have to have all three of them at once, and I'm starting to think, I might just be strong enough for it.

25

Oliver moped around for a few hours, clearly unhappy about missing out on the fun. Sullivan and Banks made sure to tease him relentlessly about it too. After taking a shower, I returned to find Banks checking his phone again. It wasn't long before he delivered bad news. My parents had gone to the police and filed a missing person's report because they hadn't heard from me, and the *guards* my father had sent, as well as Shelby, hadn't seen me for three days. Now there are police asking questions all over campus.

I guess I should start carrying my phone with me. I just didn't see the point until now, since I didn't have anyone to call or expect anyone to call me.

"We want you to come and stay with us at our house. It's not safe for you at the dorms alone, and since we don't live on campus, if something happens, it's going to take us a bit to get there."

"Okay, just drop me off at campus first. I'll talk to the police and clear this up. Then I can swing by the dorms and pick up some clothes, and a couple of other things."

"I don't think that's a good idea, we can just drive by the police station on the way to our place," Oliver says.

"I really need to go to the dorm and get something," I urge. I only have two birth control pills left. I need to take it continuously, or I'll be in trouble. More than trouble, my life will be over.

Oliver and Sullivan exchange a look, and I'm not sure what they're discussing in their weird sibling communication, but I wish they'd let me in on it.

I'm almost certain they're going to say no, so I prepare myself for an argument, but I'm shocked when Sullivan says, "Okay, you can do what you need to do, and we'll stay on campus nearby."

"Thank you," I mumble, and Banks chooses then to place his hand on mine. I can't help how happy I am to have these three men by my side.

When we pull up to the dorms a short while later. Two cop cars are parked right out front, but I don't see the police officers until I get out of the car. Before I even have a chance to explain, two more cops come running toward us, guns drawn, yelling at all of us to get on the ground.

I'm so shocked, I don't know what to do, or say, or even think. I'm about to get on the ground when I realize it's not me they're talking to, but the guys.

"What... what's wrong?" I ask one of the cops, who is currently slapping a pair of handcuffs on Banks.

"Are you alright, Miss? Did they hurt you?"

"Why would they hurt me? They didn't do anything. Please stop," I plead with him.

"We were told by your parents that three men had kidnapped you," the police officer tells me. Worry and confusion turn to anger and understanding in the blink of an eye.

"Release them now! No one kidnapped me. I went with them of my own will, and last I checked I'm an adult who can make her own choices."

Almost immediately they're released and come over to stand by my side. Banks is rubbing his wrists, giving the cop a stink eye, but doesn't say anything.

"You okay?" Oliver asks, taking my hand into his. I force a reassuring smile and nod.

"We would like to take a statement, just for our records," one of the cops tells me.

"What is there to say? Nothing happened. I went to a cabin with my friends for three days, end of statement," I snap.

I know it's not the cop's fault, but he is here right now, and my parents aren't, so I guess he'll just have to deal with my anger.

"Okay, we'll leave you to it then." The cops look at each other before getting back into their cruisers. I watch them drive away, unable to hide the dirty look on my face.

Once they're out of sight, I return my attention back to the guys. All three of them look at me with nothing but concern and only then do I realize that I'm shivering. I have this overwhelming urge to hug all of them, and since Oliver is closest, I hug him first. He holds me close to his chest for a moment before releasing me, so I can hug Sullivan and Banks too.

"I just want all of this to be over," I finally say.

"It will be soon. We'll figure it out," Sullivan says, and it almost sounds like a promise.

"Okay... you guys just wait here. I'll run upstairs real quick and get my stuff."

"I'll come with you," Banks announces, and I can tell by his tone, and the tenseness of his body that he is not going to take no for an answer. Where Oliver and Sullivan are happy for me to take the lead, Banks' concern for me overrides his usual easygoing nature. Offering him my hand, he takes it and interlaces our fingers.

We walk inside together holding hands, and it occurs to me then, is he even okay with this kind of PDA? I don't want to push this, whatever we all are, none of us have put a label on it yet, and I don't want to be the first to. I start to pull my hand away, wanting to give him some space, but I don't even get my hand moved an inch before he's tightening his grip. He looks over at me with a lifted brow, and I gulp. Okay, so he doesn't care if someone sees us holding hands.

When we reach the door to my room, there's music blasting through the heavy wood letting me know that Shelby is here.

"Shelby's here, do you mind waiting out in the hall? I want to talk to her on my own. I need to know why she lied to me about Oliver at the party."

Banks doesn't look happy, in fact, he looks like he might kick someone's ass at any given second, but he agrees nonetheless, "I'll be right on the other side of this door if you need me, and if you don't come out in a few minutes, I'll kick the fucking thing in."

I couldn't stop myself from rolling my eyes at his alpha tendencies if I tried. "Mhh, how about I just leave it unlocked, and you can come in the normal way?"

Shrugging, he says, "I guess if you want to take the fun out of it."

He lets go of my hand, and I suck in a calming breath before I grab the doorknob and twist it, opening the door. I've barely crossed the threshold when I spot Shelby running across the room, she's coming right for me, like a raging bull. Her body collides with mine, her arms wrapping around me, engulfing me in a tight hug.

"Harlow, oh, my god. I was so worried about you! Where were you and why didn't you have your phone with you? I didn't have an option. Those stupid guards your father sent wouldn't go away, and I didn't know where you were, and I tried to cover for you but..."

She's carrying on, and on, and no way am I going to get a word in if I don't get her to take a breath and stop talking.

"It's okay. I'm fine, see, alive and well."

Shelby pulls away, her eyes filled with tears, "I was so worried about you. You're my best friend, and you've had enough things happen to you lately. I can't risk losing you again."

Her words make no sense to me, especially if she is the one who put the drugs in my drink, but I can't ignore them.

They tug on my heartstrings, and I think it's because I don't want to believe that one of my only friends, my best friend, could be the one to hurt me.

"Shelby... I need to ask you something, and I want you to be completely honest with me. Why did you lie about Oliver drugging me at that party?" It seems like the longest pause in mankind occurs between us.

"What? I..." For a moment, I think she's going to deny it. Maybe come up with another lie, but then, instead of saying anything, she starts to cry. She covers her face with her hands, her whole body shaking, because she is crying so hard, and all I can manage to do is wrap my arm around her.

"I'm sorry, Harlow," she chokes out between sobs. "I'm sorry."

"Just tell me what happened. Why did you lie?"

"I'm just trying to protect you, Harlow. I swear." That sounds a little far-fetched given what she did.

"By drugging me?"

"What? No! I didn't drug you. I don't know who did. I wasn't lying about that. Some guys did distract me and kept me from going back outside... it just wasn't Oliver, and I didn't see anyone put anything in your drink."

"Then why did you say that?"

"To keep you away from them. They are bad people, Harlow. You wouldn't believe me, you never do, but it's true! They hurt you so bad. They had the whole school against you. The banner... that wasn't the only thing they did, you know? They terrorized you, and then all these other things happened to you, and every time the Bishops were there. That's not a coincidence."

"Shelby, I know you are trying to be a good friend, but you need to trust me on this. It's not the Bishop brothers who have been after me. Yes, they bullied me before the accident, but it's not like that anymore, things have changed between us."

"There is more, Harlow..." Shelby wipes some tears from her eyes, which are now swollen and red, with her sleeve. "Their parents contacted me a while back. They wanted me to spy on you. I didn't want to do it. I told them no, never would I betray you. But then they threatened me. They told me if I didn't give them information, they would hurt my family and with everything that happened with my father, I couldn't risk them hurting him, or my mother." For some reason, I'm frantic, needing to know what it is that she's talking about. Why would they go to Shelby?

"What do you mean spy? When? What did they want to know, and what did you tell them?" I'm grasping at straws here trying to fit all the pieces of the puzzle together. There are things I know now, and things I don't quite understand, or remember yet, and it's all so confusing.

Shelby exhales a breath. "They contacted me right before the boat incident. At first, they just wanted to know stuff like if you were seeing one of their sons. I told them, no, of course, you guys hated each other. Then the car accident happened, and they just kept contacting me, wanting updates. They asked if you regained your memory and stuff like that. I don't know what they wanted, Harlow, but I'm worried about you. The Bishops can't be trusted, I mean, they threatened me for information about you."

For the first time in three days, my heart is in my stomach. I don't know what to think or even feel. Have the brothers been lying to me? Do they know about this? Every time it feels like I'm getting my footing, something else happens.

"I don't know what's happening between you and them, but I felt like you should know. I think it's very likely they're the ones trying to hurt you. Why else would they want to know about you and their sons? None of these things started happening until after they approached me." *God, I hope not.* Shivers rack my body at the thought.

The brothers' parents wouldn't try and kill me over some stupid family rivalry, would they? There are so many pieces to this puzzle missing, and a headache is starting to form behind my eyes. I can't think about this anymore.

"It's okay. I believe you, and I trust you. You're really the only friend I have here. I just wish you would've told me sooner. I'm having a hard time telling who is friend, and who is foe."

Shelby nods, and takes a step back, giving me a chance to breathe. Immediately, I start gathering my stuff; a couple changes of clothes, my toothbrush, sleep shorts, and...

"Have you seen my birth control pills?" I ask Shelby, after looking where I'm pretty sure I had put them last.

"No, I haven't seen them, and where are you going anyway? You just got back. I thought maybe we could have a movie night and catch up, spend some time together. It seems like we never see each other anymore."

"Come on, girl, we haven't hung out all week." Shelby's voice echoes in my head, a memory starting to surface.

"Fine, how about we watch a funny movie?" I really need a good laugh after the week I've had.

"Rom-com?" Shelby chimes.

"That's fine, as long as the main character doesn't resemble any of my stalkers."

"Oh, Harlow... I'm so sorry you're having a hard time. Do you want me to kick their asses? Because I will!" Shelby throws her arm over my shoulder, pulling me into her side.

"The Bishops are really starting to get to me. This is not what I thought college life would be like," I lean into her, letting my best friend comfort me.

"I'll always be here for you. Don't you ever forget that."

My heart warms toward Shelby at the memory. She has been a good friend... the best.

"I promise we'll hang out soon, but not today. I'm going to stay with the guys." Shelby sighs deeply at the mention of them but doesn't say anything to stop me. "I trust them, and whatever their parents did, is not on them."

Shelby folds her hands in her lap, "Okay, Harlow, but be careful."

"I will," I tell her and keep gathering my stuff. I finally find my birth control in one of my drawers. I shove them in my bag with the rest of my belongings. "I have my phone with me this time. I'll text you."

After a quick hug, I head for the door. I step out and find Banks leaning against the wall, his lips are pressed in a tight line, and his eyes look a shade darker. I close the door behind me before I ask, "Did you hear?"

"I did," he says through his teeth. He takes my hand and starts pulling me down the hallway.

"What are you thinking?" I'm assuming he still thinks that Shelby is lying, especially now that she's accused his parents. That's why I'm so shocked when I hear what he has to say next.

"We had suspected that our parents had a spy, someone to keep tabs on you, even on us, but we didn't know who it was, and we definitely didn't know that they would go to such lengths and resort to threatening anybody."

"Do you think... they want me dead?" I don't know much about his parents or the relationship the brothers have with them, but the need to threaten Shelby for information about me has me terrified. Out of the corner of my eye, I watch Banks' face morph with pain. He looks angry and frustrated but above all, disappointed.

"I can't imagine they would. I just can't. They're good people..." his voice trails off as we reach the bottom of the stairs. The front door opens, and two girls walk inside. I don't think I know them, but they must know me, or at the very least Banks, because they both stop to stare at us. A sickening smile forms on one of the girls' lips, her eyes narrowing.

"You can't use the dorms as a place to whore yourself out, you know? Some people actually come to this university to get an education."

She didn't... yes, she did. This bitch just called me a whore.

I blink, literally shocked at her nerve. "Excuse me?"

"You heard me," she tsks, her eyes mirroring disgust.

Without even realizing it, I find my hands balling up into tight fists. I want to punch that look right off her face.

Banks shakes his head, his lips turning up at the corners.

"Ignore them, they're just jealous that you managed to bag three of the hottest guys at Bayshore." The way he speaks of them, with a smidge of snark, makes their words hurt a little less. The girls roll their eyes and carry on past us like nothing happened at all.

"Were you really going to punch them?" Banks asks, giving me a quirky look.

My shoulders raise into a shrug. "I don't know. I just wanted to make them eat their words."

When we get back to the car, Sullivan and Oliver seem tense. "What took you so long? We were about to storm up there and start knocking heads together," Oliver berates.

"Shelby says that our parents hired her to spy on Harlow," Banks announces as soon as we're back in the car with all the doors closed.

"Son of a bitch," Sullivan growls as he slams a closed fist against the dash. "It's not surprising, not in the least, but I am shocked that they went to Shelby."

Oliver speeds out of the parking lot, and we tell them the rest of the story, including the run-in with the skank squad in the hallway.

"I'm going to have a talk with Mom and Dad, and see if I can get to the bottom of this. And about those girls they're nobodies."

All I can do is shrug. I want to tell them that it's easy to say something like that when they're not the ones being called a whore or looked at with disgust. How am I supposed to let go of the things they said and did?

I know I shouldn't care about what other people think... I know that, but that doesn't mean I can just turn off my feelings or forget what they said.

"I'll try, but it's not that easy."

"Forget them," Banks assures me with a gentle hand, and something tells me it's going to be a lot harder than just *forgetting them*.

26

Walking toward the front of the class, I hand in my essay to Professor Paulson, who gives me a curt nod as I exit the room. Oliver follows in stride right beside me, our fingers interlocked as we step into the hallway together. The brothers find their way into every single one of my classes, ensuring that I'm safe. Adjusting my backpack, I walk down the long hall with Oliver in tow. I've gone maybe ten feet when a hand lands against my shoulder, halting any further steps.

Seriously. I half expect it to be one of the stupid guards, so when I turn around there is nothing but barely restrained rage painted on my face.

"Hey, guys..." Caroline greets and immediately my features soften.

Not Bert, or Ernie, thank god.

"Hey, sorry, I thought you were one of the guards my father assigned."

Oliver looks around us, scanning the area. "Now that I think of it, we haven't seen either of them for a while." He shrugs. "Hopefully they got fired. I mean, they did do a terrible job. We kidnapped you in broad daylight, and they couldn't even figure out where you were," he teases, his eyes sparkling with amusement.

"I would definitely fire their asses if I was your father," Caroline chimes in. "I just wanted to see if you wanted to get coffee or something?" My stomach rumbles in appreciation of her offer. It's been nearly six hours since I last ate anything because I stupidly chose to skip lunch and finish my paper.

"Sure. I'm done with classes for the day, and I could use a cookie, and a coffee right about now."

Caroline gives me a megawatt smile.

"You okay with that?" I direct the question at Oliver.

"Anything you want," he winks and presses a soft kiss to my hand that makes my stomach quiver. At Oliver's words, she leads the way, taking us to this little coffee shop a couple blocks from the library. We sit down at a small table near the window, and I watch as Oliver walks up to the counter and orders us some coffees and pastries. Our gazes clash when he catches me staring at him, and I look away, my cheeks heating instantly.

Caroline giggles softly, and then asks, "How's it been going? Last I talked to Sullivan, he told me you were staying with them for now?" Her question has images of me curled up in Sullivan's bed last night popping into my head.

"It's been going good," I grin. "Actually, it's been great." I already know I'm blushing up to my hairline, giving my indecent thoughts away but it's not like I have anything to hide, least of all, from Caroline.

"That's good, and how have classes been? I know the rumor mill started up again, as I'm sure you've heard."

"Did someone say something?" Oliver's voice cuts through the air, as he sets two cups in front of us.

"Yes," Caroline pouts, "Tiffany and her stupid gang of barbie dolls are spreading rumors about Harlow again."

Oliver's gaze turns murderous, "I'm so fucking tired of them spreading lies about you." He speaks through gritted teeth as he slams down into the seat beside me. He looks like a hungry lion, ready to strike down his prey. Placing my hand against his thigh, I give it a reassuring squeeze.

"It doesn't bother me," I lie. "They can say whatever they want. The only person who knows the truth is me."

Oliver's eyes move away from me and to something behind me. A moment later, a group of guys enter the coffee shop, their loud laughter and talk filling the quiet space. Sipping at my coffee, I try to ignore them, but it seems to get louder and louder.

"Dude, that's Oliver Bishop, and *Harlow*, you know the one who likes to be double stuffed," one of them snickers, and I can see the anger pouring out of Oliver like a river.

"It's okay," I whisper, even though it's not. It's not okay for them to say such shitty things, or to talk about me in such a degrading way like I'm not even here.

"No, it's not," Oliver growls, his leg bouncing up and down incessantly.

"Think he would share her with us? Let us take her for a spin?" Another guy laughs, his voice low and a little closer than the other guys.

"Never know unless you ask."

My eyes roll to the back of my head. This is nauseating.

Caroline cringes. "I'm sorry."

I shake my head. "Don't be, none of this is..."

My words are cut off as a heavy body slams into the back of my chair, causing hot coffee to slosh out of my cup and onto my hand. A yelp slips past my lips, and I place the mug down on the table, before turning around in my seat, but there's no point in scolding this guy because Oliver is already out of his chair, standing toe to toe with him.

"What the fuck, dude?"

"Sorry, it was an accident, not that it matters..." The asshole scuffs, like it wasn't a big deal or rude as fuck.

"It matters, and you're going to apologize for what you did."

The guy's eyes bug out of his head, and then he's laughing, his voice bouncing off the walls inside my head.

"This prick thinks I'm going to apologize to his skank." He elbows his buddy, who also joins in on the laughter. A knot of worry starts to form in my gut when I see Oliver's balled up fists, they clench and unclench. *Shit.* He's going to get himself into trouble for nothing. All because of some stupid idiots.

I'm so caught up in my thoughts that I don't notice Oliver moving until it's too late. His fist connects with the loser's face right as I'm getting up, the wooden chair clattering to the floor, drawing even more attention. But I don't care. I've got to stop him before he gets himself into trouble. Moving fast, I curl my hand around his bicep and pull him back toward me, but it's like trying to move a brick wall. Pointless.

The asshole stumbles backward, his posse of friends catch him, as he holds a hand to his face, fury brewing in his eyes.

"Fucking prick just punched me, and all for some stretched out pussy."

I don't even let the words he's saying affect me. They mean nothing, not a damn fucking thing. Oliver, however, thinks otherwise and lunges forward, hoping to get another punch in but I'm quicker this time and instead, put myself between him and the enemy.

"He's not worth it. He's just some idiot listening to a rumor that's been spread more than Tiffany's legs." Wrapping my arms around his middle, I hug him tightly, resting my head against his chest, the sound of his erratic heartbeat filling my ears. His chest vibrates with anger as he makes the decision to stand down.

"Get out, assholes," he growls.

"Whatever, she's not worth it." One mutters, and another says, "Keep the whore." Again, I ignore them and hold on tighter to Oliver. The dinging of the door tells me they've finally left, and only then do I peel myself from his chest.

"I want to rearrange their faces," Oliver snarls, looking devilishly handsome as he does so. My insides heat, my core pulsing with need. Damn vagina always getting in the way. A loud ringing pierces the air, and it takes me a minute to realize that it's my phone that's ringing.

Pulling the device from my pocket, I look down at the screen and see Shelby's face and name flashing across it.

"Hold that thought," I tell Oliver, and press the green answer key.

"Hey," I barely get out before Shelby's voice cuts me off.

"Oh, my god, Harlow! Our dorm it's been... it's..." There's muffled crying, followed by a shriek. Instantly, I stand, ready to make my way toward the door, needing to make sure that Shelby is okay.

"What happened, are you okay?" The words come out in a panic.

"I'm fine, but our room is not. Get here soon, please," Shelby pleads.

"I'm on my way. I'll be there soon." I hang up the phone and notice that Oliver and Caroline are both standing now. They look at me confused, and I know I have to explain.

"Shelby said something's happened to our room." Fear radiates down my spine like a never-ending trickle of ice water.

"What do you mean?" Oliver questions, as I grab my bag, and we walk out of the coffee shop.

"I don't know," I answer, my distress evident in the three simple words. "She just said something has happened to our dorm."

"God, I have a bad feeling about this." Caroline sounds like she might be sick.

"Me too."

It doesn't take long for us to make it to the dorm, and when we arrive, Banks and Sullivan are standing outside the building, waiting for us. Oliver called them on the way, and they got here in record time.

"What's going on?" They both ask with equal amounts of fear in their eyes. Oliver opens his mouth, answering for me.

"We don't know, but we're going to find out." Entering the building, dread fills my gut, and it only mounts with every step I take, until it's damn near suffocating me. By the time I make it to the room, I think I'm going to vomit. I'm about to open the door when it is pulled open by Shelby, her tear-stained cheeks and somber face greeting me.

"Harlow!" She cries and pulls me into her chest, wrapping her arms around me. It's then that I notice all of my stuff destroyed, my bed flipped over, my belongings thrown around the room. But nothing could have prepared me for what I see next; the word SLUT spray-painted across my mattress in bright red paint, the same color as the one that was used to make the banner. I remember seeing the same word... in almost identical writing before. Someone wrote it on my T-shirts when I was doing laundry.

"I think it was Tiffany and her friends, it has to be," Shelby cries. "Look at the handwriting, the paint, it's all the same."

"Fuck!" I hear Banks say.

"Bitch," Sullivan says at the same time.

"She will pay for this, no doubt about it. I'm going to make her life hell," Oliver says next, but I don't even feel the effect of his words. I know he'll do exactly as he says, but right now I feel humiliated, so damn humiliated.

"I...." I pull from Shelby's embrace, my chest rattling, as I suck air into my lungs. I'm angry, but I'm sad too. I hate these people. Say what you will about me, but don't touch my things, and don't mess with the people I care about.

"I'm sorry, Harlow. I don't know how she got in," Shelby says, and I can tell that this is all affecting her on a deeper level. "I've let you down," she confesses a moment later.

"Shh, it's going to be okay," I tell her because I know it will be. "You didn't let me down, never."

"Should we call the cops? Or at least campus security?" Caroline asks.

"You think they would do anything? Investigate a prank, even if it was taken way too far?" Banks has a good point. What are the cops going to do?

"Let us clean this up, you and Caroline can go back to the house," Oliver suggests, but I don't want to leave yet. I want to help. I need to help. Those bitches may have hurt me, but they didn't break me. I'm not going to go home and hide.

"No, I'll help. Shelby needs me, she's always been there for me, and I can't leave her now, especially since it's my fault our room got destroyed."

"Okay," Sullivan responds this time, and I can tell he's unhappy with my answer but doesn't push for me to leave. He knows I need this right now.

As we all clean up the room, I plot my revenge knowing someday soon I'll make the bitch wish she never knew my name.

27

"Why can't I just sit in this class?" Banks is basically yelling at this point, his hands clenched at his sides. The professor looks beyond annoyed, his almost always calm face starting to turn red with anger, while my own is becoming red for an entirely different reason.

"Because you are not enrolled in this class anymore, Mr. Bishop," Professor Brown barks, his voice strained, like he's about to lose his last thread of patience. "You need to leave my classroom now, or I will call campus security, and have you removed."

His words come out as a threat, but something tells me he'll do exactly what he says. Not wanting the situation to blow up further, I turn to Banks.

"Hey, it's fine. I promise I'll be okay," I whisper, trying to calm him down, all while he continues to scowl at Professor Brown. A few moments pass, and I worry Banks will push the matter, but then he looks over at me, his eyes softening as they connect with mine.

"Fine," Banks growls, the single word dripping with suffocating disdain. "I'll pick you up at the end of class," he directs the words at me, before shoving out of his seat. Then he leans forward and gives me a quick peck on the lips before turning toward the door.

Once he's left the room, I force a smile, but it's not returned by the professor, or anyone else, for that matter. Well, at least Tiffany is not in this class. It's a small positive, but I'll take it either way.

Prof. Brown goes back to the front of the class, and a heavy silence blankets the room. Half-way through class things have finally settled down enough for me to actually learn something. I might not be able to pass this class, but I can pick up some stuff, at least, to make next semester easier.

When a loud knocking interrupts the professor's speech about different research methods, I half expect the door to open and there to be one of the Bishop brothers. Instead, the door frame is filled with my two bodyguards, Ernie and Bert. At the sight of them, I slouch down into my chair, picking up one of my textbooks, lifting it and holding it in front of my face.

"Can I help you?" Prof. Brown sighs in frustration.

"Yes, we need one of your students to come with us immediately. It's a family emergency," Bernie says.

Family emergency?

"Miss. Lockwood..." He scans the room and finds me almost immediately. "Please, this is very important," he urges. I'm waiting for the feeling of dread and worry to hit me. He said family emergency that usually means someone is hurt.

I should be worried and scared, but neither feeling comes. Instead, I feel... annoyed. Nonetheless, I gather my things up and stuff everything into my backpack, before flinging it over my shoulder, and making my way to the door.

As soon as I reach the door, my security flanks me, as if they are protecting me from some imaginary threat.

"What kind of family emergency is it?" I question.

"Let me carry your bag for you," one of the guys suggests and takes my bag from my shoulder before I can respond. Blinking slowly, I stare up at him.

I can carry my own things.

Annoyed as hell, I follow the two goons out, hoping that Banks is waiting outside the door for me. Disappointment fills my gut when he isn't there, and I'm left alone with the security guards my father sent. It isn't until we're outside, and walking toward the parking lot that I realize they're not trying to keep someone from getting to me, they are trying to stop me from leaving.

I dig my heels into the ground, stopping instantly. They must have expected the move because they stop a split second later, each grabbing onto one of my arms. Instantly, I'm restrained.

"What the hell are you doing?" I yell, demanding an answer. Instead of answering me, they just tighten their grips. My lip curls in anger.

"Tell me now, or I'll scream."

Bert, I think, squeezes my arm, "Your dad asked us to bring you to him, he is very worried about you...and your safety."

My safety?

"I don't give a crap what my father asked you to do or what he is worried about. I'm an adult. You can't just pull me out of class, and force me to go with you. It's kidnapping."

Before I know it, I'm being dragged across the parking lot, the two guys tugging me along by my arms. Try as I might to dig my feet into the asphalt, nothing stops their movements, and soon we're at a black SUV.

For some reason, only then do I think about screaming and calling for help.

"Help! I'm being kidnapped!" I yell at the top of my lungs while attempting to stomp my feet into the ground and make as much noise as possible. The two men don't even blink at me.

One of the guys opens the door to the SUV while the other one pushes me inside, holding my head down, so I don't bump it against the door frame. As soon as I'm in the car, he closes the door behind me. I grab the handle and pull on it frantically, but of course, it's locked. I scoot across the bench and over to the other side and try that door.

"You can't do this," I growl, when the men get into the car a moment after depositing me inside.

Ignoring my comment completely, Bert turns to me. "Please buckle up, Miss." Crossing my arms over my chest, I shake my head.

"No, you can't make me." Both men shrug as if they don't care, and then they speed off. With their attention on the road, I search my pockets hoping to find my phone.

Shit! It's in my backpack.

Ugh, I could kick myself for being so stupid. I never should have gotten up and walked out of that classroom. I should have just kept my ass glued to my chair, refusing to go anywhere, what's the worst they could've done? Sinking deeper into the leather seat all I can hope is that someone saw me leave and maybe, just maybe told one of the guys what happened. Angrily, I stare out the window, and as soon as they turn right onto the highway heading North, I know they're taking me back to my parents' house... back to *North Woods*.

"What kind of *emergency* is this?"

"Your father told us that it was important that we not inform you of the matter. Instead, he will share the details with you when you arrive at the house."

I want to scream, to punch the seat. Do anything but sit in this godforsaken seat like a child and wait for my father to *inform* me as to why he had his bodyguards pull me out of class.

"Can I at least have my backpack?"

"I put it in the trunk. I will return it to you once we are back at the estate."

Of course, he will.

I spend the rest of the drive moping, letting the anger simmer just underneath the surface, and thinking about all the things I'm going to say... no, scream at my father, once I'm in his presence.

We pull up the long winding driveway of my family's estate, and my fury just intensifies. We park right in front of the house, just as the door opens and my parents appear on the front steps. My goons get out quickly opening the door for me so I can get out as well.

"Lloyd, Milton, thank you for getting her here," my father greets the two men who dragged me here. Lloyd and Milton must be their real names, well, I like Ernie and Bert better... fits these two puppets. Pushing that unimportant thought away, I get ready to release my anger.

Waltzing up to the front door like I'm on a mission, I start yelling, "What the hell is this? Why are you having me kidnapped from school?"

"Harlow, calm down, and don't be ridiculous. We didn't have you kidnapped. We simply had you picked up from school." My mother's dismissive tone has my blood boiling.

"Picked up? Is that what you call dragging me across a parking lot, shoving me in a car against my will, and refusing to let me have my stuff? Because, to me, that is kidnapping!"

"Don't be so dramatic, those Bishop boys were the ones who kidnapped you and held you hostage for three days," my dad snaps. He might be right on the initial kidnapping part but, of course, I won't admit to that.

"They didn't hold me against my will, I stayed with them because I wanted to." At my words, my mom sucks in a loud dramatic breath and holds her hand to her chest, as if she just had a mild heart attack.

My dad's face turns slightly red, and there is a vein popping out on his forehead, but besides that, he is keeping a composed expression. "Let's go in and talk," he grits. I take the cue and stomp past my parents and inside the house.

They follow me into the living room, where we all sit down on the couch.

"You will not be returning to Bayshore, and you will not see those Bishop boys again," my father's voice is eerily calm. "You will stay here, you will be a part of this family, and you will marry Matt next week."

For what seems like minutes, we all sit there in silence, then I start laughing, really laughing.

I throw my head back and hug myself, I laugh so hard my belly hurts. It takes a minute for me to compose myself enough to answer my parents, who are just sitting on the couch stoically not getting the joke.

"And why would I do any of that? I'm an adult, you can't boss me around. Or force me to marry someone of your choosing."

"Of course, it is your choice to make, Harlow, but there will be consequences to your actions. If you refuse to marry Matt, something might happen to Sullivan... or maybe Banks this time." I let my father's threat hang in the air for a moment before I respond.

"You can't do that! You can't frame them, again, you already destroyed his life once."

"There are other, more permanent ways to take care of someone..."

"Very well, Xander," my mom's voice suddenly fills my head, and I hold on to that memory, knowing in an instant that it's an important one. *"Thank you again for helping us with the Bishop situation."*

"No problem at all, framing people is my second favorite work," the man named Xander said.

"Oh, what's your favorite?" My dad chimed in and I could already tell the answer isn't one I want to hear.

"Killing people..." My heart stops in my chest, leaving an ache behind, that I've never felt before. My skull is vibrating with pain from the force of the memory, but I don't care. All I can think of is how my father is threatening to kill one of the men I love.

The memory slips away, but I know there is more to it. I search my brain, willing myself to find that hidden compartment where the information I need is stored.

Xander... who is Xander?

Xander Rossi... it finally clicks in my head. Xander Rossi, the head of the local mob.

My parents are working with the mob. The realization leaves me stunned. This isn't someone that I can just remove from the situation. This is the mob, and with them in my father's pocket, it's either do as I'm told or face the consequences.

"Harlow, dear, we are not the bad guys here," my mom explains. "We are trying to do what's best for you. You have to trust us on this.

Matt is going to be the perfect husband for you. He'll take care of you and make you happy."

"You don't want what's best for me, you want what's best for you, let's at least admit it." I get up, unable to sit here with them another second. "I guess it doesn't matter what I want, you win. I'll marry Matt."

Ignoring the sadness and defeat in my voice, my mom smiles.

"Perfect, I'll start planning right now. You've made the right choice, sweetie."

"And I'll call Matt to deliver the good news," my father speaks smugly, as I turn away from them and head toward my bedroom. I won't give them the satisfaction of seeing me cry. I hold back my tears until I close the door behind me, locking me inside the room with nothing but my thoughts. I'm going to marry Matt, a man I don't love, so the people I do love can stay safe.

ALL NIGHT I find it impossible to sleep, the tears flowing freely down my face. It's hours before I'm so exhausted that I finally fall asleep, and don't even wake up later that morning when someone enters my room and sits down on my bed. Only when they touch my shoulder, shaking me gently, do I peel my eyes open.

"Hey, you," Matt's face greets me, his voice is low, sugary sweet, and I think I might be dreaming. I blink, and then I blink again. Then like a stack of books falling over, everything comes crashing down on me. Sitting upright fast enough to give myself a head rush, I clutch the heavy blanket to my chest and scoot back against the headboard.

"What the hell are you doing here? Who let you in?" My voice rises with each question, still brimming with sleep.

He smiles, showing off his perfectly white teeth, "Your parents let me in, of course, and I'm here to see how my future wife is doing?"

My heart sinks into my stomach, and I feel a little like puking. All I want to do is pull the blanket over my head and go back to sleep... a long, long sleep where I wake up and all of this is nothing more than a dream.

"You look thrilled to see me," Matt points out, his face crumbling like a broken piece of rock. "I'm guessing it wasn't your idea to get married, after all."

"It doesn't matter, I agreed to get married, so we're doing it."

"Sounds like the start of an epic love story." The words come out more like a joke, but they hit their mark. As if I hadn't cried enough already, one single tear slips from my eye, rolling down my cheek, and splattering on the white sheet I'm clutching to my chest.

"Harlow, shit, sorry. Why are you crying?" Matt reaches for me, but I shake my head, halting his movements.

"It's nothing," I murmur, wondering if I can trust Matt. Maybe I could tell him? *No*. I can't. I quickly decide against it. His family and mine are business partners. He has to know what kind of people my father works with, the things he's done. I look down at the blanket, fiddling with the fabric nervously.

"I already told you once, but I'm going to tell you again... we can make this work. We can have a great life, and I'll protect you, even from your family, if that's what you need."

His response causes me to look up at him.

"What do you mean, protect me from my family?"

He shrugs, but even I know better than to assume that's a shrug of ignorance. "Looks like you are under their thumb. If you marry me, you'll have more freedom. I don't care what you do as long as it's nothing that makes me, or the business look bad. You want to go study... get a job? Marry me, and you can do whatever you want. I won't stop you or try to lock you up like your parents do. With me, there is freedom."

Don't do it, Harlow... don't fall into the trap.

Before I can stop myself, I'm asking the one question that's been weighing on my mind since he started to talk.

"What... what if I'm in love with someone else? Would you care about that?"

Matt's face doesn't fill with shock or even anger, in fact, he looks, well, like he doesn't care. "Honestly? As long as you pretend to be my wife publicly. I really don't give a shit who you fuck on your time." He's being brutally honest, and even though I do appreciate his honesty, it still shocks me to the core.

"I don't know if I can do that. If we get married, then I'm all in. It wouldn't be fair to you or to who I love to step out."

"We'll make it work," Matt says encouragingly, his hand coming to rest against my blanket-covered thigh. "You'll see, it will eventually all work itself out. You still have my number, right?"

"Yeah, in my phone." It dawns on me then. *My phone.* My eyes dart around the room, scanning the space for my backpack. I was so distraught, and in shock last night, I didn't even think about my phone. I suck in a tiny breath of relief when I spot my old backpack in the corner of the room. Matt's eyes follow mine, but he doesn't say anything about my reaction.

"Call me if you need anything. I'll come and rescue you from your parents if they get to be too much." Matt gets off the bed and starts toward the door.

"I... I... will... probably sooner, rather than later."

"Good. Bye, Princess. Talk soon," he winks before turning and exiting the room, closing the door softly behind him.

As soon as the lock clicks in, I throw the blanket off and get up. Grabbing my backpack, I dump its content out on my bed and rummage through it until I find my phone. It's still on silent like I had it when I was in class, and that is the reason I didn't hear the 92 missed phone calls and 38 unread text messages. Most of them are from Oliver, Banks, and Sullivan, but a handful are from Caroline as well.

I scroll through the text messages.

Oliver: Where the hell are you? We are worried. Please call me.

Banks: Just text or call me, we just want to know you are okay. If you don't want to be with us, it's okay, we are just worried.

Sullivan: Did your dad make you leave? Are you at your family's

estate? Don't worry, we are coming for you. We'll find you and make this right.

Caroline: Please call me, girl, everyone is so worried.

I'm so angry. Angry at my parents, angry with myself for letting it come to this, and for some unexplained reason I'm even angry with the phone. I'm about to throw the damn thing across the room when it vibrates in my hand, and Oliver's name lights up the screen.

I answer the phone before thinking about what to say. Holding it to my ear, I wait for Oliver's voice to fill it.

"Harlow... Harlow, are you okay?" His voice hits me like a freight train. It's harsh, painful, soft, and soothing all at once.

"Yeah, it's me." My voice comes out shaky and so quiet I wonder if he even heard me at all.

"God, do you know how worried we've been? Where are you? Are you safe? What the fuck happened?" Oliver bombards me with more questions before I can get a single answer in.

"Don't yell at her," Banks says in the background. Then the sound of movement and rustling comes through the receiver.

"Harlow?" Sullivan says, his voice calmer than his brother's.

"Yeah..." Is all I can get out in this moment, too many emotions swirling around inside of me, right beneath the surface, just waiting to come out.

"Are you okay?" he asks the same question his brother asked.

"Yes," I lie. "I'm fine."

"What's going on, baby?"

"We can't be together," I say, trying to keep my voice as steady as I can. "We don't belong together, and what we did was a mistake. It never should have happened."

"What are you talking about? We belong together," Sullivan's sweet voice caresses my ear.

"No, we don't, and we never did," I force myself to say. The words leave a bitter taste on the tip of my tongue.

"Is your dad making you say this? Is he hurting you?" Oliver interrupts, the phone now on speaker.

"No, this is my decision. I came to my senses. I belong here with my family, and I'm going to marry Matt."

"You are lying," Sullivan says, and it takes everything in me not to confess the truth, but then I thought about what my father said. He will hurt them... I need to keep them safe. Because however hard losing them will be, it would be unimaginably harder to know that they will get hurt or worse because of me. I couldn't live with myself if... I can't even finish that thought.

"Harlow, is this really what you want?" Banks asks, and I can hear the pain he is feeling through the phone.

"Yes, this is what I want. You need to leave me alone, forget about me. Move on... I already have." I end the call at the end of the sentence. I can't get another word out without crying. I power off my phone before they can call or message me again.

My heart feels so incredibly heavy, like it's about to drag me down, and never let me get up again. I fall back into my bed, curl into a ball and start crying, hoping that I'll be strong enough to get through this. Hoping that maybe Matt was right that we can make this work, and that maybe, just maybe one day I can be happy again.

28

The days move slow, time passes at a snail's pace. The last week has felt like an eternity full of nothingness. My mom has been planning the wedding, acting like she is in heaven, while I'm in hell. She's begging me to pick flowers, color schemes, dinner choices and try cakes. All I want to do is yell in her face... *I don't care about fucking cake!*

Since I've been back here, small memories of my childhood have resurfaced, none of them are particularly great, but neither are they alarming. It seems like on paper, I had an okay childhood. I remember actually loving my parents at some point. I remember the feeling of wanting to please them and the need for their affection. I still don't remember even close to everything, so I don't know when exactly my feelings toward my family changed, all I know is that those feelings of wanting them close are long gone, and I doubt I'll ever get them back.

"Harlow, which one do you like the best?" My mother interrupts my thoughts. I look at the three wedding dresses the seamstress hung up to show me. Shrugging my shoulders, I can't even bring myself to feel a smidge of happiness. I don't care what I'm wearing to get married. I'll get married in a pair of jeans and a tank top for all I care.

"Just pick one," my mom urges impatience lacing her words, "or I'll pick one for you."

"The one in the middle," I say quickly, not wanting to give my mom the satisfaction of being able to pick. If this is all I have left to rebel against, then I'll take it.

"Okay, try it on," she crosses her arms over her chest.

Maria, the seamstress, helps me into the pearl white designer gown while I move my body on autopilot. She zips me up in the back and turns me gently to face the mirror. Staring at my reflection, I know I should feel something, anything... but I don't. My gaze moves over the mirror. The dress fits like a glove, hugging my waist, and my thighs, and at my knees, it flails out. It's beautiful, but it's not me.

"It's a mermaid cut, and it's the dress to have this season. Not everyone can pull it off though. You, however... well, let me just say you look gorgeous in it," Maria gushes. I try and smile, but my lips refuse to pull up. I know it's not her fault, that she's simply trying to be nice, but I don't care.

"It's perfect," I say, my voice monotone.

"Liven up, Harlow. You're getting married, not being sent to the slaughterhouse."

I can't withhold my eye roll a second longer.

"Maybe not, but I would much rather be sent to the slaughterhouse at this point."

"Maria, please give my daughter and me a moment." Like the good little slave, she is, Maria slips from the room without a word.

My mother crosses the space that separates us, her menacing eyes finding mine in the mirror.

"Maybe you don't want to get married to Matt, but sometimes we have to do things we don't want to do. Life is full of choices, and sometimes those choices aren't always the ones we want to have to make, that doesn't mean you have to be so bitter about it. Do you know how many girls would kill to be in your position right now?"

A bubble of laughter escapes my lips, "You mean there are others who want to be forced into a loveless marriage? Maybe you should go find one of them?"

"Don't act like a spoiled brat. You made the right choice by coming home and agreeing to marry Matt. Now make the best of it."

"Funny, you act like this is a choice that I got to make. This was never a choice. It was forced on me. It was do this or face the consequences of the men I love being injured, or worse, that's not even close to it being a *choice* I get to make."

Her red-painted lips curl upward with disdain, and I can feel the anger vibrating off of her, slamming into me like waves against the shoreline. Her anger threatens to pull me under and into deep dark waters.

"You did have a choice, you could have let your father take care of those Bishop boys, better yet, maybe if we get rid of them, you will finally forget they exist and come to your senses."

The mere sound of their name makes me shiver, and the inky dread of her confession coats my insides with darkness. "You wouldn't..."

My mother smiles at me, but it isn't a smile of happiness. A dreadful chill runs down my spine at her coldness. "I'm just saying, maybe you should put more effort into looking happy. Smile a little. No one wants to see such a beautiful bride moping around, least of all, one with the entire world at her feet."

She acts as if I'm being a hormonal teenager that's throwing a tantrum because I can't get my way when in reality that's not the case at all. She's the one delusional, and, I can't stand to be in this room a moment longer with her. Without a care for the ten-thousand-dollar material, I strip out of the dress and put my own clothes back on.

Shock colors my mother's features, "Where do you think you are going? We are not done here. We have to find matching shoes and a veil still."

"I'm going to call Matt and ask him to take me out for a few hours. It's been some time since we've seen each other." I didn't think I would ever end up taking him up on his offer, but I need to get out. I need to get away from here, and most importantly, her.

"Oh, splendid," my mother sounds genuinely happy and pleased with herself, "That will be great. I'll just pick whatever I think will look best, don't you worry. Come your wedding day, you'll be the prettiest bride this side of the Mississippi."

Rolling my eyes once again, I escape the suffocating room and suck in a breath of fresh air or at least one that isn't filled with bullshit. Pulling my phone out, I find Matt's contact and cover my thumb over the green call key.

Do I really want to do this? The thought of hanging out with him, of getting close to him. It leaves me feeling sick, it makes me feel like I'm betraying the brothers, and in a way, I guess I am. Still, it's this or something far worse, and I'd rather hurt than ever let something happen to them. My love for them is endless.

Pressing the green call key, I swallow down the pain and remind myself that I have to do this. I have to...for them, always for them.

Twenty minutes later, Matt pulls up in a sleek sports car outside the dress shop. I open the passenger door and slip in the car before he has the chance to unbuckle. Sinking into the leather seat with a deep sigh, I look over to him. He's staring at me with a mixture of surprise and curiosity.

"What's going on? Needed saving?" he asks.

"Yes, I really just need to get away from my mom for a few hours, and my parents won't let me out of their sight unless I'm with you so..."

He nods in understanding before asking, "Are you hungry?"

"God, yes. My mom has me on a ridiculous diet, so I'll be extra skinny for the wedding," I explain while buckling myself up. Matt's eyes leave my face and briefly roam my body, making me immediately feel exposed even though I'm fully dressed.

"I don't know how much skinnier you can get without looking sick." He turns his attention back to the road and pulls out of the parking spot. "So, burger place?"

"Hell yes."

After a short drive, we pull up to a little diner. Matt parks upfront, and we both get out at the same time. The hostess greets us with a friendly smile as we walk in, and then seats us, handing us menus as we sit down. I flip through it right away, my mouth watering at the pictures I see. I want one of everything.

"I'm glad you called. I had planned to ask you out tonight or tomorrow anyway, so it was perfect timing," Matt tells me.

"Yeah, I'm glad I called too," My eyes stay glued to the triple bacon burger. I can almost taste the savory goodness on my tongue. Shit, hopefully, I'm not drooling.

"I was going to give you this," Matt's voice is soft, and I peek over the menu and look down. In his hand is a small black velvet box. That isn't... lord, please tell me that isn't what I think it is. At the thought, I lose my appetite.

"I figured people would raise eyebrows when they get to the wedding and realized I never gave you an engagement ring."

My throat tightens, and my ears swoosh with the sound of my heartbeat.

I drop the menu, laying it flat on the table as Matt slides the ring box across the wooden surface. Pausing, I stare at the box like it's going to jump up and attack me.

Part of me still wonders if all of this is a dream. Hesitantly, I reach out and grab it. The box is soft, but the meaning of what's inside it is what terrifies me the most. It makes all of this real, it's not just something inside of my head anymore. It's real, physically real. Opening the box slowly, I gasp at the first sight of the ring. Massive, glittery, with enough diamonds to weigh my hand down. How will I even wear this thing?

"It's beautiful," I whisper. "It really is."

"Are you going to put it on?" he asks after I stare at it for a few more seconds. I nod and take the beautiful piece of jewelry out of the box gently like it might break. It feels just as heavy as it looks. Slowly, I slide it into place on my ring finger.

Of course, it fits perfectly, almost like magic... *almost.*

"My mom must have measured my finger while I was sleeping or something."

Matt chuckles as he brings his cup to his lips, "Honestly, I wouldn't doubt it. Your mom's a little on the crazy side."

You have no idea.

"Oh, my god, did you just get engaged?" Someone next to us squeals, looking up, the waitress is standing by our table, pencil, and notepad in hand, ready to take our order.

"What? No! We've been engaged for a while," I say quickly, wanting to defuse the situation before it gets worse. Judging by her excited facial expression, she is ready to bring out a celebratory cake and have the whole staff sing us a song. That would be embarrassing and draw way too much attention.

"Oh, well, congratulations. That ring is to die for. He must really love you a lot," the waitress giggles, her eyes big, and her cheeks red like she just walked in on some secret. *Yes, tons.* I look up at Matt, who is watching me, his face is a mask of nothingness. He's impossible to read, and I'm not sure if I should even respond. *Does he love me? Will he ever?* Through all of this, I never really bothered to ask what his feelings on our marriage were? He just always seems okay with it.

"I'll take the mammoth burger, and she'll have the bacon cheeseburger, both with fries."

"Of course." The waitress doesn't miss a beat, as she jots down our order and then grabs the menus practically skipping back to the kitchen.

Placing my hands down in front of me, my eyes catch on the ring again. It's going to take some time before I get used to wearing this thing.

"Do you like the ring?" Matt asks.

"Yes, I do. It's... it's almost too much. You didn't have to get me something extravagant. A simple band would've been fine."

"Not for my girl. You deserve the best, and I told you, I would take care of you. This is merely the start. The moment you have my last name, I'll provide you with everything you need and more. You'll never go without."

My heart thumps heavily in my chest. I'll be taking his last name soon, forever sealing my fate of never being with the Bishop brothers again. It hurts, bad, so bad, but I have to remind myself that this is what must be done. I'm doing this for them.

"Hey, are you okay?" Matt's gentle voice interrupts my thoughts, and I blink them away, my heart still heavy in my chest as I find his hand resting against mine. I should feel something, anything at his touch, but I don't.

"Uhh, yeah. Yeah, I'm fine. Just lost in thought." I force a smile.

We make small talk until our food finally arrives and after that, I'm so busy stuffing my face with greasy goodness that I don't have time to talk.

"Wow, I didn't think you were really going to down that whole burger," Matt's eyebrows lift in surprise, as I stuff the last few French fries into my mouth.

"I didn't either, but I was starving," I point out. "Not anymore, though, I'm stuffed. I'm gonna go to the ladies room, and wash my hands. They smell like bacon, and I don't want my mom to have a heart attack when I get home," I excuse myself while Matt finishes up his burger.

Walking through the restaurant, I follow the large restroom sign above me. When I enter the bathroom, I find it empty and sag against the sink, thankful for a calming moment alone. I wash my hands, lathering them with soap thickly, all while my eyes are glued to the diamond ring that now adorns my finger.

The door opens behind me suddenly, and I look up from my hands and into the mirror, ready to fake a smile for whatever woman just walked in. But it isn't a woman. My face falls, my gut tightening, my heart beating furiously.

"Banks?" I gasp, as he closes the door behind him, turning the lock into place, trapping me in the small space with him. "What are you doing? You can't be here?"

Banks doesn't say anything, instead, closing the distance between us in one stride. I'm dizzy with need, wanting his touch, even though I know nothing can come of it. Lifting his hands, he places one on each side of my face, cradling my cheeks. His unique scent fills my nostrils, he smells spicy like cinnamon, and clean, and a warm fuzzy feeling spreads throughout my whole body at the familiar scent.

"It's just us now, tell me what really happened. Tell me what's really going on." His voice is brimming with emotion, and the intensity of it shakes me to the core.

"Banks..." My heart aches in my chest. I want to tell him the truth so badly. I want to tell him that I love him and that everything is going to be okay... but I can't. If I tell him the truth, he will kidnap me again, in an effort to keep me safe. And no matter how badly I want to go with him, I can't let that happen, because if we anger my father again, there is no telling what he'll do.

"Tell me, baby," he coaxes, his thumb gently rubbing over my heated cheek.

"This..." My throat tightens, the words almost refusing to come out. "This is my choice... I *want* to marry Matt. I will marry him." At my words, Banks' hands fall away, and a disbelieving look overtakes his features. He blinks slowly, almost like he's willing all of this to be a dream.

"You are lying, you don't want that prick. Tell me the truth. Tell me this isn't what you want, Harlow." Desperation drips from every single word, and I can hear the pain in his voice. I feel it like a knife is slicing through my heart.

"It's the right thing to do. He'll take care of me..." I start.

"You don't think we'll take care of you?" Banks interrupts, his voice taking on an angry edge. "We will protect you, all you have to do is let us in. Tell me what happened, and I can make this right. I'll have Sullivan and Oliver here in a heartbeat."

No. I can't let them get hurt. Shaking my head, I take a step back, putting some distance between us. Having him this close makes me want to agree to everything he says.

"I don't want you to take care of me or try to protect me. I want you to leave me alone." Tears form in my eyes as the words I'm about to say roll off of my tongue, "I don't want you anymore. You and your brothers are nothing to me."

Banks shakes his head, his chest rising and falling rapidly. I can see the shock and sadness taking root. "Why? Why are you saying these things? I know we didn't tell you before, but we love you, and we know you love us. Don't do this."

It feels like my heart is physically being ripped from my chest, each beat intensifying the ache. "I remembered some things that happened between us. Things I can't forget, that I can't get over." I need to make him understand that I'm serious. I know it's a low blow, but I need to get my point across. I need to make the lie more believable.

"Like what?"

"I remember you threatening me, and I remember how you bullied me in school." Banks lowers his head in shame, his eyes go blank and gloss over as if he's remembering that terrible time. I hate myself, and my father for making me do this. I hate him so much.

"I'm sorry, Harlow, I wish I could change the past, but I can't, and the past doesn't change the way I feel about you now."

"You made my life hell, and I can't forgive you, or your brothers for that." It's only partially a lie. I do remember some of it, but I forgave them long ago. We all made terrible mistakes, and I chose to forgive them for theirs. There was no point in holding a grudge or holding it over their heads if there was ever going to be a chance of all of us being together. But that ship has sailed now. There is no future for us four, at least not with me in it.

Banks looks up, his gaze clashing with mine, and for a moment, I'm overwhelmed with sadness. He opens his mouth to say something, but before he gets a single word out, a loud knocking noise fills the room.

"Harlow, you okay in there?" Matt's muffled voice carries through the door.

I take in a shaky breath before yelling, "Yeah, I'll be right..." Before I can finish the sentence, Banks turns around and heads for the door, unlocking it and pulling it open all at once. I can't move, I'm standing there like a statue, my knees shaking.

"You have got to be fucking kidding," Matt seethes when he sees Banks inside the small bathroom with me.

"What did you do to her? Are you forcing her into marrying you?" Banks accuses Matt, his voice dripping with hate, while his biceps tighten and his hands curl into fists.

Those always playful eyes of Matt's turn cold, making me shiver. "Don't be fucking ridiculous. She agreed to marry me. Get over yourself and take the hint. She doesn't want you, asshole," Matt spits back.

Banks' gaze narrows, and he takes a step forward. "She sure as hell doesn't want you either!" The room is thick with tension making it hard to breathe. Before this can escalate any more, I wedge myself between the two of them. With my back to Matt, I raise my hands up, showing Banks my palms, making an ill attempt to calm him down. I didn't realize—until I see the anger and hurt on his face—that with this stance, I'm clearly taking a side. *Matt's side.* Shit. I'm just digging myself a deeper hole. I have to stop this, end it before it's too late.

"Banks, I already told you... I want to be with Matt. Now please just let me go and stop following me. This is the end; it has to be." I take a step back until my back is flush against Matt's chest. I can feel the heat of his body radiating into mine, and as if he's trying to drive the point home, Matt lifts his hand and rests it on my hip. The pain and disappointment in Banks' eyes are almost too much to bear. My entire body is begging me to go to him, my heart nothing more than a bleeding mess. Putting the last nail in the coffin, I turn away from him and look up at Matt, who is still staring holes into Banks.

"Please take me home."

"Sure, Princess, let's go," he says, moving his hand to my lower back as he leads me out of the bathroom and through the restaurant until we're outside. I don't dare look back at Banks. I couldn't, not knowing how much I just hurt him.

Matt opens the door for me and helps me into the car. As soon as he closes the door behind me, I let the tears I was holding back go. They slip from my eyes and down my cheeks with ease. I'm so ashamed, so heartbroken. I wish things could be different.

"Hey, it's okay," Matt tries to soothe me when he gets into the car, but that just makes me cry more. It's not going to be okay. Nothing is okay. Everything is hopelessly broken, and there is nothing I can do to make things right again. The Bishops are no longer mine, and that realization hurts more than I ever thought it would.

"I'm guessing Banks is the one you love?"

All I can do right now is nod. I do love Banks… and Oliver and Sullivan. God, this is bad, so bad. My heart is breaking, shattering into a million pieces, and there is nothing I can do to stop it. "I love all three of them."

"What do you mean all three? Like… you were with all three of the Bishops?" I don't miss the condescending tone in his voice at my confession, but I still stand by my statement. I might not ever be theirs again, or them mine, but I will freely admit my feelings for them.

"Yes… I was… well, still am, in love with them."

Matt's grip on the steering wheel tightens, "Well, hopefully, you can move on because no wife of mine will be seen with a Bishop. I won't allow it, Harlow." There's a finality to his words, and I know I can't screw this up. If I'm going to protect them, then I'll need to do everything I can do to make sure things with Matt work out.

29

It's the day of the rehearsal dinner, and the house is buzzing with excitement. Excitement that I don't share. It seems as though I'm the only person unhappy about this wedding. No matter what I do, I can't seem to come to grips with what my parents have done. They've taken me out of school, threatened the only people I've ever loved, and then forced me into a situation where there is no escaping. It's like I'm sinking in quicksand, and the more I struggle, the faster I sink. There is no plan B, no fix for this situation.

It takes me forever to get dressed, and even longer to do my hair and make-up. My mother pops her head into the room just as I'm zipping up the lavender-colored V-neck mini-dress that she picked out for me. It's shorter than I would like, but it's very pretty.

"Gorgeous. The lavender really brings out the color of your eyes."

"Thanks," I somehow manage to say. Directing my attention to the mirror in front of me, I stare at my reflection for a few long seconds. I don't recognize the girl looking back at me. She's weak and missing a backbone, but I'm not sure how to help her, how to make her stronger, without putting those I care about in danger.

"Are you ready, sweetie? We're all waiting for you."

"I'm ready," I say, my voice somber.

Together with my mother, I walk out of the bedroom, down the hallway, and to the grand staircase. As we descend the stairs, my mother leans into me. She's smiling at Matt, his father, and my father, who are waiting at the bottom of the steps.

"Do not do anything to mess this up; otherwise, you know what will happen." The warning is clear, and I wish so badly that I didn't have to play by their rules. My jaw clenches, my teeth grinding together at the effort it takes me to keep my mouth shut. I want to tell her off, but what's the point? It won't change what's going to happen.

When we reach the bottom of the steps, my jaw is aching, and my stomach is twisted in knots. Matt reaches for me, and I place my hand in his, the heat of his touch radiating through me. I wish I could hate Matt, but I don't. As bad as all of this is, he's been the only person to show me even a tiny bit of compassion.

"We will meet you at the church." My father's authoritative voice rains down on me like acid. I ignore him completely, uncaring to what he has to say at this point.

"Are you okay?" Matt whispers into the shell of my ear as we walk out the front door, and toward the car that's waiting for us.

"Yes," I lie. I'm not okay, not even close, but complaining about it won't change anything.

"Good, you look beautiful tonight, and even more beautiful with that engagement ring on your finger. I can't wait to show you off to the world as my wife," Matt teases, a hint of flirtation to his words, but I don't have it in me to even make an effort to flirt back.

"I'm sorry, this is just... it's hard for me," I say as he helps me into the car.

He climbs in behind me and places his hand against my bare thigh. I drop my gaze to where he's touching me. It seems wrong, like he's taunting me with his touch or something. I can't want Matt, not when my heart belongs to another.

"We're going to be married tomorrow, and though our love isn't real, we have to pretend to an entire room of people today and tomorrow that it is."

He's right, but I just don't care. I don't want to pretend anymore. I just want to get married and escape the tower my parents have locked me up in.

As if he can sense my uncaring attitude his lips press into a hard line, making him appear almost angry. Great, I've just pissed my soon to be husband off, the only person that seems to care about my wants. Maybe I should be a little nicer to him... more grateful that he is not a total jerk to me, because truthfully if he were, there would be nothing I could do. I would still marry him to protect the Bishops. I would do anything to ensure their well-being.

"I'm sorry," I say softly. "I really am. I wish things were different."

"Yeah, me too..." He says with a shake of his head as he turns and directs his attention out the window, like the passing trees are better company than me or something.

The rest of the drive is uneventful, as is the rehearsal. Shelby is there too, as my maid of honor, and even though her presence gives me comfort, it is not enough to make me feel anything else besides dreadful.

We run through the events that will take place for the day tomorrow, and it takes everything inside me to follow through with every step, and every word. Matt doesn't skip a beat, and even smiles at me a few times, but in his eyes, beneath the fake façade, I can see anger brewing.

And slowly, the realization starts to sink in...

Am I really going to marry him tomorrow?

Before it was always, yeah, I'm going to do this, but now it's really happening. In just twenty-four hours I am going to be married to a man I don't love.

As always, Matt is attentive and caring, though his eyes say otherwise, and by the time we make it to the dinner party my parents have put together for us, I'm feeling a little less nauseated. My mother is beaming, she's over the moon as we enter the reception area that's filled with members of both sides of our families.

Many faces are unfamiliar to me, so I keep my eyes down and let Matt guide me around the room. He introduces me to nearly everyone he knows, as I fake a smile and pretend like I care what they have to say to me.

Pretending is exhausting, and I find myself reaching for a flute of wine without even thinking. The cold bubbly liquid slips past my dry lips and into my cotton filled mouth, soothing the dryness there. I down the contents of the entire thing, and reach for another, sipping the second glass, rather than downing it too.

I hate this place. I hate my father. I hate that I'm being forced to do something that I don't want to do. I just want to run away and forget about everything.

"Would it hurt you to smile a little?" my mother growls as she passes by me.

Would it hurt you to care a little? I want to say but don't.

We eat a light dinner, and Matt converses with his father, and a few of the other businessmen. I do my best to block out most of the conversation and just stand there like a statue, letting him hold my hand, and show me off, like I'm some rare jewel.

"Here, have another," Shelby walks up to me, whispering in my ear as she hands me a flute. "You look like you could use it."

"Thank you," I say, and for the first time tonight a ghost of a smile that isn't forced, plays on my lips. I'm so glad Shelby is here, my one friend who has always stood by me. "I don't know how I can ever repay you for being my friend. You've been there for me through everything."

"Don't mention it," Shelby waves me off and gives me a kiss on my cheek. "That's what friends are for."

We talk some more before Shelby excuses herself and leaves. I wish I could have left with her, but since it's my party and all, I guess people expect me to stay.

Time passes by slowly, and I watch as Matt orders drink after drink. It seems like I'm not the only one trying to drown my sorrows. The difference is, I stopped after the third flute of champagne, even though I want to drink more. I didn't like how the alcohol clouded my mind, so I forced myself to stop.

As the evening goes on, Matt becomes more and more intoxicated, but his hand stays wrapped around mine, keeping me close to his side. It's not ideal, but if I'm being honest, it's better than walking around on my own. At least this way, I have Matt to act as a buffer between my parents and me, and anyone else I don't want to talk to.

After a short time, my bladder starts to protest, the champagne running through me faster than I anticipated. Pulling my hand out of Matt's I excuse myself to the bathroom. I can feel his eyes on me as I walk away, burning through the fabric of my dress and embedding into my skin.

When I make it to the bathroom and into the stall, I all but sag against the wall. Tears sting my eyes. I want to cry so badly, to let all the things I'm feeling out, but I can't. I have to hold it together. I have to be strong. The instant I show weakness my mother and father will pounce.

Swallowing down the tears, and pain, I use the toilet, flush, and wash my hands. Exiting the bathroom, I keep my eyes trained on the floor. Failing to notice the person walking toward me, I run head-on into them.

"I'm so sorry..." I apologize and lift my gaze hoping, it's not one of my parents' friends. My eyes take in the expensive black suit and then the handsome face attached to it, it's an extremely drunk, Matt.

"Sorry enough to give me a kiss?" he slurs, his eyes are bloodshot and glassed over, I didn't realize he was this drunk before I left. Licking my lips, I'm ready to tell him no when he reaches forward and gently pushes me back against the wall.

Worry gnaws at my insides, but a tiny part of me knows that Matt isn't a bad guy. He wouldn't really hurt me.

"I don't want to kiss you," I tell him as he leans forward, blowing hot breath against my lips. He smells like a distillery and my nose wrinkles at the odor.

"Of course, you don't. Why would you want to kiss your future husband? Why would you want to show even an ounce of affection?" Bitter laughter slips past his lips and into the space between us. I try to shrug off his hold, but his fingers dig deeper into my skin, holding me in place. Pain radiates down my arms from where he's holding me, and I can't stop the whimper that passes my lips.

"You're hurting me," I whisper, hoping the words will break through his foggy mind, but they don't, in fact, they do the opposite. Without warning, his lips descend on mine, crashing against my lips with a fierceness that terrifies me.

There is no escaping him, his lips, his hands, they hold me in place. My lungs burn as I forget to breathe and instead, start to struggle against his hold, pressing my palms against his chest in an effort to put space between us.

My efforts are pointless, and instead of moving away, he steps closer, his chest pressing against mine. Deepening the kiss, his tongue enters my mouth without permission. Angry fire blooms inside of me, and somehow, I find the strength to fight back. I nip at his tongue hard, and instantly, he pulls away, taking a staggering step backward.

Shock paints his features before rage overtakes them, and I'm left cowering and shaking, like a puppy left out in the middle of winter.

Maybe I shouldn't have bitten him? It was just a kiss, and he is my soon to be husband, after all. But the words feel wrong, all of this feels wrong. I said I didn't want it. Tears start to fall without warning, staining my perfectly painted cheeks.

"Don't be such a cry baby, it was only a kiss."

"I said I didn't want to kiss you."

"You expect us to be married and never kiss? You can't be that naive."

"If I change my mind about wanting to kiss, you'll be the first one to know."

"Whatever. We will still be married tomorrow, and you will be my wife. You'll have to sleep with me eventually. I might not be a Bishop, but you'll come to love my cock as much as you loved theirs..." His face twists into a cruel smile. The kind man I had met not long ago, has become someone I don't know, and without even thinking about it, I cross the space between us, pull my hand back and land a hard slap against his cheek.

My skin burns at the contact against his, but I don't care. I don't care what happens next. All I know is that he will not talk about me like that. I won't allow him to belittle what we had.

"You don't know them, and you don't know me," I sneer, finding the strength to speak up for myself. I'm tired of being a doormat. "I might marry you on paper, but that doesn't mean I'll sleep with you. Especially not when you act like an asshole, like you are now."

Matt's jaw clenches, and his once soft eyes darken. He takes a threatening step toward me, with his hand raised, and I wonder briefly if he's going to hit me? Before he gets a chance to do whatever it is he planned to do, one of my father's guards appears.

"Your father has asked for your presence... alone," Bert says softly, his eyes taking in the situation before him.

Releasing an anxious breath, I say, "Of course, where would he like me to meet him."

"Outside, in the garden," he says, and I make a move to follow the guard.

"Goodnight. I'll see you tomorrow, *wife*." I shudder at the tone of Matt's words but nod in agreement. How am I going to do this? Marry a man that forces himself on me? Before tonight, I thought I could do this, but now, not so much. Matt is just as ruthless and scary as my father. His true colors finally coming to light.

Matt disappears down the hall, anger rippling from every pore on his body. I sag against the brick wall once he's out of sight, relief flooding my veins. How did I end up here? There aren't enough tears in the world. I'm exhausted, tired of crying, of pretending, of faking.

"Come with me, please," Bert interrupts my thoughts, and a moment later starts down the hall without even looking to see if I follow. It takes a second, but I get my legs to work and follow behind him cautiously, unsure of where he may be taking me.

He did, after all, kidnap me once before.

"Thanks..." I almost say Bert, but I know that's not his name.

"Milton," he introduces himself, making me feel stupid. I really should have made an effort to remember his real name.

"Thank you, Milton."

We walk down the hall, and then another until we reach a pair of French doors. Bert opens them and leads me outside. The night air is cool against my bare skin and goosebumps ripple across my arms.

"Where is my father?" I question, crossing my arms over my chest. Bert doesn't respond and instead turns to head back inside. Fear trickles down my spine, worry consuming me, and then I see him.

Sullivan. It can't be. This has to be a dream. All of my previous feelings fade away, and I race toward him, wrapping my arms around his middle, and burying my nose into his shirt, inhaling his familiar scent into my nostrils. A soft chuckle escapes his lips, and I peer up at him through my hair.

"Banks was so sure you had moved on, but you wouldn't be hugging me like this if that's true." His arms wrap around me as well, tightening almost as if he's trying to embed me into his chest. I can hear him inhaling my scent, my body melting into a pile of mush at his feet.

And then I realize... *Shit.* I just gave myself away.

"I...." Is there any point in trying to hide it anymore?

"It's okay, I know. We knew all along that it was an act. Whatever you're trying to protect us from, that shit ends now."

Pulling away so I can look up at him, I ask, "How did you get here? How did you know I was even here?"

Sullivan smiles, and I swear my core clenches a hundred times over. I miss that smile, his touch, his scent. I miss him and his brothers, and the way they make me feel, so cherished, so loved. I just miss them, so damn much. I have so many more questions I want to ask him, but all those things fall away now that I'm in his arms. Without breaking our hug, he walks me down the stairs and into the garden. There is a tiny maze, and we hide behind one of the ivy-covered walls. This way, we remain hidden from any wandering eyes.

As soon as we're hidden, Sullivan pulls away, his hold on me loosens, and his fingers trail up my skin, stopping once they reach my cheeks where he cradles them. "I've got connections, people helping me. Now I need you to tell me what's going on? I don't know how much time we have, and I need to know everything. Don't lie to me or spare me any of the details. We're going to get you out of this."

"No, you can't." I gasp, crippling fear overtaking me. "My father will hurt you; he'll destroy you and your brothers. He won't stop at framing you this time. I can't let that happen. I won't." I cry, realizing a moment too late that I've given him all the information he needs.

Tears start to fall from my eyes again, and Sullivan wipes each of them away with his thumb, his sea-blue eyes bore into mine, as he does. He looks conflicted, like he might want to kiss me but also throttle me at the same time.

"Fuck, Harlow, don't cry," he pleads with me, and the ache in his voice only makes me cry harder.

"I can't help it. I don't want to do this. I want to be with you guys, but there is nothing I can do, and I won't let him hurt you any more than he has." By now I'm sobbing, my make-up is completely ruined, and I look like a mess, I'm sure of it, but I don't care, not when I'm in Sullivan's arms.

"Shhh, there is no need to save us. We can fight our own battles against your father. Right now, I need you to do something for me. We're going to stop this wedding..."

My fingers dig into the expensive suit he's wearing. "No. You can't. He'll find a way to hurt you. I can't let him." I'm frantic. Trying to protect them. I know my father, and I know he'll do whatever he can to get his way.

"Stop, Harlow," Sullivan whispers and then shuts me up with a kiss that's hard, fierce, and needy. In that kiss, I feel every ounce of pain, every drop of need. I feel the love he has for me, and I never ever want to let it go. Grabbing onto him, I deepen the kiss, becoming crazed with need. My hands roam over every inch of him, as he does the same, holding me close like I'm a fragile piece of glass.

"I need you," I pant against his lips as I break the kiss a moment later. Looking up at him, I can see the hunger flickering in his smoldering gaze. He wants me just as badly as I want him, and if this is going to be our last time together, forever, which it has to be, then I'm going to take it. I'm going to take my fill of him until there is nothing more to take.

Without an ounce of hesitation, Sullivan undoes his belt and pushes his dress pants down, freeing his cock. My mouth waters at the sight, and I shiver as his hands move to the hem of my dress, before disappearing beneath it. A moment later, the sound of fabric tearing fills the night air, and the thong I was wearing is discarded on the ground.

With his hands on my hips, he lifts me, and I snake my arms around his neck, a tiny mewl of pleasure escaping my lips, as his cock brushes against my soaked folds.

"Fuck. I knew you didn't want him. I knew it," he growls against my throat as he lines us up, and I sink slowly down onto his length. In that moment, the world could explode around us, and I wouldn't care. There is nothing that compares to the pleasure that fills my veins as he enters me.

"Tell me you don't love him... tell me that you love me, and my brothers," Sullivan pleads, his handsome features haunted.

"I love you and your brothers. Only you guys..." The words come out on a pant as Sullivan bounces me up and down on his cock, his muscular thighs, and biceps holding me up as if I weigh nothing.

Sweat beads my forehead, and I already know that I need more, so much more. He's fucking me but not like I need him. As if he knows this, Sullivan moves me, so my back is against the brick wall. Then he starts to thrust upward, entering me at such a pace even my eyes can't keep up. Blood swooshes in my ears, and my lungs fill with air. For the first time since my father took me away, it feels like I can breathe again.

It feels like with every stroke he's slowly piecing my broken heart back together. His grip on my hips turns bruising, and I pull back wanting, no needing, to see his face as we fall apart together. My entire body starts to tighten like a coil, my heart races heavily in my chest. Every hair on my body stands on end, as the sound of our panting fills the air, as we come together. I need more, so much more. I don't want this moment to end, ever. Pulling at his shirt like a mad woman, I rip it until the buttons go flying, and my hands find hot bare skin. At my touch, Sullivan hisses.

"You're my home. The beginning, the end, and everything in between," he whispers, as he slows his pace, and enters me slowly, so slow it almost hurts.

The tears start to fall from my eyes again as he brings me to orgasm, my entire body shaking as pleasure ripples through me like waves cresting the shoreline. It doesn't take long before he starts to come himself, filling me with his sticky hot seed. I sigh so heavily at the feeling, trying with all my might to memorize exactly what this moment feels like.

It will forever be my most cherished memory of him. He holds me in his arms for a while longer, before placing me back down on my feet.

All I can do is stare at the ground, the cold seeping back into my skin at the loss of his body heat.

"This isn't the end, Harlow. Not even fucking close. You're not marrying that fucker tomorrow."

"I have to."

With two fingers, he tips my chin upward, forcing me to look at him. "No, you do not. Oliver, Banks, and I will not let it happen. They'll have to kill us first."

That's what I'm worried about. I think to myself but don't say it out loud. Sullivan stares at me for a long moment, before he starts to tuck himself back into his pants and fixes his shirt the best he can. As our time comes to an end, I hold the tears in, refusing to let them taint the final memory that I'll have with him.

"I love you, Harlow, we all do, and we will fight for you. I'm sorry that we let this happen, but I swear, baby, we will make it right."

Shaking my head, my hair falls into my face. I can't listen to him say these things. None of this is their fault, and there aren't enough words or time to explain it.

"I love you too. All three of you. Please tell your brothers that. I didn't mean to hurt Banks the other day, I didn't want to hurt any of you, I just…"

Sullivan's brow furrows. "Stop acting like this is the end, it's not."

Biting into my bottom lip, I suck in a shaky breath. "It's the end, Sullivan. It has to be. I have to protect you. I love you, but sometimes love isn't enough."

Sullivan opens his mouth to say something, but approaching footsteps stop him from speaking. Peeking through the bushes, I see Bert standing at the top of the steps.

"I have to go," I say, not even looking up at Sullivan as I say the words.

"This isn't the end, Harlow, it's merely the beginning."

Oh, how I wish that were the truth.

30

This isn't the end, Harlow, it's merely the beginning. Sullivan's words haunt me later that night as I lie awake in bed, unable to sleep. Tossing and turning, all I can do is think, my brain refusing to shut off.

I should be sleeping, getting some rest because tomorrow is going to be a long day, but I can't stop thinking about what he said. Maybe he's right. Maybe this isn't the end. Maybe it is just the beginning...the question is, the beginning of what? A loveless life as a prisoner?

No, I can't just let this happen to me, I need to try and save myself, without endangering the guys. There has to be a way for me to fight back, to get out of this situation. I can't marry Matt, but I also can't let my father hurt the men I love. I have to do something… anything. Filled with nervous energy, I don't even think as I tiptoe from my bed.

The house is quiet and bathed in complete darkness. My parents should be asleep by now. Which gives me the perfect opportunity to go snooping. If I can just find something, a tiny indication of my father doing shady business, I would have the leverage I need against him. I could force him to let me go, force him to let me be with the Bishops.

Like a ninja, I move through the house wearing nothing but my pajamas. I head to the most likely place I would find something... my father's office. When he is at home, he is usually in there, working or maybe just hiding from my mom. I don't know what he does in there, but he does spend a lot of time locked inside.

I push the heavy wooden door open, entering the room, I can smell nothing but his spicy cologne. It lingers in the space, leaving me with an uneasy feeling in my gut. Switching on the light the room illuminates with a soft glow, one of the walls is covered in bookshelves, there is a wet bar beneath the huge bay window, and an oversized mahogany desk is centered in the room. My gaze pauses on the bookshelves and then moves back to his desk. I decide to start there first.

Moving behind the desk, I take a seat on the soft leather chair and start to go through the drawers. The first has nothing but cigars, lighters, and cigar cutters inside. The second holds an assortment of contents, the drawer looks to be like a catch-all. I rummage through it, gagging when I find two condoms and... *lube. What the fuck?* Shutting the drawer quickly, I swallow down the puke threatening to rise up my throat.

Reaching for the brass knob on the third drawer, I pull it but find it doesn't open. It discourages me and gives me hope all at the same time. I might not be able to get in there, but it must have something worthwhile in there. Something that he is hiding.

I mean, why else would it be locked?

All I need is one thing, one piece of evidence to use against him.

Grabbing his heavy letter opener from the top of the desk, I use it to try and pry the drawer open. After a few minutes, I nearly give up, but then I hear it, a crack sounds inside of the drawer, almost like something is breaking.

Yes! Excitement fills my veins, and I give it one final shove, and the stupid lock comes undone. Thank god! I could cry, I'm so happy.

The drawer pops open, and I stare down at its contents with confusion. It's not what I expected to find. Instead of business notes or documents, I find old photos and something that looks like hand-written letters.

Digging through the contents, my confusion mounts, because I don't recognize the woman in these pictures. She's most definitely not my mother, so who is she? I recognize my dad, a younger, carefree looking version of him, standing beside the mysterious woman in the photos, there is something oddly familiar about her. Staring at the image, I try and place her in my mind. Maybe I knew her before I lost my memory, and that's why she seems familiar?

When my head starts to hurt, I decide to switch gears and open one of the letters. I scan over the words, my heart pounding in my chest as I do.

To the love *of my life,*

It's been days since I last saw your face. Every night I fall asleep dreaming of the day you'll be mine. I know that George thinks that the baby is his, but I know that it's mine. We belong together, as a family. Please come back to me, my love.

Love always,
    Lionel

Air refuses to enter my lungs. There are numerous letters, all very much like the one I just read. Letter after hand-written letter. My hands start to shake, as the confusion intensifies. Placing the letter back down, I push away from the desk. It's then that a picture out of the pile catches my eye.

I pick it up, unable to ignore the gut feeling that's swirling in my stomach. I study the dingy photo intensely. It's my dad, he must be my age in this picture. The woman from the other picture is in it too, but there is a third person... a man, one that looks just as familiar.

I'm not sure who he is, but if I had to place him somewhere in my head, I would say he could be a lost Bishop brother. He has Oliver's chocolate brown eyes, Sullivan's masculine jaw, and Banks' mischievous smile. Flipping the picture over, I read three names written in black ink on the back.

George, Phoebe, and Lionel. *George?* Then like a missing puzzle piece it clicks.

George Bishop... The brothers' dad. The questions seem to stack higher and higher with each new thing I discover. Why would my father keep a picture of him and George? Especially one where they look like *friends* instead of enemies? While those questions are weighing the biggest one is, who is Phoebe? More confused than ever, I search for more pictures, and more answers but still come up empty. It's like searching for gold and hoping to find the biggest nugget.

I find a few more photos with George and my father, some with all three of them but most have the girl named Phoebe in them. All the way at the bottom of the drawer, I find a large picture, it's the only one that's in a frame, signifying its importance.

Again, it's Phoebe. She is sitting in a rocking chair, cradling a growing baby bump, a bright, joyful smile on her lips. I examine the picture carefully, and my heart stops, my lungs cease to work, and the blood freezes in my veins.

On her lap is a folded baby blanket with pink embroidered letters on it that reads *Harlow*.

I don't know how long I sit there staring at the picture, letting all of this new information sink in, but it feels like an eternity. I'm shell shocked, desperate for more answers, answers that I know I won't get unless I go to my father. Anger simmers just below the surface. I don't know who Phoebe is yet, but I do know she is important to me.

A distant noise fills the air, soft giggling is what it sounds like. *Who is up giggling at this hour?* I force myself to look away from the picture. I can make out the sound of approaching footsteps, there are two pairs, one soft, and the other heavier. Jumping from the chair, I shove all the contents from the drawer back inside it. I close it, trying my best to make it look like nothing happened. Hurrying across the room, I flip the light switch off.

As fast as I can without falling, I use my hands and pat along the bookshelf in the dark until I reach the edge. Just as the door opens, I slip behind the side, flattening myself against the wall as much as I can, hoping and praying that I'm not visible from this position.

Holding my breath, my lungs burn for air. I expect the overhead light to come on, but instead, a soft click sounds and the lamp on the desk turns on illuminating only half the room with a faint glow of light leaving where I am bathed in darkness.

It only takes a second for my eyes to adjust, and when I see Shelby and my father together, I have to bite the inside of my cheek to stifle the gasp trying to break free.

"We have to be quiet, if Harlow hears, then we're both screwed."

Shelby smiles, devilishly, "You're screwed either way."

Oh, my god. My father is having an affair with my best friend. The person he was meeting at the hotel was Shelby. I watch horrified as they kiss, my father lifts her up and places her ass against the desk before pushing up her dress. She didn't even change; she's still wearing the same dress that she wore to the rehearsal dinner.

"Shut up and let me fuck you." My father growls, and Shelby squeals with excitement.

My mother, my poor mother. I wonder if she knows. I can feel the bile burning up my throat as I squeeze my eyes shut while they start to screw each other. The sounds they make together make my ears bleed, and I do my best to remain silent through it all.

The betrayal is like a dull knife cutting through my chest, and I know there is no coming back from this.

I can't believe them. That Shelby betrayed me, that my father is having an affair with my best friend. I can't believe it. Everything I discovered tonight weighs heavily on my shoulders. My father and Shelby. The mysterious letters and photos. It feels like I'm suffocating, drowning in all the lies that seem to surround me.

I have to find a way out of this mess, out of my father's life.

I have to escape. Break free. I did it once before, and I'll do it again.

I wait for Shelby and my father to finish.

"She can never know about this. Keep your mouth shut, and your legs closed or there will be consequences, do you understand me?"

"Yes, sir," Shelby answers softly. In her eyes, I see love for my father, and that makes me sick, so fucking sick. They leave the room a few moments later, and I remain standing, barely holding myself together.

Time ticks by slowly, and eventually, I pull myself together and escape the room, listening for footsteps, or any noises as I head down the hall and back toward my room. I've barely made it five feet when a cloth-covered hand comes out of nowhere and presses against my mouth and nose. A scream catches in my throat, and I struggle helplessly as a thick arm wraps around my middle, pulling me back against a wall of muscle.

Oh, god, no, this can't be happening again.

"Shhh, it's going to be okay," a voice whispers in my ear, but I'm too far gone, drifting off into the darkness, to tell if it's a familiar voice or not.

BOOK THREE

when
rivals *love*
BAYSHORE RIVALS BOOK THREE

USA Today Bestselling Author
J. L. BECK
C. HALLMAN

31

Slowly my eyes flutter open, but I can barely see anything. I'm immersed in darkness. It takes me a moment before I realize that I'm in the back seat of a moving car, my face sticking to the leather. The car takes a sharp turn, and my head lolls to the side. *Ugh*. It feels like my skull's been stuffed with cotton balls. My thoughts a blurred mess like I'm looking through a puddle of water that's mixed with mud, I can't figure out how I got here.

A wave of nausea overcomes me, my stomach churning like I'm on a roller coaster. I've never gotten car sick before, but right now, I could blow chunks. Slowly my thoughts return, and as I roll over on the seat, I'm reminded that someone put a cloth over my mouth... that someone drugged and kidnapped me.

Jackknifing in the seat, my vision blurs at the fast movement, and bile rises up my throat. Sucking air in through my nose, I get the nausea to fade away, and after a few more seconds pass, my vision fully clears, and I can make out the person in the driver's seat.

What the hell?

"Ber... ah, I mean... Milton? What the hell are you doing?"

His eyes find mine in the rearview mirror, "I'm really sorry, Harlow, but you weren't safe at the house, and it's my job to keep you safe." His eyes fall back to the road. There isn't an ounce of remorse or regret in his voice, and I have to wonder how sane he is right now.

Is this a joke? Some sick twisted bullshit my father is doing.

"So, you drugged and kidnapped me to keep me safe? Seems like the opposite if you ask me!" I try to keep my voice even, but patience escapes me, and it comes out as a yell.

"I'm sorry about the chloroform, but I needed to get you out of the house fast, and I knew you wouldn't have come with me willingly," he explains further.

He is right about that, I wouldn't have come with him because by leaving I'm endangering the people I love, but Milton doesn't know that, or if he does, he doesn't care. My gaze swings around the blacked-out SUV and then out the window. It's so dark, I can't make out where we're headed.

"Why do you think I wasn't safe at the house?"

"It's not that I *think* you're not safe. I know it."

"Explain, tell me, make me understand because right now you look more like the person trying to hurt me than anyone else."

With a loud exhale of breath, he starts to speak, "Remember at the rehearsal dinner when I bumped into the waitress, making her fall and your food went everywhere?"

"What the hell does a waitress tripping and dropping my food have to do with you kidnapping me?"

"It has to do with the fact that someone was trying to poison you. I saw someone put something in your food as it was being brought out."

I blanch, the realization of what he's saying sinking heavily in my stomach.

Grasping at straws, I say, "Maybe you're wrong. Maybe you saw wrong?"

He shakes his head. "I'm not wrong, Harlow. I've been protecting you for a long time, and I've been doing this kind of work even longer. I'm trained in this kind of stuff, and I saw someone put something in your food. There is no wrong when you witness it with your own eyes."

Oh, god, maybe he isn't wrong. Maybe I am. Maybe someone is trying to kill me. It makes sense, the brothers told me someone was trying to hurt me, but I never wanted to believe it. Why would anyone want me dead?

"Why didn't you say anything? Why didn't you tell my father?" I yell while moving toward the door.

I'm scared and angry. I don't understand why someone would want to hurt me. After everything I discovered tonight about my father, and the Bishops, there is very little room left inside of me to deal with anything. I'm exhausted, both physically and mentally.

"Because I don't know if your father was involved or not. I need more information."

All of this is insane, completely insane. As badly as I dislike my father right now, I need to go to him, to tell him what happened, there is no way he could be involved, is there?

"You need to take me back right now," I order, but Milton continues driving like I didn't say anything at all. "I mean it, take me back!" I'm seconds away from kicking the back of his seat to get his attention.

"I can't, and I won't. I told you it's not safe."

Clutching a hand to my stomach, I feel the overwhelming need to vomit.

"Where are you taking me?"

"Somewhere that you will be safe." Great, that doesn't tell me anything. Folding my arms over my chest, I just sit there pouting like a teenager, because really, there is nothing else I can do. Not with the car going down the highway at sixty miles an hour.

I need him to stop so I can make a run for it. Deja vu settles in my mind, that was my plan the last time I got kidnapped. Didn't work out that great then, but what else can I do? It's not like I stand a chance fighting a man who is twice my size and works as a bodyguard, but I'm not going to let this happen without, at least, fighting back, the stakes are too high.

We drive on the two-lane highway for a while longer until Milton suddenly puts his turn signal on and switches lanes to take the exit. I perk up, my eyes catching on the rest stop sign in the beam of the headlights.

Keeping my lips firmly together, even though I have a ton to say, I wait for the car to stop. With enough adrenaline pumping through my veins, I reach for the handle just as the car comes to a stop. But all my plans change in an instant because before I even touch the handle, the door opens for me.

The cool night air rushes into the car. On instinct, I jerk back at the large dark figure that's magically appeared in front of me, blocking the exit.

A tiny squeak slips past my lips when he bends down and starts to climb into the back seat. *Oh, hell, no.*

Lifting my foot, I'm about to kick this bastard in the face when my eyes catch on a familiar pair of chocolate brown ones. *Oliver.*

"Oliver..." I gasp as I lean back in the seat. I'm caught between wanting to hug him, and throat punch him all at once. When I see his trademark smirk that usually makes my insides tingle, anger wins out. All I'm feeling right now is simmering rage.

"Were you in on this?"

He had better not be, though, I'm certain he was.

"In on it? Baby, it was my idea," he chuckles.

Yup, definitely want to punch him now.

"You didn't actually think we were going to let you marry that asshat *Matt*, did you?"

"It's not your choice, and you don't know the danger you're putting all of us in by doing this... *again.*" My heart starts to break all over again. Every time I think I'm moving forward, learning to let go of the feelings I have for the Bishop brothers, one of them decides to reappear in my life.

"Drive," Oliver orders when he is in the car.

Milton throws the car into drive and pulls out into traffic. Oliver reaches for me, his fingers interlace with my own, and I can't bring myself to disconnect from him. I need his touch, need the warmth of his skin. It's like it gives me strength.

"We have evidence against your father. Leverage. You don't have to marry that prick to protect anyone. You aren't under your father's thumb anymore."

My face falls, my eyes move to where our fingers are joined. I don't understand how. I couldn't find any evidence, nothing to stop my father from hurting the Bishops. If I don't go back now...

"Stop thinking, I can see all the thoughts running through your head. You're safe, we're safe, nothing is going to happen."

Looking up into his brown eyes, I ask, "How can you be sure?"

Even in the dark, I can feel his eyes burning a path over my skin.

"I thought you would be happy to get away from him," he whispers in defeat.

Moving closer to him, I lift a hand and force him to look at me. "I am, but I'm scared. I don't want my father to lash out at you or your brothers for this. I can't let anything happen to any of you."

"And we can't let anything happen to you either. Besides the whole scam marriage thing, you weren't safe there. Someone is trying to hurt you." The pain in his voice cuts through me like razor blades, and all I can think about is making him feel better. Crawling into his lap, I wrap my arms around his neck and bury my face into his neck. He immediately wraps his arms around me, crushing me to his chest. All I can hear is the heavy thump of his heart in my ear as it beats against his chest, his intoxicating scent filling my nostrils.

I spend the rest of the drive cradled in Oliver's arms, forgetting that Milton's in the car completely. I'm so content that the exhaustion wins out, and I don't even realize that I fall asleep until Oliver wakes me up with a gentle kiss to my forehead, we've pulled up in front of a hotel.

"We are here," he murmurs into my hair as I stretch my arms.

"Where is here?"

"We'll stay in this hotel, for now, there is security everywhere, and no one would expect us to be here. It's safe," Oliver promises. He takes my hand and helps me out of the car. We close the car door, and Milton drives off to who knows where. Right now, I'm too tired to care. Oliver leads me inside, and only then do I realize I'm wearing pajamas. Luckily, there is no one in the lobby when we pass through. I'm not sure what time it is, but it's still dark outside, so it must be very early in the morning.

We ride the elevator up to the ninth floor, the ding of the door opening wakes me up a tiny bit more, but by the time we are walking down the hallway to our room, I'm half asleep again. Oliver has an arm wrapped around my waist, and I'm leaning into his side, my legs are getting heavier with each step.

He stops and swipes a card through the door lock, making it click open. Together we enter the room, which looks more like an apartment. There is a large kitchen that opens up into a living room with a sitting area, huge TV, and even a fireplace.

"Wow, this is nice..."

My words are trail off when what I assume to be the bedroom door opens, and two familiar faces enter the room. Oliver releases me so Banks can pull me into his arms. He holds me tight for a few seconds, burying his face into my hair, breathing in my scent as I do the same with him. A calmness overtakes me, all the anxiety, fear, and sadness fading away.

He releases me and lets Sullivan have his turn. Sullivan circles my waist with his arms and hauls me up against his chest, giving me a bear-like hug.

"I missed you so much," he whispers against my hair, his breath tickling the fine hairs on my neck.

"You saw me yesterday," I giggle.

"That's too long, we need to see you every day," Sullivan replies thickly.

"Hey! I didn't see her yesterday, so move along..." Banks complains, grabbing my arm and pulling me away from Sullivan. "You look tired. Do you want to go to bed?"

The right thing to do would be to stay up and talk to them since I need to know what kind of evidence they have against my father, not to mention telling them about the things I found in my father's desk and what happened with Shelby in the office.

There are so many questions that need to be answered, so many things that need to be said, but all I can think of doing right now is closing my eyes and falling asleep.

Exhaustion is winning out, and after everything, I need some time to rest my brain.

Nodding my head, I admit, "I could go for a couple hours of sleep."

"Yeah, you look pretty tired," Sullivan says, admiring my face.

"Thanks," I say, laughing softly, "I have so much I want to talk about, but I'm dead tired. Like dead to the world."

"Sleep, then we can talk." Banks leads me into one of the bedrooms, and I fall on to the bed, the soft memory foam mattress swallowing me up as I sink deeply into the cloud-like material. A heavy blanket is pulled up to my chin, the weight of it against my body, making it hard for me to keep my eyes open.

I'm vaguely aware of Banks sliding into the bed next to me, and I sigh heavily when his arm snakes around my waist, and he pulls me back against his chest.

His warmth engulfs me, and with his steady breathing against my neck, I feel myself drifting off into the nothingness of sleep, wondering if when I wake up, this will all have been a dream.

WAKING UP THE NEXT MORNING, it takes me a few seconds to wrap my head around where I am. I'm in bed with not one but two of the brothers.

Banks still has his arm wrapped around me, his face buried into my neck. Oliver is lying on his side next to me, his brown eyes meet mine and hold my gaze.

"Were you watching me sleep?"

"Yes," he admits shamelessly. "It feels like it's been an eternity since I last saw you, and all I can think to do to make the ache hurt less is be near you."

I can't help myself. I reach for him and watch with anxious butterflies as he scoots closer until our faces are only an inch apart. I can feel his hot breath against my lips. I want to kiss him so badly it hurts, but the hunger flickering deep in his eyes tells me that it wouldn't stop with just a kiss, and we need to talk before we do anything else.

"What kind of evidence do you have against my father?"

"Milton recorded a meeting between your father and Xander Rossi, do you know who that is?"

"Yes," I admit, a small shudder runs through me at the memory. "I recently remembered overhearing a conversation between him and my dad years ago."

"Milton took a huge risk, but luckily your father never had a reason not to trust him."

"Why is Milton doing this? How did he even start working with you?"

"He actually came to us," Banks says sleepily from behind me.

"Sorry we woke you," I say, twisting my head around to meet his eyes.

"It's okay, I don't mind waking up as long as you are in my arms." Banks pulls me closer into him, and I can feel his hardened length pressing against my cheeks.

"So, Milton came to you?" I say a little flustered but trying to stay on subject.

"Yes, when you came back to Bayshore after your accident. He told us that he had been on your personal detail for a long time and that he couldn't stand how your parents treated you and lied to you."

"He disagreed even more with you marrying Matt," Oliver cuts in. "He didn't like how your family were pushing you into that marriage, and he knew Matt was an asshole with only his own gain in mind. So, he helped us keep you safe."

I suddenly feel horrible for not even calling him by his name for weeks. I was kind of a bitch to him when all he was trying to do was keep me safe, and not because my dad paid him to do so, but because he actually cared. I make a mental note to apologize for my behavior the next time I see him.

"So, what are we going to do now?" I ask curiously.

"It's up to you," Oliver says. "We have two choices. We can either go to the police with what we have, or we can use it as leverage to get your dad off your back."

I don't answer right away, I let both scenarios run through my head, both have huge risks, neither one is great. I'm not sure what's the right thing to do here, but I know one thing. Before I make a final decision, I need to talk to my father, I need to know about Phoebe and the connection between my father and George Bishop.

"Before I can even think about that, I need to tell you what I saw in my dad's office last night. I need to tell all three of you."

32

"Your dad and *Shelby*?" Sullivan asks, equal amounts of surprise and disgust lacing his voice.

"I don't know what I'm more shocked about. Shelby having an affair with your father or our dads being friends," Banks adds. "Even if it was a long time ago, I just can't wrap my head around it."

We are all sitting in the living room of the enormous hotel suite, and I just got done telling them about everything I saw last night. About my dad having an affair with my best friend, as well as the pictures and the love letter in the desk.

"Who do you think Phoebe is? You think she could really be your mother?" Oliver asks carefully.

"I don't know," I shrug. "I need to talk to my father."

"We got a burner phone, you can call him from it, but you can't tell him where you are or that we are with you. Not until we're sure that he is going to leave you alone," Banks warns as if I would do either thing.

"Got it." I reach out my hand, and Oliver places a phone in it. When I look at the screen, I realize it already has a number pulled up. "Is that my dad's?"

When Banks nods, I hit the dial button and put in on speaker, so the guys can hear too. He answers after only two rings.

"Hello," his voice comes through the phone, and I can already tell he is aggravated by the deepness of his tone.

"Dad, it's me."

"Harlow, where in the world, are you? We have been worried sick. Are you with those Bishops again?"

"I saw you and Shelby last night," I cut my father's rant off, rendering him speechless for a few seconds.

"It's not what you think." My father tries to talk himself out of it.

"Hearing you fuck my best friend on your desk is pretty much confirmation, don't you think?"

"Jesus, Harlow," he says, sighing into the phone. "Okay, it is what you think, but I swear we never meant to hurt you, it just happened."

It just happened? I don't understand how that can just happen, but I don't think long on the matter. I don't care who my father fucks.

"Who is Phoebe?" My question seems to render him speechless once more. Proving to me just how important this Phoebe person is.

"How do you know that name?" he asks after a moment, his voice changing into a weird tone, almost nostalgic.

"I found the pictures and the letter in your desk," I explain.

"I can't do this over the phone, Harlow. Come home, and we'll talk. I'll explain everything to you." At my father's words, all three guys shake their heads no.

"I'm not coming home. Not today and maybe not ever again. Not after you tried to force me to marry someone for your own gain."

"I want you to marry Matt for your own good, not my own gains. Everything I've ever done was for you. Why is that so hard for you to understand or see?"

I roll my eyes so hard, I swear, I see my brain.

"It's hard to believe you when I know you're working with the mob. You are a criminal, and even worse, you made me into one too, when you had me plant drugs on Sullivan. Was that for my own good as well? Was it just training for a future job? For college?"

"We can't talk about any of this on the phone, Harlow. You need to meet me so I can explain everything. You don't know the whole story, and I'm not going to let you believe some lies that those Bishops are telling you."

"I have proof, you know. Proof that you are working with Xander Rossi."

"Harlow, listen to me. Do not get involved in this. Xander is not someone you want to mess with. If you have any involvement with him, anything against him, you need to destroy that proof right now."

"I'm sure you would like that."

"Harlow, this is not about me," my father's voice grows more frustrated. "I'm serious, you don't want to mess with Xander."

"I'm not destroying the evidence against you. I'm keeping it so you can't blackmail the Bishops or me ever again. I want to know more about Phoebe, but I'm not meeting you."

"Then I guess you will never get any answers—" The line goes dead, and for a moment, I just look at the phone in shock.

Did he just hang up on me?

Dumbfounded, I look up at the guys. "I need to go talk to hi—"

"No way," Oliver says before I can finish my sentence, his face stern and his arms crossed over his chest.

"I agree," Banks cuts in his eyes narrowing. "It's not safe."

My gaze swings to Sullivan, and I already know his answer is going to be no, as well. It's three against one here, but that doesn't mean I'm giving up. I need answers, all of them.

"What if you all come with me? Or Milton? Or everybody?"

"Your dad has a whole army of security, plus the mob behind him. The safest place for you is to be with us. We are not budging on this," Sullivan announces, and I can hear the promise in his statement. He's not going to change his mind.

"Fine..." I huff in defeat. "What about Shelby? Maybe I could talk to her and get some answers that way?"

"I guess we could see if she went back to Bayshore. As far as I know, she still has that job at the gallery. Maybe we can find her there or at class," Oliver suggests. "But if she isn't there, we are not going back to North Woods."

"Deal... let's go back to Bayshore." I stand up, ready to get moving when I realize all I have on is my pajamas.

"I don't have anything to wear."

"We'll get you some new clothes, but first..." Banks gets up, taking my hand, and with a mischievous smirk, he says, "We need to make up for lost time."

Sullivan and Oliver follow suit and stand.

"We need to show you just how much we missed you," Sullivan smiles, his voice deeper than normal, and the sound vibrates through me, awakening something deep inside me.

"And we did miss you a lot," Oliver says, and I suddenly feel like I'm burning up. The air around us changes like it's suddenly thicker. He extends his hand out to me, and I take it without hesitation.

"We don't have to do this. All three of us, I mean... If it's too much, you just have to tell us. We'll understand." I appreciate Banks trying to give me a way out, but he doesn't have to. I want all three of them, and I know they won't hurt me or test my limits. This isn't about just sex. It's deeper than that. This is about forging a connection that cannot be broken.

"Don't. This is what I want. To be with all three of you, together." I admit wholeheartedly.

"We want that too, but if you change your mind, you can tell us," Sullivan reminds me.

"I'll tell you if I do," I promise, and we all make our way to the bedroom. Once we reach the bed, Oliver and Banks start to strip me of my clothing. Their hands moving at breakneck speed. Once naked and bare to them, I watch each of them quickly strip out of their own clothing, my mouth watering in anticipation.

I've been with each of them, and with two of them at once but never all three, and while I'm only a little nervous about what's to come, there is an entire kaleidoscope of butterflies taking flight in my stomach. Warmth tingles low in my belly at the sight of the three of them shirtless—chiseled muscles that look like they could be carved from stone. As they climb up on the bed, no one says a word. Mainly because there are no words to be said.

Sullivan is the first to make a move, his hands gently cradle my cheeks as he comes in for a kiss. As soon as his lips meet mine, a fire sparks in my belly. I need him. I need all three of them. Out of the corner of my eye, I watch as Banks moves behind me, pressing hot mouthed kisses against my flesh.

I'm practically melting, and they haven't even reached the most important spots yet.

"I need to taste you..." Oliver all but growls, moving to his knees.

Breaking the kiss with Sullivan for half a second, I release a gasped, "Yes."

In a second, I'm moved to my back, all three of them hover over me with their eyes overlooking my body like I'm some kind of sacrificial lamb. Sullivan trails his hands down my body, while Oliver spreads my thighs. An electrical current ripples through me. It feels like I've been struck by lightning.

Banks leans forward his hot breath fanning against my hardened nipple. The look in his eyes screams hunger. He wants to devour me from the inside out. And I'll let him. I'll let him and his brothers do whatever they want to me.

"Oh, god..." The words just fall from my mouth when Banks' lips circle my nipple, and Oliver licks me from ass to slit.

"Fuck," Sullivan exhales, licking his lips one last time before they crash against my own. Oliver worships me with his tongue, feasting on me like I'm his last supper. Banks alternates between each breast flicking furiously against the tight nub before slowing down, teasing me at a treacherous pace.

While Sullivan may seem as if he's doing nothing, he is kissing me like a woman should be kissed, with love and adoration. I moan between our kisses, feeling my pulse pound in my ears, and my body shudders as red hot heat spreads through my limbs.

"Do you have any idea how pretty you are when you're coming?"

Sullivan whispers into the shell of my ear as he peppers kisses along my throat. "Your pale cheeks are tinted the color of roses, and your chest rises and falls so rapidly. I've never seen your eyes so big and bright. Fall apart, sweetheart, and I promise, we'll catch you."

I'd never before thought that the cliché come on command thing worked, but it's like my body is tethered to his words, waiting with bated breath for his next command. Colorful spots of light appear before my eyes as they drift closed, my entire body shaking, a whole array of fireworks going off inside my belly.

"Fuck," Banks exhales, "holy shit..."

Oliver continues to feast on me, even as I drift down from my orgasm like a feather floating in the wind. From that moment on, I'm melting, becoming a goopy mess of soul-searing post-orgasmic bliss.

I can feel the sheets growing wet beneath my ass. I'm soaked, lying in a puddle of my own arousal. I should be embarrassed by how wet I am, but that's the last thing on my mind. My hands move to his hair, and I hold him in place between my thighs, needing him and the pleasure he gives me like it's my next breath.

Oliver spreads me with his fingers and licks my clit with an unbridled hunger. I feel the tingling build deep inside my core again, my back slightly arching off the bed, when Oliver's fingers move down to my other opening. Before I can think about how wrong this is, his finger is massaging me there, and all that's left in my mind is how good it feels.

"You like that?" Banks asks, his voice low and husky.

"Yes," I admit in between heavy panting. My moans become even louder when Oliver pushes the tip of his finger inside, probing the tight ring of muscle while simultaneously working my clit with his tongue. Banks and Sullivan have their hands on me too, I have lost track of who is touching me where. All I know is that I feel like I'm being worshiped by these men.

When Oliver dips his finger into my ass even further, while sucking on my clit for all he's worth, I'm tipped over the edge once more. I go off like a rocket, soaring through the air, shattering into a million little pieces in the night sky. Tremors wrack my body post-orgasm, and I whimper like a wounded animal as Oliver releases his hold on my thighs.

He climbs up the king-size bed and lies down next to me, he turns my head so I can see him. I'm still coming down from the second orgasm, my limbs feel heavy and feather-light all at once.

"I want you to ride me, baby, and while you do that, Banks is going to claim your ass," Oliver orders, beckoning me with his finger to come to him.

None of the brothers speak as I crawl on top of Oliver, who is obviously leading the show tonight.

"What about Sullivan?" I groan as he fills me up with his thickness. It's so hard to think about anything but the burning fire that snakes up my spine as he bottoms out inside of me.

A mischievous grin appears on Oliver's full lips. "Don't worry about him, sweetheart. He'll be coming down your pretty throat while you fall apart over and over again."

My chest expands and fills with oxygen, but it doesn't feel like I'm actually breathing. In fact, none of this feels real at all. Them, me, us being together like this.

Oliver reaches up and cradles my cheek gently, his touch drawing me from my rampant thoughts. "Is that okay? Is this what you want?"

Nodding my head, I watch as the brothers arrange themselves on the bed. Banks coming up behind me, his cock pressing against my ass, and Sullivan moving to just above Oliver's head. Saliva pools in my mouth as my eyes catch sight of Sullivan's thick cock bobbing in the air. I want it. I need it.

Air swooshes from my lungs as Oliver enters me deeply, at a new angle, the head of his cock brushing against the back of my channel. I lean forward and wrap my hand around Sullivan's cock, my insides tingling with pleasure as he releases a hiss through his teeth.

"Fuck, if your mouth feels anything like your hand, I'm done for."

Smiling, I stroke his dick up and down while the pleasure in my own core burns hotter and hotter.

Oliver lifts one of his hands, keeping the other firmly in place on my hip, and plucks at my overly stimulated nipples, and then I feel it... something warm and sticky sliding down my ass crack. Banks' fingers move through the unknown liquid, and I shudder as he reaches my puckered asshole, his thumb pressing against the tight muscles of my hole.

"Relax, baby, I won't take this virgin hole until you're ready. Till you're spent, nothing but a withering mess." His thumb presses against the tightness, and without thinking, I push back against him, wanting him there.

My ass pulses and, even though, there is pressure, and a tinge of pain, it lessens as Oliver strokes me deeply with his cock. Banks moves his finger in and out gradually, so slowly that I almost forget that he's there.

The grip I have on Sullivan's cock tightens, and I lean forward, bringing my lips to the smooth head. He groans as I wrap my lips around him and drag my tongue on the underside. A drop of salty warm liquid hits my tongue, and there is something so erotic about that, I can't help but moan around his length.

With Sullivan in my mouth, Oliver in my pussy, and Banks playing with my ass, my whole body is on fire. My senses are overwhelmed, and my brain is flooded with endorphins, making it impossible to think about anything besides what I am feeling right this moment. And what I'm feeling is every nerve ending in me being charged and ready to burst, sending me into oblivion.

Banks adds a second finger, stretching my tight hole just as Oliver picks up speed. Sullivan is also growing more eager. His large hands cupping my head, holding me in place as he thrusts into my mouth, his hard length sliding in and out over my tongue until he hits the back of my throat and I gag a little.

I didn't think I could possibly come again since I'd already come twice, but somehow, I am already teetering on the edge again. I'm consumed with need for them. My body screaming for their touch. My mind is on the verge of insanity. I feel like I imagine a drug addict must when they're trying to get their next fix. Oliver, Banks, and Sullivan are my drug, a fix I crave more than anything else.

Overwhelmed with need, I suck Sullivan as hard as I can, wanting him to come, wanting to give him pleasure like he gives me. He growls like some kind of animal while his cock swells in my mouth, his fingers twist in my hair, pulling on some strands. I don't know what it is about that small pain on my scalp, but it sends me over the edge. Pain and pleasure mixing together, creating a beautiful symphony of pleasure. I come hard, moaning around Sullivan, and like a chain reaction, he comes apart as well. Salty warm seed fills my throat as ecstasy ripples through me.

Oliver's fingers are digging into my hips as he buries himself so deeply inside of me, I can feel him in my belly. Banks pushes two of his fingers inside my ass deeper than before, the foreign feeling only prolonging my orgasm.

My vision goes blank, and my body goes limp as I come down from my third climax. Sullivan slips out of my mouth slowly, leaving a salty train of cum behind on my tongue. He still cradles my head when he kisses me softly before climbing off the bed. As soon as he disappears, I collapse on top of Oliver.

"I think you are relaxed enough now," Banks announces, chuckling behind me. "Are you ready for me, baby?" He runs his hand over my ass, and up my lower back, his simple touch feels so intense.

"Yes..." I half moan.

Banks removes his fingers and replaces it with the smooth head of his cock. He pushes against the tight ring, and all I can feel is pressure. His cock is much bigger than his fingers, and for a moment, I don't think it's going to fit.

"Relax," Oliver whispers in my hair and thrusts inside me, rubbing against my clit as he does. The sensation relaxes me more than his words, and I loosen up enough for Banks to slip inside of my ass.

"There you go," Banks growls, his voice strained like he is trying to hold back. Slowly, he inches his way inside of me while Oliver momentarily stills. "How does that feel?"

"I feel... full, so full..." My voice comes out breathy, just like my whole body feels right now. "But it feels good... so good."

At my words, Banks starts moving a little more, and a small whimper escapes my lips.

"Are you sure?" Oliver asks, running his hands over my arms and shoulders.

"Yes, I want you to move. Both of you," I urge, and they don't need another invitation. Oliver starts moving, thrusting again, and Banks starts to match Oliver's pace. The feeling is new and almost too much, but I don't want it to stop.

"Fuck, Harlow," Banks groans behind me as they fall into a rhythm. "You don't know how good this feels..."

"I'm not going to last long like this," Oliver says, his voice strained like he is barely holding on.

"Me neither, I'm about to come," Banks growls, and shortly after, I can feel him growing even bigger inside of me, his movements growing frantic, and his hand landing flat between my shoulder blades, pushing me down on to Oliver's chest. I bury my face into the crook of his neck. Oliver tries to match his brother's strokes. Both of them thrusting inside of me furiously now, and all I can do is lie there and take the enormous amount of pleasure they're giving me.

They come almost simultaneously. Oliver holding me close to him, and Banks leaning over my back, kissing my shoulders until he stills inside of me.

I've never felt so spent in my life. I'm physically drained but emotionally full. This was so much more than sex; it was us becoming one. Four people coming together and proving how much they belong as one.

"I love you," I murmur into Oliver's skin.

"I love you too," Oliver replies.

"You have no idea how much I love you," Banks says in between kisses to my heated skin.

"I love you too, Harlow, we all do." Sullivan appears next to the bed. I turn my head to look at him. "I ran a bath for you. It's ready when you are," he smiles, and all I can think of is how I got so lucky?

33

It's weird to be back in Bayshore, maybe because I didn't think I would ever return here. It all looks the same, like the college town I remembered it to be. With bars, coffee shops, bookstores, and small 24-hour convenient stores on every corner; to fill every student's needs.

"We're going to drop you off at the gallery, but we won't leave you there alone. We'll be right outside in the car," Oliver explains as if we are planning some kind of super-secret mission.

"I'll be fine. It's an art gallery, and it's not like anybody would expect me to be here. I'm just going to walk in and see if Shelby is here so I can talk to her. If she isn't, I'll walk right back out, and we'll think of another plan, okay?" I look between the guys and wait for all three to give me a small nod before I open the door and get out of the car.

I can feel their eyes on me as I walk down the sidewalk toward the storefront of the gallery. A pounding forms behind my eyes and the sense of deja vu overcomes me. I continue walking until I'm in front of the glass door, my hand on the handle ready to pull the door open when the memory rushes in like water flooding a basement, seeping in through all the open cracks.

"I'm looking for Shelby. I'm sorry to show up here, I know she is working but this is kind of an emergency."

"Who?" The woman looks genuinely confused, her eyebrows drawing together.

"Shelby," I say louder, she must have not heard me clearly.

"Doesn't ring a bell. Is she one of our artists?"

"Oh...ah, maybe... maybe I'm at the wrong gallery, I'm sorry," I say embarrassed, before turning on my heels.

"This is the only gallery in town, miss."

I freeze with my hand hovering inches away from the doorknob. My mind goes blank and then this feeling of utter dread creeps its way up my spine and settles into the base of my skull.

Nothing makes sense, everything I thought I knew is wrong. My life built with building blocks of lies and deceit and like a Jenga tower someone pulled the one piece that has it all crashing down.

I feel like I'm trapped in this moment, my mind frozen in time. My thoughts hovering somewhere in between disbelief and unbelievable despair.

"Are you okay, miss?"

When I shake out of the memory, I'm not sure how long I've been standing there, but it feels like an eternity. I don't know why I'm so surprised by this lie. I already knew she was lying to me about numerous things, so why does this feel even worse?

"Harlow? What's wrong?" Banks comes out of nowhere, his hand coming to rest on my lower back.

"She never worked here," I answer. "I just remembered it. She lied to me about this too."

"I'm sorry... come on, let's get you home," Banks coaxes, his voice laced with concern. I let him lead me down the sidewalk, my mind still reeling from the recovered memory.

For some reason, I can't shake the feeling that there is more... more to this story... more I need to remember. It isn't until we are about to cross the road that it hits me. The most important memory of all. The final piece to the puzzle...

I look up, the scenery changing around me, the ground beneath me suddenly seems different. Sounds piercing through the fog surrounding my brain. Someone is screaming, but I can't make out what is being said. Then something catches my eye. I look up to see two bright lights heading straight for me. But I'm not fast enough, there is no time.

I watch in shock as the engine revs up, the car coming at me, and all I can do is stand there like a deer caught in the headlights... literally.

There is a moment, just before the impact, where the headlights are so close that they don't blind me, I can look above them, see through the windshield and get a look at the person who is trying to kill me.

It's only for a split second that I see her eyes; cold and detached, full of hate, and I don't understand why? Why does she hate me that much? Why would Shelby try to kill me?

"Harlow?" Banks is suddenly right in front of me, his hands on my shoulders, shaking me gently as if he is trying to wake me up from some nightmare. But I'm not asleep, this is not a dream, this is reality. Shelby, the person I thought of as my best friend my entire life, hates me, hates me so much that she wants me dead. My chest heaves, and it feels like a piece of my heart is breaking off.

Why? Why would she want me dead? Did I do something that I don't remember?

"Harlow? Harlow! You're freaking me out. Please tell me what's wrong," Banks questions frantically. I can see him, but not really. It's like I'm lost in my thoughts, trying to thread them back together.

"It was Shelby... I... I remember. Shelby was the one that tried to kill me. She hit me with the car on purpose. I saw her, it was her," I continue rambling on more to myself as Banks leads me to the car, halfway carrying me at one point.

He helps me into the back seat and buckles me up. Oliver and Sullivan twist around in the front seat their faces conveying a similar concern to Banks.

"What happened?" Oliver asks, but I can't say the words out loud again, they hurt too much.

"Just find a hotel. I'll explain everything there. We need to take care of Harlow first. She's remembering things," Banks explains, and Oliver takes that as his cue to drive off, pulling into city traffic with ease, leaving the gallery and the memories behind us, but not forgotten. *Why? Why would she do that?*

Banks slides across the bench seat and closer to me until his body is practically against mine, his body heat seeps into every pore of my body, soothing me in an instant like a blanket wrapping around me on a cold winter night.

Unable to resist, I turn to him, seeking the comfort he gives, burying my face into his chest. Without realizing it, I start to sob, letting all the anger, frustration, confusion, and hurt out. The tears fall from my eyes rapidly, and I don't even attempt to wipe them away.

By the time we get to the hotel, my vision is blurry, and there is a throbbing pressure inside my skull that seems to expand with each second. Oliver goes inside to check us in so that when we get out of the car, we can go straight to the room.

When we make it up to the room, Banks leads me over to the sectional, and the guys circle around me. All I can do is stare down at my hands, the same thoughts circulating in my mind.

"Why? Why would she want me dead? Why would she do something like that? We were supposed to be friends. She was my best friend, and..." I continue to mumble beneath my breath like a crazed person.

I can feel the brothers' eyes on me, and when I look up, I see nothing but anguish and worry flickering in their gazes.

"Shhh, baby, it's okay." Oliver soothes this time. What would I do if I didn't have them right now? If I was stuck back in my father's mansion? Shelby could easily get to me there. Then it hits me.

"I could've died. She could've killed me and gotten away with it, and no one would have known." The weight of that knowledge feels like an elephant sitting on my chest.

"If it was Shelby who hit you with the car at the art gallery, then I'll bet anything that she was the one to push you off the boat the night you almost drowned." Banks says.

"I can't believe this. I didn't particularly like Shelby, but I honestly didn't think she would be capable of something like this. I don't hit women, but I really want to hurt her for doing what she did to you," Sullivan hisses as if he's in pain.

"I just want to know why? What did she have to gain from killing me?" The tears start to fall again, and I don't understand why I'm crying over her. She doesn't deserve my tears.

"No one knows, but you can bet we'll figure it out. From here on out, it's us versus everyone else. We're not trusting anyone outside this room. No one is going to take you away from us or hurt you again."

Opening my mouth to say something, the words disappear, sticking to the roof of my mouth like peanut butter, and then I realize it wasn't words I needed to expel. I feel my stomach churning like I've just been on the longest roller coaster of all time. In a second, I'm flying from the sectional and heading for the nearest door.

Oh, god. I'm not going to make it.

I don't even get halfway to the bathroom before vomit erupts from my throat, splattering across the pristine floor. I empty the entire contents of my stomach while someone holds back my hair and someone else rubs soothing circles over my lower back. I don't look back to see who it is, mostly because I'm too embarrassed to look at anyone right now.

When my body is done convulsing, my throat burns, my eyes tear up, and my head throbs in pain. I feel disgusted and ashamed when I straighten back up to see all the guys standing around me while there is a puddle of vomit in front of me.

"I'm sorry..."

"Don't be ridiculous and apologize for being sick," Sullivan tells me. "Come on, we'll get you cleaned up." He gently takes my arm and pulls me toward the bathroom.

"I should clean this up," I complain, trying to pull my arm away.

"I'll call room service. Don't worry about anything, just go take a bath," Oliver waves me off, and Banks falls in step with Sullivan and I. Flanking me on both sides, they take me to the large master bathroom.

Banks turns on the water, filling up the large garden tub while Sullivan starts to take off my clothes he just bought me this morning.

"I don't know what happened. I was fine one minute, and then I wasn't."

"It's okay, that was a lot to take in. I don't know if I could have stomached all of this either. Seriously, don't feel bad because there is nothing to feel bad about," Sullivan soothes, trying to calm me down.

When I'm completely naked, Sullivan takes my hand and helps me to get into the now half-filled tub. The water is the perfect temperature, and I sink into the bubbly goodness with a sigh. It feels like I'm sinking into a bath of heaven. Banks gets two washcloths, handing Sullivan one. They each squirt some soap on to their cloth and start washing me with it. Sullivan starts at my feet while Banks starts at my shoulders.

Closing my eyes, I let them massage and clean every inch of my flesh. Their hands move over my skin, and as if there is some kind of magic involved, all the tension and worry evaporates into thin air.

In this space, no bad feelings or worry can get to me. Nothing can touch me right now. By the end of my bath, my body is so relaxed, I feel boneless, my muscles have turned to jelly sometime in the last thirty minutes, and now I can barely keep my eyes open.

"You ready to come out?"

"Yeah," I barely nod.

Banks offers me his hand and helps me out of the bath while Sullivan grabs a bathrobe, holding it open for me. My arms slide into the fluffy fabric one at a time, and Sullivan closes the belt around my waist, tying me up like a perfectly wrapped gift.

"I like this," I giggle. "You guys taking care of me. It makes me feel like a princess. Like I'm important."

"You better get used to it," Banks tells me, right before he surprises me by picking me up bridal style. Letting out a startled squeal, I throw my arms around his neck. "'Cause we're not planning on stopping any time soon."

He carries me out of the bathroom, and the strong citrus odor of cleaning solution tickles my nostrils. Room service must have already come and cleaned up the mess I made earlier.

Banks places me on the bed, and as if on cue, Oliver walks in, holding a tray of food and puts it on the bedside table, I look at it wearily. Crackers, an assortment of prepared fruit, hot tea, and ice water sit before me. None of it looks all that appetizing, but then again, I did just barf all over the floor.

"I had them bring up stuff that I know will ease an upset stomach," Oliver explains as if he can read my mind. I don't know what to say, so I just push from the bed a little and wrap my arms around his middle. Oliver bends down and returns the hug.

"Thank you, no one has ever taken care of me the way that you all do."

"Stop saying thank you. We do it because we want to, not because we're obligated to."

"We love you, Harlow, and nothing has, or ever will change that. Not our parents. Not yours. Nothing. The circumstances of our relationship might not be perfect, or even common, but that doesn't make what we all have any less special." Banks intercepts, and my heart swells, growing bigger with each beat.

Tears well in my eyes. I'm consumed by them. My heart beats for them each in its own way. There is no me without them.

"We're supposed to hate each other, but it seems all we've ever done is love each other."

"Because we weren't meant to. Before, we just let our parents dictate our lives, but that won't happen again."

"Good, because I don't know what's going to happen next," I admit while nibbling on one of the crackers. Not only do I feel like crap, but I truly have no idea where to go from here. Do I stay hiding out with the Bishops for eternity? Not that I wouldn't like that, but it's not really all that feasible of an option.

Out of the corner of my eye, I see Banks rubbing at his chin. He looks to be lost in thought, and I wonder what he's thinking about.

Each brother is handsome beyond measure, how the hell did I end up with all three of them?

Sullivan clears his throat, drawing all the attention in the room to him.

"You said our father was in the photos you found in your father's desk. The one with the mystery woman... Phoebe?"

Swinging my gaze to him, I stare in confusion. "Yes. Your father was in some of the photos. I had planned to ask my dad more about it, but as you know, he hung up on me before I had the chance. He won't talk to me again until I go back to North Woods, and none of you will allow that."

"Because your father is crazy," Banks chimes in.

"Because Shelby is still out there walking free," Oliver adds another brick of worry on their ever-growing pile. "We need to tell the police, Harlow. Are you up for that?"

All of their concerns weigh heavily on me, weighing down my heart. I don't take them lightly because I see how much I mean to them now and how dangerous things really are, but I didn't escape one ivory tower just to be trapped in another.

"Yes," I sigh. "I'll call them, but I still want to talk to my father. Staring down at the comforter, I say, "I understand why you don't want me to see him right now, and I'm okay with that, but I'm not some fragile piece of glass. I don't just want answers... I need them, which means eventually I won't have an option but to see my father again." Silence blankets the room, and I peek up through my lashes to see if they've disappeared into thin air.

Nope, they're still inside the room, and currently staring holes through my flesh.

"I have an idea." Oliver is the first to break the silence.

"Well, what is it?" Banks asks impatiently.

"We could bring you to our father..." His voice trails off, and I wonder if he's being serious or not.

"Your father would let you bring me to your house?" I ask, trying to hide the surprise from my voice.

Sullivan shrugs, "What's the worst he could do? Tell us to leave? We can't let you near your father right now, so the next best thing would be our father."

"Maybe he can piece the missing pieces of your puzzle together?" Oliver adds.

"Or he could be a huge prick and make things ten times worse," Banks mutters under his breath. Oliver and Sullivan look at him, their features hardening.

"You aren't helping."

Banks lifts his hands as if to say he's innocent. "Look, I'm not trying to be a negative nelly here. I want Harlow to get all the answers she needs just as much as you both do, but Dad isn't going to take well to us bringing a Lockwood home." Our gazes meet as he says the next words, "Last names don't mean shit to us, but Dad still sees her as the enemy, and I don't want her caught in his crosshairs."

To many, I might be weak, but I am mighty, and if I want answers, I may have to cross bridges that shouldn't be crossed. I may have to do things that I shouldn't do, but I'll do what I need to do. No one is going to dictate what happens in my life anymore.

"Let's do it."

"Seriously?" Banks runs a hand through his hair as if he's agitated. Was he not expecting me to go along with this?

"Yes, I want answers. Your dad has some. Let's do it. What's the worst that could happen?"

"'Kay, I'll make the arrangements, and tomorrow we'll visit our parents," Oliver announces as if it's final to his brothers.

Banks leaves the room a moment later, and Sullivan walks over to the bed and crawls into the vacant spot left beside me.

"Is he going to be okay? I ask. I kind of want to chase after him but know he needs the space.

"He'll be fine. He's just worried about what our dad will say or try to do to you."

I nod, understanding completely.

"Our father won't touch you. Not if he wants to live." Oliver's words have a sharp edge to them, and I shiver wondering if he really means that. Would he, and his brothers go against their parents for me? Would they risk it all for me?

I guess we'll find out.

Oliver gets out his phone and hands it to me. "Now to the hard part. You need to call the detective investigating your hit and run case and tell him what you know."

Looking down at his phone, I realize the detective's number is already pulled up. "How do you have his number?"

"We had to make sure they knew the whole story and were doing their jobs. We regularly talked to the detective and checked in to see if there were any updates."

"Oh." I probably shouldn't be surprised by that, but somehow, I still am. I just can't get over how committed they are to me. Even when I didn't even know who they were, they took care of me, watched out for me.

Hitting the green call button, I hold the phone to my ear and wait for someone to answer while trying not to think about what I'm about to do. The person I thought was my best friend really isn't, and I'm about to send her to jail... maybe for a very long time.

34

The drive to the Bishop estate isn't that long, but it seems like an eternity when you're as nauseated as I am.

"Are you sure you're okay?" Sullivan asks, his forehead scrunched up in concern.

"Yeah, I'm good. Like you said, it's just a little hard to stomach all of this. All these emotions, all these questions surrounding my life, it's really weighing on me. Hopefully, your dad can clear up at least some of the confusion."

Banks grunts next to me, his gaze fixed on something outside the window. He's barely spoken since we decided to come here. I know he is unhappy with it, but I can't think of another way to actually figure out what's going on, at least not one that doesn't involve going back to my father. I need some answers, and right now, George Bishop is my best bet.

Reaching across the back seat for Banks, I latch on to one of his wrists and pull him closer. I half expect him to pull away and tell me, no, but he lets me interlace my fingers with his without complaint. When he finally turns his head, his sea-blue eyes find mine, and the worry swimming in their depths crashes into me like a tidal wave.

"We're going to be okay," I assure him. It sounds like a promise, and even though I have no way of actually keeping the promise, I don't mind saying it this way. Maybe because I will do whatever I can, whatever it takes, to make it happen. We have endured too much heartache to not get our happily ever after.

He gives me a halfhearted smile and a slight nod. I wish I could do more, take his worry away. Take all of our worries away, but I can't.

"We're almost there," Oliver says from the driver's seat, and Banks stiffens next to me. I squeeze his hand, hoping to calm him down, but the closer we get to the house, the more on edge he seems. His body goes rigid, tightening like a rubber band that's being pulled tighter and tighter.

"You sure it's a good idea to just show up without calling first?"

"We're their kids, we don't have to announce our visit," Sullivan tells me.

"Yeah, but you usually don't bring me along."

A few minutes later, we pull up to a large brick suburban home that looks a little bit like a small castle. It's beautiful, and I can't help but stare at it. It's gorgeous with high walls, and perfectly sculpted hedges. If it looks like this on the outside, I can't imagine what it looks like on the inside.

"Wow, that's your house?" I ask while continuing to gawk at the building.

"My mom likes to pretend she's a queen," Sullivan says, throwing me a wink.

We get out of the car and start walking toward the front door. Suddenly the reality of being here hits me, and I start to get really nervous. Looking over my shoulder, I catch Banks watching me. His gaze softens, and he extends a hand out to me. I gladly take it, letting his touch calm the storm inside of me.

"Don't worry, we won't let anything happen to you, and if my dad dares to talk down to you, we'll be out the door," Banks soothes me. Our roles reversed now.

Oliver and Sullivan walk ahead of us. Opening the front door with a key, we all walk into the house, which opens to a large grand foyer that matches the outside of the house. A gigantic, fancy chandelier hangs in the center of the entrance, a rounded staircase leading to the upper level, worthy of a queen to walk down.

"Mom... Dad..." Oliver calls loud enough that everybody in the house should here, even considering the size of it. A moment later, the sound of high-heeled shoes against the tile floor echoes through the foyer.

"Oliver?" A shrill voice fills the space a moment before a petite blonde woman appears in the doorway. "Boys..." Her tone is upbeat, excited to see her sons, she smiles widely. That is until she sees me standing behind Oliver and Sullivan.

Her smile falls and is quickly replaced with a frown. That frown deepening further when she looks between Banks and me and sees that we are holding hands.

"Hey, Mom," Sullivan greets, walking toward her and giving her a kiss on the cheek. She grabs on to his arms, holding him to her and whispers something in his ear. I can't hear from where I stand, but I can imagine she is asking him what the hell I'm doing here.

Sullivan straightens up, refusing to whisper, he says out loud. "We were hoping to talk to Dad and ask him some questions about the time when he and Harlow's dad used to be friends with Phoebe."

I can practically see the blood drain from Chloe Bishop's face, her eyes go wide, and she takes a step back as if she is trying to get away from the situation.

"How... how do you know... about that?" She stumbles over her words, looking uncomfortable and wary.

"From Harlow's dad. Well, he didn't tell us, but Harlow found some pictures and some letters in his desk," Oliver explains.

"I see," she says, and as if she remembers to compose herself, she perks up. A fake smile spreads across her face. "Well, come on in boys... and *Harlow*." Banks' grip around my hand tightens at the way she says my name, but I give him a look that silently tells him it's okay. I can hold my own. I won't let anyone hurt the men I love or me, for that matter.

She waves us inside, and we follow her through the house like little sheep.

"Your father is in his office working, but I'm sure he can make time for you," she chimes, her voice high-pitched and strained somehow. She is obviously nervous about taking us to her husband. The tension between all of us grows thicker. I have to force air into my lungs now. It's getting harder to breathe.

When we get to a large set of double doors, she stops and looks back at us one more time, as if she's waiting for somebody to say something. Maybe she's hoping we'll tell her *just kidding* or something like that. When no one says anything, she lifts her hand and knocks on the door lightly.

"Yes, come in," A muffled male voice carries through the closed door.

Mrs. Bishop opens the door and walks in hesitantly, all of us following closely behind her. George Bishop sits behind his desk, holding a phone to his ear, scribbling something down on a piece of paper. His eyes are trained on whatever is in front of him. I now see where his sons get their looks from. Even though he is as old as my father, he still manages to look young and fit.

"Okay, and what's their counteroffer?" he says to the other person on the phone. He looks up, his face an unreadable mask. The pen which was dancing over the paper a minute ago stills in his hand as he takes us in. "I'm gonna call you back."

Mr. Bishop hangs up the phone and sits the device on the table next to him.

"Chloe... Kids... what's this all about? he asks carefully.

"Who is Phoebe?" I blurt out my most pressing question.

George's eyes find mine, and I'm surprised by the way he looks at me. I was expecting animosity, resentment, maybe even hate. Instead, all I find is sadness and reminiscence. Almost like I'm an old friend he hasn't seen in years, and he is sad about the fact that it's been so long.

"Chloe, dear, do you mind leaving us to talk for a while," he asks his wife, who seemingly is more than happy to have the opportunity to get out of here.

"Of course, I'll be in the kitchen preparing dinner if you need me. Will you be staying for dinner?" she asks, looking at her sons, but avoiding my gaze.

"That depends on the outcome of this conversation," Banks mutters.

"Very well," his mother sighs before leaving the room, closing the door firmly behind her.

"Why don't you all take a seat," George offers, waving his hand to the seating area in the corner of the oversized office. "This is kind of a long story."

Never letting go of my hand, Banks tugs me to one of the chairs. Sullivan and Oliver are right beside us. We all take seats in the leather chairs. George joins us, sitting down right across from me.

"First, I have to ask, not that it matters because you know now, but how did you find out about Phoebe?" George starts the conversation.

"I found letters and some pictures in my dad's desk. Pictures with you, my dad, and Phoebe in them."

"Yes, we used to be friends growing up… all three of us. Best friends, actually."

"How is that even possible?" Sullivan asks. "How were you friends, and why is this the first time we've ever heard of it?"

"Some things are just better left in the past, son. We were just kids when we were friends. That all changed when we grew up, and friendship turned into more between Phoebe and me."

"So, you and Phoebe were together?"

He smiles, his eyes twinkling, "Yes, I was in love with her. I was her first boyfriend… or so I thought. See, your father was in love with her as well and Phoebe… well, she was in love with both of us, and that led us to the biggest mistake of our lives…" George trails off, looking out the window, his eyes turn glassy and unfocused as he speaks.

"What happened?" I ask when I can't take the silence anymore.

"We told her she had to choose one of us. We fought over her, both of us terribly jealous of the other one. We were so selfish in our fight for her that neither one of us realized how unhappy she was and how much us fighting hurt her."

"One of the letters I found said that she was pregnant..." I hold my breath, waiting for the truth to come pouring out.

"Yes, Phoebe got pregnant. She was with both of us at the time, so there was a question of who the father was for a while, but it turned out it was Lionel."

"Am I..." My voice cracks at the end. I don't know if I can ask the question out loud. It's still too surreal.

"Yes, Harlow. You are Phoebe's daughter. Your dad met his new wife when you were just a baby. I always wondered if he told you about your mother. I guess he didn't."

To my surprise, I am not as shocked as I thought I would be. I guess part of me was expecting it already. Or maybe the revelation that my life had been a lie doesn't bother me as much because in some ways my life was already a lie, it was messed up long before I lost my memory.

"You okay," Banks asks, his voice concerned and gentle as if he has this need to soothe me.

"I am, surprisingly... I'm not that shocked. I don't know, I can't explain it. I guess deep down, I already knew."

"Your father and I have had a lot of differences over the years, as you are well aware, but I can tell you that he did love your mother, your real mother... and so did I. I was devastated when she died."

"How did she die?"

George sighs deeply and leans forward. With his elbows on his knees, he lets his face fall into his hands. Clearly, he's still torn up over it. Even after all this time, he looks like reliving the memories is extraordinary hard on him.

"At the end, it was our rivalry that killed her," he admits, and the pain in his voice is almost too much for me. "She loved us both, and even though she had a child with Lionel, she would come to see me. He tried to forbid it, of course, but she was a bit untamable. That was one of the things I loved about her...like a wild horse, she would gallop wherever she pleased..." he trails off seemingly lost in his memory.

"She would frequently sneak out in the middle of the night to meet me somewhere," George continues after a while. "One of those nights she had a car accident on her way home, a drunk driver swerved into her lane, hit her straight on... she died instantly."

A tear trails down my cheek as I mourn the death of a woman I didn't know and never will. The woman who gave me life. The mother I didn't even know existed. The mother I would only ever know from stories and pictures.

"Your father blamed me, of course. If I had stayed away from her, she wouldn't have been on that road. What he didn't understand is that I tried, but she wouldn't let me go. She loved me, and she wasn't going to give me up. If your father would have accepted that fact, then she wouldn't have snuck around in the middle of the night. He tried to control her, and he drove her away with that. She would have eventually come to me anyway."

"So, you blamed each other for her death," Sullivan points out.

"Yes... it was the seed that started it all, the seed that sprouted into hate and resentment over the years and led to a rivalry that has now touched the next generation, or so I thought. Obviously, you have somehow overwritten the hatred between our families." George looks at Banks and at our intertwined fingers.

"But at what cost?" Oliver blurts out. "We were fighting for years, Sullivan almost lost everything, Harlow has been through hell and back... Christ, she almost died, and for what? Because you two couldn't share the blame? Because from where I'm standing, it was everybody's fault."

"Maybe you're right, but you can't change the past, and I accepted that a long time ago. We can only control our own paths now and steer into the future we want. Now the question is, what kind of future do you want?"

"I want a future where I remember my past. I want to know where I came from, and I want to know where I belong," I admit.

"You belong with us," Oliver says, making his dad shift in his chair uncomfortably. I wonder if he knows what kind of relationship I have with his sons? Maybe he is trying to figure it out, or maybe he already suspected it. Either way, he is not saying a word about it.

"You know what I want for the future? I want Harlow to be safe," Banks barks. "I want Shelby and whoever has been trying to hurt Harlow behind bars for good. And then I want everybody to leave us the hell alone and let us live our lives as we please."

"Wait, why do you want Shelby behind bars? Isn't she your friend?" George asks, looking between all of us with confusion.

"I remembered something... about Shelby. She was the one that hit me with the car."

George looks genuinely shocked. "Did you go to the police?"

"Yes, we called the detective on my case. They are looking for her right now. But last we checked, they hadn't found her yet." I contemplate telling him about seeing Shelby and Dad together but decide against it. There is no real reason for him to know that part. "I wanted to talk to my dad about all of this, but the guys think it's a bad idea.

George's gaze collides with Banks' when he speaks again. "I want you to stay out of this. All of you," he looks to Sullivan and then Oliver. "I know you want to help Harlow, but you really need to stay out of it and let the police handle it."

Banks sighs beside me, his fingers tightening around mine. He doesn't answer, but I already know what he would say if he did. Something along the lines of, don't tell me what to do because I'll do what I want.

Surprisingly, Oliver is the one who speaks up. "We will do anything that we can to help Harlow. There is no staying out of it, we're already involved. Harlow's life is intertwined with our own, and we won't stand by and watch her be attacked or hurt."

George shakes his head, looking thoroughly displeased with Oliver's statement. "Are you boys staying for dinner?" George asks after the silence has stretched between us. I don't miss how he only invited the guys to dinner; does he expect me to leave?

"I think it's time for us to go," Oliver announces and shoves out of his chair. His body is vibrating with an unknown emotion. The brothers follow Oliver's lead, and I stand as well, slowly, my knees knocking together gently. I'm so exhausted.

"Thanks for the chat," Sullivan says, heading for the doors. We all follow without anyone saying a real goodbye. George stays in his office, and we don't see anyone else on the way out. The guys don't look for their mother to tell her goodbye either. It's kind of sad and fucked up and wrong, and somehow, I get it.

When we get to the car, I feel guilty. Am I the reason the guys have a bad relationship with their parents? When Oliver starts the car and pulls away, I can't wait any longer. I need to know if this is all because of me. "Do you guys fight with your parents because of me?"

"We fight with our parents because they are pricks," Banks growls, "They shouldn't treat you the way they do, they shouldn't treat anyone like that."

"But if it wasn't for me, you would be okay?"

"Harlow, don't you dare think it is your fault that we barely talk to our parents. I can assure you, it's not," Oliver promises.

"He is right, it's not on you. It's their own fault," Sullivan chimes in.

I'm not completely convinced, but it's enough for me to let it go for now. Relaxing into the leather seat, I realize how tired I am again. This meeting was emotionally draining. I unbuckle my seatbelt and lie down across the back seat, resting my head in Banks' lap. He immediately starts running his fingers through my hair, giving me a little scalp massage.

"That feels nice," I murmur before I can't keep my eyes open any longer, and I quickly fall into a deep, dreamless sleep.

35

The days with the brothers blend together, and while I'm happy and content staying with them in a rental house far away from the world, I know this won't last forever. We can't hide from everyone for the rest of our lives.

As I sit in the kitchen staring into my coffee, my mind wanders to the questions that still plague me. It's been a while since I talked to my father. He hasn't tried to contact me or seek me out, at least not that I'm aware of. Maybe the guys are not telling me that he is, which I wouldn't put past them. They want to protect me, and my father is the last person they want me speaking to.

"What are you doing, beautiful?" Sullivan's husky voice tickles my ear, and goosebumps blanket my skin at the tone.

"Thinking..." I reply, "Do you think my father knew that Shelby was the one that tried to kill me?" I can't imagine him knowing and not doing anything, then again, this is the same man that tried to marry me off to someone as if I was a business contract, and not a human with feelings, and choices of her own.

"I don't know." He plucks an apple out of the fruit basket in front of me, his toned body presses against mine, and a spark of electricity zings through me into my core. "I wouldn't be surprised if he did."

Swallowing thickly, I try and push the fluttering of butterflies in my belly away. I can't be thinking about crawling all over him when there are bigger things that I need to be thinking about.

"Eventually, I want to go back to classes, but as long as Shelby is out there, I'm not safe to do so."

"You think we would let anything happen to you?" Oliver enters the room, his laptop in his hand.

"No, but I would feel better if she was locked up. I don't know why she did the things she did, but I'm terrified of something happening again, and I can't expect one of you to always be with me." I don't try and hide my anxiety from the brothers. There is nothing to hide. They know how worried I am.

"What do you want to do?" Sullivan asks, biting into his apple.

"I don't know, but I need to find her."

"You aren't doing shit," Banks growls, walking into the kitchen, the look on his face says, *fight me, I dare you.*

"Yeah, I'm going to have to agree with Mr. Alpha over here." Oliver hooks a thumb in Banks' direction. "Over my dead body will you get within ten feet of that bitch."

All I can do is roll my eyes at their protectiveness. Like I was really going to go out and search for her? A part of me wants to find her and ask her why she did the things she did, while the other part of me is afraid to know the answer. Why would my best friend of over 10 years want to kill me? Yes, she was having an affair with my father, but that can't be it.

"I don't mean I'm going to physically seek her out."

"Better not or I'll take you over my knee," Oliver says, the tone of his voice serious, and when I look over at him, even his face says he would do it. "And I'm dead serious, Harlow, if you do something to risk your life for us or put yourself in danger, I will blister your ass so bad you won't be able to sit for a week. You mean the world to us, and losing you would kill us." His confession makes my heart beat a little faster.

"I'm not going to do anything. Don't worry, please," I murmur softly.

"Stop scaring her with your overprotective tendencies," Sullivan shakes his head and cups my cheek. Leaning in, his lips gently graze mine. He smells like apples and sunshine, and I want more. Greedily, I reach out and grab on to his shirt, clinging to him. Before I get the chance to deepen the kiss, he's pulling away. *Damn him.*

I need some air, air that isn't filled with Bishop scent, because right now my body is on fire, need pulsing through my veins.

"I'm going to go sit outside," I announce.

"I'll join you," Banks offers, but I shake my head as I get up from my chair, my coffee mug in hand.

"No, I need some time to myself," I announce, cringing as Banks' handsome face falls. "It's not you, really it's not. I just..."

"We get it, don't feel like you have to explain yourself," Oliver answers before either of the other brothers can, and I nod, sliding past Sullivan, and then Banks on the way out. Walking out the French doors attached to the kitchen, I close them behind me and settle on to the porch swing. Sullivan's phone sits heavy in my pocket. Sipping the coffee from my mug, I know what I have to do, and I hope that the brothers don't get angry with me for doing it.

I don't think they're trying to keep me away from anyone or control me. They just want to make sure I'm protected, but there isn't anything my father can do to me through the phone, and I'm done sitting around here doing nothing while hiding from the world. I need to know.

Setting my cup down, I pull out the phone and stare at the screen. It feels a little bit like I'm betraying the guys, sneaking around, and taking Sullivan's phone while he wasn't looking, but just like they are not trying to hurt me, I'm not trying to hurt them.

I type my father's name into the search bar and watch as Google pulls up multiple pages, the first one being my father's company. I look through it until I find my father's office number and dial it. A high-pitched female voice answers my call on the second ring.

"Lockwood Real Estate, how may I direct your call?"

"Mhm, hi... this is Harlow Lockwood. I was wondering if you could connect me to my dad?" The line goes silent for so long that I pull the phone away from my ear, worrying that the call got disconnected. "Hello?"

"Ah, yes. Could you hold, please?" the woman on the other end asks, sounding a bit frazzled.

"Sure." I'm immediately put on hold, classical music filtering through the line. I don't have to wait long before my father picks up.

"Harlow?" His deep voice fills my ear a second later.

"Yes, it's me."

"Christ, Harlow. Where are you? Tell me, right now," he demands as if I would tell him.

"I'm fine, thanks for asking," I answer sarcastically. "I will not tell you where I am, and I definitely do not need you to pick me up. I'm just calling to ask you one thing..."

"I already told you if you want to know about Phoebe, you need to meet me."

"I already know who Phoebe was... and that I'm her daughter." Even though I've known for a few weeks now, the words are still foreign in my mouth.

"Who told you?"

"It doesn't matter. All that matters is that you've been lying to me my whole life. But that's not why I'm calling. I just want to know one thing, and then you can go back to your perfect little life. Did you know? Did you know that it was Shelby who tried to kill me?" I hold my breath, the seconds ticking by as I await his answer.

"She wouldn't..." He finally says. "Who told you it was her? Did the Bishops tell you that? I swear, I will end them for good this time." Contempt drips from his words.

"No one told me. I remembered. She drove through the intersection right as I was crossing the street. She tried to kill me."

"No... it-it must have been an accident." My father sounds a bit flabbergasted, and for a moment, I try to figure out if he is really surprised or faking it. Then, as if he gathers his thoughts, he says with a stronger voice, "I don't believe you. You either saw it wrong, or it simply was an accident."

Now it's my turn to be flabbergasted, I can't believe him. "Are you serious, right now?" My voice rises with each word, my anger simmering, threatening to boil over. "I guess I shouldn't be surprised that you would defend her, not when she's spreading her legs for you."

"What proof do you have?" My jaw aches as I grind my teeth together.

"Proof? What proof do I need? I saw it with my own eyes. She drove through the stop sign... she sped up! She hit me with her fucking car. I know she saw me, how couldn't she?"

"Are you sure?"

"Yes, I'm sure, and if you see her, let her know the police are looking for her. I can't even go back to classes because I'm worried she's going to hurt me, or worse."

Silence lingers between us, making the space heavy.

"I... I believe you, and I'm sorry. Your mother and I have been worried sick about you. Will you please just come home?"

"No, and that woman you married is not my mother. My mother was Phoebe, who you refuse to tell me anything about. But that's okay..." I can feel the smile curving at the corner of my lips, "I went to Mr. Bishop and got all the information I need."

"Harlow," the desperation in his voice makes me pause. "I... I can't do this over the phone. We need to meet in person, and I'll tell you everything. I don't know what George told you, but I'm positive that not all of it is true."

"There is nothing left to say, and I'm not sure I would believe anything you have to say now anyway." The only reason he wants to see me in person is so he can drag me back home and lock me in my room. Does he think I'm stupid?

"I know where Shelby is," he blurts out, shocking me once again. "Would you forgive me if I tell the police where she is?"

Forgive him? I have to suppress a laugh. "How about you tell the police where she is because it's the right thing to do?"

"I'll do it, but know that I'm doing this for you. Everything I've done is for you. You're my daughter, the only thing I have left of your mother, and I can't lose you."

I wish I could believe him. I wish I could love my dad like a daughter should love her father, but too much has happened, and I don't think we can ever repair our broken relationship.

There are too many lies, too many secrets. I can't trust that he'll protect me, that he'll take care of me. The thought brings tears to my eyes. My emotions are all over the place, and talking to him isn't helping things.

"Goodbye, Dad," I say before hanging up the phone.

36

A few days have passed since the phone call with my father... a phone call that the guys still don't know about. I feel bad about hiding it, but I don't want to disappoint them or hurt their feelings either. I know they just want to protect me, but I had to talk to him.

With all of that, I find myself getting cabin fever, the same four walls of this rental house close in on me a little more every day. Crawling out of bed, I strip out of Banks' shirt and walk into the bathroom connected to the bedroom. I've been bed hopping since we got here, each brother getting their own time with me. Last night, I fell asleep on the couch and woke up in bed with Oliver, all while wearing his brother's shirt. Strange, but normal for us.

Turning the shower on, I let the bathroom start to steam up before I step under the hot spray of water, letting it massage my neck and shoulders. A moan escapes my lips as my muscles relax under the spray.

"I like that sound very much, but I'd prefer you making it while I'm in there with you," Oliver murmurs, chuckling as he does. Before I know it, he's stripping out of his clothes and joining me in the extra-large shower stall. I'm not surprised to see his cock already hard, pointing at me angrily. The veins popping out, throbbing and begging to be touched.

"That looks... painful," I say quietly.

"It is. I'm so hard it hurts. It's what you do to me, Harlow. Always. Every time I'm in your presence, my cock is hard."

"Maybe I can do something about it?" I try my most seductive voice, and judging by the growl coming from Oliver's chest, I'm doing pretty good.

"Fuck yeah," he groans as I wrap my fingers around his length. Giving him a hard squeeze, I revel in the way his eyes squeeze shut, and his hands curl into fists.

"I never thought it would be possible for me to want all three of you, but I do. Each of you do something to me that I can't explain."

Oliver's eyes open then, the brown in them almost black, leaving only a small ring of brown behind, "You make us whole." He hisses out, his muscular chest rising and falling as he inhales. There is nothing like the power I hold over these three men. The way they fall to their knees for me. Stroking him faster, I swirl my thumb over the head of his cock and down his slit. Pre-cum beads the tip, and I smear in over his length, my eyes mesmerized with the motion.

"I need to fuck you, Harlow," Oliver's voice is raw with emotions and reaches down inside of me, sinking its claws deep into my core.

"I want you so bad..." I murmur, as I release his cock, and take a step back. His eyes smolder as he stalks toward me, lifting me in one fluid motion. In seconds, I'm in his arms, my back pressed against the tile wall of the shower, my legs wrapped around his middle. His swollen cock bumps against my clit and I suck a labored breath in through my teeth. Oliver stares down at me, watching me, knowing that he holds power over my body and my heart.

"Every night...." His cock brushes against my soaked entrance, and I sink my nails into his shoulder, urging him on. "I think about stealing you from my brothers' beds to have my way with you."

Feeling as if I might die if he doesn't start fucking me, I grin and say, "You should."

That must set him off because he pulls back and slams into me, making the air in my lungs still, and my entire body shake with tremors of pleasure.

"Fuck, there is nothing like sinking into you. So tight, so warm, so fucking perfect," he pants, pistoning his hips, sinking deeper inside of me. His fingers dig into my flesh hard enough to leave bruises, and I want him to. I want him to mark me. Everything around me fades away as Oliver fucks me into oblivion. My nails rake down his chest, and he hisses at the pain.

Then he starts to swivel his hips between thrusts, the head of his dick brushing against what I now know is my g-spot.

"Ahhh, Oliver..." I mewl. Strands of wet hair stick to my face, but I couldn't care less how I look in this moment. All I can do is hold on for dear life as Oliver takes from me, fucking me to the brink of insanity. The orgasm I've been chasing for the last couple of minutes stirs deep in my core and slithers up my spine.

"I'm going to come..." I whimper, staring into Oliver's eyes. He's looking at me with a determination I've never seen, a wicked grin on his handsome face.

"Fuck yeah, you are, all over my cock..." His dirty words only add to the pleasure, and within seconds I'm going off, launching into space like a rocket. My pussy clenches around his length, and just from the grunts and pants that he's making, I know he's close, and strangely, I want his come like I've never wanted it before. I want it inside of me, marking me, claiming me.

"Fill me with your come, Oliver, fill me..." I plead through the sound of blood swooshing in my ears. With a steel grip and a growl, I'm pretty sure his brothers can hear, he comes, his thighs shaking, his head tipped back, exposing his throat. Acting on impulse, I nip at that unmarred skin and smile when I feel his cock jump inside of me.

Sucking the pain of my bite away, I wait for him to come floating back down to me. Seconds later, he's staring down at me and gently placing me back down on my feet, and with the loss of his cock inside of me, I feel like I've lost a piece of my soul.

"I love you, Harlow, and I'd love you even if you didn't fuck me like you love me back. You're it for me." He peppers kisses against my face, and I start to giggle.

"You're welcome, and the feeling is mutual, you definitely know how to make a girl feel good."

Oliver grins. "All for you, baby, all for you." He gives me one more kiss, a kiss that makes me want to climb him like a tree, and not shower at all. But then we wouldn't get anything done, and as much as I love being here with them, I really want to get back to living a normal life. So instead of begging him to take me again, I focus on washing my body and hair, and less on the pulsing between my legs.

Once we've finished showering and are dressed, we make our way out to the living room. Sullivan and Banks are already lounging on the couch, both with shit-eating grins on their faces.

They heard us, or at least Oliver.

"Have a nice shower?" Sullivan asks, chuckling.

"Yeah, did you get all clean?" Banks chimes in, "It sounded like you did."

"Yes, don't worry. I was thorough... made sure I got *every* spot clean." At Oliver's words, my face turns about five shades redder.

"Don't be embarrassed," Sullivan tells me, rubbing my back when I take the seat next to him.

"Can't help it," I say, even more embarrassed. While I've become more outspoken sexually, it's still a lot for me. After all the bullying and hate I've gotten about being with all three of them, it's hard for me to handle any type of teasing without feeling like caving in on myself.

Oliver opens his mouth, and it looks as if he is about to say something when his phone starts ringing. He takes it out of his pocket and looks at the screen with his eyebrows drawn together. "It's the detective."

Before anyone can say anything, he answers the phone, placing it on speaker for all of us to hear. "Hello..."

"Good morning, Mr. Bishop. How are you doing today?"

"Very good," Oliver answers, grinning at me while he does.

"Good, good... Is Miss. Lockwood still with you?"

"Yes, I'm here," I say before anyone else can answer.

"Great. Hello, Harlow. I hope you are doing well. I know you've been through a lot, so I wanted to call you right away to let you know that we arrested Shelby a few hours ago."

"Finally," Banks mutters under his breath.

I know I should say something. I know I should probably be happy and relieved that I'm safe now, but for some reason, I feel neither. All I feel is the need for answers.

"Did she say why she did it? Why she wants me dead?" Not knowing has been eating me up. I thought she was my best friend before all of this, so why did she want me dead?

"No, I'm sorry. She didn't give us a real reason as to why, but she did confess to wanting to hurt you."

"You put her in jail, right?" Oliver asks impatiently. "And she won't be getting out any time soon?"

"Actually..." The detective pauses, and I feel the air in my lungs still, "She's not in jail, we had to bring her into a closed psychiatric ward after what happened."

"What? Why? What happened?" I mean, I know she had some mental issues given what she did to me, but still. A psychiatric ward seems to be a little too much.

"Harlow, do you know that it was your father who called her location in?"

Almost absentmindedly I nod, before realizing he can't see me. "Yes," I say, after a moment. "I talked to him about Shelby and..." I trail off, not wanting to say the words out loud. *Shelby and my father.* I'm still so disgusted by the thought, and now I'm even more embarrassed... embarrassed about what kind of man my father is.

"When we arrested her, and she realized that your father was the one who had called us, she had a complete mental breakdown. She was yelling and screaming, saying that she's in love with him and that she needs to kill you to have him for herself. Then she tried to hurt herself, we had no choice but to send her in to have her mental state evaluated."

"So, she'll be there for a while or what?" Banks interjects.

"They're going to do a full evaluation on her, and then make a decision, but as of right now, that's where she will be staying. If I have any further updates, I'll be sure to give you a call and let you know."

"Thank you, detective," I can't explain the pressure that's been lifted from my chest at knowing that she's somewhere far away, somewhere that she won't be able to escape from, and that my father was the one who helped put her there.

A small piece of my heart beats for the man that gave me life because, in the end, he did choose me over her, but it took all of these bad things happening to me for him to do it.

"No problem, have a good day." The line goes dead, leaving me with nothing more than my thoughts and the three men that own my heart. When I look up, I find all three of them staring at me. Each carrying their own confused expression.

"I was going to tell you," I start, a pang of guilt hitting me.

"If you wanted to call your father, all you had to do was ask. You didn't have to sneak around behind our backs." Oliver says, and the tone of his voice makes me shiver. I know without even looking at him that he's disappointed in me. Hell, I'm disappointed in me too.

"What Oliver means to say is that we want to protect you, and we can't protect you when you're doing stuff behind our backs. We're supposed to be a team," Sullivan's voice is soft and nurturing, and for some stupid reason, I want to cry. I don't understand why, but I do. When I look up from my hands again, there are tears in my eyes, and no matter how much I try and blink them away, they continue to fall.

"Fuck," Oliver mutters under his breath and comes to stand in front of me. He wraps his arms around me, and I breathe him in. My body lights up at his touch. This is what he does to me, what they all do to me.

"I'm... I'm sorry. I wasn't hiding it. I just wanted to know if he knew that Shelby was the one to hurt me. I know I should've come to you guys, but..."

"Shhh, no. I'm sorry. I didn't mean to yell at you." Oliver soothes, his hand moving up and down my back. It feels good, too good, and I let my eyes drift closed for a second.

"I don't want to disappoint you guys," I sob into his shirt.

"Shhh, baby, you're not a disappointment. You're as far from a disappointment as it gets." Banks' strong voice pierces my ears, and I feel him along my back, his hard body brushing against mine. He brushes the hair from my neck away and presses hot kisses to my shoulder and neck, sucking on the tender flesh along my collarbone. Instantly, I melt into a pile of mush, the tears stopping all at once.

"Can't cry when my lips are on you?" He teases, and I can feel my insides turning to molten lava. That connection I have to each of them burning hotter and hotter.

"No," I whisper hoarsely. I'm only vaguely aware of Oliver releasing me, and turning me to face Banks.

"I'm sorry my brothers are assholes. I'll make it up to you." Banks' pink tongue flicks out over his bottom lip, his blue eyes blazing with unbridled need beneath the amusing glint. I want to give in to him. I want to let all three of them have a chance at me all over again... but...

Out of nowhere, a wave of dizziness hits me, and I'm overcome with nausea. Bile rises up my throat, and I know what's going to happen next. Without even thinking, I shove against Banks and make it to the kitchen sink just in time to vomit up all my breakfast. My stomach twists and I continue to puke until there is nothing but green bile coming up.

"We need to get you to a doctor," one of them says, but I can't tell who it is. All I can do is focus on the stupid need to vomit. Banks takes my hair into his hands and holds it away from my face. My fingers grip on to the counter as everything pours out of me. By the time I'm done, my eyes are watering, and my throat is burning.

I know they're right; the vomiting and exhaustion aren't normal, and I should get checked out, but a part of me doesn't want to know what's wrong. A part of me hopes whatever is happening goes away. Maybe it's just stress? I mean, what else could it be?

"I think it's just stress, this is all too much..." I groan, taking the paper towel that Oliver offers me. Wiping at my mouth and eyes, I do my best to make sure that there isn't any puke on my chin or lips.

"Even if it is stress, you've been getting sick a lot lately, and it wouldn't be a bad idea to get checked out."

"What if it turns out to be something more?" I ask, fear ringing my voice. "The doctors told me that I could possibly run into more problems from the accident down the road. Maybe that's what he was talking about."

"Then we deal with it." Sullivan answers, his voice soft and warm, and all I want to do is go to him and let him wrap his arms around me.

Knowing there isn't any point in trying to fight it, I agree. "Okay, I'll make an appointment."

"Thank you, that's all we want. You are the most important thing to us, and if you're sick, then we need to find a way to fix it."

"Sometimes, things can't be fixed." I drop my gaze down to my hands. Shelby has been caught, life is good, and yet somehow it all seems temporary like at any minute the rug is going to be ripped out from underneath our feet.

Banks cups me by the cheek, and I nuzzle into his touch. "When it comes to you, everything can be fixed. Let's get you a shower, something small to eat, and some rest."

"Sullivan and I will get everything figured out so we can go back to classes," Oliver announces.

That makes me perk up. Excitement bubbles through me. This is just what I needed to hear.

"Yes, we're finally leaving and going back to classes. Now that Shelby has been caught, we have nothing to worry about."

"We can finally all be together, and attend classes like we were meant to. Everything will go back to normal now. We'll get to be normal, or as normal as we can be as college students."

I smile because deep down, I am happy, but I can't shake the inky dread that something bad will happen. It always does. It always finds a way to ruin the good in my life.

37

"I thought you would be excited to be back in classes?" Caroline says from her seat beside me. She must see the permanent scowl that seems to have taken up residence on my face this week.

Things have pretty much gone back to normal, even Tiffany and her cronies are treating me the same as they always have, no matter how much I try to ignore their jibes, I just can't seem to. Merely thinking her name makes my brain scream.

"Earth to Harlow, you're looking at Tiffany like you want to rip out her throat, are you okay?" Caroline's soft voice fills my ears, and I look away from Tiffany before I do just that. She's bitchier than I remember her being, and it's taking everything in me to bite my tongue when she or her barbie brigade walks past me and calls me a slut beneath their breaths. It's petty and childish, and I just want them to go away.

"I'm fine, just a little... aggravated," I hiss, trying not to look in Tiffany's direction.

"Could've fooled me. I thought you were plotting Tiffany's murder there for a second."

"That's because I was." I peek up at Tiffany again. She tosses her hair over her shoulder and laughs loudly at something one of her friends says. *Bitches.* Mean stuck-up bitches. That's all they are. "I don't understand why they have to be such assholes. It's not like what I do with my life has any effect on them." I'm merely venting now, and even though I should stop and save it for when I get back to the house, it feels good to let it out right now.

At least I'll be less likely to reach out and bash Tiffany's head against the wall this way.

"She'll forever feel like you stole Oliver from her." Caroline's response makes me grit my teeth. "Before you bagged my cousins, she had her sights set on him, and from the look of it, she still does. I bet she hates you for having their hearts when she can't even get their attention. Never could. Even when they were pretending to like her, all they would talk about was you."

"Well, maybe if she wasn't being a raging bitch all the time, she could get a guy to like her for more than her mouth or the thing between her legs."

"Amen to that," Caroline mumbles. "Maybe we should tell her that..."

Grinning, I shake my head. The last thing I need is more encouragement. I spend the rest of the class trying to ignore Tiffany and concentrate on the outline for my English literature paper instead. When the professor announces we're free to go, I'm so relieved I practically sag in my seat. Who knew ignoring someone could be so draining? Then again, I guess the ignoring part wasn't my problem. It's more holding back my anger, so I don't end up getting booted from the school.

Gathering my stuff quickly, I start to get excited when I realize that I'll be seeing the guys in a few minutes. Like every day, we all meet for lunch, something that's slowly becoming my favorite part of the day.

"In a hurry to get to your *boyfriend*?" One of Tiffany's friends snarls, her voice condescending.

"Please, Claire, don't be ridiculous and call them her *boyfriends*," Tiffany decides to add her input. "She is nothing more than their little plaything. Don't you remember how they used to talk about her? How we used to make fun of her with the guys? They don't want her, at least, not like they would want you or me." I can't help myself. I look the bitch right in the eyes and just stare, wishing I could show her just how much they don't want her.

"Why don't you guys get lost," Caroline snaps. "You're just jealous because she has what you want."

"Ha, jealous? Of *her*?" Tiffany's nose wrinkles and I clench my free hand into a tight fist. *Don't slug her.* My muscles burn, as anger pulses through me. Concentrating on not wiping the smug smile off her face... with my fist.

When they move to leave, Tiffany digs her shoulder into my arm in a feeble attempt to knock me over, but my body is too rigid, and the only thing she accomplishes is making my backpack slide off my shoulder.

"Oops," she snickers and walks off as the bag slides down my arm and on to the floor.

God, I hate her.

"Congrats on having as much self-restraint as you do. I thought you were about to fight her for sure," Caroline tells me when they leave, and we are the only two people left in the classroom.

"Yeah, I'm surprised myself," I say with a shrug. "Maybe I just didn't want to be late for lunch. I'm starving. My stomach's been growling for the last hour."

"Girl, you've been all about the food lately. That wouldn't have anything to do with you meeting the guys for each meal, would it?" Caroline giggles.

"Maybe," I grin.

We speed walk across campus to get to the sandwich shop where we are meeting the guys. As it turns out, a walk is exactly what I need. The fresh air helps me clear my head and cools my simmering anger toward that witch. When we arrive at the shop, all three of the Bishops are standing out front, waiting for us. Banks spots us first and gives me a panty-melting smile, and my mind goes blank for a moment, forgetting all about Tiffany and her group of barbies.

"Hey, you two," Oliver greets us when we are only a few feet away.

I have this animalistic urge to give each of them a kiss, but we haven't been that comfortable with public affection while we are out in the open like this, and it's not because we don't want to be seen with each other or because we're hiding that we are together.

It's more because we don't want to draw any type of attention to us, and having three boyfriends will definitely do that.

Walking into the restaurant together, Oliver spots a table in the back that will fit all of us.

"How was your class?" Sullivan asks as I take a seat and read over the menu.

Before I can answer, Caroline opens her big fat mouth, "Tiffany was being a major bitch last class, but other than that, today has been fine." I give her a side-eye.

Why can't she keep her mouth shut? This is just going to worry the guys further.

"What do you mean she was being a bitch? Is she bothering you again?" Sullivan asks concern etched into his handsome features. Part of me wants to sweep it under the rug and tell them it's nothing, but if I don't tell them and they find out later, I'll feel bad for having not been honest.

"Well, it seems as if she is under the impression, I stole Oliver from her, so she's trying, like always, to pick a fight. That's all. There's no reason to worry. Can we eat now? I'm going to eat my left arm off if I don't get something in my belly soon."

"I'm sorry, Harlow... This is all our fault," Oliver huffs, looking away from me as if he is too ashamed to look at me. My eyes catch on his shiny brown hair as he runs a hand through the thick strands. When he looks back at me, I can see the regret pooling there. "I kind of pretended to like her."

"It's in the past, this is the present, and we are only looking ahead, and from where I'm sitting, the future is looking pretty good," I smile. "I mean, I do see a delicious Italian sub in the near future...so..." The waitress must have heard me, because just then she walks up to the table, a tablet in her hand, ready to take our orders.

For the rest of our lunch together, we don't talk about Tiffany or anyone else we don't like. Everything seems to feel better when I'm with the guys. Being with them reminds me that no one here is worth risking my happiness for.

Only after I've finished every bite of my sub, do I realize that Sullivan seems oddly withdrawn, barely looking at me and not even finishing his sandwich. I'm about to ask him what's going on, when he pushes his plate away and gets up from the table, his chair scraping against the floor. My eyebrows draw together in confusion.

Where is he going?

"I'm gonna head out. I want to get to my next class a little early. I'll see you later," he doesn't really speak to anyone in particular and starts walking away before any of us can respond. It feels like someone has stabbed a tiny knife into the corner of my heart. It doesn't really hurt, but it leaves a noticeable ache behind.

That's what Sullivan has just done to me. He's left an ache behind, and I know without even asking that something is going on with him.

"What's wrong with him?" Oliver asks out loud what I was wondering silently.

Banks shrugs, clearly not worried about his brother's behavior. "His grades are probably slipping. His mind has been occupied as of late," he grins at me, and I can tell he's trying to lighten the mood. "You know how worried he gets about his perfect GPA."

"Yeah, but that doesn't mean he has to be rude," Oliver growls, shoving a spoon full of soup past his lips.

"I just hope he's okay. I'll talk to him later tonight," I announce before taking a sip of my soda.

"We better get going too," Banks leans over and whispers into the shell of my ear. His hot breath fans against my skin and goosebumps erupt across my skin. The next class we have together, and the thought leaves me feeling all warm inside. I'll be able to hold his hand for the next hour, and if that's not a good way to make it through calculus, then I don't know what is.

EVEN WITH BANKS by my side, calculus is unbearable. Numbers are just not my thing, and while I luckily have Banks here to give me a little extra help, it's not going to help me pass the tests that I'll have to take on my own. I need to focus, to digest the words that are being spoken.

If Banks can sense my confusion and disappointment in myself, he doesn't let on. Class seems to go on forever, and come the end when I'm gathering my things, the only thing I want to do is go back to the house with the guys and sleep.

With everything in my backpack, I step into the aisle and head for the door. I've made it a total of five feet when Professor Clarkson calls my name.

Gritting my teeth, I walk to the front of the room where his desk is. As soon as I reach his desk, my stomach starts to churn. The smell of his cologne is overpowering. It's like I'm stepping into a cloud of some cheap masculine fragrance. The odor is so overwhelming that I don't even want to open my mouth and talk.

"Miss. Lockwood," Mr. Clarkson greets, "I just wanted to make sure you are doing okay with the work now. Your homework from last week was inconclusive, and you seemed to be having a difficult time in class today as well."

Great. Of course, he needs to point out how horrible I am at this.

"Yeah, I'm fine," I say, concentrating on not throwing up all over his brown suit.

He looks at me like he doesn't believe me, heck, I don't even believe me.

"Are you sure? I can recommend you to some study groups or assign you a student tutor. If you start to fall behind, catching up will be difficult, and I don't offer extra credit. I would hate for you—"

"I'll help her with her homework," Banks cuts in his blue eyes blazing. "She'll be fine."

Mr. Clarkson's eyes narrow, and it seems like he wants to say something else, but instead, presses his lips into a firm line. He stares at me for a long second before speaking again.

"Very well, then. I expect your grades to be up in the coming weeks. I'll see you next week," he says while closing his laptop.

I take that as my cue to go, and hastily leave the room holding my breath along the way. Only after I've taken a few steps into the hallway do I release the burning air in my lungs and suck in an even larger breath of oxygen.

"Hey, wait up. Are you okay?" Banks calls after me.

"I'm fine," I gasp, my lungs still burning as I lean against the nearest wall, my body swaying like a building during an earthquake. "I just couldn't stand the smell of his cologne. It was so strong, he smelled like he poured the whole bottle on himself."

"Are you sure that's it?" Banks eyes me wearily, "Because you look like if the wall wasn't holding you up that you'd be on the ground."

Letting my eyes fall closed, I focus only on my breathing for a moment. Once my chest has stopped rising and falling like I've run a mile, and my stomach isn't churning anymore, I open my eyes again. When I do, I find Banks has boxed me in with his body, his muscled arms frame my face, and suddenly my pulse starts to race for an entirely different reason. My cheeks heat at the indecent thoughts filling my mind.

Him taking me against the wall.

Me calling his name out as he brings me to orgasm over and over again....

"Is this too much for you?" Banks' husky voice fills my ears and interrupts my thoughts. He's staring at me with a hunger that only I can quench, and I want him, even now, right here in the middle of the hallway. Then it hits me, he asked me a question...

"God, no... this is... I feel better already," I whisper, just before his lips descend on mine, making any discomfort I felt moments ago vanish into thin air. He kisses me with so much love like I am the earth, and he is the sun. Like I'm his first taste of water after months of drought.

When he pulls away, I whimper and grip on to his shirt, wanting to keep him close.

"That's not what I mean, baby. I mean, me, my brothers, is all of this too much for you? All this shit with Tiffany, with our parents and yours. No one, including me, has stopped to ask how you're handling all of this. If you're okay?" He whispers the last part, his hot breath fanning against my lips as he pushes his forehead against mine.

This close I'm simply breathing him in, soaking him up like a sponge.

"Of course, I'm okay. I've wanted this, wanted each of you for so long, and I don't want to give you guys up. You're all I have left. You're the only people who care about me, who don't try and control me."

Banks' tongue dips out of his mouth and on to his full bottom lip, and all over again, my thoughts shift.

"If this ever becomes too much for you, I want you to tell me. Please, Harlow…" The desperation in his voice reaches inside me and sinks its claws into my heart.

"You'll never have to worry about that because it will never be too much for me. You and your brothers are all I want. All I'll ever need."

Banks stares at me for a long moment, his ocean blue gaze piercing my soul, fracturing it. He looks as if he doesn't believe me, and the thought of that kills me. It makes me want to die a slow and painful death. He has to know that I mean what I'm saying. My heartbeat thunders in my ears, drowning out every other sound around me.

"I love you. You believe me, don't you? That this isn't too much? That I want you and your brothers?" Air stills in my lungs while I await his response.

"I do believe you, and I love you too." His voice is soft, softer than normal, and when he presses a kiss to my forehead, it seems like everything is going to be okay. Taking my hand into his, we walk out of the building, and I feel a little better with every step I take. I don't know what's going on with me lately, but I need to figure it out. The dizziness, fatigue, and vomiting. None of it is normal, but after everything we've already been through, the last thing I want to do is add more to our already overflowing pot.

A smile pulls at my lips when the high hanging sun meets my skin. The warmth radiates through me, leaving me feeling warm all over. I can't wait to get home and relax with my guys, curled up on the couch, where no one can judge us or look down on us just for loving each other. When we are at home, it's just us, and that's the way I prefer it to be.

As we head to the car, we pass a group of people standing outside the library. Immediately, I recognize Tiffany's annoying giggle. I try to ignore her, but still can't help but glance over there. What I see has me stopping dead in my tracks.

Sullivan is standing with Tiffany and her friends. Even worse, he seems to be talking to them, saying something that made her giggle. *What the hell?*

I turn to Banks and find him staring daggers at his brother. He wraps his arm around me a little tighter than necessary, and I lean into his touch, seeking much-needed comfort. I don't know why Sullivan would do that, talk to her, befriend her, but I know that I can't stand here and watch this. I need to get away. I have to.

Luckily, Banks has the same idea. With his arm around me like a security blanket, he walks me to the parking lot, my legs move on their own, and when we get to the car, Banks helps me into the passenger seat.

"What the hell was he doing?" I ask when Banks gets into the driver's seat.

"I don't know, but he can ride home with Oliver," he grunts angrily. "Or he can stay here, for all I care."

We drive to the house in silence, every time I glance over to Banks, his face is set in stone, and he's gripping onto the steering wheel so tightly, his knuckles are completely white. I almost wish he wasn't so angry about it. I wish he would tell me that it was nothing, that Sullivan would never go behind my back. Seeing Banks so upset about this only makes this whole thing worse.

When we pull into the driveway and Banks cuts the engine, we don't get out right away. Banks take a few deep breaths like he is trying to calm himself before he opens his mouth to speak. "I'm sorry, I don't mean to be angry. I mean, I am angry, but not at you. I don't want to let my anger out on you. I don't know what the fuck Sullivan was thinking, but it really pisses me off seeing you hurt. You've been hurt enough, and it's our job to prevent you from being hurt any further." I'm still mad at Sullivan, but having Banks tell me this, has me feeling a whole lot better.

"Maybe it wasn't what it looked like. Let him come home and explain himself before we jump to any conclusions," I suggest, and Banks nods in agreement.

"In the meantime, we do have the house all to ourselves for the next two hours." A mischievous grin spreads across his face. "What could we possibly do with all that free time?"

The mood inside the car turns swiftly. All concerns disappear and are replaced with an aching need to go inside and get undressed.

"Mhm, I'm not sure. Let's go inside and think of something. You know how I can think best?" I ask, tapping my chin.

"How is that?" Banks asks with a grin.

"Naked."

38

When Oliver and Sullivan walk through the door, Banks and I have just finished putting dinner together. The whole time we've been waiting, my emotions have been all over the place. I try not to interpret the scene I witnessed earlier wrongly; I want to talk to Sullivan before I give it any more thought.

"Hey, guys," I greet them, forcing a smile on my face.

"Hey, beautiful," Oliver says with a grin, walking up to me and kissing my cheek.

"Hey," Sullivan mutters, walking up to me next. He places a chaste kiss on my other cheek. I expect him to say something more, anything more, to explain himself, maybe even apologize. But he does none of those things. Instead, he grabs a soda from the fridge and turns his back to me. Literally and figuratively. Part of me is screaming inside, telling me that I should say something, anything.

"I'm going to head to bed," Sullivan says, out of thin air, and my hands clench into tight fists. *Of course, you are.*

"You're not gonna eat?" Oliver questions.

Sullivan shakes his head. He can't even lift his head to look at his brother as he speaks.

"Nah, I don't feel good. I'll see you all in the morning."

"No fucking way," Banks yells, causing everyone to look his way. Anger spills out of him as he lifts a closed fist, slamming it down on to the marble island. "You're going to explain to us, but more importantly, to Harlow, what the hell you were doing with Tiffany earlier?"

"What?" Oliver's eyes widen in shock. My throat tightens as I await Sullivan's answer. He still loves me, right? He still wants this? Us? All these questions hang on the edge of my tongue, but I just don't have the courage to ask them.

"I wasn't doing anything," Sullivan answers defensively. His eyes swing around the room before coming to a stop on mine. In his blue depths, I see despair and anger, "Just talking. Am I not allowed to talk to anyone anymore?"

"Jesus, what the fuck, dude?" Oliver yells, his carefree, happy mood changing with every second that ticks by.

"Just calm down, I wasn't doing anything wrong. You're blowing this whole thing up!" He growls, waving us off before walking out of the room. I listen to his footsteps as they recede into the other room and then up the stairs. My mind is blown, my heart shattered. What is going on, and how in the world am I going to fix it? Is Sullivan really befriending the one person who hates me most?

Tears well in my eyes, but I blink them away. Crying isn't going to do me any good right now. Banks curses under his breath and follows behind him, only to return minutes later.

Banks stomps into the kitchen, "He locked his door and is refusing to open it." I don't understand. How did we get here? I thought everything was good. I thought we were all happy. I must be wearing my emotions on my face because a moment later, Banks is at my side, his arm wrapping around me, "If you want me to, I can go back up there and kick the door in, but I don't think it's going to do any good."

I shake my head, "No. If he wants to talk, he'll talk. We can't make him do something he doesn't want to do, and if what he says is true, then there isn't anything more for him to say."

"Would someone tell me what the hell happened?" Oliver's gravelly voice pierces my ears, and I look over at him, nearly having forgotten he was in the room.

"It's nothing," I answer because honestly, the last thing I want to do is rip the brothers apart. They're brothers. They should be there for each other, not be at one another's necks.

"It's not nothing," Banks objects, "it's a big fucking deal, especially because it involves Tiffany."

Oliver looks between us, bewilderedly, "What did he do?"

Before I can shut him up, Banks is talking again. "We saw Sullivan, Tiffany, and her friends standing outside the library earlier. He was just standing there talking to them, and though it seems harmless, it's wrong. After everything she did to Harlow, after all the things she said, and continues to say."

I can practically feel the steam rolling off of Banks.

Oliver just stares at both of us, drinking up every word that his brother gives him.

"I'll talk to him. I'll figure out what the hell is going on." The gusto in his voice gives me hope. If anyone could talk some sense into Sullivan, it would be his oldest brother, but even if he does, it doesn't really change anything. Sullivan still made the choice to converse with Tiffany, and I can feel him pulling away from me. Putting distance between us.

Oliver dishes up the meal, and the boys dig in, but all I do is stare down at my plate.

We're all supposed to be sitting down to eat, but instead of being together, it feels like we're falling apart, and there isn't any way I can stomach a meal with the way I'm feeling right now. Not with the amount of distance and tension between us all tonight.

"I think I'm just gonna head to bed," I say, shoving the food on my plate around with a fork.

"You sure? You haven't eaten anything," Banks says, placing his hand on my arm.

"Yeah, I'm fine. I just want to go to sleep and let this day be over with." Hopefully, tomorrow will be a better one.

"Why don't you two go on to bed. I'll clean this up and join you in a few," Oliver suggests with a smile, and I'm all for that. Banks nods and gets up with me. Together we climb the stairs and enter his bedroom.

He sets me on the bed and helps me undress before undressing himself. I'm so upset I can't even fully enjoy the little striptease he's giving me. When we are both mostly naked, he climbs on the bed and pulls me down next to him. Spreading the blanket over us, he tucks me into his side, and I bury my face into his chest. He smells like soap and man. Slowly his body heat seeps into mine, and I relax deeper into the mattress.

I'm almost asleep when the door creaks open, and light from the hallway spills over into the room. I glance up, hoping it might be Sullivan after all, he's never gone to bed without saying goodnight to me first. When I see that it's Oliver instead, a slight wave of disappointment washes over me, and my heart stills in my chest.

Why is he doing this?

I try to push it away, the pain, the anger. I try to be happy that Oliver is here, as he climbs into the bed and lies down next to me. As he wraps his arm around me and cuddles me. I know I'm being ridiculous and spoiled.

Here I am with two guys, two men that love me, but still, I can't be happy about it because I'm missing a third. Sullivan is meant to be here, and without him, it feels like there is a huge piece of who I am, who we are, missing.

I just can't help it... no matter how much Oliver and Banks mean to me, I don't feel complete unless I have Sullivan too. Having him pull away from me... away from us, it hurts. It hurts more than anything else I've been through thus far.

THE NEXT TWO days aren't any better, unfortunately. Sullivan seems isolated and cut off from his brothers, and I. Annoyance slowly turns to jealousy as I try and figure out why he's changed so suddenly. One minute everything was fine, and the next, he's avoiding me at every turn. He doesn't even look at me anymore, and if I try and speak to him, he pretends as if he hasn't heard me. It's like he is actively trying to distance himself from me.

All morning, I was looking forward to our afternoon class together, hoping that maybe then he would talk to me, but as I sit in the classroom waiting for him, the seat next to me remains empty. Of course, he would ditch me.

Chewing on the end of my pencil, I look around the class absentmindedly, because let's face it, I won't be able to concentrate on anything written on the whiteboard anyway. When nothing inside the classroom holds my interest, I let my gaze wander to the windows.

For the next few minutes, I let mother nature calm my mind a little as I watch how the wind makes the leaves dance in the trees. I'm finally starting to breathe a little better, the ache in my chest easing a bit when my gaze catches on something in the distance.

For a moment, I just stare, my mood souring as I watch Tiffany walk out of the building across the street and down across the lawn. When I spot Sullivan walk up and greet her, that sour mood turns to red hot anger.

Leisurely, he strolls beside her, as if they're the best of friends. Of course, I can't hear what she is saying, but from her body language, I can tell that they are having a friendly conversation... too friendly when it comes to her. Maybe I wouldn't react this strongly if it was somebody else... anybody else. But *Tiffany*? It feels like a thousand tiny knives are stabbing at my heart right now.

He skipped class with me to meet up with her?

Jealousy burns through me, rushing to the surface, leaving a bitter taste on the tip of my tongue. Unshed tears sting my eyes as I gather up all my stuff and shove everything inside my bag. I can't do this right now. Not ever actually. The professor briefly glances up at me but doesn't say anything as I get up and start descending the steps. I can feel eyes on me as I reach the doors and escape the confines of the room.

By the time I make it down the hall, the tears have started to fall, each one leaving a stain against my cheek. My vision goes blurry, either from all the tears or something else. Before I can grasp what is happening, my head is spinning, or maybe it's the world around me. I can't really tell. It feels like I'm on a roller coaster, my body going up and down, up and down.

On autopilot, I reach into my back pocket and fish out my phone. Unlocking it, I scroll to Oliver's number. With my eyes closed, I hold the phone to my ear and wait for Oliver's voice to fill my ear. The sound of his voice instantly calms me, grounds me, reminds me that everything is going to be okay.

"Can you come and get me," I ask, breathlessly. "Building eleven."

"Is everything okay?" I can hear the concern etched into his vocal cords.

"Yeah, can you please just come get me." The floor sways beneath my feet, and I'm not sure how much longer I can hold on.

"Of course, I'll be right there." He hangs up before I can say anything else, and all I can do is hope that I'll be okay, that everything will be okay. Because if it isn't, I'm not sure what I'll do.

39

"You need to tell us, right fucking now, what you were doing with Tiffany?" Oliver speaks through his teeth, greeting Sullivan as soon as he enters the living room. Of course, my body starts to physically ache when our eyes lock. His brows pinch together with worry as he looks between his brothers and me. Oliver is next to me on the couch, Banks on the other side, both of them are holding on to me, holding me together.

"What's wrong? Are you okay?" Sullivan questions urgently, looking directly at me. He sounds almost frantic, and though I want to tell him, to reassure him that everything is okay, it's not. With everything going on, with all the added stress. It's wearing me down. Eating away at my resolve.

"Since when have you earned the right to ask her a question? She's been trying to talk to you all week, and all you do is ignore her." Banks lashes out at Sullivan next. Deep down, I don't want them to fight, even over me.

"Harlow," Sullivan takes a hesitant step toward me, and I can't stop the tears from forming in my eyes. I blink them away, but they remain there, a reminder of how out of control my emotions have become. "Are you okay? What happened? Tell me, and I'll make it better. I'll do whatever I need to fix it."

To fix it. For some reason, my ears catch on those three words.

"Do you want her? Do you not want..." The words lodge in my throat. After everything we've been through, the mere thought of us not all ending up together. It kills me, physically kills me.

Sullivan looks as if I've slapped him, his nostrils flare and his eyes flicker with anger.

"Who? Tiffany?" All I can do is nod.

His body visibly trembles, and in nothing more than a second, he's crossed the space separating us. "No, no way in hell. I don't want her. You've got it all wrong. I don't give a fuck about her. I've been trying to get close to her, so I can find out what she's doing and who she's been talking to."

What? I don't understand.

"What are you talking about?" Banks asks the same confusion filling his face as mine.

"Last week, I went to talk to her to tell her to leave you alone. She told me that she's not the one we need to worry about; that there were other people looking for Harlow, asking questions about her..."

"And why the hell didn't you tell us any of this?" Oliver yells, his cheeks heating.

"Because I didn't know if Tiffany was even telling the truth or if she was just trying to get to us. I didn't want to worry you, Harlow." Sullivan's gaze drops to the floor, and I swear it feels like I can breathe again. At least now, I know he didn't really want her. He was only doing it to protect me.

"I guess I worried you just as much by not telling you what I was doing," he says, sounding completely defeated.

Before I know what is happening, Sullivan pushes the coffee table out of the way and is on his knees at my feet. His hands move up my legs, coming to rest on my hips, where he gives me a firm squeeze. Burying his face into my jean covered thighs, he inhales, and I do the same, moving my hand to his head, so I can thread my fingers through those long chocolate brown locks.

Suddenly my entire world realigns, and it's like all the planets in my solar system are back in order and no longer on a course for collision.

"I'm so sorry, baby, so sorry..."

"It's okay, but you could've told me. I would've understood."

Sullivan lifts his head, a dimpled grin appearing on his lips, "But would you have? If I had told you what I was going to do, you would've freaked out and told me not to, and while it was hard as hell not to look at you or tell you what I knew. I needed to be strong if I wanted answers."

Nibbling on my bottom lip, I nod my head, "You're right. I wouldn't have let you do it because we're a team, and we're supposed to do this all together. What if something happened to you? I thought..." I force air into my lungs, so I can say what I need to. "I was sure you were done with me."

Sullivan stares at me in shock like he can't believe I would think something like that. His blue orbs are bright, and brim with sadness, a sadness that I'm sure is reflecting back at him equally.

Turning to Oliver, I say, "Can I have a moment alone with him?"

Oliver nods his head, and then I turn to Banks. He looks at his brother with a mixed bag of emotions before speaking. "We'll leave you guys alone for a little bit." Banks narrows his eyes at Sullivan. "But if you make her cry again, I will personally rip one of your balls off and play golf with it."

Oliver snorts and releases me to get up off the couch. "You don't even play golf."

Banks chuckles, "Yeah, I know, but that's beside the point."

Each of them, press a kiss to my forehead before disappearing out of the room, leaving Sullivan and me completely alone.

"Why would you think I was done with you?" he asks.

I shrug, "I'm used to people who I thought loved me, turning their back on me. I didn't want to think the worst, but it's hard when I've been disappointed so many times. My own parents got tired of me, so it's hard to believe that you guys wouldn't."

"I'm so sorry, I didn't think about it that way. I would never be tired of you, and as for your parents... well, there is seriously something wrong with them, so you can't use them as an example.

"Honestly, Harlow, the last few days were horrible for me. I was so wrapped up in finding out what was going on, so I can protect you, that I thought it was better to keep my distance. But I didn't think me distancing myself from you was going to be a big deal for you."

"Why would you think that? I was miserable the last few days."

"Well, I thought, since you still had Banks and Oliver, you wouldn't be alone, and you wouldn't miss me much."

"Sullivan, that's not how this works. I need you; I need all three of you, and I love you. When you are not here, I don't feel complete, it's like a part of me is missing. Promise me you won't do this again."

"I promise you, I won't do anything like this again, and I will never be tired of you."

"Good," I say, leaning down and kissing the top of his head. "'Cause I will never be tired of you either. Now can you please tell me what Tiffany said that has you so worried about me?"

"I will, I swear, but first, I need you to do something for me," he says, lifting his head to look up at me.

"Anything," I say without thinking.

A wicked grin spreads across his face. "I was hoping you'd say that. God, I missed you so much." With his hands moving up my body, sparking a fire of pleasure, he presses his lips to mine. The kiss consumes me, and I claw at his shirt like a ravenous animal.

In seconds, he has me in his arms, flipping us around, so he is sitting on the couch, and I'm on his lap, straddling him. I need him right here, right now.

"I want to take my time with you, but I can't. I need you now." He groans into my neck, and my heartbeat spikes, my insides turning to liquid.

"Same. I need you just as badly," I mumble as we take each other's clothes off before finally coming together. Sinking down onto his cock, I revel in the way it spreads me, the girth of his cock filling me as my channel swallows every inch of him.

I'm mesmerized by the pleasure, consumed with a fiery need. Sinking my nails into his flesh, I watch as his head tips back against the couch, his fingers grab onto my hips with bruising force, and strangely that's what I want. I want Sullivan to leave his mark on me.

The bite of pain leaves me greedy with need, and I start to rise, only to slam back down. I keep my pace slow, enjoying the way the head of his cock brushes against the tender tissue at the top of my pussy. With every slide down his length, I can hear our combined juices coming together, coating both of us.

"So, fucking beautiful, so fucking mine." Sullivan's words hold me hostage and encourage me all at once. Bouncing up and down on his length, I swivel my hips, and we both sigh at the ripples of pleasure that zing through us. Our bodies are like livewires, the energy between us teetering near explosive.

Sullivan must feel the heat, the pleasure rising, because with a feverish need, he threads his fingers into my hair and pulls, forcing my lips to his. He nibbles on my bottom lip, all while jackhammering upward, thrusting into me so hard that if it weren't for his grip on me in that moment, I would be off his lap.

My core clenches, pulses, and I know I'm nearing the edge of the cliff, slowly inching closer with each thrust.

"I'm close," I pant, bucking my hips, needing more, always more. I'm sure Banks and Oliver can hear us now, our sounds spilling over into other parts of the house, but I don't care, and I don't think they do either.

"Yes, come on my cock, squeeze me, let me feel you when you fall apart." He growls against my lips, and my eyes flutter closed, but only for a moment as he tugs at my hair, forcing me to open my eyes again.

"I want to see you when you come, see the heat in your cheeks, the color of your eyes. I want to see what I do to you..."

"Shit," I'm fumbling, swiveling my hips feverishly, searching for that spot, that one single... when I feel his thumb press against my swollen clit, it's all I need to push me over the edge. My eyes widen, and my mouth forms that perfect O you always hear about. Sullivan watches me intently like a man on a mission.

Like a kite in the sky, I soar into the air, riding the waves of pleasure, floating away without a care in the world. My orgasm causes a chain reaction, and as I start to come, so does Sullivan, his cock slamming into me ferociously, until I'm positive I'll still be feeling him tomorrow. His eyes remain on mine, though, unfocused, and I bare down, squeezing his length, ensuring that he's lodged deep inside of me.

A second later, sticky warmth coats my insides, and I shiver as I slowly come down from the high of my orgasm.

"I'm sorry," Sullivan shudders beneath me.

"Don't be. I love you, and it's in the past now." I nuzzle into his chest as he wraps his arms around me. With him and his brothers, I feel invincible like I can do anything, but without them, I feel broken. Like I'll never amount to anything. I know I shouldn't rely on them as my sole reason for happiness, but they're the one and only choice I've ever been able to make.

"It isn't fully in the past. There are still things we need to talk about, but none of that matters right now. The only thing I care about is getting you upstairs so we can do this all over again."

Pulling away just enough to look at him, I smirk, "Ready again so soon?"

That grin, it's the same one he's always given me, the one that makes my knees weak, and my heart do somersaults in my chest.

"When it comes to you, Harlow, I am willing and ready for anything... anytime."

And if those aren't the truest words I've ever heard, I don't know what is. There isn't anything the brothers won't do for me, and there isn't anything I won't do for them, and if we want to make it through this, if we want our happily ever after, we're going to have to continue down this path.

We're going to always have to be each other's support system.

40

The next morning, we all take a seat at the kitchen table. After Sullivan and I caught up on a week of missed sex, we were too exhausted to talk about the whole Tiffany thing, but we can't put this off any longer.

"Start from the beginning," Oliver orders, looking at Sullivan.

"Like I already said, it started with me going to Tiffany just to tell her to leave Harlow alone. When I did, she told me that I shouldn't be worrying about her when there were bigger things going on. Supposedly, there are these guys looking for Harlow. I asked her what the hell she was talking about, and she went on to tell me that there have been these rough-looking guys on campus asking around about Harlow."

"What kind of guys?" Banks asks.

"Well, that's what I've been trying to find out. Every time I talk to Tiffany, she only reveals a little bit. It's clear she was enjoying having me around, so she made sure she only gave me a smidge of information each time I saw her. She told me if I wanted any more information, I needed to be *nice* to her." Annoyance laces his words, and I can only imagine how hard this must have been for him. I hate Tiffany, hate her so much right now.

"I wasn't even sure if she was telling the truth or just playing games, but the more I listened to her and talked to others, her friends and a couple of guys around campus, the more I started to believe her."

"Fuck," Oliver says under his breath.

"According to Tiffany, these men were showing pictures of you and asking what classes you had, and where you were staying. I was so consumed with finding them that I even talked to campus security, but like I expected, they completely brushed me off. I'm pretty sure they think I'm some crazy, overprotective boyfriend now." Sullivan sighs, and all over again, I want to crawl into bed with him and forget about our crazy life. But I can't ignore this, no matter how much I want to. Someone is out there looking for me, and I don't know why.

"Do you think my dad sent them?"

Sullivan shakes his head, "I don't know why he would. I mean, he knows where you're staying, right?"

I nod, "Yeah, you're right... but who else would be looking for me, and why?"

"I don't know, but I think we should consider hiring some kind of security again. Just to make sure you are safe in the moments that we aren't with you." It's a shame Milton is in hiding.

Frowning, I say, "I had hoped that we were past this, but it seems like every time things start to get better, something has to happen. I just want to be happy."

"You can still be happy. We're all together in this, Harlow. Where you go, we go. If we have to hire a little more protection, then that's what we do. Like always, your safety is the most important thing to us." Oliver speaks this time, giving me a dazzling smile that melts my heart.

"I know, but when does this stop, when do we get to be normal people. I'm not anything special, and yet I've come closer to dying more than the average person."

Banks laughs, "Well, I can tell you right now you're pretty fucking special. As for why people are out to hurt you, no one really knows why people do the things they do. Shelby is just mental, and now that she's been put away, the biggest risk is gone. Now, we just have to figure out who these guys are and what they want?"

Oliver places a hand on my shoulder and gives it a gentle squeeze. "Everything is going to be okay. Nothing is going to happen to you. Not now, not ever."

Just as I'm starting to calm down, and feel a little better about the shit storm called my life, a knock sounds against the door. The brothers exchange a look before Oliver pushes away from the table. The loss of his touch leaves me cold, and for some unknown reason, this inky dread starts to tug at me. I'm not sure why, but it feels like something bad is about to happen.

Sullivan moves closer to me, and Banks watches Oliver as he walks slowly to the front door. The knocking grows louder, harder, more insistent. Whoever is on the other side of that door is growing more impatient by the second.

"Are you guys expecting someone?" I ask Sullivan, just as Oliver makes it to the door.

"No, which is why I don't have a good feeling about this." His words have barely left his mouth when I look up and see Oliver opening the door. All hell breaks loose then. Immediately the door is forced open, knocking Oliver back against the wall.

I stand up so fast, the chair I was sitting on falls back and crashes to the floor. My head is dizzy, and fear has a tight grip around my throat, making it hard to breathe. I want to go to Oliver, but that would only put me in danger.

Two large men dressed from head to toe in black enter the house. One of them closes the door behind him, while the other one pulls out a gun and aims it at Oliver's chest.

A gun. No, no, no.

One of the intruders starts yelling something, but somehow my brain can't decipher what he's saying. My hands start to shake, and my lips wobble. Maybe I'm in shock, or maybe it's the fear I have of watching someone I love being hurt or worse.

Banks grabs me and shoves me behind him and Sullivan, building a wall in front of me. Because they are so much taller than me, I can barely look past them and over their shoulders, but that doesn't mean I'm panicking any less. In fact, my panic has reached new heights, because now that I don't have a clear view of what's happening, I don't know if Oliver is okay, or if one of these men are coming for Banks or Sullivan.

"Everybody, calm down," a gruff voice orders. "You do what we say, and no one needs to get hurt. You do the opposite, and well, I'm sure you know what's going to happen." A coldness sweeps through me, and I do my best to continue breathing, tiny little black spots form over my vision, the bubbling panic residing inside me is only getting worse.

"What the hell do you want?" Banks speaks, his tone defensive.

"Right now, I want everybody to slowly grab a chair and sit down with your back against that wall over there." Peeking around Banks, I can see that the man is pointing to a spot in the dining room. "We're going to have a nice little chat."

I try to step around Banks and Sullivan, but they don't let me pass. They're like an immovable mountain. Instead, they push me back against the wall, keeping me shielded from the man making demands.

"Just relax and take a seat," a second voice orders, and only then does Banks pull up a chair and motion for me to sit down. Oliver comes up on the other side with two more chairs, a menacing look in his eyes. A moment later, all four of us are lined up against the wall.

The two men each grab their own chairs and sit down in front of us, with their guns in their hand, but they're not pointed at us, not right now, at least. My eyes stay trained to the weapons. I know it wouldn't take much to raise a hand and shoot one of us. *All of us.* Just the thought of it has my heart beating against my ribcage with the force of a sledgehammer.

Now that I have a better view of the men, I allow myself to take a good look at them when they're facing away. Both of them are tall and muscled like brick walls.

Something tells me they probably don't need those guns to inflict major damage on their enemy. One of them has a huge scar across his face, making him look like some kind of ancient gladiator. The other one has tattoos all over his hands, neck, and even some on the side of his face. At a glance, I can tell you that I would turn and walk the other way if these guys approached me at any time.

My breathing is ragged, and even I can tell I'm close to passing out.

"You need to calm down, or you're going to hyperventilate," one of the men barks. I can feel his dark gaze on me, and that only makes matters worse.

"What do you want?" Oliver grits out, diverting the attention away from me.

"We've been made aware that you four have been making threats against our boss, and we do not take threats of any kind lightly."

"There must be a mistake, we don't even know who your boss is, so how the hell could we possibly be making threats to him," Sullivan interjects, and I want to tell him his condescending tone isn't going to help us, but I can't even get my lips to move.

"No?" The guy with a million tattoos cocks his head to the side. "Your little girlfriend here should know. Or are you denying having a video of your father and Xander Rossi doing *business*?"

Business? The way he says it. In an instant, everything comes crashing into me. Just when I thought I couldn't get any more scared, the name Xander Rossi is mentioned. *Shit*. That is who sent these men. That is who is looking for me.

Somehow finding my voice, I say, "I- I wasn't threatening him. I just wanted my father to leave me alone."

Scar face smiles, and maybe it's meant as an actual smile, I don't know. But it's menacing like if a lion showed you its teeth right before ripping you to pieces.

"We don't really give a fuck what your motives were. Fact is, you have something you shouldn't have, and we are here to collect it."

"That's all you want? The video?" I force the breathless words out.

"Yup, that's all, sweet cheeks," tattoo guy winks, and I hear Oliver grunt next to me, making the two men chuckle.

"You can have it," I tell him, "it's on my laptop in my room." I point up the stairs. "And there is a copy on a thumb drive on my desk too."

"There is a copy in my dresser as well, bottom drawer on the right," Oliver admits.

Scar face nods toward his friend, who gets up and heads up the stairs.

"You sure it's not anywhere else? Some place online, maybe? On one of your computers?" His gaze sweeps over Sullivan and Banks.

"No, that's all we've got," Banks snarls, and I can see from the way he's sitting with his back ramrod straight, his muscles straining, and his fists clenched tightly that he's barely dealing with these guys without losing his shit.

"Look, we won't release it," I assure him, surprised at how strong my voice sounds. "We really weren't going to use it to hurt your boss. I just wanted something against my father, that's all. I can see now that we made a mistake. We don't want any trouble, we told you where it is, and we'll even help you destroy all of the files."

The guy in front of us nods and strokes his chin as if he's thinking about something intently. A moment later, tattoo guy returns, holding three laptops in his arms.

"That's all I could find," he tells his friend.

"And the thumb drive?" Scar face pins me with a look.

"It was on my desk, and I haven't touched it since I put it there." Terror starts to take root again. It has to be on the desk, that's the last place I put it. The thought of it not being there, oh, god. I can't think about that...

He turns back to his partner, who gives him a head shake.

"Okay, let's go for a walk, blondie. You can find the drive for me, and we can get the hell out of here."

"No, you can't take her..." Banks shoves from his chair but is immediately pushed back down when scar face crosses the space and presses the barrel of his gun into his chest. A gasp catches in my throat. Time seems to stand still. My entire body starts to shake, and I already know the image before me is one I'll never be able to forget.

Leaning into Banks' face, the crazed man whispers, "I didn't ask what you want. I *said* I'm taking her with me upstairs to find the drive. As long as I find it, no one gets hurt. I'll return her back to you without a single hair out of place." He gestures to the other guy to come over by us. "You just sit tight and don't make any more stupid choices, and she'll be just fine."

Banks doesn't say anything, thankfully. I'm not sure that I would be able to protect him, to save him if he did something stupid right now.

When scar face moves the gun away and points it back down at the floor, I finally start breathing again. Sucking in a ragged breath, I push from the chair and slowly come to stand. My legs wobble, and Oliver wraps an arm around my hip to steady me. I don't dare look at him. The thought of something happening to them because of me… I would never forgive myself.

On shaky legs, I walk out of the kitchen without looking back. I don't have to turn around to know the man is walking behind me. In that moment, all I can hear is my thundering heartbeat and the sound of his heavy footsteps against the wooden floor.

Grabbing onto the railing to steady myself, I climb the stairs, but the crushing fear makes my head spin, and I have to stop once I reach the top step. A wave of dizziness overcomes me, threatening to pull me under and into the maddening darkness.

All at once, I'm swaying like a tree branch caught in a storm. I can feel the railing in my clammy grip. Blinking away the dizziness, I try and steady myself, but my legs are still wobbling, my knees knocking together. When the guy behind me places a gentle hand on my shoulder to steady me, I almost let out a scream. If I didn't think I might tumble down the stairs right this second, I would shove him away.

"Just take it slow and find me that drive. No need to get yourself all worked up, sweetheart. I'm not going to hurt you unless I absolutely have to."

"What about the guys? Are they safe? Are you going to hurt them?"

"Only if they do something stupid. Now isn't the time to be a hero. As long as they follow directions, I promise nothing bad will happen."

I swallow down my fear and give him a tiny head nod. Taking the last step up, I start down the hall and into my room. My feet are heavy as I head straight for my desk. With trembling fingers, I open the top drawer searching frantically for the drive. Pens, pencils, sticky notes, everything inside that drawer goes flying.

Every second I can't find it feels like an eternity. Fear rapidly mounts, and for a moment, I wonder if maybe it's lost.

What happens if I don't find it? No. I can't think like that. I'll find it. No matter what. When my fingers scrape against the back of the drawer, I start to think of another place I might have put it... but as I move across the back, and to the other side, my fingers graze against something metal and tiny.

Sweet baby Jesus.

Wrapping my fingers around the small device, I almost sag to the floor in relief. "Here it is. That's it," I'm basically panting as I hand it to him.

He smiles, and it leaves me feeling cold rather than warm. "There you go. See, that wasn't so hard, was it? Let's go back downstairs. You walk ahead of me," he orders and points his gun toward the door. I'm only feeling a little better as I walk out of the room, down the hall, and then the stairs. When we enter the kitchen again, I find all three brothers staring at me. One gaze more intense than the next, and I force the tiniest smile because right now, that's the only way I can let them know that I'm okay.

"Got it," scar face tells tattoo guy, a satisfying grin appearing on his lips.

"Great. Well, thanks for having us over at such a late hour," the man snickers. "I hope it goes without saying that we were never here, the video never existed, and you forget the name Xander Rossi for good. I don't have to tell you what happens if you don't, right?"

"We'll be happy to forget this whole thing," I say quickly, wanting this moment to end.

"Perfect. You mind seeing us out, lover boy?" he asks, looking to Oliver. The way he's looking at him gives me the creeps and makes me feel like something bad is going to happen. Everything inside me tells me not to let Oliver go with him, but as Oliver gets up from his chair, I find that I'm stuck in place, my feet sinking into the wooden floor like it's quicksand.

With Oliver leading the way, I watch as the three men walk to the door, the dreadful feeling that something bad is about to happen only expands with each step they take.

Just before Oliver reaches the door, scar face steps in his way, and without saying a single word, he pulls his fist back and punches Oliver in his stomach, the force of the blow causes him to stumble backward.

"What the fuck?" He wheezes out, doubling over, pain etching deep into his features. He wraps an arm around his stomach just as the second guy delivers another hit, this one onto the back of his head. Oliver slumps forward, landing on the floor in a heap.

My heart sinks into my stomach. I have to do something. Looking to Banks and Sullivan for some type of guidance they both wince, and give me a head shake. I can see they want to do something, but the risk of me getting hurt outweighs what Oliver is going through to them. I don't care, though, not with Oliver on the floor.

"Stop!" I scream, and jump up from the chair, my body floods with adrenaline, letting me move at speeds I didn't know were possible. I'm across the room in seconds, but the guys are right behind me, grabbing me by the arms, and hauling me backward before I can tend to Oliver.

Scar face swings around then, pointing his gun at us. He shakes his head as if I've somehow disappointed him by not staying in my seat.

"Stop, you promised you wouldn't hurt them!" I yell, my vision blurring from the onslaught of tears. I struggle against Banks and Sullivan, but there's no point. Their hands are like heavy iron shackles around my limbs.

"I promised nothing bad was going to happen. This isn't that bad... not considering what we could have done to you for threatening the Rossi family."

More tears slip down my cheeks, my chest rising and falling rapidly as I watch them land another kick to Oliver's stomach.

"Okay, okay, you made your point. Please, just... just leave," I barely get the words out as I speak between sobs. "I swear, it will never happen again."

Scar face lifts his hand, and his partner stops mid-kick. "Next time, it won't be a little ass-kicking. Next time you'll pay in blood."

"We understand," I pant. All I want them to do is leave so I can take care of Oliver. Staring at his unconscious body, all I can think is how this is my fault, if I hadn't threatened my father then maybe none of this would have happened. This is my fault, all mine.

"Excellent," scar face smiles, and gestures for the other guy to come over by him. "It was a pleasure doing business with you. Have a good rest of your night."

Together the two men leave as if they were never here. As soon as the door closes behind them, Sullivan and Banks release me.

"I'll lock the door," Sullivan tells Banks, "make sure he's okay."

The guys bustle around me, but I'm too consumed with a need to get to Oliver that I don't even pay attention to what they're doing. Scurrying across the floor, I drop down to my knees near Oliver's head. A whimpered sob escapes my lips when I see his face. He looks as if he's sleeping, no pain on his features, but I know once he wakes up, he is going to be in a world of hurt. I just hope he is going to be okay... he has to be.

Holding his head in my lap, I run my hand over his forehead before spearing my fingers through his hair. I find a bump right away, and do my best not to press against it.

"He's got a pretty good bump on his head," I tell Banks, who is kneeling on the floor beside me. He's got Oliver's shirt pushed up, and I try my best not to flinch when I see that his ribs are already swelling, taking on a deep red, bluish color.

"He's got some bruising, but he'll be okay. He'll be in a lot of pain, but he'll live," Sullivan tells both Banks and me, and even though, I know he'll be okay, it doesn't make the fact that none of this would've happened had it not been for me, any easier to handle.

"This is my fault, all mine. I'm sorry…I'm so sorry, Oliver." I start to sob uncontrollably, my heart crumbling in my chest.

"Stop, Harlow. Don't blame yourself. None of this is your fault. Not every bad thing that happens is your fault." Banks tries his best to soothe me, his voice soft and kind, but I don't want to hear him tell me it's not my fault, not when I know deep down it is.

"This could've been much worse, so we're lucky that it ended like this, and not with you hurt, or one of us dead. People get their houses broken into all the time." Like always, the guys pretend that these bad things would've happened to them even if I wasn't part of their lives. This wasn't a random break-in. These people were here because of me. I'm a poison, destroying and infecting everything in my wake.

Holding Oliver's head in my trembling hands, I pray he wakes soon, and that I can find a way to make the Bishops' lives safe again.

Every time I need saving, they're there for me, rescuing me like white knights, but I don't want to be a princess that needs to be saved anymore.

I want to save myself and them.

41

"Would you stop, you're worse than a mother hen." Oliver slaps at my hands as I inspect his ribs for the fiftieth time today. The guilt of what happened a few days ago is still fresh. Like a newly stitched wound, it stings and burns.

"I'm sorry," I pout, "I just feel terrible about what happened, and you wince every time you walk. It makes me..."

"Stop," Oliver orders his voice strong, powerful, and way too loud for the library. "You've been beating yourself up for days over this, and it's not your fault." Leaning into my side, he twirls a strand of my hair around his finger. "I'm glad it was me. I would much rather feel this than ever see you bruised and in pain. If it were you that was hurt, you know damn well my brothers, and I would most likely be dead by now, trying to kill those fuckers."

I shiver involuntarily, the gruffness of his voice, the truth in his words. They light a flame of pleasure in my core. I still want to be the one to rescue myself, but there isn't any harm in letting a man cherish my body, my heart. Or letting three do so, all at once.

"I know, you've said that a few times now, but I still feel bad."

"Well, don't... in fact..." He presses a kiss to the sensitive spot right below my ear, and I already know what he's thinking. Mostly because I'm thinking it too. Tenderly he sucks on the flesh, and I find my fingers circling around the pencil a little tighter.

"I can't focus with you doing that..." My voice is breathless, my thoughts swirling, heading to a place that involves both of us naked, sweating, and not doing homework.

"That's the point, baby," he whispers into the shell of my ear, before scraping his teeth across the flesh that he just sucked on. The sensation is like fire and ice. Pain and pleasure.

My nipples harden against the fabric of my bra, and I drop my pencil. Oliver lets out a low chuckle, and together we shove everything into our backpacks. Before I can start walking toward the exit, he takes my hand in his and tugs me toward him.

Giving him a confused look, I let him guide me wherever it is he wants to take me. A short walk later, we're in what looks to be an upper part of the library. Old books surround us, and dust clings to the air like it's a second skin. Oliver pulls me over to a door that has a little sign on it that says DO NOT ENTER.

"What are we doing?" I whisper, afraid that we'll get caught being somewhere that we clearly shouldn't be.

"Fucking," Oliver grins at me over his shoulder, "that is if you want to." The way his teeth sink into his bottom lip, and the deepness of his voice as he speaks, it all acts as a firework to my already throbbing center.

Closing the door behind us, I don't wait to ask him any more questions. I want him, and I want him now. Like a hungry kitten, I pounce, gently shoving him against a nearby bookcase. He grins down at me, two beautiful dimples appearing on his face.

"You're so fucking beautiful and perfect, Harlow. I know you think that everything bad that happens is your fault, but you don't see the joy that you bring. You don't see how happy you make us; how much better our lives are because of you."

I gasp, because his words touch me, not in a sexual way, but in a way that makes the gnawing guilt a little more bearable.

"I don't deserve you," I whisper, pushing up on to my tiptoes. Slanting my lips against his, I kiss him with a hunger that rivals all others. And he gives it right back to me, biting at my bottom lip, and squeezing my hips in a way that makes me groan deeply into his mouth.

Our tongues collide, and in this moment, he's thunder, and I'm lightning. The perfect elements for a storm. Brushing my chest against his, I wonder if he can feel how hard my nipples are, how much they ache to be in his mouth?

Breaking the kiss, he nudges me backward until my ass hits the edge of a desk. I'm grinning like a fool, my hands slip under his shirt, and move over the perfectly sculpted muscles there. He's ripped, and all I can think about is kissing each and every little bruise, tending to his every want and need.

Before I can get that far though, he's on me, his hands tugging at my shirt, his mouth sucking at my flesh. All I can hear is our heavy pants and my own pulse in my ears. With my shirt off, he pushes my bra straps off my shoulders and removes each breast from its cup before taking a pebbled nipple into his mouth.

My fingers cut through his hair, and I hold his head in place as pleasure flickers deep inside my core.

"Don't stop, don't stop," I pant, wondering if he's going to get me off with nothing but his tongue on my nipple.

"Oh, don't worry, I won't," he smirks around my nipple, releasing it with a loud pop so he can pay the other side the same attention. I can feel how wet I am for him already and know it won't take much to make me come.

"Pants," he orders, reminding me that I've still got them on. While he peppers kisses against my chest, I undo the button on my jeans and slide them down my thighs, kicking them away once they reach my feet.

Oliver breaks away to undo his own bottoms, and within seconds we're both naked. Even in the dim lighting of the room, I can see that his cock is swollen and angry looking. There's a drop of pre-cum on the tip that I crave to lick away.

"My eyes are up here," he says, chuckling, and I can't help but smile.

His hands trail down my body until they reach my hips, once there they come to a stop, he squeezes my flesh before lifting me to place my ass at the edge of the table.

"I have to taste you right now." The urgency in his voice confirms his need, and with a gentle nudge, I'm on my back and lifting my hips for him to pull my panties off. Peeling the silky fabric down my legs, I can't help but grin as he tosses them to the floor and presses my knees to my chest. Leaning in, he gives me one long lick.

"Oh, god..." I mumble at the onslaught of sensations. My fingers grip on to the edge of the table as he does it all over again, spreading my lips with his fingers. That skilled tongue of his flicks against my swollen clit, and I gush like a waterfall, my legs shaking as he sucks the tiny bud into his mouth. Heat rises in my cheeks, and my entire body warms as lightning rods of pleasure zing up my spine.

"Come for me, come all over my tongue." Oliver's husky voice vibrates through my core, and within seconds I'm falling apart, my hips bucking against his face as he continues licking me, savoring every last drop of my release as if it's a fine wine.

Like a wave, I come crashing back down, my body a liquid mass against the table. Oliver moves from between my legs, coming to stand. There's a carnal look in his eyes, and in that moment, I'm ensnared, trapped in his web, a willing victim to the pleasure he'll bring me.

Through hooded eyes, I watch him stroke his cock. One stroke. Two strokes. My mouth waters. I want him. Need him.

"Please," I whisper, my eyes pleading.

He smirks, "Please, what? Say it. Ask me."

My cheeks flame, but I say it anyway because I'm no longer a shy, naive, virgin. I'm a woman who is loved by three different men. "Please, fuck me."

"Gladly," he growls, gripping on to one hip with a possessiveness that makes me warm inside. Bringing his cock to my wet entrance, he enters me in one thrust, and for one tiny second, all is right in the world. Nothing but us matters. Not what could happen tomorrow, not my father, not anything. There is just us and our joined bodies.

"Fuck me, you're so tight, and warm, and shit, I'm not going to last if you keep squeezing me like that."

All I can do is whimper as he thrusts in and out of me, expelling every last ounce of carnal need that he has. Reaching for him, I let my fingers roam over his perfectly sculpted abs and chest. We're both burning up, on the verge of combusting.

The telltale signs of an orgasm start to snake up my spine. My toes curl, and my chest rises and falls rapidly, and though air fills my lungs, it feels like I can't breathe. Like I'm free-falling out of the sky. It's coming faster than usual, and Oliver must know it because he too starts to thrust harder and faster, bringing me to the edge of the cliff in nothing more than a few strokes.

"I'm coming," I pant, my nails raking across his flesh.

"Yes, come for me. Squeeze me. Milk my cock." His filthy mouth only encourages me, and within seconds I'm shattering like glass that's been squeezed too tightly. My hips buck, and my eyes flutter closed as euphoric pleasure consumes me, wrapping me in a blanket of warmth.

As I'm coming down from my high, floating through the sky like a feather, Oliver starts to fall apart, his movements grow jerky, and I open my eyes to stare up at him, needing to see him come undone.

The brown of his eyes is darker now, and he bites on his bottom lip to stifle a groan. Damn is he sexy. I want to make him feel the same way he made me feel.

"Come inside me, please..." I lick my lips and wait with bated breath for him to fill me with his come.

"Fucking Christ, Harlow," he curses, squeezing my hips with both hands. His hips piston, and all I can feel is him impaling me, breaking me apart to piece me back together again. And I love it. I love him. Three thrusts later and with a groan, I'm pretty sure the entire library heard, he starts to come, his cock pulsing deep inside of me, filling me with his sticky release.

Completely spent and satisfied, he sags against me, his sweaty forehead pressing against mine. Holding him close, I smile, feeling as if I'm on top of the world. I can feel the heat of his release dripping out of me and on to my thighs, his cock still inside of me, still partially hard.

"That was amazing," Oliver pants, "are you okay?" Always so sincere, so caring. That's Oliver, though. He always makes sure that I'm okay. That I came.

"Yes. I'm more than okay," I smile.

"Good, because it's been a while since I came apart that easily," the blistering smile he gives me warms me from the inside out. After a few minutes of lying together, we get up, and he helps me put my clothes back on, minus my panties. He puts those in his pocket as a souvenir.

As I'm sliding my backpack on, he pulls out his phone.

"Shit," he mumbles under his breath. "We're going to be late."

"Ugh, not again," I groan, all while smiling. After what we did, I would say showing up late to class was worth it.

"I won't have time to walk you in to your class if I want to get to my class without being scolded by the professor. So, I'll walk you to the building and then head across the street."

"Okay," I grab onto his hand, and together we walk back down the stairs and into the lower part of the library. As we pass by people, it feels like they are all staring at us, almost like they know what we were doing. Maybe they heard us? But since none of them snicker or smile as we pass, they must not have heard us. I tell myself it's all in my head.

Exiting the library, we hurry across campus and to class. When we reach the sidewalk, we part ways, Oliver pressing a hurried kiss to my lips before seeing me off. As I walk down the sidewalk and enter the building, I give him a little wave and smile before disappearing from view.

When I'm in the building, I realize how late I really am, and instead of walking up the stairs, I basically run, taking two steps at a time.

By the time I reach the top, I have a hard time breathing. *Shit,* I didn't realize how out of shape I am. Maybe I need to start working out.

Taking a few steps, slower this time, I try to regulate my breathing, but it seems to only get worse. This weird feeling that something is wrong overcomes me. I'm not sure what I'm feeling. Not sure what's going on, so I continue onward, hoping that it'll pass. I'm about halfway down the hall when a wave of dizziness crashes into me. It comes out of nowhere and nearly takes me out at the knees. Closing my eyes, I lean against the cold brick wall.

Maybe I just need to do some deep breathing. Forcing air into my lungs, I try and focus on nothing more than my breaths. Sweat beads above my brow, the breathing obviously not helping as my entire body suddenly starts to feel like it's been lit on fire.

Knots of worry tighten in my gut. I don't know what's going on with my body anymore. Another wave of dizziness sends my mind spiraling. I can't even open my eyes without the world spinning around me, and the panic I feel seems to only make it worse.

All at once, my vision goes black, my eyes grow heavier and heavier until I close them again. My mind slowly slipping into unconsciousness. I try to open my eyes again, but I can't. They just won't budge. Faintly, I'm aware of footsteps approaching, and someone asking me if I'm okay. I want to tell them no, that I'm not, but my tongue won't work. All words refuse to be coaxed from my mouth.

Another wave of dizziness overcomes me, and this time when it crashes down, it brings with it the power to snap me in two. Reaching out, I attempt to find something along the wall to support my body. I know I'm going to go down, I can feel it in my gut.

A hand brushes against my arm just as my knees give out and my body folds in half. I'm only partially aware of my body sagging to the floor, my knees slamming against the tile. I don't even feel the impact, there is no pain.

There is nothing but darkness.

42

*D*amnit. I have to stop waking up like this. I know before I even open my eyes where I am. The steady beat of the heart monitor fills my ears, and the smell of antiseptic and bleach tickles my nostrils. *The hospital.* I've put myself in the hospital again. Blinking my eyes open, I'm momentarily blinded by the overhead lights.

My thoughts are fuzzy as I try and recollect what happened.

"Oh, my gosh, she's awake." My mother's voice is the first that I hear, and already I know this is going to be bad. *Why are they here? And where are the guys?*

Nothing serious happened... I just fainted.

"Back up, sweetheart, give her some space." My father orders, and I look up at him, taking note of the dark bags under his eyes and worry in their depths. He looks distraught, but that can't be right. Why should he care about me? He hasn't any other time before now.

"What are you doing here?" I question, squinting my eyes because the light is still blinding me.

My father crosses his arms over his chest, his gaze hardening with each second. "I expected better from you, Harlow. I didn't think you would be this irresponsible, but after everything, I suppose I'm not really surprised."

Whoa, all I did was faint. Maybe I need to take better care of myself. Be less stressed, eat more... I don't know. What I do know is that it's not anything as bad as he's making it out to be.

"Please leave, the hospital was wrong to have called you." I murmur, shaking my head with disappointment. I don't want them here. Neither of them. I'll call one of the Bishops to come and be with me. As I shift against the scratchy sheets, a throbbing starts to pulse behind my eyes. A migraine is forming there, and having my parents here is only making it worse.

"Excuse me, but I am your father even if you don't want me to be, and I have every right as the person who pays for your medical insurance to know what is going on."

I can't help it; my eyes roll to the back of my head on instinct. "Just because you pay my medical bills doesn't mean you're my father. You have to actually act like one to be considered one, and in my eyes, you aren't one, at least to me. Besides, I didn't ask you to pay for anything. Leave the bill and leave me."

A vein bulges in his neck, his cheeks fill with blood, and he starts to look like a red balloon more and more.

"Your mother and I are the only ones here. I don't see your precious Bishop brothers standing next to your bed, checking up on you. Like always, they've done wrong and left the mess for someone else to clean up."

"What are you talking about? There is no mess. I'm fine. I just need to take a little better care of myself. This has nothing to do with them, and the only reason they are not here right now is because they don't know I'm here." My defenses are up. Like always, my father finds a way to make me feel small and insignificant.

A smile like I've never seen before appears on his lips. It's not a kind smile, nor is it really a vicious one. It's more of a, I know something you don't smile, and that leaves my stomach churning, twisting, and knotting.

"Oh, this has everything to do with them. Everything." The way he speaks, with so much disdain, so much vile hate toward the Bishops makes me want to hurt him. How dare he speak about them in such an ill manner. How dare he come here and act like he cares.

"I want you to leave, now," I growl, fisting the sheets to stop myself from getting up and slugging him. He might be my father in the sense of his name being on my birth certificate, but he might as well be a dead-beat. I don't want or need him in my life. All the lies, the secrets, the way he tried to manipulate me. I'll never forget or forgive him for that.

"And I want you to get an abortion."

The room spins around me, my mouth pops open and stays that way as I flounder like a fish out of water. He can't mean... No, it's not possible. How? I'm on birth control. He's lying. He has to be.

"What... what are you talking about?" I ask, finally finding the courage to speak. My voice wavers between barely restrained panic and fear.

"Do you even know which one of them is the father? Wait, don't answer that. It doesn't matter who the father is. You'll be getting an abortion either way."

"I'm pregnant?" I say the words out loud as if I didn't already put the pieces together. Of course, I'm pregnant. How did I not see this before?

"Not for much longer," my father chides, looking down at me like I'm a disappointment to the world. Well, likewise, dearest dad.

"It's a good thing you don't have a say in it, isn't it? Now leave. I never asked for you to be here, and I won't let you dictate any more of my life!" I yell, gathering up every ounce of strength I have to sit up a little taller. Maybe he could push me around before, make me be his little puppet, but not anymore.

I'm about to yell, to tell them to get the hell out again when someone knocks on the door, interrupting my little outburst.

"Come in," my mother answers before I can make a sound. I watch the door as the unknown person pushes it open. Every fiber in my body hoping and praying that one of the guys is on the other side of that door. But when the door swings open all the way, all I'm left with is more disappointment.

Even though it's someone I know, it's not one of the Bishops like I had hoped it would be. My stomach drops, and I feel like I might throw up as I watch Matt leisurely walk into the room. His gaze sweeps over the room before coming to rest on me. He doesn't even look like he cares. All over again, I'm reminded of how I'm nothing but a pawn to my father.

"Matt, thank you so much for coming," my father greets him, making it sound more like a business arrangement.

"No problem. How are you feeling, Harlow?" he asks, coming to stand beside the bed.

"Terrible, and you being here doesn't help," I snap at him. Not caring how rude I must sound. The last thing I want is to be surrounded by these people that don't care if I'm happy or not, people that only want me to play a part in their shitty story.

"Ouch," Matt smirks. He's clearly not offended by my words.

"Be nice," my mother scolds, and I barely restrain the growl as my lip curls with anger. "We're going to give you two a moment. Don't mess this up, Harlow. This might be your last chance to save yourself from complete destruction. Make the right choice, so that we don't have to make it for you."

My last chance? What the hell is that supposed to mean?

My parents leave the room, and Matt grabs a chair dragging it over to the bed. It scratches against the floor loudly, but he doesn't seem to care. He takes a seat, the chair creaking under his weight. He's only a foot away from me now, and I shiver at the thought of him being this close, especially after the way he treated me the last time I saw him.

Giving me a boyish grin, he says, "So, I heard you got knocked up by one of those Bishop brothers."

"I don't see how this is your business."

Matt shrugs, "Your dad wants you to get rid of the baby, but I've got a better idea. A way that will allow you to keep it. Since the beginning, I've told you I was here to help."

I'd laugh if I didn't already have a headache the size of Texas, and it didn't hurt to move. "Ha, doubtful. You've never wanted to help me. You're a disgusting, selfish prick, and I want you to leave and never come back."

What I have to say doesn't matter to him. I know this. I've known it all along. Maybe I had hoped he would be different, that he would become a friend to me. That turned out to be nothing but a lie too.

Crossing his arms over his chest, he stares me down, his gaze hardening. "I'm being very generous to you and your family, Harlow. I'm still willing to marry you. I don't mind that you're having a baby, in fact, it's one less thing I have to do." He winks at me, and I gag, the thought... it makes me want to barf all over the floor.

"No one has to know who the real father is. I'm willing to raise it as my own, give it, and you a home, a life. I'll protect you, ensure that you're happy and healthy."

I can't believe him. Does he even hear himself?

"You're a lunatic if you think I'm going to go along with this. I'll never marry you. With or without this baby. It's not happening," I snarl. I have this impulse to scratch his eyes out, to do whatever I can to get him out of this room and away from me. I don't need him or my parents. I can do this all on my own.

Matt chuckles a humorless laugh, "You are the crazy one. If you don't do this, your father will make you get an abortion. He's not going to let you have this baby any other way." He pauses, and I'm hoping he'll shut the hell up and get out, but he doesn't. Instead, he opens his mouth again. "Do you know what kind of embarrassment this would be to him? A baby with his sworn enemy's son? Hell, you don't even know who the father is."

"I don't care. I don't care what any of you think or say..." I whisper, all the emotions inside of me swirling together.

He unfolds his arms and runs a hand through his hair, before exhaling a deep breath, "Look, he's not going to let you leave this hospital with that baby inside of you. Not unless you agree to marry me. The abortion will happen today, you have no say."

"He can't do that! He wouldn't..." I argue, but even as the words leave my mouth, I know the truth is, he would. He is probably paying this hospital half a fortune to do this without my consent, or maybe he is just threatening them with whatever sick thing he can come up with. The lump in my throat thickens as I weigh my options. It feels like all hope is lost.

"I'm just trying to help," Matt tells me, and anger overwrites my fear momentarily.

"Like you were trying to *help* me the last time I saw you. When you threatened me?"

He shrugs like it's no big deal at all, but his eyes hold his emotions inside. Like a glass house, Matt is the type of person that will crack, snap, shatter if you hit him enough times.

"I admit, I was drunk and out of line. I'll try not to let it happen again."

"You'll try?" I snort. "Well, at least you are honest."

"I try to be, but that doesn't mean I don't make mistakes. In all seriousness, you don't know what your father is willing to do. You don't know the lengths he'll go to get what he wants. I'm your best choice right now. Actually, I'm your only choice." Only then does the reality of this all hit me. I'm pregnant. I'm carrying a child inside me, and my father wants to kill it. Fear settles deep inside my bones, and I know I need to do everything I can to save the life inside of me, but marrying Matt can't be the answer.

"You might be the lesser of two evils, but that doesn't mean I will just marry you," I whisper. "I'm in love with someone else." A coldness fills the room, and dread clings to my bones. "If you really wanted to help me, you would give me your phone and let me make a call. You would help me get out of here."

Matt blows out a frustrated breath, "And how would that benefit me? Didn't you listen to anything I've said to you? Going against your father never ends well, that doesn't exclude me. If I go against him, if I try and save you, he'll retaliate, and I can't afford that. He would—"

A knock on the door interrupts Matt mid-sentence, and we both turn toward it.

"We need a few more minutes," I yell before the door can open.

"Okay, take your time," my father's muffled voice filters through the door, and even from here, I can hear the triumphant tone in his voice. He already assumes that he's won. He thinks I'm agreeing to Matt's proposal. The joke's on him though. I'll die before I do a single thing, he wants me to.

Instead, I know I'm going to have to convince Matt in whatever way I can.

"Matt, please help me. Really *help* me. Don't let him do this. Don't let them kill my baby, please..." I don't care that I'm begging or how desperate I might sound. I'll get on my knees if that's what gets him to help me.

For the first time, I see real empathy reflecting back at me. He gets up from the chair and steps really close, taking my hand into his.

"I won't let him kill the baby, okay." He lowers his voice and leans into me. "I'll tell him that I want you pregnant, but you have to agree to marry me now, even if it's only to buy yourself time. I won't be able to help you contact your boyfriends, and if they don't show up on their own, then you might have to marry me, after all. I can't go against your father."

"Okay, thank you..." I can't believe what I'm about to say next, but like he said, right now, he is my best bet. "Will you stay here with me. I don't want to be alone with my parents."

He nods and sits back down, just as someone knocks on the door once more.

"You can come in now," I call out, and the door opens. My parents walk in, my father has a smug grin on his face, and it takes everything inside of me to bite my tongue.

"Did you two come to an agreement?" he asks even though I know for a fact that he already knows.

"I'll marry Matt," I grit out. That sinister grin on my father's face only grows.

"And I'm okay with her having the baby," Matt announces. "No one needs to know that I'm not the father."

"Great," my mom cheers and claps her hands together. "I'm so excited. The wedding is back on then."

I force a smile and nod slightly, hoping with all my heart that the guys find me before it's too late because if they don't... I don't even want to think of the mess that will come when all the pieces fall.

43

My parents left after our talk yesterday, and even though I felt fine after they pumped some fluids in me, the doc insisted on keeping me overnight for observation. Matt ended up staying with me in the hospital the whole night, sleeping on a pull out chair the nurse brought in. Part of me is glad that he is here, and I'm not alone with my father's goons who are posted outside my door. But there is another part of me that has a hard time trusting Matt, considering the way he's treated me in the past.

I'm trying to hold on to the fact that he has never lied to me... at least, not that I know of. Assuming he is telling me the truth, he won't let anything happen to the baby and me, and right now, that is the most important thing. As much as I love the Bishop brothers, I already love the life growing inside of me just as fiercely, maybe even more.

After breakfast, one of the nurses comes in to take my tray. Smiling at me sweetly, she asks, "Is there anything else you need this morning?"

"Actually, I could use a little help going to the bathroom. The IV makes it hard to get around," I say, glancing over at Matt, who frowns at me. I'm sure he knows what I'm up to, but to my relief, he doesn't say anything when the nurse helps me out of bed and into the bathroom. As soon as she closes the door behind us, I turn around and look at her.

"Please, I need your help," I whisper. "I'm here against my will. I need to make a phone call. Can I please use your cell phone?"

I see the brief shock in her eyes before she lowers her gaze to the ground. "I'm sorry. I can't help you." Her apology sounds genuine, and I know my father must have threatened the staff here. "I am sorry. Really."

"It's okay, I know you are," I say in defeat.

"Do you need help to use the bathroom?"

"No, not really..." As soon as I say the words, she scurries out of the room, whispering another *sorry* on her way out.

I use the toilet on my own before brushing my teeth and washing my face. Every move I make is on autopilot, my mind too busy being worried and scared about what's to come.

When I get back into the room, Matt is still sitting in the chair, only now he's reclined it and his feet are propped up.

"I'm guessing she didn't go for it?"

"My father must have really freaked her out. She couldn't get away fast enough after I asked to use her phone."

"You don't give up easily, I'll give you that. You think after three times, you would stop trying," Matt says, tucking a blanket over himself. "I'm taking a nap; I hardly got any sleep last night with you snoring so loudly."

"I do not snore!"

"Whatever you have to tell yourself, princess," Matt chuckles, closing his eyes.

I crawl back into my bed, careful not to tug on the needle still sticking inside my arm. Turning on the TV, I flip through the channels, landing on some cooking show. I don't really care about it, but I need something to take my mind off the reality I am in.

After twenty minutes, Matt starts to snore softly, letting me know he is asleep. I keep glancing at the door, wondering if my father's guards are still there or if they left. After five minutes of inner dialogue, I talk myself into trying to leave.

Carefully, I remove the tape around the IV in my arm before pulling out the needle slowly. Blood starts to puddle on my skin, and I quickly take my bed sheet and press it onto the spot until it stops bleeding.

Trying to not make any noise, I slowly slide out of my bed and tiptoe toward the door on sock covered feet. I'm in my own clothes, which my mother brought me last night, but I don't have any shoes. I don't have to get far, anyway, only far enough to find someone who isn't on my father's payroll or has been threatened by him.

I'm almost at the door, my hand already reaching for the doorknob when I freeze. Holding my breath, I listen to a man's voice right outside my door. A voice I know all too well.

My father. Shit.

His voice is coming closer, and I hurry back into bed with my heart pounding in my chest. I barely manage to hop back in and pull the blanket over my arm, before the door opens and my father walks in without knocking.

"Harlow," he greets me mechanically, and I sit up straight in bed. Matt startles awake at my father's entrance, seeming just as surprised as I am to see him here.

"What do you want from me now?"

"I actually came to talk to Matt," he scowls at me. "However, I would appreciate it if you could stop harassing your nurses to use their phones."

God, I want to throw something at him. Preferable something heavy.

"Matt, a word outside."

"Sure," Matt answers, getting up from his chair, he gives me a look that says *behave* on his way out.

You behave yourself. I yell after him in my head. The door closes, leaving me all alone in the room. I throw the blanket back, jump up and tiptoe back to the door, pressing my ear to the wood so I can hear better.

"Telling her you wanted the baby was stupid, Matt," My father growls. "I don't want her to have that child. If she wants a baby so badly, you're gonna have to do it, I can't watch a child of *theirs* grow up under my nose," my father spits. "We are going through with the abortion. I don't care what she wants. If she didn't want this to happen, then maybe she should've kept her legs closed."

Fear trickles down my spine. *No! He can't!* There is no way I'll let him do this, and if he does, then I'll never forgive him.

Matt's voice cuts through, "I'm worried about her, and I don't think it's a good idea to do this. Harlow and I are in a good place now. She's just started to warm up to me, and doing this would mess everything I've worked toward. You don't have to do this. I'll raise the baby as my own. No one has to know who the father is, and no one would dare question my family and me."

"I'll know, and that's all that matters! And I don't care about *feelings*. I care about my reputation, and what this will do to me, and so should you. It's already been decided. We're going through with this. End of story." My dad barks, and I stagger back.

The door opens a moment later, my father and Matt appearing in front of me with three nurses right behind them. Two females and one male. Shaking my head profusely, I watch Matt's face contort into a mixture of both sorrow and shame.

He can stop this. I know he can, so why isn't he?

"No, you can't do this!" I scream and take a few steps back, only to hit the wall. I'm trapped. There is no place to go. "Please," I beg, but no one listens. Their faces are blank like they're not even here mentally.

The male nurse grabs one of my arms so tightly, I know there will be bruises. Still, I struggle, trying my best to fight them off. I won't go down without a fight.

"Please don't do this," I look to my father who is staring at me with nothing more than disappointment in his eyes. He's supposed to be my father. He's supposed to care about me. How could he do this? To me? To his unborn grandchild, and all because of a last name?

"You brought this on yourself, Harlow," my father says, his voice clipped.

Tears sting my eyes, and I wince when the female nurse grabs on to my other arm, her fingers biting into my flesh with the same harshness.

It's then that I spot the syringe in the third nurse's hand. *No. No.* I shake my head, wishing that this was nothing but a bad dream.

Subdued against the wall, I watch helplessly as the needle pierces through my skin, pain followed by a cold tingling sensation spreads through my veins. "Stop!" I scream as loud as I can, my throat throbbing.

Even with the syringe empty and the fact that I've given up fighting, the nurses still hold on to me like I'm going to bolt for the door, then again, if they released me, I would do just that.

"Okay, that's enough. Let her go," Matt growls the look in his eyes is murderous, and immediately the hands on me disappear, but I can still feel them. Still, feel the pain. Still, feel the needle in my arm.

My body starts to sag toward the floor like goop, but Matt steps in and grabs me at the last minute. His arms come around my waist, supporting most of my weight, and I can't help but seek his comfort in that moment.

He's the only thing I have right now, the only person who cares if I live or die. And as badly as I want to hate him, in this moment, I can't bring myself to. We're both pawns in this war. Burying my face into his chest, I start to cry. Sobbing uncontrollably, I can feel the medication they gave me kicking in. My limbs are getting heavier, and my mind fuzzier by the second.

"You promised..." I whimper, clutching on to his shirt. A warmth courses through me, my cheeks heat, and my whole body starts to tingle. All the discomfort in my body starts to fade.

"I know," Matt whispers back. I've lost all hope now. I'm going to lose this baby; this tiny little human is going to be taken from me before I even get the chance to tell the guys about it. Leaning down, he nuzzles his face into my hair. "I need you to trust me, okay. I won't let this happen. I'll find a way to fix this."

Shaking my head, I try to speak, but my tongue feels heavy.

I want to tell him that I wish I could believe him. That I want to believe him and his words so badly, but I can't. I can't trust anyone. Still, a part of me hangs on to the hope that maybe, just maybe he won't let me down this time. But how? How can he help me? How can he stop this from happening? He said so himself, he won't go against my father. No one will. Not the hospital staff, not Matt, not the Bishops. I'm doomed. My child will die, and there is nothing I can do about it. Spots form over my vision, and no matter how much I try to hang on to that last shred of light, it slowly dims out, getting lighter and lighter.

My last thought before everything goes black is that I hope the guys will forgive me for this. Forgive me for failing to protect our child.

WHEN I WAKE UP, the same heaviness I felt earlier remains in my limbs, and the fuzziness engulfing my mind only increases. I feel like my brain has been run through a blender and has been poured back into my skull, but even with my head being in utter disarray, I remember what happened before I passed out.

The pain in my chest only gets more prominent, the emptiness expanding and leaving a hollow space behind.

I pry my eyes open, just to squeeze them shut again when I see my father standing at the end of the bed. I thought I hated him before, but the hatred I feel for him has grown into a colossal amount over the last few hours. I can't put into words how much I despise my father for doing this, how much I loathe him for taking this child from me... for killing the life inside of me.

I never considered myself a violent person before, but if I had the strength to do so now, I would kill him. If I never again see this man who called himself my father, I would be a happier person... that is if I can ever find happiness after what was done to me.

"I'll leave you to deal with this," my father's voice cuts through the fog surrounding my head like clouds surround the top of a mountain.

"Since you two seem to get along so great now," he continues, and for a moment, I don't understand who he is talking to.

"We *did* get along, but after what you did to her, she is never going to trust me again," Matt barks.

"Trust is overrated. There are other ways to keep people in line. More effective ways," my father declares. I can hear him turn, his expensive leather shoes making a squeaking sound against the hospital floor as he does. I listen to each of his steps as he is leaving the room. The door opening and closing, leaving me alone with the man who promised to keep my child and me safe.

I didn't realize how cold I was until a large warm hand comes down to rest on my icy cold fingers. Even though the warmth feels good on my frozen skin, I pull my hand away at once, not wanting to feel an ounce of relief and comfort. Because I don't deserve either one. I deserve to be cold, alone, and in pain after I failed… I failed everybody I loved.

"Harlow," Matt whispers as he tries to capture my hand once more. Again, I pull away, and when he tries to touch my cheek, I turn my face away as well.

"Don't touch me," I croak, barely able to make the words come out at all.

"Harlow, listen to me…" Matt pleads with me, but all I do is shake my head. "Open your eyes and look at me."

"No," I sob, realizing I'm already crying again. Tears roll down my cheeks, leaving cold tracks behind. "Leave…"

"I won't leave you here," Matt tells me as he places a hand on my stomach. My eyes fly open in shock, and a wave of all-consuming anger engulfs me. How dare he touch me there… how dare he touch me at all?

Like a wild fury, I start shoving at his arm, slapping, scratching, and hitting him wherever I can, letting out all the burning anger inside of me.

"I said, don't fucking touch me! I hate you!"

Matt catches my flailing arms mid-air, wrapping his fingers around my already sore wrists and pinning them next to my body.

"Listen, Harlow!" Matt whisper yells. "Just listen! It didn't happen, okay?"

It didn't happen? What is that supposed to mean? Is he telling me to just forget about it? Forget what he and my father did to me?

"Do you feel any pain?" he asks next. "Any discomfort?"

Other than the suffocating ache in my chest, he means? "Yes, my whole damn body hurts."

"But your stomach doesn't hurt, does it?"

I blink some of the tears away, trying to look at his face, and make sense of what he's trying to tell me. A smile tucks on his lips, and when I finally stop fighting him, he released my wrists. No, now that I'm concentrating on feeling each part of my body, I realize that he is right. My lower abdomen doesn't hurt, and there is no soreness between my legs. If I'd had an abortion, wouldn't I feel both?

"The baby?"

"Still inside of you," Matt says. "I paid off the doctor. He just pretended to do the abortion. The baby is fine." I watch his face carefully, looking for any indication that he is lying, but his eyes are genuine, his smile is kind, and his voice is gentle.

"I'm... I'm still pregnant?" I ask again, needing to confirm, even though deep inside, I already know the answer.

"Yes, you are still pregnant, and now with your dad off your back, you should be able to stay that way too."

I tuck my arm under the blanket to put my hand on my still flat stomach, rubbing the skin there like the baby could somehow feel it. "Why? Why did you help me?"

"I told you I would. What your dad did was unforgivable, and I couldn't watch him go through with it. He went too far, even for my standards, and I'm a pretty big asshole."

I used to think so too. I thought Matt was a huge jerk, and maybe he still is by other standards, but after he risked going against my father to help me, I can't feel anything but gratitude toward him.

"So, what now? He is going to find out eventually."

"Honestly, I haven't thought that far ahead. I don't know how to get you out of here without your father knowing I helped you."

"Thank you, really, thank you, I don't know how I can ever repay you for what you did. It's not your fault that my father is this way, and I'm not your responsibility. I'm no one's responsibility. Not even the Bishops. I will get out of this on my own. I will fight my father. I won't let him control me and the people around me anymore. I won't let him continue using you, or anyone else for that matter. I'm going to be the one to put an end to his reign."

"This is dangerous, Harlow, going against your father. He has resources, money, people." Matt sounds almost afraid, and that strikes something inside of me. Even the most powerful of people have a weakness, and while my father has all the things he needs to destroy me, I have the determination needed to fight back.

I'm done being afraid. Done worrying about what might happen next. If I don't, at least try to fight him, I'll never escape. I'll never really be free.

"I can't stay here, Matt, I can't stay with you, you know that. Not only because of the baby, but because of my father. I won't be stuck under his thumb. I won't be married off or tossed away like garbage."

Matt scrubs a hand down his face in frustration, and a little piece of my heart feels bad for putting him in this situation.

"I won't force you to do anything, and I'll do what I can to help you, but I can't make any promises," he finally says.

"That's all I'm asking for. That's all I need. I'll do the rest on my own."

Now all I need to do is come up with a plan.

44

Neither one of my parents came back to the hospital today, and I am more than happy they didn't. I don't think I could stand to be in the same room with either one of them right now.

"Are you sure you're going to be okay on your own?" Matt asks for the third, and hopefully, final time.

"Yes, I promise. They need you at that meeting so go to work. I've held up enough of your time." The truth is, even though I now value Matt's company, I want him to leave. I don't want my father to think that he helped me escape. The last thing I want is anyone else to get hurt.

"I'll only be a few hours, then I'll come back and pick you up. Your father has reluctantly agreed on you staying with me," Matt says while slipping his arms into his jacket.

"Okay..." I try to force a smile when he glances my way, but I don't think it's very convincing.

"You know, your dad has two guards posted outside that door at all times?" Matt sighs. Of course, he's figured it out. He's intuitive like that. I'm glad he's not trying to stop me.

"I know. I mean, I figured. Thanks for the heads up."

"Be careful, Harlow," Matt warns, but it's not the threatening kind of warning, is more like the concerned kind of warning. He stops at the door, his hand already resting on the doorknob when he turns around to look at me one more time.

"Good luck," he says, just loud enough for me to hear it.

"Goodbye, Matt," I murmur, not sure when or even if I'll see him again.

The door closes, and I'm left in the large empty hospital room on my own. Loneliness and dejection creep up on me, like shadows in the night, trying to pull me into darkness. I try not to let them get to me, knowing that this is only a momentary state. I am not really alone, not as long as I have people who love me out there waiting for me, probably worried sick about me.

I wait about twenty minutes before I start moving. This is probably long enough for no one to suspect Matt helped me in any way. Grabbing my empty food tray, I stick it under my armpit and grab two boxes of orange juice, that I saved from breakfast. Opening them up carefully, I walk to the door, holding them in one hand, and grabbing the shiny silver doorknob with the other.

My pulse is racing, and my knees are shaking, but my mind is sharp as a blade. There might be some truck-sized men on the other side of this door, but my determination to leave this place is stronger than any two-hundred-pound man.

Sucking in a deep breath, I let the plan run through my head one final time.

Then, I open the door.

I step outside and find two guys sitting on the other side of the corridor looking up at me simultaneously. "I need a nurse right now, this juice is bad," I complain like I'm an angry customer in a restaurant, and they are the managers.

"Go back in there," one of them growls at me, not hiding his annoyance at my request.

Instead of following his orders, I grab on to the tray under my arm and throw it at his head as hard as I can. Like I had hoped, I catch both of them completely by surprise. With the tray flying through the air and both of them distracted, I bolt.

As I sprint down the hall, I drop the two boxes of juice behind me.

"You fucking brat!" One of them yells after me.

Concentrating on making my legs move as fast as I can and nothing more, I continue forward. When I hear what sounds like someone slipping, followed by a loud thud, and a string of curse words, I know my plan has worked.

I can't help but smile at this small triumph, even though I know damn well that I'm not safe yet. My sock covered feet pound against the hospital floor as I let the bright red EXIT signs guide me to freedom.

Since I don't know who my father has paid off in this place, I decide against stopping for anything or anyone until I'm outside. I pass a few shocked and confused nurses and patients, but I don't stop. I continue running through the blinding white hospital hallways like a madwoman on a mission because I am.

After what seems like an eternity of running through the maze of halls, I finally make it to a pair of sliding glass doors. Through them, I can see a parking lot, cars, people... *freedom.*

I'm so close to escaping, so close to being free.

Creeping toward the doors, I finally glance behind me to see if I'm being trailed. When I find no one, my shoulders almost sag with relief. The sliding doors open, and I dart through them. Fresh air caresses my skin, and sunlight warms my face as I take my first steps outside. I want to stand there for a moment; to catch my breath and enjoy these feelings coursing through me, but I know I need to keep moving. I need to get as far away from here as I can. I'm not safe, not until I'm back with the brothers.

Ignoring the throbbing of my shoe-less feet with each bang against the concrete, I race toward the main road. Not wanting to waste any time, I cut the corner sharply, too sharply it seems, because as soon as I round the edge of the wall, my body comes crashing into another person. The impact knocks the air from my lungs, and if the person wasn't holding on to me, I'd probably have fallen on my ass.

Before I even look up from the guy's chest, I know who it is. The familiar smell of forest and rain tickles my nostrils, and like a small child, I wrap my arms around his middle and bury my face into his chest.

"Fuck, Harlow," he croaks into my hair. His arms come around me, enclosing me in a cocoon. "We need to get out of here."

I pull away from him, even though my body objects, wanting to stay here with him. Just like this, in a perfect little bubble where no one can hurt us.

Taking my hand in his, Sullivan starts to pull me away, but before we even make the first step, a car comes barreling toward us. Tires squeal against the asphalt as it comes to a sudden halt. My gaze widens when I spot Oliver in the front seat. My eyes catching sight of Banks running toward us from the other side of the road.

Sullivan pulls the door open, helping me into the back seat, just as Banks approaches from the other side, climbing into the passenger seat up front.

As soon as we are all in the car, Oliver presses his foot to the pedal, and we speed off. The acceleration pushes me into the leather seats as relief, and endless happiness engulfs me. I'm safe now.

"Are you okay?" Banks asks, turning around in his seat.

Sullivan hasn't stopped touching me. Running his hands all over me as if he was checking for any wounds.

"I'm okay, just so glad to see you. How... how did you find me?"

"Matt called us when he left the hospital," Oliver explains. "He told us where you were and that you were probably going to make a run for it."

"He did?" I ask, instantly, worry starts coating my insides. If anyone finds out what he did, my father will crucify him.

"We got here as fast as we could," Banks says breathlessly. "We've been so fucking worried; we've been looking everywhere for you."

"I promise, I'm fine. I just can't believe I'm finally out of that hospital, and I can't believe Matt called you. But, of course, I'm glad he did. I'm just worried about at what cost." Pushing the thought away, I ask something else that's on my mind. "Did he tell you anything else?"

"That's all he said when he called," Sullivan confirms before questioning me frantically. "What is it? Are you hurt? Did someone hurt you?"

"No, no. I told you, I'm fine. It's nothing bad. I mean, at least I hope you don't feel like it's a bad thing. I don't think it's a bad thing. I guess we never talked about it..." I keep rambling on nervously.

"Harlow," Banks cuts me off. "Out with it."

Clearing my throat, I say, "I'm pregnant."

Dead silence fills the car, and as it stretches on, I start to get seriously worried. Maybe they are not as happy as I am about a baby? Glancing over to Sullivan, I find him staring at me, his eye impossibly wide, his face pale, and his lips slightly parted.

"Say something," I whisper.

Sullivan blinks, almost like my voice has snapped him out of some trance. "You're pregnant?" he finally asks. "Like you are having, kind of, a baby, pregnant?"

"Erm, is there another kind of pregnant?"

Banks turns once more, so I can see his face again. To my relief, there is a huge grin spread across his lips. "We're having a baby?" he asks, his voice filled with happiness and excitement.

"Yeah, we are."

When I glance back over to Sullivan, he seems to have composed himself as well. The shock has left his face, and the corners of his lips tug upward into a dazzling smile.

Two down, one to go.

"Oliver?" I ask tentatively. "How do you feel about this?"

"I-I'm just shocked. I mean, I thought you were on the pill?" Oliver starts but stopping himself right away. "Shit, that came out wrong. Sorry, I'm not saying it's your fault or anything. Not saying it's anyone's fault...Ugh, that came out wrong too."

"Dude, just stop talking," Banks scolds his brother. "For now, just shove your foot in your mouth, will you?"

I try my best not to frown. For some reason, I thought Oliver would be the happiest with having a baby, considering he is the oldest. Apparently, I was wrong. I'm not angry or anything, and I know this was unplanned and not ideal, but this is what happens when people have sex.

Sometimes they get pregnant even while on the pill. Everybody knows this, so why is he acting like this now? Why is he so unhappy?

The whirlwind of emotions leaves me utterly confused. I'm happy to be out of the hospital and away from my parents. I'm relieved to see the guys, but I'm heartbroken and scared seeing Oliver's reaction. Does he really not want this baby? I can't imagine he would ever tell me to get rid of it, but his response isn't anything like I thought it would be.

"Hey," Sullivan reaches over and cradles my face with his hand. His touch is warm, and instantly, I lean into his touch like a kitten who wants to be petted. "Everything is going to be okay. We're not going anywhere."

He can't possibly assure me that it will be. Still, I take comfort in his promise.

"Now, please tell us what the hell happen? How did Matt end up helping you?"

I take a deep breath before explaining the whole story. Just when I'm done, we pull up to the house. Oliver kills the engine once we reach the end of the driveway and we all climb out of the car. Sullivan's hand never leaves my body as he helps me every step of the way. Like he is scared that I'm going to disappear again.

Right now, I need his touch. I need it like I need my next breath. I want him to touch me more. I want him to wrap his arms around me and never let me go again. I want to curl up in bed with all three of them, having them surround me like a protective wall.

On the way inside the house, Banks comes up to my side, while Oliver unlocks the door.

"Are you hungry, thirsty, tired?" he questions as he takes my hand into his.

"I'm fine. A little tired, but definitely not hungry. They did feed me pretty well in that hospital. Since it was a private facility, they actually had restaurant-quality food."

"I guess that's the only good thing about the place." I couldn't agree more. I hated the place and hated that my father had tried to hurt my unborn baby there.

Walking inside, Banks closes the door behind him, twisting all the locks into place. Oliver leads the way into the living room, and the rest of us follow. Once we are all situated on the couch, I direct all my attention to Oliver. I can't let this hang in the air between us. I need to know what he's thinking. If he's okay with the baby.

"Is me being pregnant that bad? Do you not want this... *us*?" My voice cracks at the end, emotions overtaking my ability to speak evenly.

Oliver's angelic face falls. "I'm sorry, Harlow. I'm still trying to wrap my head around it. You... us, having a child together. The thought of it has my heart bursting with happiness. I just..." he trails off, running his fingers through his thick brown hair. I can feel his frustration from where he is sitting.

"What's the problem? If you're happy, then why do you seem so frustrated? Why do you seem so *unhappy?*" Oliver's gaze clashes with mine, and everything around us fades away.

"We can barely protect you, Harlow. Every time we think you are safe, there seems to be another threat lurking in the shadows, ready to take you away from us." The sadness that radiates out of him is stifling. "Do you have any idea what the last few days have been like for us? Now with you being pregnant, it's only going to get worse. It's like we can never catch a break."

"Oh, Oliver," I sigh in relief. Getting up from where I'm sitting, I crawl into his lap, wrapping my arms around his neck. He welcomes me into his arms, doing the same, his giant hands rub gently up and down my back while he peppers kisses all over my face. He does want the baby; he's just scared of something happening to us.

"Oliver does have a point," Banks mumbles after a while. "There is something we need to tell you. Another thing that we have to protect you against."

Twisting around in Oliver's lap, I look up between all three of them, waiting for one of them to continue. When they don't, I open my mouth to speak.

"What is it?"

Sullivan gives me a sad look. "The police called earlier today... to warn us," Sullivan explains, "Shelby escaped from the psych ward last night."

It's a good thing I'm sitting because if I wasn't, I would be on the floor right now.

"What? What do you mean she *escaped*?" How can she escape? She was supposed to be locked up." This is bad, so bad. Already, I can feel the pressure of what this means settling on my shoulders. She escaped, she's out, free, doing god knows what. Before I know what I'm doing, my hands come to rest on my stomach, cradling my imaginary bump. There is so much more at stake now, so much more than just protecting me.

All of Oliver's worries and fears, they come crashing into me then.

He's right, as sad as it is, he is right. I can barely protect myself. How am I going to protect this child?

45

The weight of the world seems to sit on my shoulders. I do the basics; showering, eating, and trying to sleep. Days pass, and once again, I find I'm stuck in this house, hiding from the world. Oliver and Sullivan leave for class, while Banks stays behind with me. We all agreed me returning to classes again was all but pointing a bright red arrow at where I was. Shelby could easily get to me if she wanted to.

And I suppose she could get to me here too if she really wanted.

"Please stop frowning, your sad face makes me sad." Banks pouts.

That makes me smile, "It's hard to be happy when it feels like everything is falling apart. I thought she was put away forever." I drop my gaze to my hands, "I thought we were safe. Now it feels like all we were doing was lying in wait."

Banks' hands cover my own, and he sits down on the cushion beside me. "All we can do is wait for the police to find her, and right now, no one knows where she is. Maybe she ran away? Maybe she decided hurting you wasn't really what she wanted after all?"

"You really think she would escape just to be free, and not to track me down and hurt me more?" I lift my gaze and stare at him in disbelief. If he says yes, I'm going to be forced to smack some sense into him.

"No, but I can only hope. The last thing I want is for her to try and come after you."

"Same. All I want is for all the threats, all the stress to go away." Pausing, I can feel the emotions swirling inside me, brewing just like a thunderstorm does. "I'm scared, and not just for me but the baby too. What if she finds me? What if she hurts the baby?"

I'm spiraling out of control, my thoughts headed into a dark and dangerous place.

"Stop, she isn't going to touch you or the baby, and nothing is going to happen to either of you, not if I have anything to say about it." Banks' soft tone is meant to reassure me, it's meant to calm me, but nothing will stop me from worrying, nothing but knowing that she is behind bars where she really belongs.

The buzzing of my cell phone against the coffee table has me lurching toward the device. I take it into my hands and stare at the name flashing across the screen. It's my stepmom. What could she possibly want?

My finger hovers over the green answer key, but a head shake from Banks helps me make my decision. Talking to her isn't going to help me any, not when all she's going to do is hurt me more with her hateful words and tell me how horrible I am for running away. For hurting Matt.

"I don't know what she wants, but I can tell you that it's nothing good. If she has something to say, she'll leave a voicemail." Banks says. Moving from the couch and heading for the kitchen. "Are you hungry? You have to be. I know if I were pregnant, I would be eating the house down."

"You eat the house down normally, so what's the difference?" I giggle.

Banks cocks his head to the side as he opens the fridge and inspects its contents, "I suppose there isn't a difference. Maybe I would eat twice as much then? Or four times as much since I technically eat for two already?"

My phone beeps, letting me know that my stepmom has left a voicemail, and because I'm curious, I grab the device, going to the voicemail before bringing it to my ear.

"Hi, sweetie, it's me. I just wanted to call and make sure you were okay. We got word that Shelby escaped the psych ward, and I wanted to warn you and make sure that you were safe. I know that we ended things badly at the hospital, but your father and I just want the best for you. We have the police searching for Shelby and will do everything we can to protect you. We love you. Call me or your father if you need anything."

The voicemail ends, and I'm left with my mouth hanging open. How can she act so normal after everything that happened at the hospital? How can they act like they give one single fuck what happens to me?

"I told you nothing good would come from that woman," Banks interrupts my thoughts.

"She claims they want to warn me about Shelby, and that they're working with the police to catch her. They'll do everything they can to protect me."

Banks rolls his bright blue eyes, pulling stuff out to make some sandwiches, "Pfft, protect you from what? They're the reason that all of this happened. Your father and Shelby are perfect for each other, and your stepmom is a gold-digging bitch. They all should be in that mental hospital together."

He's not wrong.

"All I want is for everything to end, for my father to leave me alone, and let me be happy, and for Shelby to get what she deserves."

"It'll happen. We'll make sure of it. No one is going to hurt you anymore. You and that baby are the most important things to us, and I'll be damned if I stand by and let people hurt you again."

My heart decides to do that stupid pitter-patter thing in my chest, and I can't help but smile, my lips turning up at the sides. It feels foreign like I shouldn't be doing it, but I want to smile. I want to be happy.

Together Banks and I eat an early lunch. Afterward, we chill on the couch for a little while, where he cradles my belly and talks in a baby voice to it. I laugh so hard that my eyes tear up. For a few hours, I forget about the heartache that is behind us, all the hurdles we'll have to get over in the future, and all the uncertainties we'll have to face.

At the time, I didn't know that this was going to be the calm before the storm. A moment of blissful happiness before everything comes crashing down on me. Before, my life took a turn for the worst.

"I think I'm going to take a nap," I yawn after we've been lying still for a while.

"Go ahead, I'll clean up the dishes from earlier and maybe join you in a little bit."

"Alright, I'll try and wait up for you," I tell him and plant a quick kiss on his very kissable lips. I want to linger there longer, but I know if I do, I'll never get to take a nap, and lately, that's all I've wanted to do. Sleep, and eat, and sleep some more.

Walking into my bedroom, I realize that I don't even need to change clothes since I stayed in my PJs all day. I slip into my bed, the one I rarely sleep in. I usually spend the night in one of the guys' rooms, but they still wanted me to have my own room.

My head hits the pillow, and a wave of exhaustion washes over me. Who knew someone would be tired from doing nothing all day?

With my eyes closed and the heavy blanket wrapped around me, sleep finds me quickly, dragging me into a dreamless slumber. Before my brain can shut all the way off, the sound of glass shattering rips me back to reality. My eyes blink open, and for a moment, I think maybe I've dreamt it.

Shoving into a sitting position, I toss the blanket off. I don't know how, but I instantly know something is wrong. The rational part of my brain tells me to calm down, maybe Banks just dropped a glass. But my gut tells me something else, that something terrible is about to happen. It's only a feeling, but it's strong enough to be taken seriously, very seriously.

All the exhaustion vanishes as adrenaline takes over, pumping through me with a furious fire. Holding my breath, I listen to every single noise.

When I hear the shattering of glass again, I know my gut feeling was right. Ripping the door open, I start down the hall, my feet slapping against the wood floor in a flurry.

"Stay upstairs!" Banks yells from somewhere on the first floor, clearly hearing me. "Go into your room and lock the door."

For a moment, I just stand there, my feet cemented on the floor. I want to listen to him, I want to be safe, but how can I leave him down there all on his own. What if Xander sent more guys? What if... No, I can't think like that.

I need to... what should I do? Oh, god. I can feel the air entering my lungs, but I'm not breathing, not really. The air inside them stills. Then it hits me. I need to call the police. Patting myself down, I realize quickly that I didn't bring my phone up with me.

Shit, it's still on the kitchen table.

More glass shatters downstairs, and I find my feet moving without thought. No...wait... that wasn't downstairs. I turn around and look in the direction I think the sound came from. I think this time, it came from upstairs. Someone broke a window up here. Before I can start to move again, I see a figure appear at the end of the hallway.

Shelby.

She looks so different that I almost don't recognize her. Her normally straight, shiny hair is uncombed and messy. An unfitting gray jumpsuit is covering her slender body, and as my gaze moves down her, I notice she's not wearing any shoes. The socks on her feet are nasty, covered in dirt, and mud and have holes in them. But what makes her seem like a completely different person isn't her get up.

It's her eyes.

The look in her eyes is nothing short of bone-chilling. Cold, detached, unhinged... batshit crazy. How can this be the girl who's been my best friend all my life?

"Hello, Harlow," she greets, and even her voice sounds different, disturbing. I take a small step back, ready to make a run for the stairs to get away from her. But when she reaches around to her back and pulls out a black object from her waistband, I freeze. My heart stops. My lungs deflate. My entire life shatters.

A gun... she has a *gun*.

"Shelby, please..." I lift my hands, palms up. "Please don't do this," I beg, but she only smiles at my pleading. She smiles as if this is some kind of joke to her.

Banks must hear me, because the next thing I know, he's barreling up the stairs calling out for me.

"Don't fucking come any closer," Shelby yells. "If you do, I'll shoot her. I'll do it right now!"

I don't look back at Banks, but I can hear his footsteps falter somewhere behind me.

"Okay, okay, I won't move," Banks answers, his voice abnormally shaky. A stark contrast to his usual cocky, unfazed demeanor.

Shelby sneers, "This is all your fault, you know? Your dad and I could have been happy. I could've had it all. He loves me, and the only reason we can't be together is you." She points the gun at me as she speaks.

"What do I have to do with you and my father's relationship? If I have a say in it, I'll never see him again. You can have him."

Her pale cheeks flush with anger, "It has everything to do with you!"

"Every time I was with him, all he wanted to talk about was you. What you were doing? Who you were seeing? He was never interested in what *I* was doing. All I wanted was his attention. I wanted him to see *me*, and the only way I can have him is by getting rid of you. Then everything will be perfect." Her smile is frightening and makes the blood in my veins turn to ice.

"Please, Shelby! I'm pregnant," I sob, cradling my stomach.

"I know," she snickers. "The plan didn't go as expected." She shakes her head and points the gun at the ground.

"What do you mean?"

"How do you think you got pregnant in the first place? I exchanged your pill for placeboes. You've been taking nothing more than sugar candy," she admits, shocking the hell out of me. My mouth opens, and for once, I'm speechless. She... she did this?

"Why... why would you do that?"

Shrugging her shoulders, she says, "I thought if you got knocked up by one of the Bishops, your father would finally disown you. I guess that didn't work out. So, I'm going back to the original plan I had. It sucks a little, but killing you is all I can do now."

Shelby raises the gun again, and my mouth opens, a scream on the edge of my tongue. Then the doorbell rings. With the gun still pointed at me, she tilts her head, looking at me with shock and anger in her eyes.

"Expecting someone?"

"I-I don't know..." I really don't know. Were we expecting someone? I can't think straight with that thing pointed at me and my life on the line.

No one moves for a moment, and then the doorbell chimes once more. Then that same impatient person starts to pound on the front door, the sudden, loud noise making me jump.

"Harlow, I know you're in there. Open up!" My stepmom's muffled voice carries through the heavy front door and silent house. "I'm not leaving until you open this door and let me know that you're okay!"

Why the hell is my stepmom here?

"Well, I guess you better let her in. I can go ahead and kill two birds with one stone... Or two people with one gun," Shelby cackles.

"If you hurt her, I swear to god you'll wish you were never born," Banks threatens.

She rolls her eyes, "Go get the door, Romeo, or I'll shoot her right now, and you won't be able to do a thing to stop me."

Listening as Banks descends the stairs, I start to shake; fear and panic bubbling up.

"You don't have to do this. We've always been friends, and we still can be. Just put the gun down," I do my best to keep my voice even, but Shelby can see right through me, and instead, she takes a step closer, her eyes darkening.

"Maybe a long time ago, we were friends, but not anymore. Not ever again," tears pool in my eyes because even as crazy as Shelby is, as lost as she is, I still yearn for that person that I once knew. The person who was a friend.

I can hear someone climbing the stairs, and when I peek over my shoulder, I find my stepmother at the top of the landing. What the hell is going on? My body is caught in the crosshairs between two crazed women.

"Shelby, don't be stupid, drop the gun. Harlow, everything is going to be okay." I can hear my stepmother speaking, but I don't feel the emotion in her words. It's not going to be okay. None of this is okay.

"Me?" Shelby laughs like an evil villain, and my stepmother strolls right past me, closing in on her. "I'm not stupid. I'm not the one who doesn't even realize her husband is in love with someone else. He loves me, not you, you old hag." I can see the glint of metal peeking out of my stepmom's sleeve, the edge of it red with blood, droplets falling casually to the floor.

Slowly, I bring my hand to my mouth to stop the scream from coming out. *Banks.* Oh, god, she didn't. She wouldn't.

"Ha, then why is he with me? Why did he call the cops on you, and have you sent to a loony bin?" It's like I'm watching a nightmare play right before my eyes. I want to look away, but I can't. Shelby raises the gun to my stepmom's head, but it doesn't seem to faze her.

"Huh? It wasn't because he loves *you*?"

"Shut up!" Shelby yells her voice cracking, agony pouring out of her.

But my stepmom doesn't listen, she just continues nudging her closer and closer to the proverbial edge, "You were nothing more than convenient pussy for him. He needed you to keep an eye on Harlow and spreading your legs for him; that was just an added bonus for him."

"Stop, just stop!" Shelby screams even louder this time, the sound ringing in my ears like a siren. Lifting her hands, she presses them against her ears, and like a hawk, my eyes remain on the gun that's still in her hands. With it pointed away from us, now is our chance. Then it happens.

The moment the gun isn't pointed in my stepmom's direction anymore, she lunges for Shelby. Everything happens so fast; I can hardly make sense of it all.

A sob escapes my lips as I helplessly watch as the woman I've always known as my mother drives the already bloodied knife into Shelby's chest.

For a moment, I can't breathe, I can't move, I can't think. Time slows, and all I can do is watch Shelby die. The girl who has been my companion for most of my life stares back at me. A knife stuck in her chest, blood seeping from the wound, soaking through her gray jumpsuit. Her wide eyes bleed into mine, her face pales, and her eyes go blank.

I can see the exact moment all life leaves her. One second she is standing, the next she crumbles to the floor, landing in a heap. I don't know why, but I can't stop staring at the lifeless form on the floor. I'm unable to understand or comprehend anything that is happening. This can't be real. This has to be a dream.

A nightmare.

I know I shouldn't, but my eyes move on their own from her crumpled body, and to her eyes. I gape at the vacant look there, somehow waiting for some kind of spark to return. For her to wake up... but it's too late. She's gone, her entire life, all hopes, and dreams, every memory she ever had... gone. Just like that...

"Oh, come on. Don't act like you actually cared about her," my stepmother says nonchalantly, utterly unfazed by what she's just done.

"You-you k-killed her," I stutter. My voice coming out just as shaky as I am.

"So what? She deserved it. Truthfully, I should have killed her a long time ago," she admits. Bending down to where Shelby's body is lying on the floor, she pries the gun out of her lifeless hand. "And I should have killed you when your mother was pregnant with you. I apologize for making you go through all of this just to have it end with the same result."

Shock is all I feel. Fear. Anger. Sadness. I don't feel any of those emotions in that moment. Not like I should. It's like I'm having an out of body experience.

She killed my mother.

"Why do you look so surprised?"

Swallowing thickly, I push everything down. If I'm going to survive, I'm going to have to come up with a way to escape her.

"Why... Why did you kill her? What did she do that would make you want to kill her?"

"She took your father from me, that's what. He was always supposed to be with me. We belonged together, and she ruined it all. Just like now, how you ruined everything. I should have killed you with her, but your father and I found out early on that I couldn't have children of my own, so I thought I could raise you. I thought he would love me even more for it." A darkness overtakes her features, "I actually thought I could love you, but just like your mother, you turned out to be nothing more than an inconvenience."

An inconvenience?

The word cuts through me like a sharp knife. So many emotions flood me all at once that I can't decide which one is greater... hurt, anger, or disappointment. I'm so disappointed in myself. Disappointed that I let this woman be part of my life for so long, that I didn't see the kind of person she really was. All this time, I thought my father was the biggest monster, but as it turns out, there was a worse evil lurking.

I want to cry, to scream, to destroy the woman in front of me. I called her my mom... the woman who took my real mother from me. The walls around my fragile heart crumble as the reality of everything crashes into me.

Everything that happened, every bad thing that ever happened to me, it all boiled down to the person in front of me. It was all her fault, the rivalry, the fighting between the families, every single thing was her fault.

"I'm sorry that things have to end this way."

I don't know what compels me to do it in that moment, but I rush her, shoving at her shoulders. A look of horror flickers in her eyes, and she stumbles backward, the gun in her hand dropping to the floor with a thud. My heart races in my chest, the sound of blood pounds in my ears, and I dart for it knowing that if I don't get it, she will. It's strictly about survival now, and if anyone is going to get out of this alive, it's going to be me.

My fingers wrap around the cold metal, and I stumble backward, nearly tripping over my feet in the process. Tremors of fear wrack my body, and my wild gaze swings to my stepmother. The weight of the gun in my hand is heavy, but it doesn't stop me from lifting it, pointing the barrel directly at her.

"You can't do it, Harlow. You aren't a killer." She taunts, and my finger shakes as I move it toward the trigger.

She's right, I'm not a killer, but when it comes to protecting my unborn baby, the men I love, and myself, I'll become anything I need to.

"Harlow, don't do something you can't live with…" Her voice trails off, and before I can even think about it, I pull the trigger. The kickback of the gun vibrates through me, and I watch completely unmoved as the bullet cuts through her chest. Her eyes go wide, and her mouth opens, but the words never come out.

A second later, she falls, just like Shelby did. My entire body clamps up, and then I start to shake watching as the only person I've had as a mother figure dies. Forcing myself to move, I drop the gun and turn running down the stairs.

Once I reach the bottom step, I yell, "Banks? Banks?"

"Over here," he weakly replies, and I rush in the direction of his voice, finding him on the ground near the door. My hands start to move, inspecting him just as my eyes are. His hand is pressed to his side, the bright red blood seeps through his shirt, and I can barely breathe as I look into his eyes.

"Please don't die on me, Banks." Tears fall, skating down my cheeks, but I don't even feel them. All I can see is blood, it's everywhere, on my hands, on the floor. Death surrounds me, and I refuse to let it claim another person.

"Banks," I whimper, but he's slowly fading, the color draining from his face. He's lost so much blood, and there is nothing I can do.

"I love you," he says, but it sounds like a wheeze. His bright blue eyes fall closed, and panic seizes my heart.

"Don't. Stop. This isn't the end. Banks!" I scream, pressing harder against the wound. Sirens sound off in the distance, but it feels like it's too late. I can feel him leaving me.

"Please, Banks! Stay with me," I sob, but he doesn't listen. He doesn't open his eyes, and by the time the ambulance has arrived, I have no more tears to cry. In the end, my stepmother took more from me than I could have ever imagined. More than I think my heart can handle.

EPILOGUE

One Year Later

They say time heals all wounds, and I believe that. I think that as time goes on the heartache and loss, it all gets easier to deal with. The pain becomes less, the sadness isn't so suffocating, and slowly the anger toward it all fades away.

"You sure you're ready to do this?" Sullivan asks.

"Honestly, I'm not sure," I say, looking down at our four-month-old daughter. She is still so small, so fragile. Even though I know Caroline will take care of her, it's hard to let her go. Even if it's just for a few hours.

"I promise little Phoebe will be perfectly fine with me," Caroline chimes in. "We will have a great time watching classic movies, reading stories, and singing that baby shark song before bedtime."

"Oh, god, I can't hear that song anymore," Sullivan frowns.

"But, she loves it!" I interject. "And more importantly, it makes her sleepy."

"She probably wants to go to sleep to get away from that song," Sullivan grins.

"You guys just need a break, that's all. So, go, get out of the house. Go have fun. I'll send you updates every ten minutes if it will calm your mind. Just please, go do something." I know she is joking, but I actually like the ten-minute update idea. The last year has been crazy, and protecting our daughter is the most important thing to me. Since her birth, I've been with her every second of every day.

"Don't tempt her; she'll hold you to it," Oliver chuckles, walking into the living room.

"I will not," I lie, my lips pull into a sly grin.

"She will, and that's fine. Give us periodical updates. We'll be keeping Harlow busy enough to take the worry off her mind."

Caroline wrinkles her nose, "Ew, that's nasty. I don't want to hear about your sex life."

Shaking my head, I give Phoebe one last kiss before buckling her into her car seat.

You can do this. You can do this. It's just a few hours. I tell myself.

"Alright, we'll see you guys later," Caroline announces as she walks out the door, taking my entire life with her.

I watch from the window like a little kid as she puts her into the car, securing the car seat in the base.

"She's coming back, you know," Sullivan whispers into the shell of my ear, and a shiver rolls down my spine. It's insane how effortless they have to be when it comes to my body. With them, I'm in tune, every muscle, every beat of my heart, they own me, consume me. There is no them and me. Just *us* now.

"I know, but it's so hard. I've never been away from her, and all I can think about is if she's going to get enough snuggles. Is she going to miss me? What if she cries, and Caroline doesn't know what to do?" I'm rambling now, but these are all the things I worry about as a new mother.

"Let us take your mind off the small stuff for a few hours." Banks sneaks up behind me, wrapping his arms around me and pulling me back to his chest. His warmth blankets me, and I melt into his touch, letting him guide me into the bedroom. Since everything that happened, we got a new house in a new area, away from Bayshore. We wanted to a new life, a fresh start, and that meant leaving the past behind.

With both Shelby and my stepmom dead, things have finally become easier, safer, and much less complicated. But the past will always be a part of me, no matter how hard I try to forget it. It will always be there.

My father has tried to contact me a few times, but I never could bring myself to talk to him. The two people that surprisingly did stay in my life are Matt and George Bishop. I don't talk to Matt often, but we have stayed friends. We all hung out a few times, and the guys actually became friends as well. George has been telling me about my mom, my real mom. The chance to meet her was taken away from me a long time ago, but at least I have his stories to get to know her.

"What exactly are you going to do to *help* take my mind off of things?" I smirk, knowing damn well what they all have planned. "Didn't we tell Caroline we were going out for dinner and drinks?"

Sullivan chuckles, and I can feel that deep husky sound in my bones. "Yeah, we could still do that, but we really thought about something else... something better."

"It would have been weird to tell Caroline what we really had planned," Banks points out. "Hey, Caroline, would you please watch our baby so we can have an uninterrupted fuckfest?"

Oliver punches Banks in the arm, making me giggle.

"You are such a romantic, but you do have a point," I tease, "So... what exactly do you have planned?"

"Follow us, and we'll show you," Oliver says, holding out his hand to me. I take it eagerly and let him lead me up the stairs. Banks and Sullivan follow close behind.

They lead me to my bedroom, the one I hardly ever sleep in, and Oliver motions for me to open the door. I grab the brass doorknob, turn and push the door open. When I see the inside of the room, I can't help but gasp.

The entire space is decorated beautifully. There are candles set up on the dresser and desk, illuminating the room with a dim, romantic light. Fresh cut flowers are sitting on my nightstand, giving the space a fresh, flowery scent, and rose petals are artfully laid out on the bed in a heart shape, making the whole thing just perfect.

"Oh, you guys. I love it," I say, having to hold back tears. Tears of happiness, of course. I'm just so happy and incredibly lucky. Not only did I find one man of my dreams, but I found three. Three wonderful men who love me and would do anything for me and my happiness.

We enter the room, and like always, Banks is the first one to lose his patience. I giggle as he pounces on me like a wild animal. His lips crash against mine, stealing the air from my lungs. I'm consumed by his kiss as I pull up his shirt while he undoes my pants. We only break the kiss to pull his shirt over his head. The fabric landing somewhere on the other side of the room.

As soon as Banks' upper body is free, I run my hands across his chest, stopping at the tiny raised scar where he was stabbed.

It's hard to believe that something that is so small now, barely noticeable even, almost cost him his life. I shudder just thinking about it, reliving those moments of when he was in the hospital, fighting for his life while Sullivan and Oliver promised me that everything was going to be okay. I remember falling apart, not knowing if I was ever going to come back together again.

Someone moves behind me, starting to pull up my shirt, and Banks moves from my mouth to my breasts. Pulling my bra cups down and freeing my boobs, he closes his lips around one of my nipples. My head falls back, and I moan, just as my shirt is being pulled over my head.

"You smell divine," Oliver whispers against the tender skin on my neck as he undoes my bra, letting it fall to the floor. He starts peppering open mouth kisses all along my neck, shoulders, and down my spine while his brother pays special attention to my chest.

"Lay her on the bed, so we can show her the other surprise,"

Sullivan urges, and the next thing I know, Banks is wrapping his arms around me, and picking me up. I throw my arms around his neck and start to giggle like a schoolgirl.

He gently deposits me on the bed and pulls my panties off in the next moment, leaving me completely naked. When I look up, I see Sullivan holding a small bottle of lotion or maybe oil, I can't really tell.

"We're going to give you a relaxing massage," Oliver grins, letting Sullivan pour some liquid into his palm.

"Yes, a very, very relaxing massage," Banks adds with a wink, while he also gets what looks to be massaging oil poured on his hands.

I smile again, but the smile turns into a low sigh when Banks' warm, oily hands land on me, slowly working into my tight muscles.

"Where did you learn to do that?" I sigh, melting into the mattress. Banks' hands move up my body, while Sullivan crawls up onto the bed and starts massaging my shoulders and neck. Oliver tends to my feet, and right then, it starts to feel like what I imagine heaven feels like.

Their big hands work my tight muscles and tender flesh until I'm nothing more than a liquid mass floating in the center of the bed.

"I hope you're ready for us," Sullivan whispers as he leans down, and nibbles on my earlobe. Banks takes that moment to suck one of my pebbled nipples into his mouth and Oliver, well, he spreads my thighs and settles between them. I can feel the heat of his breath against my core, and I shiver.

"Oh, god. It's not going to take me long with all three of you," I complain, even though it's not really a complaint. "But still, I can't get enough of you. I don't think it will ever be enough…"

"That's fine. We've got hours and days, and if that's not good enough, we've got years too." Sullivan says, sucking at my throat hard enough to leave a hickey behind. I open my mouth to speak, but the words are lost on me when I feel Oliver's rough tongue against my slit. At the same time, Banks pinches one of my nipples, and I can't help myself.

My pussy gushes and my thighs quiver with the impending pleasure that's about to be brought on me. With my clit in his mouth, Oliver enters me with two fingers, pumping in and out of me with an ounce of resistance.

"Fuck me, my cock is harder than steel right now," Banks says, his voice muffled from my breast. I try to focus on each of them individually, but I can't. The pleasure builds rising second by second, and it doesn't take me long to start going off.

"Come, baby, come all over my brother's tongue," Sullivan's filthy words only encourage me onward, and with a gasp, I lift my hips and fall apart, grinding my core into Oliver's face. Like a wild animal, he continues to feast on me, leaving not even a drop of my release behind. By the time he's done, I'm completely spent, and the brothers move away from me to slip out of their own clothing.

Watching through hooded eyes, I admire each of their bodies, my mouth watering as their rock-hard cocks come into view.

"You ready to get fucked?" Banks growls, and I nibble on my bottom lip seductively before nodding my head. He strokes his cock up and down a few times with the oil that they used on my body earlier. Then they're moving me.

Banks lifts me, and I reach out, pressing my hands down onto his impeccable chest as he impales me on his cock in one single thrust. My gaze widens, and my tongue darts out over my bottom lip. *Sweet baby Jesus.*

He stills inside of me, and I swear it's like he's grown, gotten bigger. It doesn't hurt, but I feel fuller. Oliver appears in front of me, and Sullivan presses against my back, bending me to his will. Banks fingers dig into the flesh at my hips, holding me in place as he bucks his hips, his cock slicing me in two. At the same time, Oliver starts to stroke his cock, the mushroom tip is red and painful looking, and all I can think to do is ease his pain.

"You want my cock in your mouth?" he questions, his thick, heady voice shooting lightning bolts of pleasure through me.

"Yes," I gasp, just as Sullivan starts to lather my ass, and my puckered asshole with the oil. His fingers probe at the entrance before slipping in with ease. Slowly he fucks my ass with his fingers while Banks moves steadily in and out of me.

Like a cat in heat, I mewl, the sound radiating through Oliver's cock, which I suck on like a lollipop. Teetering back and forth between Sullivan and Banks, we slowly find a rhythm that works for all of us.

"Fuck, yes, suck me, baby. I want to come down your throat. Fill your belly with my cum." Mmm, yes. Sucking him harder, I take him deeper into my mouth, gagging when he threads his fingers through my hair and holds me against his groin. My lungs burn, and my eyes water, but as soon as he pulls back and I see the pleasure pooling in his eyes, I'm doing it all over again. With every hole filled, it doesn't take long for me to fall apart, and with my orgasm brings the brothers' orgasms.

Banks is the first to come, groaning as my clenching pussy rips every drop of sticky hot seed from his cock. Oliver is next, and I fondle his balls as he holds my head in place, fucking my throat until he finally reaches climax. I suck him off until he grows soft and slips from my mouth. Pressing a kiss to the corner of my mouth as he moves off the bed, most likely going into the bathroom.

With two out of the three done, I push back against Sullivan, and he meets my thrust, slamming into me with the same intense need. His touch is rough, and all I can feel is his cock taking my ass.

"Please fill my ass with your cum," I whimper, knowing how he loves it when I talk dirty. Peering at him over my shoulder, we lock eyes, and his thrusts become harder, almost painful, but like a volcanic eruption, I feel my own climax sneaking up on me. Thrust. Thrust. The sound of our skin slapping fills the room, and my mouth pops open, a delightful moan escaping.

Banks smirks at me, and I can feel the bite of pain as he rolls my hardened nipples between two fingers.

"Come on, baby, you can come again. I know you can…" Banks encourages, the look in his eyes is dark, heated, and like waves cresting the beach, my orgasm slams into me. At the same time, a roar that could wake the dead pierces the air. Sagging against Banks' sweaty body, I smile floating down from my own orgasm while Sullivan fills me with every drop of his release.

My lids start to grow heavy immediately after. It's been a long time since we did a threesome, and with a baby, there isn't much time for sex, let alone with all three of them.

"You okay?" Sullivan asks, his fingers caressing my back.

"More than okay. I'm pretty sure I've become a pile of liquid mush."

"No worries, we'll let you sleep for a little while before we go for round two."

That causes me to perk up, "Round two?" I roll off Banks, and sit up on the bed, my eyes moving between all three of the men I love.

"Yes, round two, and three, and four, and..."

Oliver rolls his eyes, "I think she gets it. We want to fuck her."

"Oh, that's not the only thing we want," Banks snickers and jumps off the bed. Confusion isn't even a word I would use to describe how I'm feeling, still my brow furrows, and I try and comprehend what is happening.

"What do you mean?" I direct my question to all three of them.

"We started as enemies," Oliver says.

"We became lovers," Sullivan says next.

"We have saved each other, and had a baby," Banks adds.

"And?" I say, my heart beating out of my chest.

The brothers look to each other before Sullivan pulls out a black velvet box. It's then that I know what is happening.

"Will you do us the honor of becoming Mrs. Bishop?"

What? How? What do I even say to that? After all we've gone through? After everything that's happened, there is no way I could ever say no.

We're more than just fated rivals.

We're lovers, we're a family, and together we beat the odds. We got our happily ever after, and so much more.

"Of fucking course. I'd love nothing more than to be tied to the three men I love for life."

Something that resembles relief appears on each of their faces, and within seconds the heavy, three stone diamond ring is placed on my finger. Nestled between the three diamonds is one smaller one, and I know right away the symbolism of that ring. It was designed with a purpose. Our story.

Three Brothers.

One love story.

A lifetime of love.

The End

Made in the USA
Monee, IL
12 May 2023

33163275R10256